LUST FOR REVENGE

LUST FOR REVENGE

Komil Sindarov

Library of Congress Control Number:		2025901535
ISBN:	Hardcover	979-8-3694-3920-3
	Softcover	979-8-3694-3919-7
	eBook	979-8-3694-3918-0

Print information available on the last page.

Rev. date: 01/28/2025

To order additional copies of this book, contact:
Xlibris
844-714-8691
www.Xlibris.com
Orders@Xlibris.com
863609

PREFACE

Every genre follows its own set of rules, principles, and patterns. Love, as the saying goes, is as old as time, yet every lover expresses it in their own unique way. Similarly, the detective genre—renowned for its widespread popularity in Europe and beyond—has distinct characteristics. However, a notable distinction exists between European and Russian detective stories. Fyodor Dostoevsky's *Crime and Punishment*, for instance, is often interpreted as an adventure or detective novel, but its strong social themes distinguish it from the typical focus on crime alone.

That said, the detective genre has evolved according to certain conventions, primarily established by American and European authors. These include:

1. The motive for the crime must take precedence.
2. The crime (usually murder) should occur early in the narrative.
3. The investigator must demonstrate exceptional perceptiveness.

4. Both the investigator and the reader should be equally informed about the crime.

5. Themes of love or family should not overshadow the central mystery.

6. The criminal's identity must be deduced through analysis and inductive reasoning rather than luck.

There are approximately 25 such rules in total. Yet, literature from every culture selectively adopts these norms, imbuing the genre with a unique national character. This is evident in works such as *Dzhura* and *Slepy Dozhd* by Ulmas Umaybekov, *Shaytanat* by Tohir Malik, and *Orly Vzrosleyut v Gorakh* by Nuriddin Ismoilov.

This dynamic particularly struck me while reading Komil Sindarov's *The Thirst for Revenge*. The narrative begins, as any intricate detective story should, with the mysterious disappearance of Bahrom Safarov, the diligent and respected head of the prosecutor's office. Naturally, questions arise: where has this exemplary official gone? Was he kidnapped, murdered, or did he vanish of his own volition?

The uncertainty leads to panic and speculation among colleagues, family, and friends, setting the stage for the mystery essential to any detective novel. As the story unfolds, the criminal demonstrates exceptional cunning, attempting to evade capture and conceal their actions.

Readers are drawn into the suspense, wondering: who is more clever—the suspected criminal Akhad Batyrov, adept at evasion, or the seasoned investigators Fakhriiddin Karimovich and Sanjarbek, who tirelessly pursue justice?

The narrative skillfully immerses readers in the unfolding drama, making them partners in the investigators' tense decisions and challenges. The suspense builds as the author adheres to the conventions of the detective genre, gradually revealing the criminal's identity. Ultimately, readers discover that the supposed culprit is, in fact, an honest and decent individual.

Through vivid storytelling, the author explores the psychological depth of the characters, their emotions, grievances, and joys. Sindarov highlights how a single misstep by an investigator or prosecutor can lead to devastating, irreversible consequences.

The romantic subplot involving Bahrom and Vazira adds further richness to the narrative. Notably, Sindarov adopts a technique seen in the works of Agatha Christie and Georges Simenon, where the plot momentarily stalls. These pauses encourage readers to step into the characters' shoes, propose their own theories, and engage more deeply with the mystery.

Three years pass in the story—enough time for the events to fade from memory. However, the introduction of a journalist, Vazira, revives the cold case. The arrival of Marziya, Ozoda, and Lailo near the story's climax further heightens the tension, keeping readers on edge as the complex web of events is unraveled.

Detective fiction in Uzbek literature remains so scarce that one could count its works on a single hand. Komil Sindarov's *The Thirst for Revenge* stands as a remarkable addition to this rare genre. I am confident it will be a treasured gift for fans of detective fiction. I wish the author continued success in his creative endeavors.

Khudoyberdi Tukhtaboev
National Prize Writer of Uzbekistan

FROM THE AUTHOR

Dear Reader,

The book you hold in your hands is the culmination of twenty years of experience in the prosecutor's office and the courts. Within these pages, I share my observations and insights, drawing from real-life events. Naturally, I have woven these accounts with artistic embellishments, crafting a narrative that blends reality with imagination. My personal and extensive experience in solving crimes has served as a valuable foundation for writing this story.

The events depicted take place in the 1980s during the Soviet era, extending into the years of independence. Based on the real-life experiences of dedicated and conscientious prosecutors, this book demonstrates how even the smallest mistake can lead to significant consequences.

While this work is rooted in the detective genre, I have also sought to explore universal themes: love, loyalty, devotion, encounters and separations, friendship, humanity, and the sanctity of family. My hope is that these elements will inspire readers to reflect deeply and draw meaningful conclusions.

As an amateur writer, I leave it to you, dear readers, to judge whether I have succeeded in tackling such a significant endeavor. For any creative person, their work is like a beloved child—no artist would willingly call their creation flawed. Nevertheless, I trust your attentive reading will provide an honest assessment of my efforts. Your objective evaluation holds great importance to me.

As this is my first major prose work, I kindly ask for your understanding if you encounter any shortcomings. I eagerly welcome your feedback and letters, which can be sent through the publishing house.

Thank you for embarking on this journey with me.

Sincerely,
Komil Sindarov

It's easy to go from minor mistakes to major vices.
Lucius Annaeus Seneca

Bakhrom Safarovich went to bed late, so he could not sleep well. He turned from side to side: his thoughts were not resting. Toward morning he still managed to take a nap and had a long dream.... He was walking somewhere. It was a long way. At some point the road split in two, and he stopped at a crossroads in bewilderment, not knowing where to go. Suddenly an old woman appeared beside him and advised him: "If you want to reach your destination safely, go to the right, if you want adventures on your head, go to the left". She said and disappeared. As soon as he took a step to the right, wishing to reach his destination safely, a second old woman dressed in white clothes appeared. She advised the opposite, "If you want to reach your destination safely, go left, if you want adventures on your head, go right." He hesitated, not knowing which of the old women to believe. Then he took a chance and went to the left. He walked for a long time, it seemed that there was no end to the road. At that moment a black sandy whirlwind rose in the distance, which picked him up and carried him into the sky. And then everything went quiet. After a while he flew downward at the speed of light.

...He woke up in a cold sweat. For some time, he could not move under the influence of the nightmare. Which old woman was right? Both spoke convincingly. Which one was the angel and which one was the devil? But for what reason had he made the decision without much thought? Why did he go left anyway? Can a man be so indifferent to his fate? No, it's a dream! Let everything be for the best! Oh, by the way, his wife is good at dreams. No, it's better not to. She's an alarmist. She won't rest until we slaughter the chicken. So it's better not to say anything to Vazira. Maybe when he gets back from his trip, he'll tell her everything in detail.

When Bakhrom washed his face and entered the kitchen, Vazira (Bakhrom's wife), having sent the children to school, was waiting for her husband for breakfast. They sat down to breakfast together. Seeing the anxiety on her husband's face, the wife thought: "He must have slept badly!". She tried to cheer up her husband by chatting about everything.

Bakhrom Safarovich told her that today he would probably go on a business trip to Khorezm and instructed her to take good care of the children. It was as if he was saying goodbye to his wife. When he left the house, he turned around as if he had forgotten something and came back. He tried to say something important to his wife, but he opened his mouth and could only babble:

- Watch the kids!

- You will be back in a couple of days, why are you so worried about the children? - Wazira said.

They said goodbye again on the threshold. The wife was surprised that her husband turned back several times as he descended the stairs. "Maybe he doesn't want to go on a business trip," she thought...

Bakhrom Safarovich was appointed to the position of the Head of Department of the Prosecutor's Office a year ago. He managed to gain respect among his colleagues by his determination, knowledge, straightforwardness and modesty.

He entered his office and was about to take the documents necessary for the trip out of his desk drawer when the internal telephone rang. Deputy Prosecutor Tahir Gafurovich briefly informed him that the trip had been postponed and that in a few days he was to act as a public prosecutor in a trial that would begin in the Supreme Court against a group of criminals who had committed grave crimes against the state. The plane ticket was refunded. On the one hand, that's even better. Because he has to spend most of his life on business trips. His wife and kids worry about him all the time. And he doesn't like to be away from his family. But service is service. He chose this profession himself...

He immersed himself in work that he didn't even have time to warn his wife about the canceled trip. He began to scrutinize the twenty-volume criminal case that would be tried in court.

At half past one, Laziz's secretary informed him that a woman who wished to remain anonymous was asking for him on the telephone. She insisted that she was a close friend of Bakhrom Safarovich, who was waiting for her call. The chief picked up the phone in his office.

Two seconds later, Bahrom locked his office and hurried outside.

-Lazizjon, I'll be back soon, don't go out to lunch yet! - he said to the secretary, who followed him out into the corridor.

The sun was shining outside, but even so, the autumn air was quite cool. The secretary thought that if the chief ran outside without a jacket and hat, he might be back quickly.

Half an hour passed; Laziz became worried. He went outside but did not find the chief. "Maybe he's somewhere nearby talking to a guest. He won't go without his outer clothes for lunch," he thought and decided to wait a little longer.

At about 1:30 p.m., Laziz had had enough. Since he had not been able to have a solid breakfast in the morning, he decided to have a quick lunch in the service canteen. That way, the supervisor would be able to find him easily if he wanted to look for him.

Laziz hurriedly ate and went upstairs. The door of the reception room was still closed. His jacket and hat were also in place. "So, the boss still hasn't returned yet. Maybe his friends came by car and called for lunch somewhere nearby," he thought.

Around three o'clock in the afternoon, Bakhrom Safarovich was asked by the head of the personnel department and then by the head of the organizational and control department. Laziz covered for the chief as best he could, coming up with all sorts of excuses: "He was just here, he's out now, I'll tell him that you asked for him". This was repeated several times, but he tried not to set the chief up. At the end of the working day the chief was demanded by Tahir Gafurovich himself.

Laziz struggled to get out of it as best he could. On one hand, the guy was angry because he didn't know where his boss was, and on the other hand, he was afraid he'd set him up.

"Weird, where could he have gone? I mean, he could have warned me! I wouldn't have gone to the trouble of fooling everyone. Had he forgotten all about it while talking to his friends? But you could have called! Or couldn't he have? But he didn't have that habit! Even if he had to go somewhere for half an hour, he would call and find out about the situation! What will I tell my superiors now...?" With such thoughts, Laziz ended his workday. "Anyway, the chief will stop by the office," he thought and went on with his business. However, the chief had disappeared with the ends. Convinced that there was no point in waiting any further, he left work around twenty-one o'clock. "Probably he got tired of sitting and went straight home without stopping by the office," the secretary thought to himself...

Laziz, who was used to coming to work early, opened the door of the reception area and saw that the boss's outerwear was still hanging there. "So, he didn't come into the office during the night," he thought and went about his duties. However, he began to worry as there was still no word from the boss even though working hours had already started. He didn't know what to answer if the management asked the chief. "He probably stayed up late with friends last night and went to bed late, so no wonder he'll be late today," he thought.

As expected, at ten o'clock in the morning the management asked Bakhrom Safarovich again. Now Laziz did not know what to answer. He knew that the boss took his work very seriously and had never been late. In moments of dire need, he would at least notify the management by phone of his absence for a valid reason. "So what happened to him? Or did he end up in the hospital? Or maybe he was in a traffic accident? No way. In that case, the hospital would have called." Laziz was alarmed at his thoughts. "Maybe we should call his house? What if he wasn't home? What should I do then? That way I'll scare Wazira opa. I know her well. She'll panic at the drop of a hat and then she'll put everyone on edge. In that case, I'll end up worrying everyone. I'd better wait a while. If the chief doesn't come at lunchtime, I'll slowly find out everything from Wazira opa.

After lunch, the anxiety of the leadership grew. Meanwhile, only Laziz suffered. He was now definitely at an impasse. Finally, gathering his thoughts, he called Wazira opa's workplace. After the usual greeting, he informed him that Bahrom Safarovich was eagerly awaited at work today.

- Uh, Lazizjon, don't you know, he left for Khorezm yesterday. But he hasn't called me yet either," Vazira opa added carelessly.

The chief's wife's reply put him in a stupor. After all, the trip to Khorezm had been canceled yesterday. So he didn't even go home.... All sorts of thoughts ran through his head.

The same question from the chief's wife, "Didn't you know?" ran through his mind, to which he murmured uncertainly, "No, I didn't know." "If I tell her now that the trip has been canceled, and the chief left the office yesterday close to lunchtime and did not return, there will be a scandal. It's better to wait until the end. Chief is still a man, who knows, maybe he found someone else! Whatever it is, let it end well...," he thought.

The working hours were over, but the boss still hadn't shown up. He was tormented by the question: "Should I go home or wait?! He had to do something. We can't just sit idly by! What should I do? Or should I tell the management? Wouldn't he hurt the chief in that case? Or should we wait until morning? What if we consult with Hasan Aliyevich? He is, after all, Bakhrom aka's deputy and might give good advice.

Lazizjon, satisfied with the idea that had occurred to him, went to the deputy.

-Come in, Lazizjon, are you still here, haven't you gone home? - Without taking his eyes off the papers, Hasan Aliyevich gestured to him to sit down.

-I was just leaving. You've got a visitor.... - Laziz hesitated, not knowing where to start. Because every time he'd asked his boss since yesterday, he'd lied to him.

Fortunately, the deputy handled the situation himself:

- What happened, Lazizjon, the chief didn't come back?

- From where?

-You said yourself that the chief was away on an errand and would be back soon!

- Yeah, no, he's not back. But to be honest, I don't even know where the chief is....

- What do you mean you don't know? What does all this mean? - Hasan Aliyevich stood up and looked questioningly at the secretary.

- I wanted to cover for him while he was away...

- What are you talking about, bro? Who's being covered up and why? Calm down and explain! -said the deputy, sitting down on the chair opposite.

Laziz told everything in order. Hearing what had happened, Hasan Aliyevich was also puzzled.

- Maybe he told his relatives that he was going to Khorezm and spent the night at another's house?

- Then he would have warned me. After all, today is the second day he's been gone. Even if he went out yesterday, he should have come to work today! You know very well that the boss gives a warning even if he's gone for half an hour.

- You are right, today is the second day. But in any case, it is necessary to inform the management about it, - said

Hasan Aliyevich and got up from his seat. - Sit here, I'll talk to Tahir Gafurovich.

- Hasan aka, I hope the chief won't get hurt by this," Lazizjon said, not hiding his concern.

-We cannot sit idly by! - The deputy replied and, adjusting his uniform, headed for Tahir Gafurovich's reception room.

The deputy prosecutor, having heard that Bakhrom Safarovich had not come home yesterday, was thinking. It was not hard to guess from his focused gaze where he was concerned.

- I must report this to the prosecutor. And you call all the relatives and acquaintances. Invite his wife. We'll meet in an hour," the deputy prosecutor commanded, standing up.

Laziz was instructed to invite Wazira opa. What reason could he think of to call a woman at night and invite her to her husband's office? With such thoughts he started dialing a familiar number. Vaziraopa herself answered the phone.

-Assalom alaikum, opazhon[1], sorry to bother you again," Laziz tried to speak confidently so as not to show his excitement.

-Walaikum assalom, ukajon[2], how are you doing? Any news from Bahrom aka? I was expecting a call from him all day today, but he must have had a lot of work to do to find time to call me. Have you talked to him?

---

[1] opazhon - sister
[2] ukajon is a brother

Lazizjon was taken aback: "No, I guess he didn't have time." Then, as if nothing had happened, he added:

-Opajon, Tahir Gafurovich is asking for you. Do you have time now?

-What's the question?

-I don't know, I guess I wanted to consult with you about something.

- Can I come by in the morning?

- It's just that he is waiting for you now. It is possible that he will leave for the region in the morning," Lazizjon said, ashamed of his lie.

-Okay. I'll be right there," Vazira's voice changed, as if she sensed something wrong.

"It's not for nothing that the deputy prosecutor asks to come to the office at this late hour, is it? What advice could there possibly be at this hour? Laziz also has a strange, agitated voice. You can sense some anxiety. The important thing is that her husband is alive and well. He hasn't called once since he left on his business trip, and it's been a day and a half. That's not like him. Everywhere he goes, he calls to say he got there safely. Oh, God, save and preserve us from trouble!". In her musings, Wazirahon did not even notice when she reached her husband's office. Laziz was waiting for him downstairs. The two of them went up to the fourth floor, to the reception room of the deputy prosecutor. The secretary must have been warned in advance, because he didn't ask who the woman was and immediately invited her to the office.

Tahir Gafurovich stood up and greeted the guest. Letting her sit down, he poured tea from the kettle on the table into a bowl. He asked her about her health, business, family and parents.

Though Wazirahon had seen and greeted this man before at weddings or various events of the prosecutor's office, she did not know him intimately. So she preferred to answer his questions briefly: "yes," "no," and "thank Allah." The fact that he had started the conversation from afar finally got to her. In addition, he was too condescending. "How long he's dragging on! I wish he would get to the heart of the matter. God forbid something should happen to the father of my children!". A thousand questions tormented her.

- The purpose of inviting you here... - Tahir Gafurovich hesitated, not knowing where to begin....

- Will you please tell me the truth, what happened to my husband?"-Wazirahon turned pale and jumped up from her seat: - "Don't hide it, please, tell it as it is....

-Wazirahon, please calm down, nothing has happened yet. But we haven't been able to find your husband for two days.

- How can't you find it? My husband left yesterday on a business trip to Khorezm!

- That's the thing, the trip to Khorezm was canceled. Bakhrom Safarovich was at work yesterday until lunchtime. Then he went out. No one has seen him since then. Perhaps he called you yesterday or today. Or maybe he had something urgent to do... It's strange.

- No, he didn't call me. Yesterday morning he left saying, "I'm going to Khorezm." All this time I thought he was on a business trip... - said Vazirahon, unable to hold back her tears.

- Please, Wazirahon, calm down. There's no need to panic. He'll be found, where will he go? We'll find him. Someone called him yesterday around noon. Maybe a classmate, maybe a classmate. Anyway, it was a close friend of his. Maybe he's out partying with them right now. Or maybe he had too much to drink.

- But he wasn't in the habit of going somewhere without telling me! Wherever he was, he always called.

- Who knows, maybe he didn't have time to call or there is no phone where he is now.

Vazirahon seemed somewhat relieved. He really could have been in a no-phone zone! They said he had gone out with his friends! Maybe he'd gone with them to the mountains or to a cottage where there was no antenna. God, let it be true!

- Yes, by the way, Bakhrom Safarovich's parents seem to live in the village. Can you contact them? It's possible that he went to visit them. Perhaps one of his relatives had a disaster and left without informing you. Do they have a telephone?

- Yes, yes, yes! - said Vazirahon, trying to believe his words herself.

Tahir Gafurovich dialed the number of Bahrom's parents, which Vazirakhon called, and handed her the receiver.

-Assalomu alaykum dadaajon[3], how are you doing, everyone is alive and well? Allah be praised, your

---

[3] dadajohn - dad, father

grandchildren are fine, Bahrom aka is fine too.... I'm calling you because I'm worried about Bahrom aka. He's late. He didn't come to see you?

-No, he didn't. I talked to him the day before yesterday. He didn't say he was coming, but he said he was going on a business trip. Daughter, what's wrong? - Safarak's voice was clearly heard by everyone around him.

-It's okay, Dadajohn. -It's okay. It's just that a business trip got canceled. I thought he'd gone to the country since he hasn't called. I'm sorry for disturbing you. If he comes back, I'll call you. Don't worry. Say hello to everyone for me, take care of yourself, Dadajohn! "He didn't go to the village either!" she muttered unhappily as she put the receiver back down.

-Wazirahon, you go home and calm down. We'll try to find him ourselves. If possible, ask his relatives, friends, acquaintances. Who knows, maybe he'll come back tonight. We'll talk in the morning, the guys will take you home," the deputy prosecutor walked the woman to the door.

Laziz, escorting Wazirahon home in his car, on the way told the whole story of yesterday from beginning to end.

- Has this woman called before? Maybe her voice sounds like that of common acquaintances? - Wazirahon asked, peering into the face of her interlocutor.

- No, it was the first time I'd heard that voice. Perhaps because I had a short conversation on the phone, I couldn't figure out who she was. But she didn't even introduce herself! I wish I had asked who she was! But it was obvious that it was a close acquaintance. Because Bahrom aka wouldn't go out to a stranger. And anyway, who knows?

-Just something...

-Vazira opa, don't worry, you'll see, everything will be fine!

- God willing.

When she entered the house, Vazirahon looked for her husband's shoes. When she did not find them, she thought disappointedly, "Then he has not come!" and went to the nursery. Jahangir and Jawahir had long since fallen asleep.

Vazirahon found her husband's phone book in her desk drawer and quickly began running her eyes through it. "So, where do I start and what do I tell them? I can't just ask, 'Have you seen my husband? Or is it better to tell it like it is? But in that case, it might damage the husband's reputation. What will people think when they hear about it?"

Since it was late, Wazirahon first called only the closest family friends. She called four of them, but did not hear any encouraging response from them. None of them had seen her husband in the last two days and he had not called anyone. Though the time was late, Wazirahon kept calling. She spoke to almost every acquaintance of her husband's that she knew. But not a single call yielded the expected result. On the contrary, she became more worried and found herself in an awkward position. Because many acquaintances knew her as an overly jealous wife. What would people now think of a woman who searches for her husband at night and disturbs the peace of others?

Every moment seemed to take Vazirahon farther away from her husband. As the minutes passed, the small spark of hope in her heart seemed to fade away and her dreams crumbled to dust. The woman lay awake all night and met the morning with the darkest of thoughts. In the morning, the phone rang unexpectedly. Vazirahon shrieked with joy: "Well, at last! Thank God!" and picked up the receiver. On the other end of the line was Safar aka - her father-in-law. Judging by yesterday's call, he had not slept either. When he heard that his son still hadn't come home, he coldly said goodbye to his daughter-in-law, saying that he was leaving for the city immediately....

Wazira went to her husband's office without waiting for work hours to start, thinking, "Maybe they have news!" Laziz came to work early, too, but it was easy to see from his face that he hadn't slept last night either. They both looked at each other, trying to see something reassuring.

-Oops, any news? - Laziz spoke first.

- No, I called all his friends and close acquaintances, no one has seen your boss in the next two days," Vazira could barely hold back her tears.

- Opazhon, sit down, now we're going to visit Tahir Gafurovich, surely, he has good news! - Laziz didn't know how to calm this woman down.

After a while, the deputy prosecutor invited Vazira into the office again.

- Hello, Vazirahon, how was your rest? - Tahir Gafurovich gestured for the woman to sit down. - Is there any news?

-Called his friends and acquaintances all night. No one had seen him for the past two days. In the morning my father-in-law also left for Tashkent, perhaps he will arrive by noon. Tahir Gafurovich, what news do you have? What should we do now?

- I reported it to the prosecutor yesterday. He's got everyone on alert. We've sent people to all the hospitals and morgues just in case. We're questioning all our colleagues and acquaintances; I think we'll get results...

-What-what-shall-I-do? - Tears came to Wazira's eyes again.

-You stay here for a while. I'll have the boys look around Bakhrom Safarovitch's office with you. Maybe there will be some clue in his clothes, notebook or notes!

Tahir Gafurovich pressed a button, inviting the secretary, and instructed him to escort the woman to the office of the deputy head of the department on the third floor.

They were met downstairs by Bakhrom Safarovitch's deputy Hasan Aliyevich.

-Vazira opa, how are you?

-Thank you, Hasanjon, who knew these troubles would fall on our heads?" said Wazirahon, wiping her tears with her handkerchief.

-Opazhon, just don't cry, God willing, everything will work out!

Hasan Aliyevich took the woman to her husband's office. The hat and jacket were still hanging on the hanger in the reception area. Vazira took the jacket off the hanger and searched its pockets. In the inner pocket of the jacket there was change - three or four thousand sums, and in the outer pockets there were scraps of paper with phone numbers. They entered a cozy and clean office. Everything was in place. A large safe stood in the corner. On the desk were stacks of papers. Next to the phone was an open notebook. They carefully studied all the papers, on which were written someone's phone numbers and other records. Everything as it should be. Nothing unusual was found in the office.

Hasan Aliyevich ordered Laziz not to let anyone into the office yet, not to touch anything and, leaving Vazira waiting in the reception room, hurried to Tahir Gafurovich.

Vazira was now gripped by panic fear. She wished it were a dream that would end sooner! She recalled the vivid moments spent with her husband. What a happy time it had been...

Their acquaintance was very interesting. At that time, she was a first-year student at Samarkand State University. Classes at the university were hard, there were not enough textbooks. For this reason, she had to go to the university library every day. Vazira remembered the day when they first met. As if it had been yesterday. One spring day she had stayed in the library for a long time and had been so absorbed in reading that she hadn't even noticed how dark it had gotten outside. Unfortunately, her friend Mashhurakhon was not around. She went outside alone.

The university dormitory was not far away, but to get there one had to walk one or two stops through the park. It was usually crowded during the day, but much quieter in the evening. Spotlights shone dimly in some places, illuminating only their circumference. Vazira regretted staying up so late and tried to walk quickly. After walking a little, she noticed two young men sitting on a bench on the side of the sidewalk. To avoid attracting their attention, she crossed to the other side.

-Girl, what time is it? - one of them asked. Vazira pretended not to hear and continued on her way.

-Are you deaf?! - The other guy got angry, jumped up from his seat and blocked the girl's path.

- Get out of my way, I don't have a watch! - Vazira's voice trembled for some reason.

-Where is beauty in a hurry? If anything, we can take you by car," said a tall, mustachioed guy approaching the girl.

-Thank you, I live in that dorm over there," the girl said, pointing ahead.

-Ah, are we students? Hunting? Here we are in your trap. Look at that, it's not hair, it's a waterfall! - said the short guy, touching the girl's long hair.

-Hands off, you idiot! -Vazira slapped the young man's arm. Sensing that these guys' intentions were not good, the girl looked around, hoping to see someone who would come to her aid. Unfortunately, no one was visible in the alley.

-Please, guys, let me go, I must go," the girl pleaded.

- Where are you in such a hurry, you are a student, don't you want to have fun with us? We'll give you as much as you want, - said the mustachioed man, taking the girl's hand and pulling her to him. Vazira vomited from the smell of booze and screamed at the top of her voice:

- Let go of my hand, you bastard! Ouch. Ma-ma-a-a-a-ah!!! - The girl pushed the guy's chest with all her might and punched him in the face.

- You bitch! Did you hit me? I'll fucking show you! -the mustached man lunged at the girl with a roar.

The girl fought back as hard as she could and continued to scream exhaustedly, looking around.

- Don't shout, no one can hear you. If you don't agree nicely, I'll have to stab you! - The short guy took something out of his pocket and held it to the girl's throat.

Vazira noticed that the thing that glittered in the moonlight was a knife, and now she realized that the situation was very dangerous. Her hands and feet went cold. Thousands of thoughts ran through her mind, "What to do? Will she die at the hands of these scumbags? Will she let herself be dishonored by these thugs! What will happen to her dreams?! How will she face her parents, relatives, friends, classmates?! No, no, no, even if she dies, she won't let them dishonor her! Die with honor!".

These thoughts gave the girl confidence, and she pushed the mustachioed man away from her with force. The young man staggered and took a couple of steps back. At that moment, the second guy clasped the girl's hands and started pulling on her. No matter how much the girl tried to break free from the vise, the guy's strong hands squeezed her harder and harder. The girl screamed desperately with her last strength, but her voice became hoarse and completely silenced. The young men dragged the girl to the Zhiguli standing on the roadside. At that moment, someone's silhouette appeared in the distance.

- Po-mo-help, please! Po-mo-help...! -she shouted in his direction.

One of the guys clamped a hand over the girl's mouth. The silhouette seemed to hear the girl's voice, and he ran up to them.

- Let the girl go, you bastard! - The stranger rushed at the boys with anger and snatched the girl out of their hands. The trembling girl staggered back and took shelter behind the back of her savior. The mustachioed man, like a dog from whom a piece of meat had just been taken away, rushed at the stranger in a frenzy.

- If you want to live, don't meddle in other people's business, or I'll gut you!

-Calm down, buddy! You think you can do anything? If you're so brave, come on, be a man, go one-on-one! - said the stranger, not backing down.

- Go away, I say, nicely! We don't spare those who stick their noses in unnecessary holes! -the short man grabbed the stranger by the collar.

The young man pushed him down in one motion. Now the mustachioed man, playing with the knife in his hand, began to attack the enemy. With an unusual blow of his left hand, the savior knocked the knife out of the villain's hand. The knife fell nearby. The bandits with bloodshot eyes now two of them pounced on one.

Vazira was now worried not only for herself but also for her savior. Most of all she was afraid that an innocent man might get hurt because of her. At that moment two people appeared at the other end of the sidewalk. The girl, gathering her last strength, began to call them for help. When they heard the girl's voice, they went towards them. But it seems that they did not have enough courage, because they turned back and disappeared from sight. Despite this, the girl continued to cry out for help at the top of her voice. But there wasn't a soul around. The girl bent down to help her savior, but nothing came under her hand. The bandits tried to crush the poor young man's resistance with their hands and feet. But the boy was not a coward either ...At this moment the mustachioed man began to look for a knife that had fallen into the grass. The girl wanted to stop him, but her legs did not obey her, no matter how hard she tried, she could not move. The mustachioed man found the knife and ran towards the fighters, who threw strong blows at each other. No sooner had the girl shouted, "Be os-too-horrible, he has a knife..." than the mustachioed man plunged the knife into the side of the boy who was pinning his opponent to the ground. For a while everyone was silent. The lean man, bringing himself to order, shouted to the mustachioed man, "What have you done, you fool! You killed him!". The mustachioed man froze for a moment, and the bloody knife fell out of his hands. The stranger turned back and collapsed helplessly to the ground.Then one of the bandits shouted: "Run!" Both ran to their car. Wazira stood like a stumbling block. Then, gathering all her strength, she rushed to the boy's aid. No matter how hard she tried, she was unable to straighten the young man's torso. Her hands and all her clothes were covered in blood. She placed the boy's head in her lap and covered the bleeding wound with her palms. Despite the fact that his life hung in the balance, the young man looked intently at the girl for the first time and whispered: "Those scumbags didn't hurt you?!" His voice grew quieter and quieter, and the light in his eyes seemed to fade. She heard people's voices and called for help again, "Please help, help is needed here...".

The doctors fought for the young man's life for a long time. Even after the operation, which lasted more than three hours, the danger was not completely over. Vazira ran up to everyone in a white coat coming out of the intensive care unit and repeated the same questions: "How is he? Is he all right? Has he regained consciousness?". Not hearing a positive answer, she was losing her strength. Even though the doctors were saying that everything was fine and he would regain consciousness soon, she could see some worry in their eyes. "So something bad has happened. No, no. He must survive and he will definitely live! If God wills it, it will all go away like nothing ever happened!" Wazirahon spent the whole night without washing her eyes in the corridor of the hospital. She would have called his relatives, but she didn't know his name or where he lived. "The poor guy's parents and relatives are probably out of their minds. He probably has a wife and children. Imagine what would happen if such a nice young man, for no reason at all, didn't come home! How would his family feel now?! O Almighty Allah, help this innocent brave man who risked his life for me! Do not make me the cause of his death!"

Meanwhile, first the police arrived, and later the prosecutor's office arrived. Someone must have tipped them off! Three or four people took turns interrogating Vazira, who at that moment was concerned not with the investigators' meticulous questions, but with the condition of the man whose life the doctors were fighting for behind the wall. Therefore, she tried to answer the questions briefly, but the investigators, on the contrary, urged her to tell everything in detail. They wrote down everything she said on paper and drew up some documents.

Thankfully, the prayers of Wazira, who had spent the night on her feet, were answered, and towards morning the nurse on duty reported that the young man had regained consciousness.

-Opajon, let me go in to see him for a moment, please! - the girl begged the nurse.

-Unfortunately, that's not possible. The doctors said not to let anyone in.

-Sister, I will pray for you forever. -Sister. Please allow me to, uh.

-All right, just for a minute, but if they see this, it will be bad luck for you and me! - said the nurse, slipping her robe over Wazira's shoulders. -Follow me.

They tiptoed into the intensive care unit. The nurse carefully closed the door of the room.

-Okay, I'll give you two minutes! - she said and walked out the door.

The girl slowly approached the bed of the sick man. The young man lay with closed eyes, his breathing was imperceptible. His whole body was connected by wires to some apparatus. Last night in the darkness she had not even had time to see his face. "And he's handsome!" thought the girl. Seeming to hear the sound of footsteps, the young man opened his eyes and turned toward the girl. At first, he thought it must be one of the nurses, and closed his eyes again.

-Hello, how are you? It's because of me.

The young man recognized the girl by her voice, opened his eyes wide and stared at her:

-You've been here all night? -You've been here all night?

-Wait for me- Because of me.

- Don't worry, it's fate and no one has ever escaped from it. Everything that is done is for the best!

- Anyway, I blame you. If it weren't for you.

- Don't say that. Anyone in my position would have acted the same way. Oh I didn't even ask your name," he said, smiling slightly.

-Wazira.

- You have a beautiful name. My name is Bahrom. So we've met. You're at university, aren't you?

- Yes, in the Philology Department.

-I'm in law school. I think I've seen you a couple times in the library.

- Yes, I was on my way back from the library yesterday, so engrossed in a book that I didn't even realize it was dark. It cost me a lot of money. Now I owe you one. Forgive me, Bahrom aka!

The guy was thrilled that the girl addressed him respectfully "aka[4] ".

-Vazirakhon, please stop reproaching yourself, I'm fine, I'll be discharged in a couple of days, God willing, but at least we've met. And as for the debt, I've forgiven it! I have forgiven it! -Bakhrom joked.

At that moment a nurse appeared in the doorway:

-Wrap it up, sister, it's time to go out, the patient should be left alone, he can't talk at all right now.

Wazira, reluctant to say goodbye to the young man, turned around leaving the chamber:

-Bahrom aka, I could call your loved ones if you give me the number," she said.

- No, no, my parents live in the village, it's better they don't know about it yet. Better tell my friend Olimjon, who lives with me in the second dormitory, what happened. He must be worried too.

-Okay, get well soon!

Wazira left the hospital, embarrassed because she could not find the right words to comfort her savior. When she saw that the young man was in a satisfactory condition, she felt a great relief. It was as if a mountain had been lifted off her shoulders. "Fortunately, everything ended well, he will recover quickly. Did he say his name was Bahrom? And he's cute. He didn't get depressed even at such a difficult time. And his eyes are always smiling. He lives in a hostel, so he's not married yet...," she thought on the way.

---

[4]   aka brother, a respectful address to a man.

Blushing at her own thoughts, the girl left the hospital grounds and headed straight for the university dormitory...

Remembering the moments of meeting her husband, she tried to convince herself that a man who had gone through such a difficult ordeal could not be accidentally lost and that he would surely be found.

-Opazhon, aren't you bored? -Hasan Aliyevich's voice interrupted her thoughts.

-No, is there news, Hasanjon?!

-Silence for now, опажон. Shall we go see Tahir Gafurovich?

Wazira followed Hassan, hoping to hear good news from the deputy prosecutor. In the reception area, the secretary again greeted her as warmly as last time, invited her to sit down and handed her a cup of[5] tea. The chief was talking loudly to someone on the phone. His words were not clearly audible, but it was clear that he was talking about important business. After a while, the secretary, having spoken to the chief on the internal phone, invited them to come into the chief's office.

Tahir Gafurovich's face showed his bad mood, he was very nervous. Vazira, afraid to hear cold news from him, kept silent, not knowing where to put herself.

-Vazirakhon, you know, it seems that the case is much more serious than we thought. That's why the management

---

[5] piala, pialushka - an oriental cup without a handle, from which tea is drunk

has decided to initiate a criminal case, a special group of the most experienced investigators and operatives has been formed, the group is headed by me personally. You will see, we will soon find Bakhromjon....

Wazira couldn't stand it:

-What criminal case? What group? You think someone killed Bahrom aka? I don't understand anything.

-No, no, you misunderstand me. Bakhromjon has been missing for three days and his whereabouts are unknown. In such cases, according to all rules, a criminal case is initiated on the fact. This has also been reported to higher authorities. The progress of the investigation will also be monitored by them. You go home and reassure your relatives. I'll call you when necessary. Hasan Aliyevich will be in touch with you. If you know anything, inform him immediately!

As she left the prosecutor's office, Vazira felt weak in her body. She was haunted by the darkest thoughts. Could it be that she would never be able to see her husband again, and her children would remain orphans like she herself had once been?! Lord, so many trials on our heads! They said it's a criminal case, so it's more serious than that. Something happened to her husband and they're hiding something. What do we do? What do we do?

Laziz drove Vazira home in his car. She was met on the doorstep by her father-in-law Safar aka.

-What's wrong, my daughter, where's Bahromjon?

Wazira, couldn't contain herself and sobbed.

-Wai, my child, what has happened to my son, son-no-ok, Bahromjon, is he alive? -now wailed Safar aka.

- Father, Bahrom aka is missing, for three days now they have been looking for him and can't find him.

-Daughter, sweetheart, don't panic. He must have gone somewhere, he will be back soon, as long as he is alive and well! - Safaraka said, trying to reassure his daughter-in-law.

-If only, if only, Father!!!

-What do they say at work?

- A criminal case has been initiated, an investigation is to be carried out. When Safar aka heard the word "criminal case", he was also frightened. "Something is wrong!" thought the old man. Although he was shaking inside, he tried to remain calm in front of his daughter-in-law, who was in an even worse situation:

-Daughter, a criminal case doesn't mean anything, don't panic, I'll go talk to them. A grown man can't just disappear suddenly!

Despite his daughter-in-law's resistance, Safar aka left the house and went straight to his son's office.

Tahir Gafurovich warmly received the old man. He reassured the father that the search was underway, that all the agencies were involved, but there was no news yet, and promised that in a couple of days the results would be in, that they would find his son and bring him back to his family. He said goodbye to the old man, instructing the guys to escort him home, and said that he would immediately inform him as soon as there was news.

Safar aka did not object to his son's superior and returned home with some confidence, but at the same time his anxiety did not leave him....

The next day Laziz called Wazira and asked her and Safar aka to come to the prosecutor's office. The father-in-law and daughter-in-law, who had not slept a wink at night, quickly arrived at the prosecutor's office hoping to hear good news. Lazizjon, as always, greeted them warmly and took them to Hasan Aliyevich's office.

- Hello Safar aka, hello opa[6], how are you, did you have a good rest? - greeted Hasan Aliyevich, inviting them to sit down.

- Thank God, but we barely made it to the morning," Safar aka wanted to get to the point of the conversation.

- Is there any news, Hasanjon? - Wazira intervened impatiently.

- Now Takhir Gafurovich is holding the first meeting of the investigation team. The guys have been working all night and gathering all the information. Several versions are being put forward. When the investigators come out, they'll talk to you. We need your help to clear up some questions. You'll have to wait a while. Soon Laziz said that the meeting was over and Fakhriddin Karimovich, an investigator for especially important cases, was waiting for them in his office. Five or six people met them in the investigator's office. After a greeting, a young man sitting in an armchair in the back of the office spoke:

- Safar aka, Wazira opa, we understand your situation and are doing everything in our hands. In a couple of days everything will be clear, we will definitely find Bakhrom Safarovich. Therefore, you should not worry for the time

---

[6] opa is a sister, respectful of women.

being. As you know, an investigation team was formed yesterday. I, Fakhriddin Karimovich, am the deputy head of the group," the investigator introduced himself. Then, pointing to the people sitting next to him, he continued: - These people are our experienced investigators on especially important cases, most of them are Bakhrom aka's disciples. The group also includes operatives from the Interior Ministry, KGB and other agencies. They need your help.

Safar aka put his hand to his chest in approval of the investigator's words and said: - "Okay, I see."

Wazira couldn't find a place to sit as events grew more complicated by the hour. She was eager to hear something reassuring from the investigator's lips. But as there was no news about her husband's fate, she could not help herself: -Fakhriddinjon, is there any news about Bahrom aka's fate? If something happened, don't hide it, please tell me the truth, I'm sick of it! - Wazira said, wiping away her tears with her handkerchief.

Opazhon, please pull yourself together, we're not just sitting around, either, we're working on some assumptions right now. God willing, everything will be fine," Fakhriddin Karimovich said with the calmness typical of investigators. - Most importantly, Safar aka, opazhon, there is no bad news related to Bakhr aka yet. It means he is alive and well. For this alone, we should already be grateful to God.

- God willing," Wazira said, sighing heavily.

-All hope is in you, may the Almighty support you! - Safar aka said, breaking the silence.

-Sanjarbek, take the guests to your office and talk to them in detail, and make sure that no detail is left out! Ask them if they noticed any changes in Bakhrom aka's behavior during the last year, with whom he communicated, whether he quarreled with neighbors, acquaintances or anyone else, who came to visit him, whom he himself went to, whether he had enemies, find out everything from thread to needle, and if you have any questions, come to me, understand? - said Fakhriddin Karimovich, standing up.

- Yes," replied Sanjar.

-By the way, I have one more request for you, when you get home, check all the things belonging to Bahrom aka, one by one, if you find anything dubious, like a phone number or a letter, call us immediately," the chief finished his instructions.

Vazira nodded her head in agreement.

Sanjarbek first questioned Safar aka in detail and then Vazira. From time to time he asked questions to clarify the events of a particular day. Although the interrogations lasted all day, the investigator was apparently not satisfied with his work. He reread the protocols again and again.

- Good," he said, taking a break from his papers. - You haven't forgotten anything?

-No," replied father-in-law and daughter-in-law at the same time.

- Well, then sit here, I'll report to the team leader," Sanzharbek put the documents in a folder and stood up. Soon the investigator returned: "Opazhon, you go downstairs. I'll catch up with you now. We'll go to your place together. We need to examine Bakhromak's things," said Sanzharbek, gathering the papers on the table. - I've received such an assignment. I'd better go myself. Perhaps there will be some clue there.

Outside the window, the autumn sun had set behind the horizon and the streetlights on the side of the road began to flicker. A light breeze blew the last leaves off the huge maple tree and stacked them underfoot. Vazira's frustration grew as today too had yielded no results. "Could it be that no one has seen or knows how such a prominent man could have disappeared without a trace. It is mind boggling! O God, save the life of my Bahrom aka! Give me back the father of my children! O century-old maples, tell me, where is my dearest man now? Didn't you last see him and escort him somewhere? I beg you, answer me...!" Somehow just today the last spark of hope seemed to have gone out in her heart. It felt as if she were losing her first and last love forever.

Sanzharbek did not wait long, he came out with another young investigator....

The investigators thoroughly examined the room, the desk and Bakhrom Safarovich's clothes. They even went through the books, magazines and albums on the shelves one by one. Except for a few scraps of paper with phone numbers and names of people, they found no significant documents or, in the language of the investigators, "physical evidence". Only one small letter found among the books attracted the investigators' attention. It read: "Hello, Bakhrom aka! I didn't manage to meet you. I will come again soon. Let's see each other. I have an important business with you. I will call you."

The letter was handwritten, and it was not hard to guess that it was a woman's handwriting. But there was no name, no signature, no date. Judging from the envelope found nearby, the letter had been mailed to Bahrom aka's office. There was no information about the sender on the envelope either. Sanjarbek carefully examined the envelope and found out that the letter was sent from Tashkent on October fifteenth and arrived at the address on October sixteenth.

The investigators, observing all formalities, took this letter as "evidence".

-Vazira opa, if you find anything else like this letter, call me," Sanzharbek warned as he packed his things. - That's enough for today. We will go and report to the leadership.

-Good day, -Wazira, seeing the guests off, looked at them questioningly, "What should we do next?"

-You stay at home for now. It is desirable that Safar aka should stay here as well. If there is any news, I will inform you at once, -Sanjarbek took his coat in his hands and hurried towards his partner, who was waiting for him in the started car.

The children came out of their rooms when they heard the guests leave. They, especially Jahangir, had already realized that these were not easy "guests". From the way they thoroughly searched their father's room, the always kind and smiling grandfather walking around very sad and their mother not finding a place to be, they realized that some unpleasant events were going on. Even so, they did not dare to openly ask their mother about it.

-Mom, who are these guests and why have they come? -Jahangir asked.

-These people work with your father. Since your dad is away on business, they were looking for some documents related to him in the house.

-Since Daddy left, he hasn't called once. Mom, where did he go? -Jawahir asked in turn.

-He called me at work and I forgot to tell you about it," the mother faked a smile on her face to hide her worries.

Although the children had long ago noticed the worry on their mother's face, they did not bother her with questions so as not to hurt her. They acted like adults: they pretended to believe their mother's words, said good night to the adults and went to their room to sleep.

"Today I was able to deceive and reassure the children, but what will I tell them tomorrow? It's hard when you contradict yourself. Tomorrow our favorite daddy could come back. So don't scare them. It is good that I was able to reassure them," thought Wazirahon.

The father-in-law and daughter-in-law were silent for a while, preoccupied with their thoughts. No one even touched the food on the table. Safar aka wanted to cheer up his daughter-in-law, who was grief-stricken, but it was difficult for him to find such words.

Daughter-in-law, hope springs eternal. Pull yourself together and don't despair. You'll see, they'll find Bahromjon tomorrow. We have no enemies. Who can harm us? You know your husband is a man who always helps everyone. Perhaps he is doing good deeds somewhere now," Safar aka smiled faintly.

-I understand, but he could have called! -Wazira had tears in her eyes again. -Wazira's tears came to her eyes again. —The most important thing is that he's alive and well, wherever he is.

- Anything could have happened, my child, there's probably no way to call. You can't find a phone in many places. There's no cause for panic and despair. Tomorrow, God willing, something will become clearer..... - Safar aka's voice trailed off as if a lump was stuck in his throat. He hurriedly took his tear-filled eyes away from his daughter-in-law.

Vazira made her father-in-law's bed in the living room and went into the nursery to see how the children were doing. She adjusted the blankets of the sleeping children and for some time admired the curls and blush on the cheeks of the sleeping children in the light falling from the crack in the door. "Will my children suffer the same fate as mine? Why has my happiness come to an end so soon? Why have I suffered this!!! Why am I so miserable?! Did I come into this world just to grieve?! Where is the justice, Lord?! What is my children's fault? Give me back my Bahrom aka, who am I without him, what's the point of my life? They say that when swans lose their mate, they throw themselves from heights onto cliffs to crash and die. Where do these animals get such devotion?! And humans? Are they capable of it? It turns out they are! Today I found myself in the position of a swan. No, Wazira, calm down! Don't extinguish the light of hope in your heart! Think of your children! Don't let them repeat your fate!" she pondered.

Vazira sat close to her youngest son, stroked his hair, kissed his cheeks, eyes and hugged him tightly, as if she wanted to snatch him from the claws of cruel fate ...

Wazira, who had not slept all night, took a nap in the morning. She dreamed that she was looking for her husband in the middle of the desert.... Sand dunes, hot. She was thirsty. Suddenly a well appeared in front of her. Wanting to drink water, she threw a bucket into the well. At that moment a voice was heard from the bottom of the well:

-Wazira, my Wazira, I'm here.

-Bahrom aka, what are you doing here? I've been looking for you everywhere!

- I fell down a well. Now I can't get out. Throw the rope!

Vazira hurriedly threw the rope tied to the bucket into the well. She bent down and gazed at the bottom of the well. She could clearly see her husband in distress. "Thank God he is safe!" she thought.

- Pull! - came a voice from the well.

Vazira slowly began to pull the rope. The rope slipped out of her hands midway. A rumbling sound came from the well.

-Bahrom aka, the rope slipped out of my hands, I'm sorry. Did you fall hard?

- No, no, don't worry. Pull again! Bahrom tied a stone to the end of the rope and threw it outside.

Vazira pulled the rope as hard as she could. This time it broke suddenly.... The woman with trembling hands bent down and looked into the well and saw no one. The water in the well seemed darkened for some reason....

-Bahrom aka, Bahrom aka, Bahrom aka!

Jawahir, awakened by the scream, started waking up his sweating mom:

-Mommy, Mommy! What's wrong with you! Mommy, get up, ma-ma...

Woken by her son's voice, Wazira looked around and hugged her frightened younger son:

-Calm down, sweetie, I'm fine. -I'm fine. I think I had a bad dream.

Wazira calmed her son and returned to her bedroom. The rays of the rising sun began to illuminate the room. Somehow at that moment her room seemed uncomfortable and cold. She picked up the photograph that stood on the table. It was taken on the day of her wedding with Bahrom: "Eh, Bahrom aka, where have you gone? Without you our house is empty! Wazira tearfully clutched the photograph to her chest and thought: "What happened? Where could he have gone? Or like in the movies, did the criminals steal it? But for what purpose? For profit... But why aren't they asking for ransom or something? Maybe they'll call now. We should keep an eye on the phone. Oh, if only that were true! I'd sell everything, house and possessions, but I'd free my husband. Maybe... no, no! It can't be. I mustn't think of bad things. There are all sorts of things in life. He may be in the most disadvantageous position imaginable. By the way, Bahrom aka couldn't get out of the well in his dream. What does this dream want to warn about?".

Vazira went out of the room and rummaged through Bahrom's study and found among the books a "Dreambook" and quickly began to leaf through it for the letter k: "sorcerer", "collage", and here she found, "well". "Who will see in a dream that in a certain place dig a well, - it is a sign that his loved ones will be deceived. If the well will be black or blue water - it is a sign of sorrow. If the water from the well goes underground and dries up, it means the death of the spouse or the plundering of his property.

Vazira felt as if she had been doused with boiling water. She hurriedly closed the book as if a scorpion had jumped out of it and put it back on the shelf: "What kind of dream was that, what kind of interpretation? What kind of deception? Who could do such evil? Did the water in the well look dark? Is it a sign of sorrow! But the water didn't leave the well. Then Bahrom aka is alive!".

Pleased with her findings, the woman took a deep breath and headed for the nursery - to wake the children...

Safar aka could not sleep either; he tossed and turned from side to side all night. All sorts of thoughts, innumerable suspicions and unanswered questions kept him awake. Getting up early, he took a walk down the street. Seeing his grandchildren off to school, he tried to appear calm and not give away the anxiety that was eating away at his heart. His father-in-law and daughter-in-law ate breakfast together in silence.

Bad news, it turns out, spreads quickly. Rumors of Bahrom's absence for several days spread lightning fast. Anwar, when he heard the news from his sister, did not pay much attention to it at first. "Maybe he is going about his business somewhere, after all he is a man, he will come," he said at that time. Because of the busy schedule at work, he could not see his sister. But after talking to her on the phone at night, his heart sank: "Something happened. He couldn't leave and not call his family for so many days. Could it be an accident? Or enemies tried to... God forbid! How could such a man have enemies? Maybe...".

Anwar, too, had hardly slept all night and went straight to his sister in the morning.

-Hello, sister! How are you, how is Jahangir, Jawahir? -Anvarjon tried to remain calm.

- Thank you, Anvarjon! How are you, how's my daughter-in-law, how's Sarvarjon? You still can't come to us! - On seeing her brother, Vazira couldn't bear it and cried.

- Sister, sister, everything will be all right. You'll see, your son-in-law will be back on his feet today. He probably wanted to play a joke and scare you! - Anwar said and hugged his sister tightly, but he was embarrassed by his own inappropriate joke.

-Whatever he's doing, as long as he's alive! -Vazira led the guest into the house.

"Poor sister, been through so much in those two days! When they talked on the phone, he didn't think it was that serious. I guess she didn't want to alarm me! The situation seems much more complicated than I imagined," Anwar chided himself for not supporting her at such a difficult time.

-You're here too?! Hello," Anwar greeted his sister's father-in-law warmly.

- Welcome, hello Anvarjon! How are you, how are you at home, daughter-in-law, grandchildren? - said Safar aka, inviting Anvar to take a seat next to him.

After the traditional greeting, Anvarjon turned to his sister:

-Sister, I apologize a thousand times. I couldn't make it yesterday.

- It's okay, brother. Don't beat yourself up! Dad and I spent the whole day at the prosecutor's office yesterday. Even if you had come, you wouldn't have been able to find us.

- What do they say at the son-in-law's workplace?

-I don't know, they're asking around and making inquiries, too. But no word yet," said Vazira with a deep sigh, tugging at the corner of the tablecloth.

-They too are trying their best. May Allah Himself support us," said Safar aka and opened his palms to pray.

Some time later Bahadir aka and Nigorakhon arrived. No matter how hard Vazira tried to keep calm, when she saw her parents, she burst into tears again.

The support of her family gave her strength, and once again a spark of hope flared in her heart. Leaving her parents at home, she went to the prosecutor's office, accompanied by Safar aka and Anvarjon....

Laziz, as usual, greeted them warmly. Sanjarbek met them on the second floor of the building and led them to his office. It was easy to guess from his face and eyes that the investigator had not slept well that night either.

- Safar aka, opazhon, how was your vacation?

-Thank you son, you had to wait a long time for dawn," Safar aka said sadly.

Wazira, eager to hear good news from the investigator, but she realized from his slowness that there was nothing yet. However, she asked:

- Bro, what's new with you, did yesterday's letter do anything?

- I can't tell you anything yet. We are working on the letter, a handwriting examination has been appointed, - - said Sanzharbek, gesturing to the paper in his hand.

The investigator, leaving the guests in his office, went to the head of the investigation team. On this day, the team met to discuss the results and analyze the available data.

Fakhriddin Karimovich briefed the team leader on the work and investigative activities of the previous day. Emphasizing the evidence found in Bakhrom Safarovich's house, he noted that a letter from an unknown person could shed light on the case.

-Are there any results of the expertise? -Tahir Gafurovich interrupted the speaker's speech.

-It'll be ready by tonight.

- Go on.

- Thank you, some work is being done on each of the hypotheses put forward. During the past period, Bakhrom Safarovich's father, wife, and practically all of his close relatives have been questioned. In addition, neighbors, former colleagues and acquaintances are being questioned. -Fakhriddin Karimovich, leave the general statements, tell us about concrete actions! - The deputy prosecutor took off his glasses and turned to the reporter.

- Excuse me, Tahir Gafurovich, - the investigator gathered his thoughts for a while and continued. - An instruction has been sent to all district and city prosecutors. All regional divisions of the Ministry of Internal Affairs are searching for him. The most experienced and professional operatives are involved in the work. At present, the collection and analysis of information on this issue has begun. In addition, all criminal cases sent to the courts, terminated, suspended and separated into separate proceedings, which were investigated by Bakhrom Safarovich, have been withdrawn. A complete list of persons deprived of liberty in these criminal cases, serving their sentences in prisons, colonies, released after imprisonment, as well as their close relatives who have a propensity to commit crimes and previously convicted, is being compiled.

- How many people can go on that list? - The chief asked.

-approximately over two hundred people.

-Deceased persons may be removed from the list," Tahir Gafurovich stood up and continued his speech. - Persons who have left for work and permanent residence abroad, as well as those serving their sentences in places of detention, should be thoroughly checked for involvement in this crime. In addition, it is necessary to find out with whom Bakhrom had conflicts before coming to the prosecutor's office, where he worked and studied, the circle of relatives of his father, wife, sons, brothers, whether they were enemies or not. What was Bakhrom Safarovich's relationship with his wife?

- Very good, the couple was very friendly," Fakhriddin Karimovich answered confidently, because he knew the family personally, and looked at the others waiting for confirmation of his words. The investigators nodded in agreement.

- In such crimes, as a rule, the main suspect is the wife," said the chief, and to suppress the surprise of those present, he added: "I know this family well too, cultured, exemplary. And still nothing should be missed. The life of Bakhrom Safarovich for the last month should be restored in chronological order. When and where he went, who he met, the whole chain of events must be reconstructed hour by hour, minute by minute. Understand? -Tahir Gafurovich stood up.

-Yes," replied the subordinates.

-Next meeting at twenty-two o'clock. Everyone dismissed.

The members of the group gathered in Fakhriddin Karimovich's office, the tasks to be performed today were distributed among them, after which everyone started their work.

Sanzharbek was assigned to work with close relatives of the family. So he went to the personnel department, took all the information from Bakhrom Safarovich's personal file and went down to his office.

43

- Are you bored? I beg your pardon. Tahir Gafurovich gathered our entire group and gave the appropriate instructions. That's why I was a little delayed, - the investigator put the documents on the table and continued to speak standing up. - Vazira opa, if you know the phone numbers of the people on this list, write them down in front of each of them.

The list included all of her and her husband's close relatives. Vazira quickly wrote down the phone numbers he knew and handed the paper to the investigator.

-Okay, now write on this paper the names and addresses of your and Bakhr aka your closest friends, their addresses and phone numbers," the investigator took a sheet of paper out of the desk drawer and handed it to his interlocutor. -You take your time, remember and write, and we'll be in the other office.

Sanzharbek gestured Safar ak and Anvarbek to a neighboring office. The investigator first questioned Safar ak in detail, then Anvarbek. The main attention was paid to the relationship of the spouses, with whom they were friends and with whom they met.

Toward noon, the investigator released the visitors.

The confusion of events increased Vazira's anxiety: "Why is the investigator approaching the issue from afar, looking for her and her husband's relatives? Doesn't it mean that the investigators don't know anything yet? It looks like they don't have any versions or plan yet. Why else would he be looking for my friends and parents? Or is that the order? Judging by the investigator's actions, he has no information about my husband's disappearance.

It seems like he wants to start from scratch. Or do they suspect me? If not, what do they want to ask my friends? Do they have reason to doubt me? What am I thinking, what are they thinking?! I'd give my life for Bahrom aka! Poor guy, where is he now and in what condition? Is he in the hands of criminals? Or is he somewhere in a deserted place, hungry and helpless, waiting for Allah's help? But does he not have the opportunity to make at least one phone call, even if only through someone! If he had such an opportunity, he would not wait, he would send a message, risking his life! Would he have flown home to his children on wings? If only he were alive! Investigators are strange people, too! They don't know where to start. Maybe they have secrets of their own that she doesn't know about. I wish everything would end well!".

Sanzharbek interrogated more than fifteen close relatives of Bakhrom's family before evening without hurry. The questions were almost identical: when you last saw Bakhrom Safarovich, did you notice anything suspicious in his behavior, what was the relationship between the spouses, did you hear that they quarreled or had disagreements on any issues, did they have housing or other problems, was there a dispute over property, were the spouses jealous of each other, and so on.

Having failed to get answers from the questioned witnesses that would have interested the investigation, the investigator realized that his intuition had not failed him. Having made a report on the work done, he rushed to Tahir Gafurovich's office.

The deputy prosecutor heard the reports of the members of the group one by one. At about twenty-three o'clock it was Sanzharbek's turn:

- Tahir Gafurovich, according to the investigation plan, relatives and friends of Bakhrom Safarovitch's family were questioned. As it turned out, the Safarovs married for love, lived very friendly, there were no disputes and disagreements between them. We did not receive any information from Vazira Opa that would give us reason to suspect her of her husband's disappearance. Nevertheless, we have placed her brother Anvarbek under constant surveillance. The telephone conversations of close relatives are being listened to. In this regard, operational and investigative measures are continuing. Relatives of the family living in the regions have been summoned for tomorrow. One more question. It turns out that Bakhrom Safarovich, being a student, saved his future wife from criminals. But then he himself was stabbed in the stomach and was taken to hospital with a serious injury. Later the criminals were caught and brought to justice.

- Recall and study this criminal case. Find out where the people who committed the crime are now, whether they are related to the criminal case under investigation," said Tahir Gafurovich, looking at Fakhriddin Karimovich sitting next to him. - Prepare a detailed report to report to the republic's prosecutor tomorrow at ten o'clock.

Everyone dispersed. The members of the group spent the night in their offices without going home.

Despite the fact that it was late, Fakhriddin could not sleep: "What a mystery this is. A man disappears in broad daylight and there are no witnesses! No one has seen or heard anything! In all my years of work as an investigator, I have never faced such a confusing puzzle. How many serious crimes have I solved, although at first glance it seemed impossible. But I've never been at such a dead end. And the clock is ticking. Every minute that passes puts us further away from the perpetrator, gives him a chance to cover his tracks. We must hurry, yes, yes, we must hurry! But at the moment, there's no one sure thing. It's unlikely to be positive either. Who is the woman who wrote the letter? Friend or foe? For what purpose is this letter written? If it is a friend, why is his name not given? Or is it the work of an enemy? If so, what kind of idiot would handwrite a letter and leave open physical evidence? Or is this letter part of a premeditated plan to distract the investigation? In any case, it is necessary to establish the author of the letter...".

The investigator started going through the stack of papers on the table. He wrote something, scribbled, crossed out on the paper and wrote again. Then he took the last cigarette left in the pack and lit it. He stood up, went to the window and opened one sash. Fresh air from outside blew into the room. It was dark and quiet outside. He remembered that he hadn't been outside since yesterday. Having had enough of the fresh air, he closed the window and with some unusual enthusiasm took a thick multi-volume criminal case from the safe and began to leaf through it: "Who is the enemy of the investigator? Definitely a criminal! A person deprived of liberty for committing a serious crime, feeling his guilt, will first of all blame the police, the investigator, the prosecutor and the judge. In his heart will appear enmity towards them. He will set a goal to take revenge on them and on this path will not stop at anything. Some people consider it their duty to avenge their loved ones. Bakhrom Safarovich has thrown many criminals behind bars during his career. How many of them are thirsty for revenge? So that's where the work should start. It is necessary to study grave and especially grave crimes that he investigated...".

Fakhriddin opened a thick file with the inscription on the cover, "Criminal case initiated under Article 119-1 of the Criminal Code of the Uzbek SSR against the officials of the Tea Packing Factory Sh.B. Shokirov, T.U. Umarov and others, 1 volume." He then went on to the next volumes of the criminal case. His attention was attracted by one phrase in the protocol of interrogation of the accused Sh.B.Shokirov: "My brother Shavkat has nothing to do with our affairs. He did not know that we added clover to tea. On my order he sent me two or three cars of alfalfa. But I told him it was for the cows. He wasn't aware of everything. My parents died when we were little. My brother and I were left alone. We grew up in need. I gave him all my brotherly love, raised and educated him. I swear on the souls of my dead parents, Shavkat has no idea of the crimes we committed. I am ready for any punishment. But I can't stand silently watching my brother being unjustly accused. Those who put him behind bars will be punished one day. But then it will be too late" ...

The investigator reread the protocol over and over again: "... I cannot silently watch my brother being unjustly accused. Those who put him behind bars will surely be punished one day...'... 'What does that mean? What does it mean? Blood for blood, death for death, or does he want to leave it up to God? "But then it will be too late...". What does he mean, that his brother will serve his sentence? Or is it a hint of revenge? Is it a threat of physical harm to someone? Or is it just a desperate attempt to intimidate a man who is genuinely worried about his family man? In any case, it is necessary to investigate this matter in depth in the morning...".

The investigator, asleep, tucked into a pile of papers, was awakened by colleagues, who came to work earlier than usual today...

This night also went badly for Vazira, who had not slept well for days. She sat awake for a long time waiting for a call from the investigator. The phone didn't ring, so she even thought of calling him herself. But since it was already late, she changed her mind: "If there was news, they would have called him themselves. So there's no news yet. Another day has passed. Another difficult day! Are so many people and agencies powerless before this test of Allah! No one can do anything! Everyone only knows how to sit idly by!".

Vazira went into the bedroom and tried to sleep, but it was no use. She hugged her husband's pillow and tossed and turned in bed for a while. Then, turning on the light again, she took out a thick album from the dresser drawer and began to look through the photos. Taking out a photograph taken during her marriage to her husband, she looked at it for a long time. Then she gently stroked her husband's happy face with her fingers and brought the photograph to her lips. Tears soaked the photograph. The trembling lips of the woman whispered: "Eh, Bahrom aka! Where are you!!! Why are you scaring us. We have missed you. Please come back home soon! Come back to your children! You said, "God made us for each other, we'll be together until our last breath!".

Remembering the words of her husband, once said in her ear, her thoughts involuntarily returned to those distant times ...

At first Vazira visited Bahromjon in the hospital as her savior, then he began to occupy her thoughts. At first she felt it her duty to feel deep respect and reverence for this young man who had risked his life for a strange girl. Sometimes alone, sometimes with her friends, she went to the hospital to inquire about the health of the young man who had almost died because of her. Some friends jokingly said, "Girlfriend, he is a handsome young man, God himself made sure that you met him. Look, don't miss him!". At such moments Vazira blushed up to her ears and joked away. Especially her best friend Mashhura, when it came to Bahrom, liked to joke: "Come on, friend, hold on tight to this guy. Look how handsome he is, and he's also studying law, and he's smart. Where will you find a better guy than him? If you refuse, I'll marry him myself, and you'll be sorry you missed him." At such moments, Vazira would reply:

-Stop joking, friend, I am indebted to this man for the rest of my life," she too wanted to say jokingly, "Take it, if you need it, marry him!" but some inner instinct prevented her from doing so.

A month later Bakhromjon was discharged. That day Vazira took leave from her studies and went straight to his hospital. She slowly went up to the second floor and knocked on the familiar door. "Come in," she heard from inside.

-Hello, Bahrom aka, how was your rest? - the girl looked through the door in embarrassment.

- Hello, Vazirahon, how are you? - A handsome young man came out to the girl, already changed from hospital clothes into his own clothes. He offered her a seat.

-Have you been discharged?

- As of today, I'm a free bird, Vazirahon! The doctors say that from now on I will live for a hundred years... Thanks to your.... - Bakhromjon apparently wanted to say "thanks to your care I have recovered", but fearing that the girl would think that he was speaking in the opposite sense, i.e., "because of you this misfortune happened to me?", he held his tongue so that he would not be misunderstood.

-Congratulations, may all the bad things be behind you, never be sick again," the girl smiled at the guy with special tenderness.

- I promise you, - for a few moments the young man looked with loving eyes at the slender figure of the girl, at her moon-faced face, at her black eyebrows apart, framing her black eyes, smiling long before her lips smiled.

At that moment there was a knock at the door and Safar aka and Halima opa entered. The parents, embracing their son, greeted him for a long time. Then Bahrom invited them to sit down. Vazira, blushing with excitement, sat down beside him.

-Ayajon[7], dadajon, meet Wazirahon, one of the most beautiful girls of our university!

- How are you, my daughter, how are your studies? - Safar aka greeted the girl warmly.

-So, this is the same Wazirahon?! -Halima opa looked angrily at the girl and continued: - Daughter, a girl should not walk alone in the street in the dark. Besides, you are a student. Your parents probably raised you with such hopes....

-Wife, stop talking nonsense, the girl is not to blame, everything happens by the will of Allah," Safar aka scolded his wife.

-Mommy, mommy, don't you know that Vazirakhon is a nice girl, she was coming back from the library that day, just like me," Bahromjon, who knew his mother's character well, tried to divert the conversation. -You sit down for a while, and we'll call the nurse and have her take the room.

The guy gestured for the girl to follow him, and they walked out.

-Vazirakhon, I apologize for my mom, but you should understand her too. She didn't really mean to offend you... -Bahrom could not find words to justify his mother.

---

[7] ayajon - mommy

- It's no big deal. No mother would forgive a man who almost killed their child. She said the right thing, but I'm not offended," the girl, who had no trace of her previous mood, smiled falsely to hide her sadness.

-Thank you," the young man sighed, as if relieved of a heavy burden. At that moment he understood what was going through the poor girl's mind, but he was embarrassed that he couldn't find the right words to cheer her up.

Bahrom walked the girl to the gate:

-Vazirahon, today I'm going to the village with my family. I'll stay there for a week and then go back to school. I'll find you myself, okay?

Vazira nodded her head in agreement and hurriedly said goodbye:

-Have a good trip, take care," the girl gave the guy a sweet smile and hurried away.

The girl's gentle smile and kind words of encouragement to take care of himself seemed to dispel the worries in the young man's heart at least a little.

Bakhrom said a warm farewell to the doctors and nurses and left for his village accompanied by his parents. Despite the fact that he had lived in the city for so many years, his distant homeland seemed blessed to him. It gave him a lot of pleasure to breathe in the pure air of the village, enjoy the beautiful nature, wander around the endless hills and rocks, and socialize with simple and kind people. Every time he came home, time flew by so quickly that he couldn't enjoy his happiness. For this reason, he did not want to leave.

Hearing that a student from the city had arrived, the whole family gathered in his house. Safar aka admonished his son: "May this be the worst thing you have seen in your life! May misfortunes pass you by!" slaughtered a sheep in honor of his recovery. A fire was lit under the cauldron, and a long line of people came to ask about his health. The guests told funny stories from their lives. It can be said that the celebration of Bahrom's recovery turned into a verbal jest between men - Askiyabozlik ...[8]

Although Bakhrom went to bed late, he woke up early. As usual, he fed and watered the cattle, did some pull-ups on a bar he had once built himself, then washed his face and took a bucket to the garden at the end of the yard. Although the apricot trees had already dropped their fruit, the branches of the tree at one end of the garden were untouched. His mother had forbidden everyone to touch the fruit of this apricot tree, which was the latest to produce a crop each year. She was saving them for her favorite son, who was studying in the city. And so it was this time.

Bahrom quickly climbed up the tree and filled the bucket with ripe apricots. Sitting on a branch, he tasted a few yellow apricots. "This is not an apricot, but honey that melts in your mouth!", he thought.

Bakhrom got down from the branch, put the bucket aside and "said hello" to his dear apple, peach and walnut

---

[8] Askiyabozlik, Askiya - a type of oral folk art formed among men in the Fergana Valley, which is an art of witty talk, requiring wit, ability to improvise and mastery of all the subtleties and nuances of the language, including knowledge of the local dialect.

trees, asking "how they were doing". He gazed mesmerized at the fruit ripening on the branches. Each time he marveled at the results of his father's labor - a consummate gardener. Ever since he could remember himself, this garden had had a special aura of cleanliness and order. Safar aka had watched over this garden, which he had once created with his own hands, with great love. He treated every tree as his child. And he taught this to his children from a young age.

Bakhrom walked through the garden and breathed fresh air. He realized how much he missed his homeland, the aroma of flowers and grass in the garden, mint and greenery near the stream. He remembered his childhood, his school days.....

When the young man returned with a bucket of apricots, his mother was laying out flatbreads freshly baked in the tandoor on the table. The whole family gathered around the dastarkhan for breakfast.

Bakhrom was busy in the courtyard until noon, but by evening he was worried. The young man, who every time he came to visit his village, was drawn to the city for some reason. No matter how he drove away thoughts of Vazira, her sad face appeared before his eyes. "Poor thing, his mother's words of yesterday must have lodged themselves in her soul and she can't find a place to go. Where is she now? What is she doing...? I couldn't even apologize to her properly! She must have a bad opinion of my mom now. How can I get out of this unpleasant situation? Maybe she wasn't offended. Perhaps she correctly understood the situation of a mother who loves her son more than life. After all, she is a smart girl!".

Satisfied with his conclusions, the young man went back to the garden again. Some of his classmates came to invite him to visit, but he did not want to go. The young man, who used to spend most of his time in the company of friends, this time wanted to be alone with himself. Of course, as any mother, the woman could not help noticing such a change in her son's character. At first, she attributed this behavior of her son to his injuries, because of which he went to the hospital. But her worry grew: "Does her son still think about this strange girl? Was she the cause of her son's unsociable and absent-minded behavior?".

The woman grinned, mentioning the famous phrase of Uzbekoyim[9] regarding her daughter-in-law Kumushbibi: "Maybe this girl is as smart and charming as Kumush!". The mother was startled by her thoughts and immediately whispered: "No, no, God forbid! My son almost died because of that foolish girl. Lord, turn her face away from our family!".

Anxiety in her heart made Halima aya[10] go after her son. Bakhrom, with a cotton chapan under him[11], sat pensively looking at the trees. The mother did not want to disturb her son's thoughts at first: "Is he thinking about her again?

When he heard footsteps, the young man stood up resolutely:

---

[9] Uzbekoyim, the heroine of Abdullah Kadiri's famous novel "Days Gone By" Kumushbibi is the protagonist of Abdullah Kadiri's famous novel "Days Gone By".
[10] aya - mother, aunt, dialect of a certain region
[11] chapan - a cotton winter coat for men

-Ayajon, let's go, I happen to miss our garden a lot, I'm sitting and enjoying the trees.

- The garden is even more beautiful, especially these days. I don't even want to leave it. Of course I miss you. You've been away so long. You see, the trees are waiting for you too.

-You can't breathe the air here!

-Okay, son, rest," said the mother, embarrassed at having distracted the child, and returned to the yard.

"Oh, mommy, mommy! If I step back a little, she follows me, because she is worried about me. Apparently, it is in such cases that people say, "A mother's heart is in her children, and a child's heart is in stone". Poor thing, she'd give her life for me. Are all moms like that? They must be. When Allah created mothers, He gave them the great power to sacrifice their lives for their child in order to leave offspring in this world. For example, birds nesting on the earth, exposing their lives to thousands of dangers, protect their eggs and engage in battle with predators several times stronger than them. They do not retreat, even if they realize that they will not overpower the enemy. By spreading its wings, the bird distracts the predator from its nest, and thus preserves the lives of its chicks. Or the chicken, for example. She flinches even if a small child says "shoo." But the Creator Himself gives her unlimited power to protect her eggs and chicks. She has incredible power to resist not only small children, but also adults, and even angry dogs who hurt her chicks. Therefore, a human mother is out of the question here! Her love for her children cannot be compared to anything. If this love turns into anger towards the enemy who attacked her child, this power can turn the earth upside down," thinking about it, Bahrom shuddered. A sort of uneasiness appeared in the back of his mind, "Does Wazirahon seem like such a 'monster' to his mother? No, no, it can't be. After all, there is nothing between us yet! We are just acquaintances, she treats me as her savior. There's nothing wrong with me treating her with warmth. Then why are my thoughts confused? Why do I keep going back to her in my mind over and over again? Why can't she get out of my head? God, what's happening to me? For some reason the whole world seems beautiful to me...".

The next morning, Bakhrom woke up with a strong conviction that he had to return to his studies as soon as possible, as the session was coming up, and he had to prepare for his exams. Halima did not like the fact that her son, who was going to rest in the village for three or four days, suddenly changed his mind. The mother's attempt to change her son's mind was unsuccessful. The husband was also on his son's side: "Wife, don't hold him back. Let him go. Indeed, he missed a lot of classes, let him take his exams, and then he will come back again!

Feeling the futility of confronting the stubborn son and the indifferent father, the mother had to agree with them. But she was more disturbed not by the fact that the son, having just arrived, was leaving at once, but by the fact that "this bastard is dying to see this girl!" ....

As they approached the city, Bahrom's heart raced with excitement. He did not understand the cause of it. A feeling of longing for something or someone seemed to grow stronger in his heart. There seemed to be a spark of hope in his soul that urged him to live life to the fullest, and everything around him seemed beautiful. This had never happened to him before: "Oh, God, what is it with me? Or has there been some change in my psyche at the hospital? Or is my heart warmed by that little brave act I did for the poor girl? Uh, what thoughts come into my head! What a deed! Wouldn't any guy in my place have done the same thing? It's not bravery, it's human duty. I just acted like a man. Then why am I not myself? Isn't it Vazirahon's fault? For some reason, I've been thinking of her a lot lately. No matter how hard I try not to think of her, her blooming face and fiery gaze appear before my eyes. What is this?! Love?! I've fallen in love with her. Is this how love shows itself?"

- Brother, we're here. Did you fall asleep? - The driver's rough voice interrupted his thoughts.....

Having almost not slept last night, Bahrom pulled out his favorite suit and pants from his clothes and ironed them with pleasure. It was because he hadn't been to class in a long time. So today he wanted to look his best. He had never looked in the mirror before, but today he didn't leave it, he spent a long time dressing up and combed his hair nicely. Hurrying to class, he warmly greeted the acquaintances he met and gave them a good mood. He felt like a young man rushing to a date with his beloved after a long separation.

Yesterday, as soon as he had returned to the city, he had planned to see Vazira the next day during the big break. Maybe it was this impending meeting that was giving him a thrill...

Even during class, his thoughts were preoccupied with her. Finally, after the second class, the bell rang for the big break. Bakhrom walked across the alley toward the Philology Department. Despite the fact that both sides of the front door were open wide, students were coming down for lunch in droves, forming a traffic jam in the aisle. The young man stared at the door for a while. Finally, two girls dressed in khan atlas[12]. came out. One of them was Wazira. Bahrom's heart pounded frantically, "How she looked so much prettier!"

-Wazirahon, hello? - a young man blocked the girls' way.

-Bahroma aka? Hello! Is that you?! What are you doing here? Didn't you go to the village?

-I went away and came back yesterday, I was waiting for you here... -Bakhrom felt awkward in front of the unfamiliar girl and blushed up to his ears.

Noticing this, the girl began to introduce him to her friend:

- Meet my friend Gulnara.

- Nice to meet you, Bahrom.

-Ah, you are that brave young man! -Gulnara looked at her friend enigmatically.

A little calmer, Bahrom invited the girls to dinner. The girl's long-suffering look made him wonder: "What did she tell her about me?

Despite the fact that Gulnara felt uncomfortable between the two lovers and, under any pretext wanted to leave, Vazira persuaded her to stay together for lunch.

---

[12] khan-atlas - Uzbek national silk fabric

The student cafeteria was full of customers. Bakhrom sat the girls at the far table and stood in line. He was generous and bought a lot of food. Gulnara, without ceremony, ate the first and then the second course. ABakhrom and Vazira picked at their plates with forks, embarrassed in front of each other.

Bakhrom occasionally glanced furtively at Vazira, but the girl did not dare to look at his face. A couple of times when their gazes met, a spark of mutual sympathy flashed between them like lightning. While the young man was busy finding some funny story to amuse the girls, Vazira was thinking about the reason why this guy, who had gone to the village for a week, had come back after two days. The silence was broken occasionally by Gulnara with her funny stories. The break was over and the girls were about to leave. The boy also involuntarily followed them. At the door of the faculty the young people said goodbye.

Only Gulnara turned around and despite the fact that her friend was pulling her by the arm, she cheerfully exclaimed: "Come visit us more often!".

Bahrom, hitherto agitated at not being able to say two words properly to the girl he had longed to see for several days now, glowed when he heard this...

The next three or four days passed in the same way. Bakhrom went to Vazira's house sometimes during recess and sometimes after class on the pretext of eating ice cream. The girl always went out to meet her friends, often Mashhura, sometimes Gulnara. In their presence Bakhrom did not dare to say anything to Wazira. Nevertheless, their relationship grew stronger and warmer day by day.

A month later the exams began. Bakhrom and Vazira met almost every day. It was as if some invisible bond had appeared between them. There is little to hide among students. Noticing the frequent visits of a law student to Vazira, they were nicknamed a couple in love. Some of Vazira's classmates bit their elbows with envy that they had missed such a girl, while others admitted their defeat: "What is the point of regret now, let the lovers be happy, they deserve each other.

In the middle of June, the studies were over and the students left for a construction team. The law students were sent to the city of Marjonbulok and the philological students to the distant city of Navoi. Although Bakhrom knew from books what the "pain of separation" was, he did not attach much importance to it. He had never imagined that this feeling would torment him so much morally. It had been a week since he hadn't eaten or slept normally. He began to shun everyone. The previously cheerful and cheerful guy had now turned into a sad and serious person. The image of Wazira kept him awake.

His only friend Zafarjon, to whom he could confide his secrets, kept telling him half-jokingly, half-seriously: "You are in love, my friend, you are in love! We must tell your parents about it and get you married as soon as possible. Otherwise, like Majnun[13], you may go to the desert.

It was at times like this that Bahrom took offense at his friend:

---

[13] Majnun is the protagonist of the romantic poem "Leili and Majnun"

- Get outta here! I share my secrets with you as a friend, and you laugh at me! You can't trust anyone!

But after a while, they continued their friendship again, as if nothing had happened. Perhaps because Zafarjon had never fallen in love before, or rather had never been close friends with any girl, he liked his friend's stories about Vazir. And Bakhrom felt relieved to share his worries with his friend.

Time stretched very slowly... The work turned out to be profitable. During the day the students spent most of their time at the construction site, and in the evenings, they made a fire in the street, organized various games, parties and other entertaining events, trying to enjoy every moment of the "golden period" of life. Only Bakhrom kept away from such gatherings and liked to walk alone or with Zafarjon.

Today was also one of those days. In the evening after work, the students gathered to have fun. Bakhrom went to a quieter place not far from the dormitory and sat down on a boulder. There was silence all around. The sky was clear. The full moon seemed to be watching him from above. The stars seemed as if they were about to fall to the ground, it seemed as if you stretched out your hand and they would come down to your palm. The barking of dogs and the sounds of night crickets could be heard in the distance. The warmth of the sun still lingered in the stone on which he sat. A pleasant breeze from the mountainside stroked his face and ruffled his hair. He took out a photograph of Wazira from his shirt pocket. The girl's beauty shone in the moonlight: "Eh, my Vazira,

Vazira! It's been twenty days since I haven't seen you. Twenty days! How I miss you, my beauty! Where are you now? I can't reach you or shout to you! How I wish I could see your pink face now, hold your hands, stroke your hair, lay my head in your lap. I have no greater wish."

Bakhrom sometimes wrote poems while at school. He would recite them at events and receive applause. Later, especially after entering law school, this talent seemed to disappear. However, for some reason now, lines, but full of suffering, began to gush out of the depths of his soul again:

Your magical beauty
I'm remembering this night.
And until dawn, looking up at the sky,
Looking for your beautiful features.
I will ask the moon in vain
To help me through the separation.
I'm looking at the look on your face in the photo,
But it wasn't comforting.

How sad I am without you,
I wish I could drown in your eyes.
Oh, mountains, throw down water from above!
I'll swim with the flow to her.

We're separated by distance,
No reaching, no calling.
Let the wind carry the beloved
My sad poems...

If only Vazira had appeared at that moment! He would read his creations to her, see her happy face, hear her praise: "Magnificent! Congratulations!". "Oh, love, love, how you make me suffer. Now I understand where poets come from.... What about her? Does she love me? I haven't even confessed my love to her yet! I'm afraid! Every time I saw her, I wanted to pour out all my soul to her, but when I met her eyes, I lost the power of speech, could not really connect two words. Because I'm a slacker! Yes, yes, a slacker! Of course, she could probably tell from my actions and looks that I cared about her. But what if she thinks it's just a friendly attitude! Maybe because of the events that have happened, she feels obligated to me, and so she only comes out to meet with me so as not to offend me! No, that can't be. I think she sympathizes with me too. The eyes can't deceive you. Didn't I see her look of love, chastity, and modesty shine every time she saw me?! Yes, you did! Perhaps she has love for me in her heart too. What is she doing now? Is she thinking of me? Is she waiting for me? Maybe I should go to see her? The city of Navoi is probably 400 kilometers away. You can go there and back in a day. But how will she feel about it? No, it's better to wait, there are only ten days left. Not without reason poets say that separation is both pain and tenderness. Pain, okay, I see. But what's the tenderness? Probably in living with hope, spending days dreaming of seeing the face of the beloved. Isn't it this hope that fills my heart with light and illuminates my life...", - Bakhrom cautiously got down from the boulder and headed towards the dormitory...".

The rest of the days also passed mixed with suffering and hope. Meanwhile, Bakhrom, as a good poet, began to gain popularity among the students. At poetry competitions held in the squadron, he impressed many by reciting his poems dedicated to Wazira....

Finally, the long-awaited moments came. The bus with the students left for Samarkand. On the way young men and women were singing songs in the bus. Only Bakhrom was busy with his thoughts. He was thinking about his forthcoming meeting with Vazira: "How will she meet him? Will she feel that I was pining for her like a madman? Has she been pining for me? Why didn't he have the courage to tell her he loved her on the day of his departure! What if she had said no? No, no, she couldn't have done that. Her eyes gave away her attraction to me! It's clear that in her heart she sympathizes with me. After all, he's no worse than the other guys!"

The young man combed his hair and, looking at his reflection in the bus window, was pleased with himself....

Bakhrom left all his luggage in his room and hurried to the dormitory of the Faculty of Philology. The old lady janitor sitting at the entrance to the dormitory recognized Bakhrom:

- Come in, son, come in, the girls have arrived, they're in their rooms.

- Thank you, aunt, I won't be long," said Bakhrom, greeted the old woman warmly, and went upstairs. He stopped in front of a familiar door and knocked softly. The door was opened by Vazira. When she saw Bakhrom, she glowed:

-Assalom alaikum, Bahrom aka, welcome..... Come in! - Wazira led the guest into the room.

-Vazirahon, how did you... how was your trip? -Bakhrom's legs were trembling with excitement.

Mashhura, after saying hello to Bahrom, came out on the pretext of putting tea on.

Taking advantage of the fact that they were alone, Bahrom tried to say what he had prepared in advance, but hesitated, not knowing where to begin:

-How was your trip? Aren't you tired, Wazirahon?

- Thank you, how are you, aren't you tired at the construction site? -Vazira quickly set the tablecloth on the table.

-I missed you so much... -Bahrom wanted to say: "I missed you," but did not dare and corrected his speech: "I remembered you a lot, even dedicated a poem to you.

Vazira blushed: "Poems, really? -The girl, who was rubbing the tablecloth, smiled with embarrassment at the edge of her lips and gave the young man a sultry look. -I didn't know you had such talent.

-Yes, I began to write poems thinking of you," said Bakhrom, and blushed up to his ears. - That's how poets are born!

The atmosphere was lightened by Mashhura entering, holding a teapot in one hand and drinking bowls in the other.

The three students talked for a long time. They were telling each other interesting stories from the construction team. Suddenly he suggested to the girls: "Girls, I have a suggestion - to go to the movies. A new Indian film is being shown in the Samarkand theater. Let's go together. The girls readily agreed.

Bakhrom had managed to earn a lot of money in the construction team. So first he took the girls to a restaurant. They had a nice conversation and ate dinner. Then, before the movie started, he treated them to ice cream.

When the guy led the girls into the luxurious hall of the movie theater, all the spectators were already sitting in their seats, only three of their seats in the front row were empty. Bakhrom seated the girls and sat down next to Vazira.

The lights went out and the movie started. Though Bahrom's eyes were fixed on the screen, he could feel the heartbeat of the girl sitting next to him with his whole body, and the pleasant fragrance of her hair made him anxious. His heart was pounding like a child caught stealing. Finally, he calmed down a little and put his hand on Wazira's arm. At that moment he felt as if he had been burned. The girl flinched and slowly released her hand, then looked warily at her friend to see if she had noticed, but she was watching the movie intently. This situation further disturbed the still shaking young man: "What have I done, you idiot! How can I grab a girl's hand right away...? I haven't even confessed my love to her yet..... What will happen now? What will she think of me? Will she say I'm frivolous and rude? No, I guess not. Then why did she take her hand away? Isn't that a rejection of my love? Perhaps she was afraid her friend would notice. What was the right thing to do?! She did the right thing. Because the girl is beautiful in her decency and modesty. Knowing that... I did wrong...".

Bahrom now began to feel even more awkward. On the one hand, he was embarrassed by his rudeness, and on the other hand, he was disappointed that he could not behave with dignity. It was good that it was dark and quiet in the hall, otherwise everyone would have seen this guy blush red with shame like a coal. The movie was coming to an end. Now the light will be turned on in the hall. How will he then look at the girl's face? What to do? How to get out of this difficult situation? Didn't he put not only himself but also Vazira in an awkward position by his careless actions?...?

At that moment, Vazira leaned over slightly and whispered something in her friend's ear. She grinned. In the light of the screen Bakhrom could clearly see the girls' faces: "Are they whispering about me? Are they laughing at me? Yes, no, probably their own conversations. I think she won't tell her friend.

Wazira then moved away from him and sat closer to her friend, then returned to her original position. This gave Bahrom confidence. Finally, gathering all his strength, he placed his palm on the girl's palm. The girl shuddered, hissed, and leaned forward slightly, as if hiding her "unfree" hand from her friend's eyes. Somehow this time she did not hurry to pull her hand away but gently squeezed the young man's strong wrist with her slender fingers, then slowly removed his "errant" hand. Bahrom's heart was ready to leap out of his chest. In this feminine action of the girl, he guessed a great meaning: "So, she loves me too! Love-be-it, yes, yes, she loves me! Wazira is my girl!" In an instant, feelings of confidence and joy replaced the sadness, despair and hopelessness in Bahrom's heart. He wished that the movie would end sooner, that the light would turn on and he would look at the painfully familiar face of his beloved. Oh, life, how beautiful you are...!

From that moment on, the life of the two young people began to shine with new bright colors. Now they met almost every day and spent all their free time together. They loved each other so much that even one day without meeting seemed like an eternity. An invisible bond had formed between them. Two years of study, spent in this university, became a real test for the lovers, for their pure love. In joy and in sorrow they were each other's support.

Fakhriddin washed his face and put his clothes in order. Then he went down to the dining room, drank bitter coffee and had breakfast. Feeling that today was going to be a more difficult day than usual, he drew up a plan of work to be done first. Despite the fact that there was still time before the work day started, he called all the members of the group. After listening to their reports one by one, he gave instructions on how to organize the activities to be carried out during the day. He sent one of the group members to the city of Samarkand to collect information about the head of the tea factory Shukhrat Shokirov and his brother Shavkat and instructed him to check their involvement in the case under investigation.

Then he sat down and began to prepare a report to the prosecutor on his work. Dissatisfied with what he had written, he crossed it out and wrote again. He concentrated hard, took one cigarette from the pack brought by the secretary and smoked: "Oh, God, what a riddle you have given us! Have we reached a dead end? Not a single theory has yielded any results! And even the handwriting examination didn't help. What if we're on the wrong track? Maybe there will be news from Samarkand?!".

The investigator gathered his thoughts and continued writing the certificate again and as soon as he finished, the black phone on the edge of the desk rang:

-Fakhriddin Karimovich, is the certificate ready? - Takhir Gafurovich's serious voice came from the receiver.

-Got it, I'll be right there.

The investigator signed the certificate and hurried to his superiors. In the reception room of the deputy prosecutor, five or six employees were waiting for their turn. The secretary, seeing Fakhriddin Karimovich, said: "Come in, they are waiting for you." The investigator apologized to his colleagues standing in line and entered the office.

- Hello, Tahir Gafurovich, how was your vacation?

-Sit down, what's new? - the warden got right to the point. - Any leads?

- We're working through all the assumptions, but... - The investigator handed the chief the papers that were in his hands.

-What "but", Fakhriddin Karimovich, do you even feel responsible? How many days have you been leading me around by the nose! There's no result. I have to report to the prosecutor now. What will I tell him?! - Tahir Gafurovich lost his temper.

Fakhriddin remained silent, for he knew his superior's temper. At such times it was better not to speak to him. If you try to argue with him, he will get even angrier and smash you against the wall.

- What about the handwriting analysis? Any results? -asked Tahir Gafurovich, not taking his eyes off the certificate.

- The letter was written by a woman, but her identity has not been found out yet. Among relatives, friends and acquaintances of Bakhrom Safarovich the author of this handwriting has not been found either. At the same time, more than a hundred samples of handwriting of women who communicated with him on various issues were taken and sent for examination.

- Where did you get the list from and on what basis?

- The list is based on the testimony of Bakhrom Safarovich's relatives, information from his colleagues, and entries in his phone book.

- Has an analysis of home and business calls been obtained?

-Yes, they were used to make the list, too.

-Okay, the author of the letter wrote that she herself would call him, right? - Tahir Gafurovich took off his glasses and looked at the investigator. - So, she called either to his house or to his office phone? Did you ask his wife and secretary about it in detail?

Fakhriddin shrugged his shoulders, saying no.

- In addition, all calls made during the last six months should be analyzed one by one," Tahir Gafurovich began to speak piecemeal, seeing that the investigator was writing down his instructions. -This woman could not have called from home or work. It is not logical. Therefore, it is necessary to pay special attention to calls made from pay phones and pay phones. Take care of it personally.

-Yes.

The chief put his glasses back on and continued reading the reference:

- Who did you trust to work on the tea factory episode?

- Sanzhar Rakhmonov traveled to the city of Samarkand with several staff members.

- Good. By the way, what about the bandits who wounded Bakhrom Safarovich when he was a student?

Fakhriddin Karimovich took a sheet of paper out of the folder in his hand and held it out to the chief:

- One of the criminals, Suhrob Azizov, was sentenced to six years in prison, the other, Temur Nosirov, to five years. They served their sentences in the city of Karshi. Azizov was later engaged in entrepreneurial activity. He opened several stores in Samarkand. Nosirov was charged with premeditated murder. He is currently serving a sentence in the city of Navoi. So he has nothing to do with the crime we are investigating. Azizov's involvement in this crime is currently under investigation. According to the information received so far, he came to Tashkent several times during the last month. Details of the visit are being investigated.

- Is there any information about whether Azizov met with Bahrom Safarovich after that incident?

- There is no information to confirm that they clashed on an issue.

- Okay, wait for me in the reception, we'll go to the prosecutor together, - Tahir Gafurovich stood up and picked up the receiver of the internal telephone with the state emblem...

The prosecutor of the republic first read the reference carefully. Then, looking at one point, he thought for a long time:

- Tahir Gafurovich, so nothing is known yet. None of the previous versions have yielded any results. Are you satisfied with the work done?

- Of course not! - The deputy prosecutor looked fiercely at Fakhriddin Karimovich, "I told you so.

- I was not satisfied with your reports either! If we have involved the most experienced staff from all law enforcement agencies and research institutions in this work, why is there no progress? Or is it a matter of insufficient organization of work? Fakhriddin Karimovich, you are an experienced investigator, a lot depends on you as a team leader. It is good that you are working on handwriting, Azizov from Samarkand and tea packing factory. But the work should not be weakened on other directions. We have enough forces and employees! It is necessary to work in parallel in all directions! Do you understand? - the prosecutor stood up.

- I see! -Tahir Gafurovich and Fakhriddin Karimovich stood up and simultaneously replied.

-What help do you need from us? No matter what, the crime should be solved very soon! - said the prosecutor before finishing his speech.

- Thank you, the conditions are sufficient for the moment. I will periodically inform you about the progress of the investigation," Tahir Gafurovich said goodbye to the chief in accordance with military custom and headed for the exit.

Fakhriddin, who had left the office earlier, apologized to his boss:

- Tahir aka, I'm sorry. I'm the reason you got hurt.

- It's not a big deal, but the prosecutor was right to object. Anyone would have done the same thing. We need to revitalize our work. Assemble the team members at 4:00 p.m.

-Yes.

Fakhriddin Karimovich headed for his office. Several members of the group were waiting for him at the reception. He invited everyone to come in and took a cigarette out of a drawer:

- Takhir Gafurovich and I have just reported to the prosecutor of the republic on the progress of the investigation. The leadership expressed dissatisfaction with our work. And rightly so. The chief demanded that we revitalize the group's work and solve the crime in the shortest possible time.

-Fakhriddin aka, I have urgent news," Sanzharbek interrupted the chief.

- Well, well, tell me, what's the news? -Fakhriddin Karimovich jumped up.

- This is about Azizov. On the day Bakhrom aka disappeared, Azizov was in Tashkent, staying at the hotel "Russia". According to the hotel staff, he was not alone, there was another woman with him and, of course, not his wife. Because they stayed in different rooms. We also found out the identity of the woman. It's Gulnara Artikova. She graduated from Samarkand State University and is engaged in entrepreneurial activities. One more thing. According to the analysis, the phone call to Bakhrom Safarovich's reception on that day, November 13, was made from a pay phone near the Rossiya Hotel. A day later, another call was made from the same place to Bakhrom Safarovich's home phone. The conversation lasted exactly one minute, - Sanzhar handed the chief the documents that were in his hands.

- I think we're getting closer to a clue. Sanzharbek, thank you! -said Fakhriddin Karimovich, standing up and quickly running his eyes over the document. - Where are they now?

- In Samarkand. We haven't touched them yet.

- You're right, you can't scare them.

-Sanjarbek, call Vazira opa to me immediately! -Fakhriddin put the documents in a folder and prepared to leave. -And you go on with your work, I'll go to the management to report.

The members of the group left the office.

Tahir Gafurovich listened carefully to the investigator's information and asked:

- After all these years, has this Azizov gotten his revenge?!

- He was sentenced to six years in prison and released after four years. He was expelled from the cooperative institute. Maybe he had something to do with all of this.

-Maybe, but revenge is a bad thing. It robs a man of his reason. What do we know about this woman? - Tahir Gafurovich looked at the investigator.

-Artikova Gulnora studied at the university around the same time as Bahrom Safarovich. I think they know each other. Azizov must have taken advantage of that. I called Vazira Opa. She can clarify the matter.

- All right, I'll report it to the prosecutor. You take some trusted people and go to Samarkand. Oh, by the way, I believe the guys there were working on the tea-packing factory episode?

-That's right.

-So put them to work.

Vazira was waiting for Fakhriddin Karimovich in the reception room. Letting her into the office, he thought: "Poor girl, in two or three days she has given up a lot, her eyes are sunken, she is all droopy. It's all because of suffering and the unknown!".

-Vazira opa, how are you? How are my nephews?

- Praise be to Allah! Fakhriddinjon, any good news? - Wazira looked hopefully at the investigator with the intention of hearing some news. After all, she had been summoned for a reason.

- Sister, do you know a woman named Gulnara Artikova?

- Yes, Gulnara and I went to school together - she's a classmate of mine. Is something wrong?

- When was the last time you saw or talked to her?

-It was a long time ago. When we lived in Samarkand, I saw her occasionally. After we moved to Tashkent, we lost contact.

- Has she called you or Bahrom aka lately?

- Uh, no.

- Look, on November fifteenth at 18:26 she called you at home and talked for exactly one minute,-the investigator handed the interlocutor a paper obtained from the PBX.

- I was at the prosecutor's office on the evening of November 15th. The children were at home. She may have talked to them. But why is it necessary at this moment? What does this have to do with Gulnara? -Vazira got nervous.

-Sister, please take your time! We believe that your friend also called Bahrom aka's reception on November 13. Did they know each other?

- He knew her through me. We went to school together. Are you saying they were secretly dating?

- We haven't figured that out yet. Do you remember the guys who assaulted you when you were a student?

- One was called Suhrob, the other Nasir or Temur? Something like that. Why?

- Could they have seen Bahr aka after serving their sentence?

- No, we don't even know what happened after they were locked up. Bahrom aka wasn't interested either. Otherwise, I would have found out for sure.

- Did Gulnara know them?

- I don't know... but... -Vazira thought for a while and continued, -one of them, I think, Suhrob, lived in the same neighborhood as Gulnara.

- How do you know that?

- Then before the court Sukhrob's father through Gulnara asked Bakhrom aka to withdraw the suit. But Bakhrom did not listen to them. Gulnara also asked me to do the same. But I also refused her. After that our relations with Gulnara slightly deteriorated.

- I see," Fakhriddin sighed with relief. - Sister, are your children at home now?

- At home.

- Here is the phone number, call them and ask them if a woman named Gulnara called on November 15 and asked for Bahrom aka.

Wazira called home. The investigator pressed the button of the phone, putting it on volume. Nigora opa picked up the phone.

-Mommy, how are you, put Jawahir on the phone!

-Are you okay, daughter? Any good news?

- It's okay, Mommy! I'll come and we'll talk... Jawahir, is that you? Son, think back carefully and tell me, please, on November 15, a woman asked for your father on the phone?

Jawahir thought for a moment and replied:

-A woman called and asked for my dad, but didn't give her name.

-What did you say to her?

-said Daddy was away on a business trip to Khorezm. I'm sorry, Mom, I forgot to tell you that.

79

- She didn't ask anything else?

- No, Mommy!

- Okay, son, thank you," Wazira hung up the phone.

- I see," Fakhriddin wrote something down in his thick notebook and called Sanzharbek on the internal phone.

- Sister, the boys will escort you out. I have to go to Samarkand. Suhrob and Gulnara's connection to Bahrom aka's disappearance is being investigated. It's too early to make a decision. So please don't tell anyone about the conversation that took place between us.

-You think Gulnara's involved in this case?

- That still needs to be proven. Suhrob had a previous conviction, he could have avenged it on Bakhromak. And Gulnara may have helped him.

- I can't believe it, no, it can't be," Vazira grabbed her collar with a gasp.

- Anything can happen, opa. We'll find out for sure. You don't want to tell your family about this yet, either. I told you everything because you're my man. The truth is, you can't divulge the secrets of the investigation.

- Thank you, ukazhon! Any word on Bahrom aka?

- Sister, let's expose the criminals first, and then we'll find Bahrom aka.

- God, may what you said come true!

Fakhriddin Karimovich said goodbye to Vazira, instructed the secretary to prepare the documents for the business trip and went upstairs. After reporting the information to Tahir Gafurovich, accompanied by several operatives, he went straight to the airport....

It was not difficult for the officers to find Sukhrob Azizov and Gulnara Artikova. At the same time, searches were conducted at their residential addresses, during which no evidence of their involvement in the crime was found. Azizov kept calm. However, Artikova was a little worried. But both pretended that they did not understand why they were detained.

Fakhriddin Karimovich himself interrogated the suspects. Sanzharbek wrote the protocol. After a couple of routine questions, the investigator got down to business:

- When and for what purpose were you last in Tashkent?

After thinking, Suhrob Azizov replied:

- Early November.

-What date exactly?

- I think I got there on November thirteenth and came back on the fifteenth. Because November 16th was my wife's birthday.

-With what purpose and with whom did you travel to Tashkent? - Fakhriddin Karimovich continued asking questions.

- I traveled alone. The reason I went, I am an entrepreneur. I go to Tashkent to buy goods.

- When you travel to Tashkent, where do you usually stay?

- The hotel.

- What hotel did you stay at on Nov. 13-15?

-You can check it out at the Rossiya Hotel.

- Did you meet any of your acquaintances from Samarkand in this hotel?

- No, I haven't met anyone!

- Do you know a woman named Gulnara Artikova? - said the investigator, looking directly into Sukhrob's eyes. The suspect shrank back and was silent for a while. Then he answered quietly, keeping his eyes on the floor:

- I know her, we live in the same neighborhood.

- When and where was the last time you saw this woman?

-I don't know! Sometimes I see her in the mahalla or on the street.

- So, you went to Tashkent alone and did not meet anyone you knew there? Fakhriddin deliberately repeated his question.

- That's right.

-According to our information, Artikova was also in Tashkent on November 13-15. She also stayed in the same hotel where you stayed overnight.

Suhrob turned pale and fidgeted in his chair:

-I was alone. I didn't see ar-ti-ko-va!

- Here is the information of the hotel administration, - the investigator opened a thick criminal case file. - According to the information received, you lived in room 415, and Artikova lived in the neighboring room 416. Are you going to continue lying?

The suspect didn't seem to think the case would get this far and froze like a stiff.

- Azizov, you are suspected of committing a serious crime! If you don't tell the truth, it will be difficult for you. Tell the truth! Confess your guilt, the court will take it into account when imposing punishment, - Fakhriddin Karimovich went on a direct "attack".

-I'm being honest, I haven't committed any crime. I'm not a criminal. Are you trying to pin someone else's guilt on me? - Suhrob began to choke.

-Then why are you lying and trying to obfuscate the investigation?

- Yes, yes, I may have seen Artikova at the hotel. But I didn't commit any crime! I went to Tashkent for goods, you know, for goods! - Suhrob exclaimed in fury.

- So you admit that you traveled with Artikova!? - concluded the investigator.

- She had business in Tashkent, too. Anyway, I was alone in the car.

-What was Artikova's business in Tashkent? Did she tell you?

- I don't know, she didn't tell me.

- Don't know or don't want to tell? - The investigator repeated his question.

-I told you, how many times can you ask me the same thing?! - Azizov's nerves were frayed.

-Calm down. We'll repeat it a hundred times if we have to! We'll keep asking until you tell us the truth! Do you understand?

Azizov continued to sit with his head down like a delinquent child.

- Do you know a man named Bakhrom Safarov? - Fakhriddin Karimovich asked seriously.

-Who's Bah-rom Sa-fa-rov? I don't know him!

-You know, I'll remind you of him. Don't you know the man who was stabbed and hospitalized for standing up for the girl you attacked?

-Ah, this one? His name was Bahrom, I don't remember his last name! Well, I know, so what of it? - Suhrob said confusedly.

- When and where was the last time you saw Bakhrom Safarov?

- I saw him then during the investigation and trial. After that, I never saw him at all. Comrade Chief, I've served my sentence for my crime. What else do you want me to do?! What did I do wrong? - Suhrob got nervous.

-Calm down! We're questioning you as a suspect! No one is accusing you yet. Your job is to answer the questions correctly and tell the truth. If you're innocent, we'll let you go! But if it's your fault.

- I'm not guilty of anything. Thank God I make an honest living.

- So you never saw or spoke to Bakhrom Safarov again? - The investigator returned to the subject.

- He is. I heard he works in the prosecutor's office in Tashkent. That's all I know.

- Who did you hear that from?

Azizov remained silent.

- From whom? From Artikova?! - the investigator answered his own question, saying we know everything.

Suhrob, without raising his head, nodded in agreement.

-Why are you interested in Bakhrom Safarov? - The investigator phrased the question differently.

- Who's interested? I didn't ask her about him! Gulnara was in the same class as Bahrom's wife. That's why she knows their family. When we talked to Gulnara one day, she told me that Bakhrom had become a big man and was working in the prosecutor's office in Tashkent. That's when I found out about him," Suhrob looked at the investigator, saying, "That's enough.

- So you weren't interested, but Artikova gave you the information herself. Is that correct?

-Yes.

- When Artikova went to Tashkent with you, did she see Bakhr aka?

- I don't know.

-What did she tell you about it? Did Artikova say that she had an intention to meet with Bahrom Safarovich?

- No. She didn't tell me that. She could have met him without me. I've been busy all day doing my own thing.

- So she didn't tell you! Azizov! I'm warning you again, tell only the truth! Otherwise, it will be difficult for you. You are suspected of committing a very serious crime! One lie can cost you a lot! -Fakhriddin Karimovich jumped up from his seat.

-Don't scare me, Warden! I did five years for my crime. I was expelled from school. It broke up my family. My life is a mess. What more do you want? Now you want to slander me and put me behind bars? - Suhrob's eyes were bloodshot.

Fakhriddin Karimovich thought: "Apparently, this man is still hungry for revenge. He has only now begun to show his resentment.

- Azizov, pull yourself together! No one is slandering you. If you're innocent, the law will protect you. You just need to tell the truth. If you lie and try to distract the investigation, no one can help you!

Azizov seems to have calmed down.

- Azizov, here is a sheet, write down in chronological order where you were on November 13-15, when, with whom and on what issues you met. Take your time, think about it. Don't miss anything, - Fakhriddin winked at Sanjarbek. - Take him to another room.

The investigator took several deep puffs of his cigarette and pressed it to the ashtray. Then he ordered the operatives waiting in the corridor to bring Artikova in.

A beautiful tall slender swarthy woman of about 35-38 years old entered the room, with a neatly gathered knot on her head.

"Beautiful broad," - thought Fakhriddin.

After greeting her, the investigator invited the woman to sit down. Gulnara modestly sat down at the table opposite the investigator.

Fakhriddin Karimovich introduced himself and printed out information about the woman's identity and biography on a printer, then asked duty questions and filled in blank boxes in the protocol.

-Artikova, we're questioning you as a suspect. All we need from you is the truth. Think about my questions and try to answer briefly and clearly. If you lie. - the investigator looked into the woman's glaring eyes and hesitated. Then he pretended to write something on a piece of paper and continued asking questions:

- When was the last time you were in Tashkent?

The woman didn't seem to have expected such a question, she was confused. Not knowing what to say, she hesitated for a moment and replied in a long voice:

-I don't remember. I think it was last year. I went on a couple of business trips.

- No, this year, or rather in November, for what purpose did you travel to Tashkent? - the investigator put the question in a straightforward way.

Realizing that the investigator knew a lot, the woman mumbled inarticulately:

- Yeah, I went there for work one time in November-January....

-Do you remember the date?

-I think it was November 14th or 15th.

- Who were you traveling with?

Gulnara blushed and took her eyes away from the investigator:

- I traveled alone.

- Where did you spend the night?

-At friend's.

- What is your friend's name and where does she live?

Apparently, Gulnara did not expect such a question, she was sweating and did not know what to answer the investigator. Fakhriddin Karimovich took a sheet of paper out of the folder and put it in front of Gulnara:

- Here is a certificate from the Rossiya hotel where you stayed. It says that you stayed in this hotel from November 13 to 15. What do you say to that?

Gulnara felt as if she had been splashed with ice water. The woman, who had not thought that her lies would be exposed so quickly, was ready to fall through the ground with excitement. She was speechless and frozen like a stone.

-Artikova, I'm warning you again! Just tell the truth! If you lie, it'll be hard on you!

-I'm, I'm.... sorry! I did stay at that hotel. But I told my family and my husband that I slept over at a friend's house named Wazira. My husband is terribly jealous. So...

-You went to a friend's house?

- No. I wanted to go, but I didn't have time.

-Have you been to her place before?

- No. Not before.

- Then how did you get her address?

- I didn't know her address, only her home phone number I got from my friend Mashhura.

-Did you talk to your friend on the phone?

- No, she wasn't home when I called. I talked to her son. Then I called her husband's office. That man wasn't at work either. They told me he had gone to Khorezm.

- Why did you call your friend's husband? Did you know this man before? Who gave you his number?

Gulnara thought for a moment and replied:

- I knew this man from my student days. I also took his work number just in case. I wanted to ask him about Wazir.

- Who told you that Bakhrom Safarovich had gone to Khorezm? - The investigator continued to question.

- I was talking to one of his coworkers. I think either he or his son mentioned it...

- So, you went to Tashkent alone, stayed in a hotel, called your friend, but couldn't find her, didn't go to her house, didn't meet them, right? - Fakhriddin Karimovich asked a tricky question.

- Hm... so, - the woman didn't understand the investigator's sarcasm or pretended not to understand it.

The investigator went on the attack: "Do you know Sukhrob Azizov?

Gulnara was stunned, a thought flashed through her mind: "So he knows everything! Realizing that it was useless to argue with him, she confessed everything:

- Excuse me. please forgive me! We went to Tashkent together...

- What was the purpose of your trip? - When he sensed that the woman had given up, he continued his questioning.

-Sukhrob had business in Tashkent, so he offered me to go with him.

- Who is Azizov to you?

- We're from the same mahalla.

- What's Azizov doing in Tashkent? Did he tell you?

- Apparently, he wanted to see the merchandise for his stores.

-What was the purpose of your trip to Tashkent?

The woman was silent. So the investigator rephrased the question:

- We're not interested in your relationship with Azizov. We don't want to interfere in your personal life. But in any case, you should only tell the truth. We need to know the reason for your trip to Tashkent.

-I...I...I...I went because Suhrob offered to go "for company".

- Then why did you call Vazira Opa's house?! You were looking for Bakhrom Safarovich! What was the purpose?

- When I arrived in Tashkent, I wanted to see my friend, but I couldn't find her.
- Why didn't you see me then? What stopped you?
- I had some free time that day. Then things got busy, I didn't have a chance.
- Who got the idea to go to a friend's house, you or Azizov?
- What do you mean?! I wanted to see a friend. Suhrob doesn't know her.
- Do you think? -Fakhriddin Karimovich ordered Sanzharbek, who was writing at a neighboring table: -Transmit that criminal case over there!

Sanzharbek opened a briefcase lying on the table and took out a thick folder.

- Here, please, meet Sukhrob Azizov and Temur Nosirov. They were accused of intentionally inflicting grievous bodily harm on your friend's husband Bakhrom Safarov, for which they were imprisoned. What do you say to this?

Gulnara froze this time. She was covered with cold sweat. As a grown woman, she was ashamed of her untruth:

- If you know everything. why are you asking me?
- Yes, we know everything, but we want to listen to you and ask you to tell only the truth! - The angry investigator raised his tone.

-That's right, Suhrob knew Bakhr aka. While we were on our way to Tashkent, we talked about Vazira. I said that she lived in Tashkent and her husband worked in the Republican Prosecutor's Office. Suhrob asked if I was in touch with my friend. I said that I did not. Suhrob said:

"Let's visit them when we arrive in Tashkent, I have to apologize to them. At the same time we'll get to know each other better, as he works in the prosecutor's office, he might come in handy. I didn't have their phone number. So I called my friend Mashhura and got their phone number. After that we made a couple of calls from the hotel, but they could not be found. I told you the rest of the story....

-Artikova, I have to warn you once again. You are suspected of committing a particularly serious crime. Do you feel that every lie works against you? You are in a very difficult situation. All the facts are against you. Only the truth can get you out of this difficult situation! - the investigator stood up and approached the woman.

- What other felony? I've told you everything I know! What do you want from me? - said Gulnara, sobbing.

-Tell the truth. You may not have committed the crime directly. But if you tell a lie and try to hide something, you're an accessory to a crime! Do you understand that? -Fakhriddin Karimovich said.

- I'm telling the truth!

- You lied from the beginning and tried to distract the investigation, so we have reason to disbelieve your words! What good is lying to you?

- I was only trying to hide my trip to Tashkent with Suhrob. I'm a married woman. In the sense that there should be no talk... In other matters, I was telling the truth...

- Did Suhrob know Bakhrom Safarovich's home and work telephone numbers? - The investigator sat down and continued the interrogation.

- No, I made the call, and he was standing right next to me. Maybe he saw a piece of paper with a phone number on it.

-When you didn't get through, did Suhrob ask you to call back again?

- No, when he heard that Bakhrom aka had gone to Khorezm, he said: "All right, introduce me next time".

- Were you always with Suhrob in those days? Did he go anywhere without you?

- Most of the time we were together, sometimes he would leave me at the hotel and go off to work.

-Sanzharbek, take Artikova to another room and prepare the documents in the appropriate order," Fakhriddin instructed his assistant, who was typing.

Sanzharbek took Artikova to a neighboring office. Fakhriddin Karimovich ordered the operatives standing at the door to bring Azizov.

Sukhrob, pale as a sheet, was brought into the office. He handed the investigator a piece of paper. The investigator ran his eyes over the paper and began to ask the questions he had prepared in advance:

- Here's the report of Artikova's interrogation. According to her testimony, it was you who came up with the idea to call Bakhromak and Vazira opa! What do you say to that?

-On the way to Tashkent, Gulnara remembered her friend Vazira. She told me that she now lives with her family in the capital, and her husband works in the Republican Prosecutor's Office. I told her: "If she has a phone, talk to her, arrange a meeting." I just wanted to apologize for the sad events in the past.

Gulnara called someone and found Vazira's phone number, then called her. But that day we failed to find the husband and wife. We were told that Bakhrom had gone to Khorezm. So we did not call again.

-Why did you want to meet with Bahrom Safarovich?

-With what purpose? Since Gulnara remembered, I said: "Let's meet them." I wanted to tell them that I had served my sentence and was doing well. I thought if he forgave me, we could get to know each other better.... After all, he works for the Republic. I thought he would be useful in the future! Suhrob looked excitedly at the investigator.

- You attacked Wazira Oppa's honor, you almost took Bahrom aka's life! What face did you want to show them? Or are you still burning with a thirst for revenge? - The investigator continued to interrogate pesteringly.

- What revenge?! We were young then. Yes, I admit we were foolish! But we were punished accordingly. That's why I never thought about revenge before or after prison. I always felt guilty. Did something happen to them? - Suhrob seemed to feel something and shuddered.

- Tell me the truth, did something happen to them?

- We want to ask you about it! Can you please tell us where and when you met with Bahrom Safarovich?! What happened then? It's time to tell us everything! Don't try to mislead us!

-I...I...I...I was telling the truth. I never met Bahr aka or Wazira. If something happened to them, I had nothing to do with it. If you don't believe me, ask Gulnara! -Sukhrob covered his face with his hands. - Oh, God, what a mess this is! Just when I thought everything was fine, now these problems appear?

-Okay, if you keep hiding the truth, we'll try to find it ourselves! -Fakhriddin Karimovich stood up. - We'll discuss the rest in Tashkent!

- I'm-I'm-I'm also going? -Sukhrob was completely confused.

- I must arrest you as a person who has committed a crime! -the investigator, pacing around the room, explained the rights and obligations of the detainees according to the law.

- Can I call my family and warn them? - Suhrob, who had a thousand thoughts running through his head, dared to ask.

- Sure, please - the investigator slid the phone toward Suhrob.

Fakhriddin called the operatives waiting at the door and told them to bring Azizov out. Sanzharbek entered and signed the decision to detain G. Artikova as a suspect in the commission of a crime.

The operatives took the suspects to Tashkent in separate cars.

Fakhriddin took out the last cigarette from the pack he had bought in the morning and lit it. He had a vague doubt: "Have we gone down the wrong path again? They don't seem to have anything to do with this case. They called his home and office! What kind of criminal would leave behind such traces? Or is it due to carelessness, or inexperience? I don't think a person who commits such a crime should be allowed to make such a mistake. Then why did they both try to lie in the beginning? Perhaps they were afraid that their affair would be exposed."

Fakhriddin remembered that he needed to call his superiors and began dialing a familiar number:

- Hello, Tahir Gafurovich!

- Hello! What's new? - came from the other end of the line.

- We caught them both. I have just completed some investigative work and sent them to Tashkent.

-Fakhriddin Karimovich, do you think there will be any results? - asked the long-awaited question of the deputy prosecutor.

- I don't know, Tahir Gafurovich! Frankly speaking, I don't believe in their involvement in the crime. In general, I don't know. Anything can happen.

-Okay! Hurry back. We'll discuss the rest when you get back.

Sanzharbek entered the office with a piece of paper. Apparently, he was waiting for the chief to finish talking on the phone.

-Fakhriddin aka, here is the report on the work done on the "Tea Packaging Factory", and this is the interrogation report of Mashhura Melieva, Vazira's friend from the institute!

The team leader glanced at the certificate:

- So Shavkat Shakirov was released after eight years. Now he has completely lost his sight. Doesn't work. His brother Shukhrat Shakirov came out of prison after five years and went to Moscow to earn money. He has not come to Samarkand for the last year.

-Just in case, we checked the phone records of both of them. Then we're looking into their circle of connections," said Sanzharbek, playing with an empty cigarette pack on the table.

-Melieva confirmed Artikova's statements?

-That's right. Artikova did call Melieva on November 13 and wrote down the home and work phone numbers of Bakhrom Safarovich and Vazira.

-What time did they call? In the morning or in the evening?

-About 5:00 p.m.

-Good. Anything else?

-I don't think so.

- Then we can go back," Fakhriddin Karimovich started collecting documents.

"Strange, what does Gulnara have to do with these events? Yes, maybe she really did come to Tashkent and called at our house. But that doesn't mean she should be suspected of anything! Why did she call my husband's office? Or was there some malicious intent? Yes, no, it can't be, most likely she didn't find me and decided to ask Bahrom aka. The investigator said she came to Tashkent with that bandit named Suhrob? How is it that Gulnara, being a married woman, gets entangled with that bastard? How to understand her trip to another city with a strange man? God forbid they are planning something bad together. After all these years, is this bastard taking revenge?! There's a reason the investigator suspects them. Then he must have a good reason to suspect them. The investigator said he's going to Samarkand? So, it's a very serious case! Here's the po-do-on-kis! They stabbed Bakhrom aka, almost killed him, and they're taking revenge again! What's wrong with them? Even prison didn't fix them. What could they do to Bahrom aka? Did they took him hostage to demand something in return? Then why haven't they said anything until now? In this time they could have called long ago and communicated the terms. I want Bahrom aka held hostage, but I want him alive. I'll give whatever they ask, but I'll save Bahrom aka.

I wish someone would call my home phone right now and say: "Your husband is alive, just pay the bail and take your husband! I'd agree to all their terms! Or ... really ... No, no! God forbid! But you can expect anything from these bastards! Can a man who stabs someone for no reason be reformed after prison? Clearly, he's even more vicious. Oh, God! Save my Bahromak's life! How did this Gulnara get involved in this story? We haven't met since graduation! How did she get my number? Nobody but Mashhura knows my contacts! She must have gotten my number from her. We should ask Mashhura about it...," Vazira shuddered at the thought and rushed to the phone:

- Hello. Kadyrzhan, is that you, son?

- Hello! Yes, I'm Kadyrjan.

- Kadyrzhan, how are you, son? It's me Aunt Vazira from Tashkent. How are your mom and dad?

- Auntie, how are you? Mom's not home.
- She's not back from work yet?
- No, she went to the D.A.'s office.
- The D.A.'s office? Why?
- I don't know, she got called away. When she gets back, I'll tell her you called.

-Kadyrzhan, have mom call me when she gets back, I'll be waiting, okay? -Vazira hung up the phone and thought: "So, they called me right away!".

Lately, Wazira had made it a habit to come home and lock herself in her bedroom. The same thing happened today. It was the only place where she could calm down and gather her thoughts and strength to withstand the blows of fate. Only in this holy corner did she find comfort and could mentally communicate with the dearest person in the world - her husband.

On the one hand, Safar aka, Bahadir aka and Nigora opa were worried about Bahrom aka here, and on the other hand, frightened relatives came in droves every day to inquire about the situation. It was not easy for Wazira to see the questioning looks of her loved ones and answer their questions, who were waiting to hear from her any minute now whenever she spoke to someone on the phone, went out for business or someone came home. She herself needed the help of a counselor. But despite this, she tried not to show that her last hope was fading with each passing day and found the strength to reassure others.

During these difficult days for the family, the housewife had a great responsibility to ensure family cohesion, to fight courageously against the misfortune that had befallen them, to be a support for her relatives and children. For this reason, Vazira tried to remain calm and not to show her worries. To some extent she even succeeded. Only Bahadir aka, Nigora opa and Safar aka could sense the deep-seated anxiety in Vazira's eyes.

Wazira was just about to leave the bedroom when the phone rang. She ran to the phone, guessing that it was a call from Mashhura.

- Hello, Wazira, is that you, friend? Hello!

- Hello. How are you Mashhura? How's home?

- Thank God, my friend. How are you? Bakhrom aka, are the children alive and well?

- Thank you! It's okay. I called you the other day, your son answered. He's all grown up now.

- Girlfriend, are you okay? I got called into the D.A.'s office. I just got back from there. What's going on?

- What did they say?

- Remember we had a classmate named Gulnara? She asked me for your contacts. So she was going to go to Tashkent and really wanted to see you! So I gave her your number. The prosecutor's office asked me about it. What happened, friend? - Mashhura repeated her question.

- It's all right-all right! - Vazira's voice trembled.

- Girlfriend! What happened? Or is that naughty girl having an affair with your husband? Why did I give her your contacts? -Mashhura felt guilty.

- Girlfriend, you know, Bahrom aka has been gone for a week....

- How not? A week? Maybe he's gone somewhere, don't panic, he'll be back.

99

- He's nowhere to be found. We've looked everywhere, we've asked everyone. I think something's happened, my friend! I don't know what to do. I'm so miserable. No matter how hard Vazira tried to control herself, she could not bear to talk to her close friend and burst into tears.

- Don't cry, my friend! You were a strong-willed girl! Where can a grown man go? Bahrom aka is not the kind of man who can get lost! You'll see, not today, but tomorrow he'll come home on his own feet....

-Let it be!

- What does Gulnara have to do with this?

- She called Bahrom aka's office. Next to her was the bandit who once attacked me. I think his name was Suhrob. They must be suspected of something. But I don't know anything.

- Rumor has it that Gulnara and that man have been taken to Tashkent. Sounds like something serious.

- I don't know.

- Come on, buddy, don't give up! Hold on! This is also a test from Allah. Everything will be all right, - Mashhura tried to use all warm words in her speech.

- Thanks, girlfriend!

- Wazira, maybe I should come to you.

- Thank you, that won't be necessary. I'll be on the phone. Say hi to your people.

- Okay, girlfriend! Kiss the kids for me.

Wazira hung up the phone and thought, "She said they were taken to Tashkent? So there is a good reason for them to come from far away and take them away...... Where are these scumbags keeping Bahrom aka? Or have they already...". Wazira was shocked at the thought. She whispered a prayer repeatedly, asking the Almighty to return her husband to her safe and sound...

Fakhriddin Karimovich and Sanzharbek drove directly to the office from the airport. The secretary said that the deputy prosecutor was waiting for them. The head of the group went into his office, took out the necessary documents from his diplomat and hurried upstairs. When he saw Fakhriddin, the secretary, who was quietly talking to someone on the phone, pointed to the chief's door, saying, "Come in, quickly. The investigator knocked quietly on the door and, without waiting for an answer, looked into the chief's office.

- Hello, Tahir Gafurovich, may I?
- Yes, yes, Fakhriddinjon, come in! How was your trip? - The deputy prosecutor stood up and sat opposite his employee.
- Go ahead, from the top!

Fakhriddin gave a detailed account of his trip to Samarkand. The chief listened to him attentively, without interrupting. Then, twirling a pencil in his hand, he thought for a while and said:

- So, it seems that Suhrob and Gulnara have nothing to do with the disappearance of Bakhrom Safarov. Is that my understanding?
- I think so.
- Then why did they both lie and try to divert the investigation from the beginning?

- The reason is clear; they both have families. They came to Tashkent together secretly and tried to hide the truth because they were afraid that their relationship would be exposed. Their phone call coincided with that fateful day. That's just my personal opinion. We still have two days. We'll go over it again just in case. We'll scrutinize their every move in Tashkent and their social circle. Only then can we come to a definite conclusion.

- That's right, you have forty-eight hours. Check everything in detail. Don't miss anything. By the way, have the versions about the heads of the tea-packing factory yielded any result? - said Tahir Gafurovich, drinking the coffee that the secretary had just brought in.

- This version also falls out. Shukhrat Shakirov has served his sentence and is now free. At the moment he has completely lost his eyesight and cannot move independently. And his brother got out of prison and went to Russia to earn money. He has not come to Samarkand for the last year. Nevertheless, we have not stopped working in this direction as well," Fakhriddin handed the certificate to the chief.

-Fakhriddin Karimovich, when you were in Samarkand, your staff informed me that on the bank of the Chirchik River in the Sergeli district they found a completely burnt body of an unknown person. Take this under your control too! Gather the members of the group tomorrow at 14:00 in my office. The report of each employee will be heard, let them get ready! - Tahir Gafurovich stood up.

-Yes! -Do you have permission to go?! - Fakhriddin stood up with the agility of a military man and started to leave.

Tahir Gafurovich nodded his head, allowing him to leave.

Despite the late hour, Fakhriddin Karimovich gathered the members of the group, listened to their reports for the day and gave instructions for tomorrow. After midnight, a company car drove him home....

The next two or three days passed for the investigation team with virtually no results. No evidence that Suhrob and Gulnara had committed a crime was found. They were released after the end of the legally required period of detention. However, the investigation team decided to follow them.

The examination of the body found in the Chirchik River did not give the expected results either. It turned out that the corpse belonged to a man aged 35-40 years old, his height when alive was 166 centimeters. Since the height of Bakhrom Safarovich is more than 180 centimeters, this version, which had worried all the members of the group and the leadership, was dropped.

Fakhriddin was dissatisfied that no matter how hard he tried, the investigation had not yielded positive results. Isn't there a single witness who will say "I saw", "I know" or "I heard"? After all, his teachers had taught him that "every crime leaves a trail." Now where's the trail, where's the evidence? What kind of professionals committed this crime?! In his years of work, he had never encountered such a confusing situation. An investigator who has solved crimes in a short time and made criminals answer to the law, when his close friend who worked side by side with him is kidnapped, he can do nothing but watch from the sidelines. All the work he does is for naught. What a nuisance this is! And time goes on. It is obvious that each passing minute takes the investigators further away from the truth. Attempts to solve the crime "hot on the trail" seemed to fail....

The next day the operatives brought to Fakhriddin Karimovich an old man living in a house near the prosecutor's office. The grandfather, who was in his seventh decade, introduced himself as Sotwoldi Ota and turned out to be a very smart man. In his testimony he said that he lived in a house near the building of the Republican Prosecutor's Office and that on November 13 a suspicious Zhiguli had been parked in front of his house since morning. He remembered that day because it was his daughter's birthday. Two men and a woman were sitting in the car. Around noon, a young man in a black suit, pants and tie came up, got into the car with them, and they drove away.

The old man's story made Fakhriddin jump up. It was as if he had found a clue, because all the events described by the old man were very similar to the story of Bakhrom Safarovich's disappearance. Fakhriddin respectfully treated the old man to tea, asked about his health, relatives, children, grandchildren, and family. Then he moved on to the target:

-Sotoldi ota, on November 13, your daughter's birthday, there must have been a lot of guests at home?

- On my daughter Dilnoza's birthday, guests were to arrive at our house late in the evening. My son-in-law was at work, my grandchildren were at school. My daughter was in the kitchen... all day long, she wouldn't leave the stove. I had to go out to the store for a little shopping. When I came out at ten o'clock in the morning, there was a red Zhiguli outside the house. I didn't pay much attention to it. The next time I went out again, the Zhiguli was still there. Inside were two men and a woman. They seemed suspicious to me. They looked like adults, what could they be doing in the car? If they were visiting someone, they could have come in. If they were waiting for someone, they could have waited on the high street. So I thought they had deliberately chosen a place away from prying eyes. When I went out for the third time, a tall guy in a tie approached the car. Then they drove off," -Sotoldi ota looked at the investigator as if to say, "That's it.

- Father, did you pay attention to the license plate number? - Fakhriddin asked, not hoping for a positive answer.

- The first digits are 22. That's exactly what I memorized. Because I was born in 1922. The next digits, if I'm not mistaken, 89 or 98. I don't remember now. The number ended in "TSH" or "TN." If it had been a visitor from the region, I would have remembered, but I thought it was a local car.

- And that's the end of it, Father. I'm delighted! Young people today don't even know the license plate number of the car they drive! You have an exceptional memory! - the investigator gave the old man another cup of tea and continued: - The color of the car was dark red?

-Cherry-colored like that book over there," the old man said, pointing to a thick book on the table.

- What did the people in the car look like? You don't remember them?
- At the wheel of the car was a fat young man, about 35 years old. Next to him sat a thin guy of about the same age. I do not remember the woman, as she did not get out of the car.
- And did you notice the man who came out to them?
- He was a handsome young man of 35-40 years of age. He was dressed neatly like an official. I even remembered his facial features.
- Father, please tell me, why did you pay attention to them? What made you so suspicious of them?
- You know, son, as a man gets older, he becomes a skeptic who looks at everything with suspicion and scrutinizes his surroundings.
- Father, thank you so much! You've been very helpful. If we need you, we will invite you again. You can go home," Fakhriddin stood up and walked the guest to the door.

Sotoldi ota's words were confirmed. The investigative team checked more than five hundred red Zhiguli cars registered in Tashkent city and the region with license plates starting with 22 and finally managed to find the car the old man was talking about.

It turned out that this car with the license plate number TSh 22-68 belongs to a resident of Buki district of Tashkent region, Kholmurod Togaev.

When the owner of the car was questioned, he confirmed Sotvoldi ota's testimony. In fact, on November 13, he went to Tashkent with his classmates Karim and Muyassar. They called their classmate Mahmud Temirov, who works in the prosecutor's office, who said he had time to meet them only during lunch. They waited for him from 10:00 to 12:40 near the prosecutor's office near the houses until he got off work. Mahmudjon came out around 13:00, and they all went to have lunch at a café near the Tashkent Hotel.

Mahmud Temirov, an employee of the prosecutor's office, confirmed the words of his classmates Karim, Muyassar and Kholmurod Togayev.

Thus, the next version also fell away, and the investigation team again reached an impasse. More than two hundred people suspected of committing the crime were under investigation. Operational measures and efforts to investigate each of them did not yield the expected results. None of all kinds of assumptions, hypotheses and versions put forward in connection with the criminal case were justified. The efforts of Fakhriddin Karimovich and the members of the group were, in fact, wasted.

Wazira put the children to bed and did some small chores around the house. Then she went into her bedroom and took out of the drawer the letters and poems that Bahrom had once written to him. She read them with special tenderness and awe. Each time it seemed to her that she was reading them for the first time. While reading, she mentally returned to the past, to the years when she had first met Bahrom. She marveled at Bahrom's wisdom and determination, who had gone through so much to be together with her, no matter what. After all, he had suffered so much to achieve her. With what difficulty he had begged for his parents' approval. He did not behave like other boys who went along with their parents but fought for his love and his happiness with special persistence and caution so as not to offend his mother.

Remembering these moments in her life, Wazira felt a tender boundless love for her husband.....

How much they've been through together.

On New Year's Eve, a message sent by agent number "2245" from Zangiata prison seemed to give hope to the members of the investigation team. The notice stated that a prisoner named Ahad Batyrov, who was serving his sentence in that prison, had said, "If I get out of prison alive, I will take revenge in any way I can on the investigator, prosecutor and judge who have treated me unjustly and made my life hell!

Fakhriddin Karimovich immediately instructed the members of the investigation team to gather all information about Ahad Batyrov and requested the criminal case against him from the court. Sanzharbek, together with three or four operatives, was assigned the task of finding out Batyrov's present place of residence and bringing him to the prosecutor's office.

Late in the evening, Tahir Gafurovich gathered the members of the group on this issue. He looked at those gathered while running his eyes over the information provided by the group leader:

- Is everyone here?

- Except for Sanzhar Rakhmonov, everyone is here. I sent him to find out Batyrov's place of residence and bring him here," replied Fakhriddin Karimovich, standing up from his seat.

- Sit down, sit down! Please tell us what we know so far about Batyrov!?

- Tahir Gafurovich, Ahad Batyrov was born in 1955. After graduating from the Tashkent State Medical Institute in 1977, he worked as a surgeon at the central hospital in the city of Bekabad. He was sentenced to fourteen years' imprisonment for the aggravated murder of citizen Ozoda Kabulova. He served his sentence in Zangiata prison.

In May this year, he was released early. At the moment we have no information about his whereabouts.

- Okay. What does Batyrov have to do with Bakhrom Safarovich? - Takhir Gafurovich took off his glasses and put them on the table, turning to Fakhriddin Karimovich.

- The criminal case against Batyrov was investigated by Ikrom Bozorov, an investigator with the city prosecutor's office, and the indictment was actually confirmed by Bakhrom Safarov, who was the city prosecutor at the time," Fakhriddin Karimovich said, leafing through a thick volume of the criminal case on his desk.

- So, it looks like the case is really serious," Tahir Gafurovich tapped his pen on the table, thought for a while, and then shuddered at a thought that came into his head. -Fakhriddin Karimovich, if this version is confirmed, then the life of both the investigator and the judge is at risk. We must act immediately. It is necessary to organize the protection of the workplace and home of the judge and the investigator.

-Yes. I'm sending officers now to take control of their workplaces and homes.

- Oh, and by the way, warn your employees to be careful! Batyrov may now show up at these addresses. You can't call the investigator or the judge here. If Batyrov is watching them, he may notice we're on his trail. In addition, organize wiretaps on both office and home phones. Don't leave a single call unanswered. Batyrov, apparently a hardened man, can call and summon for a meeting through other people, such as women. Okay?

Fakhriddin Karimovich, writing down the deputy prosecutor's instructions in his notebook, nodded in agreement.

- Who has any questions? - The deputy prosecutor addressed the members of the group. Seeing that everyone was silent, he added: "Get started!". Then he picked up one of the telephones standing nearby and asked to connect the Tashkent Oblast prosecutor.

-Fakhriddin Karimovich, do you think one doctor can do so much? Or are we on the wrong track again? - The deputy prosecutor looked questioningly at his interlocutor.

- I don't know. But revenge is a bad thing.

The phone rang. Tahir Gafurovich leaned over and picked up the receiver carefully:

- Abdurashid Mahmudovich, how are you doing? Investigator Ikrom Bozorov used to work in the Bekabad City Prosecutor's Office. Where does this guy work now?

-Bozorov, Bozorov! -Bozorov! Yeah, yeah, I remember. He quit his job a few years ago. Tahir Gafurovich, is something wrong?

- It's okay. Why did he quit his job?

- On his own recognizance. This guy was just bad at his job. He's been audited several times. Many times we warned him and punished him! Nothing worked. We had to accept his resignation. Tahir Gofurovich, did he complain about us?

- No, no! Do you know where he works now?

- No, I don't know. Since he left us. I haven't been interested. I can clarify," the regional prosecutor replied embarrassed.

- Not necessarily. Well, good luck in your work! Takhir Gafurovich interrupted the conversation and hung up the phone.

At that moment, the secretary said that investigator Sanjarbek Rakhmonov was waiting in the reception room. The chief authorized to let the investigator in.

- Hello," Sanzharbek entered the room, respectfully putting his right hand to his chest.

- Come on in, son. Well, what did you find out? - Takhir Gafurovich asked impatiently.

- After serving his sentence, Ahad Batyrov sold his house in Dombrabad, deregistered from Tashkent and moved to an unknown location.

The neighbors don't know where he went either.

- Are there children? After all, he will not leave them ... - Fakhriddin Karimovich joined the conversation.

- The fact is that while serving his sentence in prison Batyrov had a misfortune ...

- What's the misfortune? Speak quickly! - Tahir Gafurovich didn't like the investigator's artistic presentation of official information.

- Batyrov's wife and two sons were involved in a car accident while traveling to visit him in prison. The wife died at the scene, and the two children... died in hospital," Sanjarbek struggled to finish his sentence and fell silent.

Although Tahir Gafurovich did not know these people, he sincerely felt sorry for them in his heart. He repeated several times: "Yes, it's very bad!". Then he turned to Sanzharbek:

- Where is Batyrov himself now?

- We have not been able to find out yet. In Bekabad, he and his family lived in a service apartment. After his arrest, the family gave up the house and moved to Tashkent.

- Maybe he moved in with relatives? -Fakhriddin Karimovich stood up.

- Batyrov's parents died when he was still a student. I spoke to his only close relative, his uncle. I heard all this from him. But he doesn't know where Batyrov is now or what he does. He said that after losing his family, the man almost lost his mind. His uncle visited him in prison several times. But he did not want to see or talk to anyone. After he got out of prison, he came to his house only once. But he did not tell his uncle about his further plans for life. For a while he lived alone in a large mansion. It seems that he could not bear the loneliness, and, without consulting anyone, he sold his house and went wherever he went. No one has seen or heard from him since.

- We have to find Batyrov at all costs! He's like a wounded lion! We must not forget what he is capable of in such a state. Fakhriddin Karimovich, send operatives to Bekabad immediately. Batyrov worked there after his studies. Naturally, he has more acquaintances there. Just in case, we should check what other relatives, friends or buddies he has in Tashkent, and send operatives to these addresses.

-Yes!" said Fakhriddin Karimovich and Sanzharbek in one voice.

- Yes, by the way, Fakhriddin Karimovich, scrutinize Batyrov's criminal case through the eyes of an investigator. Then tell me what you think about it. Batyrov believes that he was unfairly accused. Can you imagine hatred in the heart of a man who has committed such a terrible crime? Only injustice can cause such hatred! After you have familiarized yourself with the criminal case in detail, hand it over to "USO[14]" for an official conclusion!

- Bingo!

One by one, the investigators left the chief's office. On the way, giving instructions to Sanzharbek, Fakhriddin hurried to his office. He instructed his secretary not to let anyone in and began to study Batyrov's criminal case diligently. It seemed to him that the whole solution to the mystery of his colleague's disappearance was hidden here. For this reason he began to scrutinize every document

---

[14] ODR - Division for Supervision of Criminal Cases in Courts of Law

in the case and to read carefully every statement. On a separate sheet of paper he made notes, drew diagrams depicting events, persons and their connection.

According to the documents of the criminal case, the details of this murder were simple: Ahad Batyrov had an intimate relationship with a girl named Ozoda Kabulova, who worked for him as a nurse. As a result, Ozoda became pregnant by him. The girl, not wanting to be dishonored in front of her parents and people, began to demand that Ahad marry her. She threatened that otherwise both colleagues and the family of Batyrov, who had a beautiful wife and two beautiful sons, would find out about it. And at work he had respect in the team.

Ozoda could destroy his family, his future and his dreams. For this reason, he thought that the only way to get rid of this trouble was to destroy Ozoda.

The motive for the crime is clear. Batyrov had ample reason to kill the girl. But how could a highly educated doctor prepare in advance to commit a crime and leave such a trace behind him? Why did he commit the crime in Ozoda's house? The neighbors could see him going in and out of the house! If he had such an evil intention, why didn't he choose another secluded place to realize his plan? In this way he would have averted suspicion from himself!

Batyrov may have gone to see Ozoda that day to reassure her of his words. He probably did not intend to kill her. But Ozoda apparently did not back down from her words and demanded that he divorce his wife and marry her. Then Ahad became angry and stained his hands with blood. He did not have time to cover up the traces of the crime. Because at that time Ozoda's girlfriend Lailo Shodieva came in. Realizing that he had been caught red-handed to avoid punishment, Batyrov ordered Lilo to call an ambulance immediately. Lailo ran to a neighbor's house in search of a telephone. When she came running back, Ahad said that Ozoda had died. After a while, the ambulance and the police arrived...

Batyrov maintained from the outset that he had not committed a crime. He did not recognize the charges against him. According to his testimony, he did have a good relationship with Ozoda. They had met several times. On that day, Ozoda called him in the morning and told him that she had important business to attend to and asked him to come to her after work. He came in the evening and knocked on Ozoda's door for a long time. But no one opened the door. Then he pushed the door, it was unlocked. When Ahad entered the house, Ozoda was lying on the floor with a knife stuck in her stomach, in a death agony. Being a doctor, he carefully removed the knife from the girl's stomach and tried to save her life by giving her first aid. At this time, Lilo approached....

Fakhriddin's thoughts came to a standstill. Who was interested in Ozoda's death? Did such an educated man kill a pregnant woman for such a trifle? After all, there were other ways to solve the problem! Was it so easy to take the lives of two people at the same time! Was Batyrov capable of such cruelty? Could a man who had lost his parents early, who had first-hand knowledge of suffering, who had graduated from school and university with honors and in a relatively short period of time had gained a good reputation in the workplace, and who was an exemplary family man, commit such a crime?

Or had he lost his mind because he was so afraid that everything he had worked so hard for all these years would be destroyed? Did he not think about the consequences of his actions? After all, many people knew about his relationship with Ozoda and there were rumors of disagreements between them. In this case, naturally, the first suspect in the girl's death was Batyrov! Why did such a prudent guy deliberately go for it?! Or was he hoping to get away with it?

The investigator walked in circles around the room and smoked four or five cigarettes in a short period of time. The further he dived into the criminal case, the more unsolvable questions and problems occupied his mind: Batyrov had been caught red-handed, but at the investigation and trial he had never admitted his guilt! What is this? Is it sheer audacity or enterprise? Maybe he really had nothing to do with the crime! But the evidence... His fingerprints were found on the knife found at the scene. What about the testimony of the main witness Lailo Chodieva? In her testimony at the investigation, she stated that she and Ozoda were close friends and did not hide their secrets from each other. One day she got upset and told him that Ahad aka was forcing her to have an abortion and she did not agree. At this point he got angry and said: "You want to embarrass me in front of my family and society. That's enough. The child should not be born. If you bother me, I will stab you with a knife." She was crying, at which point the head doctor, Tashmurad Sobirov, came in and asked: "Daughter, what happened?". Ozoda did not answer anything. She repeated this testimony to the investigator several times during the meeting with Batyrov. The chief physician also confirmed Lailo's words. This testimony of the witness Shodieva served as the main evidence to accuse Batyrov of committing the murder.

However, Batyrov stated at the investigation and trial that Shodieva's testimony was pure slander, that Ozoda was not pregnant, so he never talked to her about abortion, their relationship had always been good, but later on Ozoda was depressed about something, felt lonely and unhappy in life, but did not give the reason for this, that he tried to cheer the girl up. One day when he entered Ozoda's room he saw her with eyes swollen with tears. To calm her down he gave her some water and asked her: "What happened, who hurt you?" to which she replied, "It's nothing. Everything will pass." At that moment, the head doctor entered the room and asked them: "Is everything all right?" - and left without waiting for an answer.

Forensic medical examination confirmed that the deceased Ozoda Kabulova was three months pregnant....

Fakhriddin's thoughts are confused. All the facts were against Batyrov. They worked together. The relationship was good. They also met outside of work. As a result, Ozoda got pregnant. In any case, the case could become a rumor tomorrow. For this reason Ahad demanded her to have an abortion. The nurse was well aware that aborting the first fetus could deprive her of the happiness of motherhood in the future. Therefore, she did not agree to the abortion. Batyrov forcefully tried to persuade the girl, but she insisted on her own. Then Ahad had no other choice. Perhaps he did not intend to kill Ozoda that day. But the girl invited him home and told him that her decision was firm and demanded to get married as soon as possible. She threatened that otherwise she would not sit idle and would fight for her rights. Amid the quarrel, the young man became angry and could not control himself and grabbed a knife.... He was afraid of what he had done and tried to flee the scene. But at that moment Lilo appeared, which made him change his course of action. He now pretended to help the injured Ozoda. At that point, the girl was still breathing. Ahad was worried that the dying girl would say something important to her friend and deliberately sent Lilo to call an ambulance. When Lilo returned, Ozoda was already dead ....

At first glance, everything seems to be as it should be. Batyrov's guilt seems to be fully confirmed by the evidence collected in the case, the testimony of witnesses and the conclusions of experts. Yes, of course, there are certain ambiguities, contradictions and unanswered questions in the criminal case. In some cases, it seems that the investigation was conducted in a one-sided manner - towards the prosecution. During the investigation, Batyrov's motives were practically not investigated. In particular, the investigator ignored his testimony that Ozoda had recently been depressed, often cried and was worried about something. Ozoda's colleagues, friends, relatives and girlfriends, except Lilo, were not questioned. In addition, it has not been established from whom she was pregnant, the circumstances that could have caused the depressed mood of the girl have not been studied. The circle of persons interested in the girl's death has not been specified.

In addition, Batyrov's personality has not been thoroughly examined. True, if Batyrov had a criminal record, did not work anywhere and drank alcohol, there would not be the slightest doubt about the charges against him. But it is not believable that a talented surgeon, a leader with a bright future, an exemplary head of a family committed such a heinous crime. Somehow it seems that Batyrov could not have committed such a crime!

Having made the necessary notes, Fakhriddin took the documents and rushed to the deputy prosecutor's office. Sanzharbek was waiting for him in the reception room:

-Fakhriddin Karimovich, there are two messages from Bekabad. Which one should I start with?

- One's good, one's bad?

- Both can't be called good or bad...

- Then start wherever you want," Fakhriddin Karimovich said back. - Let's go and talk in the study.

- Ikrom Bozorov, who was investigating Batyrov's criminal case, died in a car accident several years ago.

- A car accident, you say? Fortunately, Batyrov had nothing to do with it.

- Clearly there is no connection because he was in jail at the time.

- What's the second news? Speak quickly! -Fakhriddin Karimovich stared at Sanzharbek.

- Batyrov also died last August.

- What... in what way?

- He went from Tashkent straight to Bekabad. He wanted to get a job. For some time he lived with a friend named Zafar, with whom they used to work together. Then he lived alone in a rented apartment. He was treated in hospital several times for heart attacks. The illness eventually led to his death. His body was found four or five days later. Neighbors were concerned about the foul smell from the apartment and reported it to the police. Doctors declared death by heart attack, and there were no signs of murder. Dr. Zafar took his body to his home and organized the funeral. They say Batyrov's personal belongings and documents are kept at his home," Sanzharbek handed the certificate to the chief.

- Wow! What's the next step? We're accusing him of committing a crime, and he, poor guy, has long ago left this mortal world and got rid of human vanity! May he rest in peace! Well, there's nothing we can do about it...

- That was his fate!

-Come on, let's report to Tahir Gofurovich," the team leader gathered up the scattered papers on the table and hurried out of the office.

Tahir Gafurovich listened carefully to the information of the investigators and thought:

- So, the dead Batyrov had nothing to do with either the death of Ikrom Bozorov or the disappearance of Bakhrom Safarovitch. That's good in one way! Because it still gives hope that Bakhrom is still alive. On the other hand, it means that the investigation has lost its way again. Now we'll have to start all over again. Fakhriddin Karimovich, as team leader and investigator, what are you going to do?

- Tahir Gafurovich, so far all the assumptions made have not been justified. Almost all possible cases have been investigated. Frankly speaking, at the moment we do not have a single worthwhile lead on our hands.

- What do we say to the management, to the Administration? Say: "Sorry, we couldn't solve this crime, we didn't have enough experience and knowledge"? I believed in you guys. It's a shame. Too bad. Well, go on. You're free to go. I'll report this to the Attorney General. We'll see what he wants me to do.

- Tahir Gafurovich, your objections are appropriate. Perhaps we're not experienced enough. Maybe we should bring in more experienced investigators to the team?

- Who do we bring in? Where are we going to find such a smart investigator? - The deputy prosecutor was indignant.

- You are right, but, as they say, "one head is good, but two are better". Takhir Gafurovich, I have studied Batyrov's criminal case... I have some comments on this case...

- Leave Batyrov alone! Why disturb the spirit of a dead man? It's better to transfer the criminal case to the appropriate department. Let them get dizzy! - Takhir Gafurovich stared at his interlocutor, saying, "I understand what I said.

Fakhriddin had no choice but to quickly collect the documents and quietly leave. Sanzharbek also reluctantly followed his boss.

-Fahriddin aka, what do we do now? Do you have any unprocessed versions left? -Sanjarbek asked the chief a question on the way.

- I don't know, I can't think of anything. I have no idea where to start now," Fakhriddin replied reluctantly.

After giving some instructions to his assistant and warning the secretary not to let anyone in, he went to his office. Standing by the window, he lit several cigarettes one after another: "What a waste of effort! Is there nothing we can do! Or, as Tahir aka says, do I lack the experience and knowledge to solve the crime? What is this mysterious criminal who left no clues behind. Did he really plan everything so meticulously and managed to realize it all? How is it that in broad daylight called from the place of duty responsible law enforcement officer and taken away without leaving a trace. And they did it in such a way that no one saw anything! But I or my other colleagues could have been in Bakhrom Safarovich's place!".

Toward evening he was summoned to his office again by Tahir Gafurovich.

-Fakhriddin Karimovich, sit down," said the deputy prosecutor to the investigator and sat down at the table opposite him. Pouring him a cup of tea, he continued. - So, you claim that there is no trace of the crime. Then tell me, what happened to our cardinal rule that 'crime does not pass without a trace'?

- Yes, every criminal naturally leaves their mark. But in my many years on the job, this is the first time I've encountered such a conundrum. The perpetrator didn't leave behind even a small piece of evidence.

- The perpetrator left no trace. Maybe there was no crime itself? - said Tahir Gafurovich, standing up.

- You don't get it, do you?

- I spoke to the Prosecutor General," Tahir Gafurovich explained. - He said something interesting. In his opinion, there are no signs of a crime in Bakhrom Safarovich's disappearance.

- How- how- how- how- how- how- how- After all, the man has disappeared. Isn't that a crime," said the investigator, unable to contain his surprise.

- I thought, there seems to be some truth in the Prosecutor General's words. It would have been more correct to declare Bakhrom Safarovich missing. There were no signs of crime in the man's accidental disappearance. All assumptions have been thoroughly investigated. Therefore, we can close the criminal case for lack of corpus delicti ...

- Tahir Gafurovich, but... but Bakhrom Safarovich... knowing everything, how can one say that there is no crime? - Fakhriddin Karimovich objected to the chief.

- No buts. The situation calls for it. I've made arrangements with the attorney general. Stop the proceedings.

- Tahir aka, give me a day or two, I'll solve the crime, you'll see!

-Fakhriddin Karimovich, come on. You've had more than two months at your disposal. It's too late. There's no point in leaving the crime unsolved. It's better if we close it. The Interior Ministry will continue the search for the missing man. Is that clear?

- Tahir aka, I understand you, but it is clear that Bakhrom Safarovich was the victim of a crime! How can we turn a blind eye to this?

- Where did you get this information? Bahrom may not have been the victim of the crime. I mean, we don't have any evidence to support that. He may have traveled abroad with someone else. Anything can happen in life.

- What will we say to Bakhrom Safarovich's relatives, his wife and father? After all, they rely on us. After all, Bakhrom aka was our colleague.

- I'll explain it to them myself. What can we do? We've been working for two months without a break, doing everything possible, but as you can see, there's no result. Our conscience is clear before Bahrom.

- Right... - said Fakhriddin Karimovich, calming down.

- Today bring me the decision to close the case file. Prepare the materials for submission to the Ministry of Internal Affairs! - Tahir Gafurovich stood up.

- Tahir Gafurovich, in the criminal case of Batyrov....

The deputy prosecutor looked at Fakhriddin Karimovich, "What else?

- I don't think Batyrov's guilt has been sufficiently proven. The investigation seems to have been conducted one-sidedly.....

-Fakhriddin Karimovich, I appreciate your sacrifice for the sake of others. But if Batyrov served his sentence and died, is there any point in reviewing his case? Do you want to scratch where it doesn't itch? Hand over the criminal case to the USO, let them study it.

- I think someone set Batyrov up pretty badly. Looks like someone needed to throw him in jail...

- All right, all right, let's say it was. But this is none of our business!

Refer it to the appropriate department, and if they deem it necessary, they will file a protest and send the case for a new hearing. And you go about your duties!

As Tahir Gafurovich's last words sounded loudly, Fakhriddin Karimovich did not dare to say extra words and left the office...

An unexpected call from Sanzharbek asking him to come to the prosecutor's office together with Safar aka alarmed Vazira: "It seems that there is news from Bakhrom aka? Or have they caught the criminals who stole him and took him away? This Sanzharbek also gave a riddle! It was impossible to give at least a hint. He simply and briefly said: "The management is asking for you." He didn't even let me ask why. Whatever it is, let it be good news! As long as he's alive. I'd do anything! Let him be far away..., let him be held captive by criminals, let him be held hostage, but let him be alive and well!".

With these thoughts Vazira did not notice how she reached the prosecutor's office. For the last two or three months, the severely drooping Safar aka had sadly and quietly followed his daughter-in-law without asking any unnecessary questions.

Downstairs, as always, Sanjarbek greeted them with an open smile. Vazira looked at him and tried to understand from his face why they had been summoned.

But unfortunately, nothing came out. "Investigators, they are like that. You can't tell from their faces what's going on inside them!".

Sanzharbek took the guests straight to Fakhriddin Karimovich's office. The chief stood up and greeted them with special respect.

After the greeting, Vazira's patience broke:

-Fakhriddinjon, what happened? What is known about Bakhrom aka?

- Sister, unfortunately, there is nothing I can do to make you happy....

- What-oh-oh, Bahrom aka.... - Wazira stood up.

- No, no! Don't get me wrong. The absence of good news is not bad news. Over the last few days, we've been working through all the remaining leads. But none of them worked. We've analyzed every possible case. Our work has been fruitless...

- Did Bakhrom aka disappear without a trace, will he never be found now...? -the tears glistened in Vazira's eyes.

- Son...what are you going to do now? Do you have any plans or speculations? - Safar aka very quietly intervened in the conversation.

- Safar aka, that's what we called you about," Fakhriddin Karimovich picked up one of the phones standing next to him: "Is the chief in? Good, we'll be right up.

- Safar aka, let's go to Tahir Gafurovich's house. We'll talk there," Fakhriddin Karimovich led the guests to the top floor.

Tahir Gafurovich met them in the reception room and invited them to his office. He asked Vazira about the health of his parents and children. He paid special attention to Safar aka and encouraged him. He told the secretary to bring coffee. The deputy prosecutor's special attention to them only increased Vazira's doubts. Remembering Fakhriddin Karimovich's words, she calmed down.

Tahir Gafurovich, noticing the excitement of the guests, got down to business:

- Safar aka, Vazirahon! We all respected Bakhromjon. He was one of our best employees, a talented and experienced investigator. We are extremely concerned about his disappearance....

The fact that the deputy prosecutor spoke in the past tense further instilled fear in Vazira's heart: "Why is he talking so much? What does he want to say... or does he have bad news? Is it hard for him to inform us about it? I wish he would get to the point soon! Otherwise, my heart won't be able to bear it!".

- We did everything we could. We even ran one percent probability tests. But nothing worked. How Bakhromjon disappeared, where he went and where he is now, we have not been able to find out. After he left on that fateful day, there was no one left who claimed to have seen or heard of him. For this reason, the Prosecutor General instructed us to close the case and declare Bakhrom Safarovich missing. Therefore, our investigative team found it necessary to terminate the criminal case.

- What does that mean? You won't look for Bahrom aka anymore? -Wazira asked, ready to cry.

- No, of course the search will continue. We will only close the criminal case. Because no evidence confirming that a crime was committed in this case has been found. This is the basis for recognizing Bakhrom Safarovich as missing. And the search, as I said, will not stop for a moment. We've called you here to inform you of this. Now we'll all have to be patient. Hopefully, one day, things will be clearer. Maybe after a while, he'll come back safe and sound. Everything happens in life," Tahir Gafurovich said calmly.

-Tahirjon, thank you very much! We have caused you so much worry," said Safar aka, who had been restraining himself all this time. - We have no doubt that you have taken all possible measures. Every event happens by the will of Allah. What can an ordinary man do. But I can't understand one thing. You say that Bahromjon is missing... But he is not lost in the desert, in the vast steppe, among the mountains, in the vast ocean or on the battlefield, but you say that he is missing! My poor son was taken from his office in broad daylight! He was taken from here right under your nose! A grown man, a responsible employee of such an authoritative agency was kidnapped by unknown persons, and you say that "no traces of the crime have been found, the perpetrator has not been caught, and now we will declare him missing!"...!

- Safar aka, please don't despair. We have no reason to call him a victim. Maybe he is alive," Tahir Gafurovich tried to reassure the old man.

- I really wish he were alive! Where has he been for three months?! Where could he have gone, leaving his wife, his children, his already weakened father, his job, his friends like you? Would he do that if his will was his own?

Yes, any situation can happen in life. But if Bahromjon were alive, if he had even the slightest chance, wouldn't he have at least warned us? - Tears came out of Safar aka's eyes.

- Father, please don't lose hope, your son will be found! We... we will find him, we will definitely find him," Tahir Gafurovich couldn't find words to calm the old man.

The first time she saw tears in her father-in-law's eyes, Wazira could not hold back and cried silently, sobbing and averting her eyes so that those around her would not notice her tears.

Fakhriddin Karimovich, saddened by such a sad situation, poured water into a bowl and handed it first to Safar aka and then to Wazira.

Safar aka took a sip of water with trembling hands and continued:

- I wouldn't wish on anyone what we have been through these months! Days and nights watching the door, flinching at any knock, not showing our pain, making each other believe in lies we don't believe in ourselves... Of course, for parents there is no pain more terrible than the death of a child. I understand if a child died, you can cry over his body, carry his tobut on your shoulders, put him in the grave, recite the Quran over his grave and cry to release your heart from suffering. Tahir, my son, tell me what should I do? My son has been gone for so many days and I can't even keep mourning for him like normal people! I can't hug him tobut! If my son is alive, please find him! And if he's dead. please find his body! I'll hold his dead body to my chest! He wasn't a stranger to you either!

Safar aka choked with excitement and froze. No matter how hard he tried to continue his speech, he could not utter a single word. He pressed a handkerchief wet with tears to his eyes and began to cry, sobbing silently.

Both Tahir Gafurovich and Fakhriddin Karimovich, who could barely contain themselves not to burst into tears, could not find words to comfort this grief-stricken old man....

They say time is the ultimate judge, but there is something that time doesn't seem to affect. It's called love. Time passes, but true love burns and ignites. It will not be extinguished by the winds of time, nor by the suffering of separation. Vazira's love for Bahrom was just as hot and sincere.

Although more than three years had passed since her husband had disappeared, there was not a day when Wazira did not think of him, look for him, or wait for him. Although on the advice of neighbors and relatives last year Safar aka did "acknowledge" his son's death and conducted the "burial rites of Bahrom" and other related activities, it seemed to Wazira that her husband was still alive, waiting for help in his imprisonment and would one day return home. This hope gave her the strength to go on with her life. She searched with her eyes for her husband among the people when she went out on the street to run errands, on her way to and from work, when she went out to fetch her children to walk them to school.

When she saw a man who resembled her husband in height and build, she would follow him, level with him, and discreetly scrutinize his face to make sure it was not him, and then continue on her way. When there was a knock on the door, it seemed as if her husband had arrived, and when the telephone suddenly rang, her heart raced as if she were about to hear her husband's voice.

Wazira had not gone to weddings and other entertaining events in the last three years. She did not want to hear people's advice. In recent years, laughter had not been heard in their house. The children had gotten used to it, too. When mom was home, they talked almost in a whisper so as not to make her angry. Now they were older and understood a lot of things, as before they didn't pester her with the question "When is Daddy coming?", they behaved like adults and considered their mother's mood. It seemed that the trouble that had fallen on their heads had made them grow up quickly.

Vazira tried not to show her pain to her children, supported them with affectionate words, tried to encourage them and not to extinguish the spark of hope in their young hearts, and to raise them as full-fledged people. She was very responsible for the education and upbringing of her children. Wazira wanted them to grow up to be educated, intelligent, polite, honest and perfect people like their father. For this reason, she spent a lot of time at home with her children and gave them all her love.

At night, when the children were asleep, she liked to look at Bahrom's picture in her bedroom, mentally communicating with him. She read over and over again the letters and poems Bahrom had once written to him. Though it had become a habit, sometimes she felt humiliated. Her heart clenched because the lines from his poem, "I look at your picture, but none of it comforts me," which Bahrom had dedicated to her when she was a student, seemed like something she would now spend her whole life reciting to the author herself. As soon as she fell asleep, she immediately saw her husband in a dream.

Each time, for some reason, she dreamed of Bahrom in an anxious, sad and helpless state. But he did not complain about life, as if he was already used to it. Once Wazira came closer to him in her dream. Her husband, as usual, paid no attention to her and spun yarn. He continued working even when his wife came very close to him. Wazira gathered her strength and shouted at the top of her voice:

-Bahrom aka, what are you doing here?! How long we've been waiting for you, the children can't wait for you! At least think about your elderly father!

Bahrom shuddered. He wanted to say something but bent down again and continued spinning the yarn.

He acted as if he didn't recognize Vazira. She got angry:

-Bahrom aka, we haven't forgotten you for a moment. We wait for you every day. We believed you were alive... Why don't you say anything? Say something! Is it really so...

- Go away, I don't know you! -Bahrom continued his work.

- Your children - Jahangir and Jawahir - are big now, they miss you very much! I promised them I would bring you back!

When he heard the names of his children, Bahrom's eyes widened, he stopped his work for a moment and looked intently at Vazira. Then he resumed his work.

Wazira realized that her husband's will is not in his hands. For this reason, he pretends not to know her and wants the family to forget him too. He hopes that if he behaves like this, Wazira will quickly forget him and will sooner get rid of her pain and suffering. So Wazira found a different approach and tried to influence her husband to bring him back to life:

-Bahrom aka! Even if you stay here for the rest of your life, I will still wait for you. I'll remember you till my last breath. Do you remember our wedding vows? We swore to be together in health and sickness, joy and sorrow, wealth and poverty! Without burying you in the ground, I keep you in mourning. This is done for the people. For you are always alive to me.

Bakhrom could not stand it. Throwing the work out of his hands, he stood up abruptly. Then she saw that his feet were shackled in heavy chains. He wanted to take a step towards Vazira, but he could not move:

- Wazira, I'm sorry! Looking at your clothes, I thought you had long forgotten about me. I didn't want you to suffer for me again, I didn't want to hurt you more! I made a mistake! I am guilty before you. I have been punished for my misdeeds. Now I will spend the rest of my life in this captivity. You must forget me and start a new life. If you love me, do as I say!

- No, no! Don't say that! For what sins can a man be chained for life? I will wait for you as long as it takes, five years, ten years. Your children are waiting for you, your father. I'll do anything to rescue you from this captivity. The only thing that matters is that you don't give up hope. Trust me," Vazira tried to approach her husband, but she couldn't move.

- My dear Vazira! Our children are young, and our parents are old. Yes, only you can get me out of here. But it's not easy! You will have to walk an incredibly difficult path. Thanks to your faith, hope and resourcefulness, we can be safely reunited again. I believe in you, I believe in you, I believe in you!

-Bahrom aka, wait, where are you going?! - Wazira woke up to her loud scream and looked around. She thought, "Was it a dream or was it real?".

- Mother! Tea is ready. Come out," came Jawahir's voice from behind the door.

The family had breakfast together. Wazira sent the children to school and began to analyze her dream: "So, Bahrom aka is alive! What could the captivity mean? And the shackles on his legs? All right, let him be captive or captive, but the main thing is that he is alive, and that is already good. He said: "Only you can take me away from here, only you can save me?". But what can I do alone?! How can I solve this riddle and find the man who cannot be found for three years now by the internal affairs authorities and the prosecutor's office, which have such limitless powers? He himself admitted that it is not easy, he said that I have an incredibly difficult path ahead of me. He said that my faith, hope and reason would help us to be safely reunited! But how to understand these words? What a man my poor Bahrom aka was! Now he needs the help of a weak creature like me. O God, show me the right path!".

Vazira took the prophetic dream seriously and decided to take a desperate step: to find a husband herself! And after all, she is a journalist by profession, which will open many closed doors for her. She has enough experience. During her career, she has done a lot of investigative journalism. But where to start?

Thinking long and hard, Vazira decided to start the investigation with a meeting with Sanzharbek and Fakhriddin Karimovich. Because they had been working on the case for a long time. Perhaps they had some information. First of all, it is necessary to get this data.

The next day Vazira went straight from work to the prosecutor's office. First she met Sanzharbek. After the traditional greeting, Vazira moved on to the purpose of her visit:

-Sanjarbek, as an investigator who was directly involved in Bakhrom aka's case, and as his friend, tell me, is there any hope of finding my husband?

- Sister, there's a saying, "hope springs eternal." We can hope. After all, the investigation found no evidence that he was dead.

That means Bahrom aka is alive. Everything takes time!

- I think so, too. That's why I want to start the search myself. You've done your best, of course. Now it's my turn. After all, it's been three years. I can't just sit around and wait!

- Wazira opa, it will be difficult for you to do what a whole army of law enforcement officers could not do. Besides, you have no materials on hand!

- This is what I wanted to consult with you about! Can I, as a journalist and as Bakhrom Safarovich's wife, familiarize myself with the materials of the investigation and take copies of them?

- You can, but...

-Can you help me in this matter? - Vazira looked into the eyes of her interlocutor.

- If your decision is firm, we will do everything. For this you need to apply to us with an application, - said Sanzharbek.

- Thank you, pointer! I will apply tomorrow. Vazira said goodbye to Sanzharbek and returned home satisfied that she had easily coped with the task at hand.

The next day Vazira spent the whole day in the prosecutor's office and familiarized herself with the materials of the criminal case. She copied the necessary documents. Then she consulted with Fakhriddin Karimovich.

- Sister, I understand you very well," he said. - And I support your decision. But I want to remind you that it will not be as easy as you imagine!

-Fahriddinjon, I have no choice. I will endure everything, no matter how hard it is! I've waited with hope for three years. I'm tired of waiting. But now my patience is over. In my heart, I believe that Bahrom aka is alive. And this hope motivates me to act! How can I sit at home when he needs my help? Do you know... - Wazira wanted to tell him about her dream, but changed her mind, fearing that the investigator would think she was "a woman who believes in omens.

- Wazira opa! I would do the same if I were you. Because it seems to me too that Bahrom aka is not dead.....

- If you're so sure, why didn't you follow through?

- Oh, sister! If it were up to us! I was against it even then. But the leadership and Moscow had a different opinion," Fakhriddin Karimovich said faintly.

-But now Moscow is out of order. Who's stopping you? - Wazira couldn't help herself.

- I am now working in a group to review the cases of people illegally convicted in the "cotton case". Hundreds of people have been acquitted. Thanks to independence, we have freed many innocent compatriots from prison.

- Thank you. We've been following your good work in the press, too. But, uh, don't get me wrong.

- No, no. I said those things just for information. It has nothing to do with you.

-Fakhriddin Karimovich, as an investigator, can you advise me where to start the investigation? - Vazira suddenly became serious.

- Honestly, I don't even know what to say. We've been through every possible theory. I'm almost out of guesses in my head.

- That letter found at home, on Bahrom aka's desk, was also left unopened?

- Yeah, we didn't find the author of that letter either. A lot of people's handwriting was examined at the time. It didn't work. Then we concluded that the letter had nothing to do with Bahrom aka's disappearance. After all, what kind of criminal would deliberately write a letter to his victim!

- What if it was done on purpose to distract you?
- Maybe! For some reason the thought hadn't occurred to me.
- I apologize for taking up your time. Fakhriddinjon, can I come to you for help if I have any problems? - Wazira stood up and left.
- Wazira opa, you're welcome. Contact me at any time. You know my phone number, -Fakhriddin Karimovich followed the guest to see her off.
- Thank you very much. Goodbye, then.
- Bless you, Sister.

As soon as Vazira opened the door and stepped outside, Fakhriddin Karimovich seemed to remember something and beckoned his guest back:

- Vazira opa, I forgot to tell you something. You know, I suspected a man named Ahad Batyrov. He had enough reason to take revenge on Bahrom aka. But then it turned out that he died shortly before Bahrom aka disappeared. Had he been alive, I would have arrested him as the first suspect ...

- Batyrov died before these events. Therefore, he cannot be a suspect," Vazira made a logical conclusion.
- That's true. But it could have been through others.
- Could it have been?
- Anything could be. For some reason, the thought has just occurred to me now. We didn't think of it during the investigation.
- It's unbelievable that a dying man could think of revenge.

- You're right. But this man. It's hard for me to explain his situation to you. Wazira opa, you should read the material yourself. Then you can come to a conclusion. By the way, when Batyrov got out of prison, he sold his house in Tashkent and lived in a rented apartment in Bekabad. What could the money from the sale of the house have been spent on?

-Batyrov's in jail for murder? You said so, but I forgot.

- Yes, he was charged with murder. But then, having studied his criminal case, I came to my personal opinion that Batyrov's guilt was not sufficiently proven. I told my superiors about it. But they paid no attention to it. Because Batyrov was dead at the time. It would be good if you studied this case too," Fakhriddin said in a whisper.

- Of course I will! Thank you for everything, - Vazira said goodbye to her interlocutor once again and left the office.

For the first time in three years, Vazira was satisfied with the work she had accomplished in a day. Today she was able to start a task that she had wanted to do for a long time but could not find the courage to do. Her friends had helped her with advice. They had also promised that they would be happy to help if necessary. So, the matter was moving forward. The rest depended on her actions. She would see this case through to the end, no matter how much time, life and money the job required. Of course, the prosecutor's office and the police have a lot on their plate. That's why they don't have the opportunity to be on the case all the time. And she has no other job besides this one. The kids are big now. They can manage on their own without her. Her official work is not so strenuous either, she writes an article and sends it to the editorial office. The rest of the time she belongs to herself. Though she writes occasionally, but many people like the way she writes. Therefore, the editor-in-chief treats her with respect.

So it's time to start looking. Such conditions and opportunities may never present themselves again. Thus began the biggest and most complex journalistic investigation in the history of...

Wazirahon once heard a story from her late mother-in-law: "A boy and a girl fell in love and got married. For many years they lived happily and peacefully. During this time they had children. The husband in the institute and the wife in the school taught young people. Due to their diligence and commitment to good deeds, both had respect in the mahalla and at work. In short, the couple were content with their lives, their happiness, their good fortune.

One day the head of the family fell ill. No matter how hard the doctors tried, they could not make an accurate diagnosis. As a result, the treatment was of no avail. Day by day the man's condition worsened, the disease exhausted him. His wife took her husband to hospitals. Even the prominent doctors of the republic could not cure the man. In the end, the doctors advised the woman to resign herself to her fate and take her husband home to spend the rest of his short life with his children.

The wife had no choice but to take her husband home from the hospital. The doctors predicted that the patient had only ten to fifteen days to live, so the woman preferred that her husband, completely exhausted and turned into a living skeleton, spend his last days in the company of his family. She began to take care of her husband, cooking a variety of delicious meals every day with appetizing seasonings. She spent sleepless nights taking care of her husband. She tried to cheer him up with kind words, to instill hope in his heart. No matter how much the woman believed in the words of doctors, no matter how much she realized that her husband's misfortune was inevitable, she somehow believed in her husband's recovery. She sincerely wished that some supernatural miracle would happen, that her husband would recover and return to his family and his favorite business. But miracles in life don't always happen....

After ten days, my husband's condition suddenly deteriorated. The next day he stopped eating and drinking. The woman realized that the time had come to say goodbye to her husband forever.... What could she do? Morally, she was ready for the fact that her husband would leave this world any minute now. She looked at him with pitying eyes and suffered from the fact that she could do nothing to help her husband and only passively watched him leave. She did not know what to do, who to turn to for help, or which door to knock on.

In desperation, she began to dig through the medical books in her personal library. The next day she went to the largest library in the city and started collecting all the materials on liver disease treatment published in Russian and Uzbek. She copied important articles and read them at night. After three or four days, the woman, who had almost no knowledge of medicine, had some idea of her husband's disease. With the help of this knowledge, she began to treat her dying husband on her own. After a while the man's condition improved a little. He began to eat small portions slowly.

Encouraged by the results of the treatment, the woman began to read Ibn Sina's Canon of Medicine. She began to diligently study treatises on folk medicine, went to the markets, to doctors, to the mountains in search of medicinal plants that could cure the human liver....

And a miracle happened. Thanks to God's help and the woman's prayers, the man was back on his feet in three months, and six months later he went to work as if nothing had happened.....

It was the power of love and the power of loyalty!".

Remembering this story, Wazira confessed that she had not paid much attention to it at that time. What was the purpose of her mother-in-law telling her this story? Did she have a premonition of something at that time? Or did she simply retell what she had heard from others? Is this a real story or did someone make it up? Why did her mother-in-law tell her this story? Or did she foresee that one-day Wazira would be in this woman's shoes? No! What mother would wish such a misfortune on her child? Her mother-in-law was totally against their marriage. Did she really could foresee the future? What if she had a premonition of these unfortunate events?

What is she thinking about? Instead of looking for ways to save Bahrom aka, she is thinking about extraneous things! In any case, one cannot help but admire the will and perseverance of the woman in this story. With no medical training, she started treating her husband who could not be cured by experienced doctors. She did not sit idly by, trusting in God. She never gave up hope for her husband's recovery. She managed to find the courage to rekindle the fading spark. Isn't this defenseless woman an example of perseverance to her? Is she any worse than she was?

As she pondered this, Vazira looked straight ahead like a falcon ready to fly far away. She clenched her fists tightly and whispered involuntarily: "Bahrom aka! I will still find you...".

Inspired by her late mother-in-law's story, Vazira started reading legal literature and detectives from her husband's library at night. After all, it also requires professional skills! Would she be able to complete this case without knowing the basics of law?

The next day, in spite of Saturday, Vazira was going to the library. At that moment the doorbell rang. Jahangir was the earliest to reach the door. It was Safar aka who had come. The boys glowed with joy at seeing their grandfather, who had been coming less and less lately. Wazira, too, breathed a sigh of relief because she did not know with whom to share her worries. And just then a man came to the house, with whom she could consult about the business she had started. Everyone was happy to see the old man. Safar aka wept when he saw his grandchildren who missed him, his daughter-in-law who was tired of all the troubles but always kept herself cheerful and firm.

But in order not to show his tears, he went into the bathroom, under the pretext of washing his hands and calmed down.

"Poor father," thought Vazira, - he had given up a lot lately. Oh, how healthy and energetic he used to be! There is nothing more terrible for parents than the death of a child. What else can be the situation of a father who has lost his son and has not even a grave?! The hope in his heart may have completely faded. I need to quickly tell him what work I have started, to cheer him up at least a little, to give him hope. By the way, how will he take it? Of course he'll be supportive. But what if he doesn't? What if he says, "Think of my peace, my children, don't do it!". Will I then go against his opinion? Or is it better not to tell him about it yet?".

Safar aka distributed to the children the gifts he had brought from the village. Vazira prepared breakfast. The father-in-law and daughter-in-law talked over tea: - Daughter, how are you doing, what news? - The old man gathered his strength and came to the main topic. Vazira silently lowered her eyes. Feeling that it was time to tell about the case she had started, she took her time and began to tell:

- Father! I haven't heard from Bakhrom aka. I went to the prosecutor's office, talked to Fakhriddin Karimovich and Sanzharbek. They did everything they could. But there is no result. According to the investigators, there is no hope that Bakhrom aka will be found. But...

The father, who had been listening thoughtfully to his daughter-in-law, lowered his head when he heard the word "but" and looked up at his companion, as if he sought salvation in her eyes:

- Well, well, well!

- Father, it seems to me that Bahrom aka is alive! I have a feeling that he is a hostage in some situation somewhere that needs our help.

- If only it were like this, daughter! - Safar aka took a deep breath.

- That's why I want to start the search myself.

- I don't understand... you... how, uh.

- Father, I can't sit still when I feel the need to act! I've waited three years. Now I must begin the search myself. Bless me, Father," Wazira looked directly into her father-in-law's eyes for the first time.

- Daughter, I understand you correctly, but how can you do alone what the competent government agencies could not do? Do you know what you're getting into? What will happen to the children? Everything happens by the will of Allah. If Bakhromjon is alive, one day he will return home on his own feet. But if he's not alive, what can we do?

- Father! My decision is firm. I want you to believe me. I started some work last week. I received a lot of documents related to this case. God willing, everything will be all right," Wazira said confidently.

-I'm powerless to say anything. If you're going to do it, it means you have a plan in your heart and enough evidence on your hands. But please, my daughter, don't let it get to the point where there are rumors about you, like "a crazy woman looking for a husband on the streets"! Don't tell anyone about it, just do your job in silence.

- Thank you, Father! It'll be just as you said.

Vazira left her father-in-law with the children and hurried to the library.

The library is like a bottomless ocean. Once a person dives into it, he or she swims deeper and deeper with curiosity. And the deeper you go, the more wonders are revealed to your eyes. The unknown world appears before you. Vazira didn't even notice how dark it got....

It had been about two weeks. Wazira was fully immersed in the "underworld".

Her thoughts were occupied with terrible crimes, criminals who dodged out of fear of being exposed, investigators who stayed up days and nights to catch them, lawyers who called "black" "white" against their conscience, prosecutors who were not afraid to call "white" "black," "witnesses" who sold their souls to the devil, and experts with incredible skill. During this period, she read more than ten books detailing more than a hundred crimes. The events are different and not the same...

Among the countless crimes, Wazira searches for something similar to her story. Ah, if only! It turns out that the types and methods of crime are myriad, and they are not alike...

One day, while reading a detective novel by a foreign writer, a case caught Vazira's attention: a woman is murdered in her own home. Investigators question her acquaintances and neighbors. But it is impossible to find out who killed the woman and for what reason. No significant evidence or traces of the crime scene are found. The efforts of the young detective are wasted. The crime remains unsolved for a long time. Then the detective decides to re-examine the scene. After re-examining the house of the deceased, he finds one letter among the books.

The letter told the woman to never tell anyone about what she had seen and to move to another city as soon as possible, or she would be sick. So the woman had accidentally witnessed some kind of crime. The criminals feared that their actions would be exposed and demanded the woman to keep her mouth shut and move to another town as soon as possible. The woman was afraid of the criminals and did not tell anyone about what she had seen, but she did not want to move to another town. The criminals didn't like that. They decided to destroy her, thinking that one day she would talk about it.

The investigator gave the letter and the enclosed envelope to the experts. But the experts could not identify its author. The investigator goes to the communication unit to find out where and how many envelopes of this stamp were distributed. It is found out that envelopes of this stamp were distributed in four districts of the region. It is found that the aunt of the deceased lived in one of these districts and visited her frequently. After examining all the recent crimes committed in those areas, the detective focuses on one related to a car accident.

In the case, the driver of the car testified that the man suddenly ran out onto the road, no matter how hard he tried to slow down the car, he could not, as a result he hit the pedestrian, who died on the spot. The criminal case was suspended due to the fact that the driver's guilt was not proven.

The investigator takes handwriting samples from the driver and his family members and appoints a handwriting examination. Then it turns out that the letter found in the house of the dead woman was written by the driver's fourteen-year-old sister. As a result, both crimes are solved.

The driver said that he had a grudge against his neighbor, so he wanted to run over and kill her, but did not notice the woman who was standing at the bus stop and saw everything. He followed her to her house and then asked his sister to write a letter and dropped it in the woman's mailbox, but the woman refused to comply with his request. The driver confessed that he killed her out of fear that his crime would be discovered.

One envelope was the reason the crime was solved.....

Vazira returned home satisfied with the idea she had come up with after reading the work. She dashed into her room and looked for a copy of the envelope among the papers in her desk drawer. Here's a copy of the letter found among Bahrom aka's books. Where was the copy of the envelope... here it was. Nothing was written on its front. In the upper left corner, there is a stamp with a majestic image of the commander and statesman Amir Temur. On the back of the envelope there was a note that it was a product of the Uzbekistan Publishing House.

Vazira got dressed, put the copies of the letter and the envelope in her bag, and went to the publishing house. On the way, as she rode the bus, she had various thoughts:

"Maybe they know something there. Maybe there are still people who worked in those times. And how many envelopes are produced and distributed in a year. After so many years, who can remember about it. Maybe we should contact the Ministry of Communications? In any case, envelopes are distributed through them! We should check it out. It's worth a try! Anyway, apart from this envelope, I don't have any guesses and versions.

Wazira went straight to the director of the publishing house. The director, aged about thirty-five or forty, received her cordially. Between words he mentioned that he read their newspaper with great interest.

- This envelope happens to be printed at your place! - Wazira handed him the envelope.

The principal looked at him carefully:

- Yes, that's our product... and what do you have to do? - he wondered.

- Do you have any information on this envelope? How many were produced, where they were distributed, etc.

- Uh-huh! The envelope was made before independence! That was so long ago. I didn't work here at that time. So I don't know anything about it. But how many were produced, we can find out from the archives. However, it's hard to say where they were distributed. We only produce them. Distribution is done through the system of the Ministry of Communications. You can get such information from them," the director said and looked at Vazira as if asking: "What's the matter?".

- Do you have any employees who worked at that time?

149

- We'll find out now," he said and called the secretary to summon Fayu opa.

After a while, an elderly woman of about 55-60 years old with glasses entered the office, breathing heavily.

- Faya opa, this man is from the newspaper. She has some questions for you," the director said, pointing to Wazira.

- Please ask," Faya said, looking at Vazira questioningly.

- Faya opa, I heard you've been working in publishing for a long time. Do you know anything about this envelope? - Wazira handed the envelope to the woman.

She looked at the front and back of the envelope and turned to Vazira:

- What do you even want?

- Was this envelope actually issued at your publishing house? In what quantity? Where were they distributed? - Wazira repeated her questions once more.

- Clearly, it was printed here. It says so on the back. But I don't know how many were issued and where they were distributed. How many of these envelopes we produced in a year, you can't remember! - said Faya opa, handing the envelope back to Vazira.

Then, as if she remembered something, she took the envelope in her hands and scrutinized the stamp on it:

-Whoa! -This is the envelope issued for Amir Temur's jubilee! It's been more than ten years... I remember there was a big scandal back then.

- What scandal? - Wazira looked at the woman in surprise.

- Before independence, there was no permission to print Amir Temur's portrait. Our late director Aziz Rasulovich was a very good manager. He was not afraid of anything. Despite the opposition of some officials, he said that Amir Temur was the pride of our nation and gave the order to print his portrait on the envelope. After the envelopes were distributed, there was such a scandal, there was a showdown! The envelopes were recalled and destroyed. And Aziz Rasulovich was fired. Where did you get this envelope?

Wazira looked at the headmaster, not knowing what to say.

- Faya opa, thank you. You have helped us a lot. You can go now," the director stood up and moved to the chair opposite Vazira:

-Wazirahon, I've heard about it too. I was told about the "historical envelope" when I first came to work here. But I haven't seen it myself, - the director took the envelope in his hands and looked carefully at the portrait of Amir Timur. - Yes, those were interesting times! They say Aziz Rasulovich was a real patriot. One could not say a good word about Amir Temur back then, when the Soviet system was still on the horse. Although I did not know Aziz Rasulovich, but after this story my respect for him increased.

- Is it true that the envelopes have been recalled and destroyed again? - Wazira, busy with her thoughts, interrupted the director.

- That's what I heard. But I think some of the envelopes got lost somewhere.

- How do we know where these envelopes are lost?

- That kind of information can only be found in the communications departments. But I think that would be very difficult to determine. Wazirahon, I'm sorry, but why do you have that envelope?

- I'm doing some investigative journalism on a case," Wazira stood up and prepared to leave. - Thank you very much. I'm sorry to have taken up your time.

- I'm glad to have done a favor for a charming employee of such a prestigious newspaper," the director smiled contentedly.

Wazira, disregarding the young man's compliments, walked out of the office with quick steps....

After spending the next two days at the Ministry of Communications, Wazira was able to study the envelope distribution system in detail. She found and interviewed employees working in post offices at the time. Although many had heard of the Amir Temur envelopes, they were unable to provide any valuable information about how they were distributed or recalled.

The next day, having lost all hope that anything would come out of this case, Vazira decided to go to the house of the late Aziz Rasulovich.

The widow of the old publisher welcomed her cordially and invited her to the table. When she heard Vazira's intention, she poured her heart out, thinking that the journalist would write an article about her husband:

- Honey, as if that envelope wasn't enough to get my husband fired, he wasn't allowed to work in other places either. He was stamped "nationalist" on his forehead. A man who had worked in government agencies all his life became bored at home and fell ill.... Fortunately, he saw independence and witnessed the rehabilitation of the holy name of Amir Temur.

-Hadicha aya, I'm sorry to pour salt on your wound. Do you have any documents or items related to that terrible event?

- I keep my husband's personal documents. But I don't remember if any document on this matter has been preserved. Because the audit was conducted secretly and without publicity. The discussion of the results of the performance audit was also conducted in strict confidentiality.

- Remember who did that performance review?

- The inspection was carried out by a Russian from Moscow, whose name I do not remember now, and from the ministry, Nikolai Kasimov, who worked as head of the personnel department. By the way, Kasimov is still alive. It is possible that some documents have survived in his personal archive.

-Ayajon, do you know this man's address?

- Of course I do. Kasimov was on good terms with my late husband. Even after his retirement, they kept in touch. We used to go to his house every year for his birthday. They lived on the first floor of a nine-story building near the Kazakhstan Cinema. Everyone in his mahalla knows this man," Khadicha aya said, sipping hot tea.

- Thank you, Ayajong! Well, I'll be going. Once again, I apologize for the inconvenience," Vazira opened her palms for a blessing.

- Amen, may the souls of the departed be in heaven and the living in health and prosperity.

Seeing her guest off, Hadicha aya asked several times to be informed if the article was published...

It was not difficult for Vazira to find Kasimov's house. Fortunately, Uncle Kolya was at home. Usually, pensioners are eager to talk to someone. When they get such an opportunity, apparently out of boredom, they tell their whole story in detail, as if they want to brag about it. But Uncle Kolya was not one of those old men. Vazira noticed at once that he was a man of few words, reserved and serious. That's why she spoke to the old man very carefully. When he heard the purpose of the guest's visit, he asked openly: "Why do you need it?". At first Wazira tried to distract the old man by saying that she wanted to write an article. But, no, the old man turned out not to be the naive type. "There seems to be something else here," he insisted.

Vazira was forced to tell everything as it was. Uncle Kolya listened attentively to the woman and softened a little. He told everything he knew about the scandal with Amir Timur's picture on the envelope. Then he went out for a moment and brought a whole stack of old documents:

-Here are those performance review materials. I used to collect documents like that all the time during my tenure. I thought it might come in handy someday. I have a lot of them in my personal archive.

Uncle Kolya looked through the documents one by one and, apparently having found the necessary certificate, began to read it carefully:

- So, 20,000 such envelopes were printed. Of these, 19,200 were withdrawn from the communications departments and destroyed. The remaining 800 pieces. never came back. Hmm-hmm, so the envelopes only didn't come back from Bekabad City Communications. Because they were distributed to the public long ago. Somebody got punished... fired...

- So the envelopes were distributed only in the city of Bekabad... - whispered Vazira. - Uncle Kolya, please tell me, could these envelopes have been sent to addresses other than Bekabad?

- No, that's completely impossible! Every envelope was accounted for. Only 800 envelopes were never returned. We destroyed the rest. That's for sure.

- These 800 envelopes could have been used by people from other districts!

- Right, it's possible, but unlikely. Who would go to another neighborhood to pick up an envelope?

- You're right. Uncle Kolya, can you give me a copy of this certificate? — asked Vazira embarrassed.

- Please. These are things that happened during the Soviet period. Nobody needs them now.

- Thank you, father. I'll go out now and copy the certificate outside," Wazira jumped up from her seat.

- What copy? Take it for good, daughter. I'll be glad if I've been of any use. So you've kept them all this time for a reason," the old man said, smiling contentedly.

- If I find my husband, the gift is on me.

- May the Almighty help you," the old man, standing up, opened his hands to pray

Vazira didn't notice when she reached home. On the one hand, she was glad that she had found the end of the ball of yarn, but on the other hand, she was confused, not knowing where to start. In any case, her efforts for so many days had not been in vain and the matter had moved forward. Now it is necessary to go to Bekabad. What can we find out there? It's a big city. It's been so long. Maybe the envelopes were distributed in specific areas. Then the job would be a lot easier. Maybe she'll meet people like Uncle Kolya. We have to go. Yes, yes, we must go to Bekabad tomorrow, without putting it off for later.

The next day Vazira saw the children off to school and left for Bekabad. Since her husband worked in this city and they had lived here together for some time, the area was not a stranger to her. Besides, they had some acquaintances here. First she should find at least one of them. At that moment, she remembered about her neighbor Zamirahon. Although they had lost touch in recent years, they had still lived in the neighborhood for three years and had a good sincere relationship. They were family friends. Even after moving to Tashkent, they kept in touch for two or three years. But lately the connection was broken.

Her husband Farrukhzhon is a sociable man. It would be better to go to them, of course. I wonder if they know about Bahrom aka's disappearance. They say bad news travels fast. They must have known for a long time.

As Wazira rode on the bus, she was overcome by thoughts: "Why Bekabad again? Bakhrom aka worked here. Naturally, he had enemies. Does the tangle of crime threads lead here?... By the way, Fakhriddin Karimovich spoke about unjust punishment of some doctor? But what was his name? Ahad Batyrov, if I'm not mistaken? Yes, yes, Ahad Batyrov. But he said that he died before the terrible events connected with her husband! Then this man has nothing to do with Bahr aka! Why did the investigator tell me all this? What did he mean? During the last meeting he wanted to say something, but.... What could he be hiding from me? What else did he say? Yes, yes. He said that this man sold his house in Tashkent after prison and lived in a rented apartment in Bekabad. If he had no one, where could he have spent the money? Could he have hired an assassin?! Perhaps Fakhriddin Karimovich wanted to tell her. But he didn't because he was afraid of scaring her.

Whatever it is, one thing is clear so far: in both cases, the thread of the tangle leads to Bekabad. Is there any connection between these events or is it just a coincidence?

Vazira, not finding her friend at home, went to her place of work. The longtime friends greeted each other cheerfully. Zamira embarrassedly apologized for having heard about the trouble with Bakhr aka, but was unable to go to Tashkent to visit her friend. Vazira tearfully recounted her ordeal. She explained the reason for her visit and asked for her help.

Zamira's heart ached to hear of the hardships this once happy family had endured. She couldn't imagine how a family that had once been admired by everyone had fallen into such a predicament. As she looked at Vazira, she felt sorry for her former neighbor, but she couldn't find the words to comfort her. She really wanted to do something to help her friend. So she took a day off work and joined Vazira.

- We'd better start with the communications department. Maybe there we'll find some information related to the envelope," Zamira suggested.

Wazira followed her friend in silence.

First they met with the head of the communications department. The thirty-five-year-old manager, Abdurahman, did not know the history of the envelope. He said that he had come to this position two years ago from another sphere and advised them to go and see Ergashali aka, who had worked in his place for many years. Then, whether he wanted to show off in front of a journalist from Tashkent or whether he really wanted to help them, he agreed to drive the guests in his Zhiguli to Ergashali aka's house. The car drove for 15-20 minutes and stopped in front of a green gate. He dropped the women off, apologized several times for not being able to wait for them and drove away.

Abdurahman was right. Ergashali aka had worked in this system for many years and knew a lot. Hearing that the journalists (thinking that Zamira was also a journalist) had come to talk about the envelope with Amir Temur's image, the old man excitedly began to tell:

- Those were strange times! It was forbidden to print an image of the great Amir Temur. I was a supervisor at the time. About six hundred pieces of such envelopes were brought to our department. We had not yet had time to distribute them, but the day after tomorrow the "alarm" started. We were asked to quickly return the envelopes.

They didn't say exactly why. But I knew right away what it was. I thought it must have something to do with the image of Sahibkiran.[15]

I got angry and distributed the envelopes to the liaison units without returning them to Tashkent. Although we were taught that our ancestor Amir Temur was a bloodthirsty and despotic tyrant, I knew that he was the pride of our people and was a just king and a brave commander. I do not regret what I did, although the leadership at the time almost skinned me. After so many years, there are brave people who remembered this incident!

-Ergash aka, your bravery in those dangerous times is nothing short of heroic," Zamira praised the old man.

- Do you remember which branches these envelopes were distributed to? - Wazira's patience ran out.

- Heroic or not, it is what I did, and I did it not to boast or to show off. I have done my duty to the memory of our great ancestor," said the old man, encouraged by Zamira's praise.

- Father, what else do you remember about the envelope? - Wazira asked, unable to find a place to sit.

- I was punished, wanted to be fired...

- No, no, that's not what I meant, I wanted to know where the envelopes were distributed.

- What does it matter? The main thing is that they went to the people, got into the hands of the people.

---

[15] Sahibkiran - in Persian and Turkic medieval sources Amir Timur was called "Sahibkiran" (Persian صاحب کران), i.e. born during the conjunction of two planets: Venus and Jupiter or Venus and the Sun, in a figurative sense - happy.

- Right, but-oh... - Vazira was confused, not knowing what to say. - It would be better if we found at least one of these envelopes. I mean, it's n-u-u-needed for the article.

- Yes, I remember, as if it were yesterday, I handed them out to post offices No. 245 and No. 246. Because I trusted the heads of these offices more.

- Do you remember what areas of the city these departments served?

- I remember, of course, they served the territories of the present mahallas "Almazar" and "Temirchi", -Ergashali aka went to another room, saying "now", and after a while returned with a map of the city in his hand:

- These mahallas are located next to each other in the southeastern part of the city.

- I know these places. A relative of ours lives there," Zamira intervened.

- The department heads are retired now, but if you want, I can give you their home addresses," my father said naively.

- That would be good," Wazira wrote down the addresses.

- We are glad to have met and talked to you. You have made our task much easier, thank you very much," said Zamira.

- I'm sorry to have taken up your time. Now, Father, we will go. Please bless us," Wazira opened her palms in prayer.

Ergashali aka said a long prayer and escorted the women to the door.

- If the article is printed, don't forget to send me a copy," my father said before saying goodbye.

Next, Zamira insisted that they go to her house for some rest.

They chatted over tea. Concerned that the children were left home alone, Vazira said that she would come again tomorrow or the day after tomorrow and returned back to Tashkent....

Since the next day was Saturday, Vazira left the children with her brother Anvar and went to Bekabad again. Zamira greeted her friend warmly and by prior arrangement they went straight to Almazar mahalla. Failing to find the house of the former head of communication department No. 245, they went to the mahalla "Temirchi". It was not difficult to find Toshtemir aka, who worked as the head of communication department No. 246. The former head, having heard the purpose of the visit of the "journalists", immediately recalled those events:

- Those were incomprehensible times! Our poor friend Ergashali almost lost his job because of envelopes with Amir Temur's picture on them. I remember Sahibkiran's portrait now. And he is the pride of our nation!

-Toshtemir aka, do you still have these envelopes? - said Wazira, getting straight to the point.

- No, because Ergashali aka told us to distribute them quickly and we distributed the envelopes to kiosks and stores. If I'm not mistaken, it was about 400 pieces. The envelopes were sold out in a couple of days. Because the inspectors went around to the kiosks and stores to recall them. The same thing happened in the neighboring branch No. 245. None of the envelopes could be returned.

- Do you remember how many of those envelopes were distributed and to what locations?

- At that point, there were a lot of dots. We gave 15-20 pieces to each one!

- What else do you remember about those envelopes? - Zamira came to her friend's rescue.

- What else could there be? Then the inspections started. We were called in a couple times. We had a meeting to discuss—

- Father, thank you very much. We will now go with your permission," Wazira made the conversation short, so as not to waste time.

- And tea.

- Thank you, Father. We're in a hurry.

The women said goodbye to old man Toshtemir and went to Zamira's house.

- Vazira, what are we going to do next? — Zamira turned to her friend, who had been driving in silence for quite a while.

- I've been thinking about that too... Remember I told you about a man named Ahad Batyrov? He lived in Tashkent. He came to Bekabad on a referral from the institute. He worked as a surgeon in one of the city's central hospitals. Later he was arrested on suspicion of murdering a nurse with whom he worked together. At that time Bakhrom aka worked as a prosecutor in Bekabad. Unfortunately, when Batyrov was serving his sentence, his wife and two children were killed in a car accident on the way to him. It was a terrible tragedy. Batyrov lost his entire family in one day.

Then he swore in prison that he would kill everyone who had unjustly imprisoned him and made his life a living hell. No one knows whether Batyrov said this out of grief or whether he really intended to do it. What if he really was unjustly imprisoned! I think any person in his place would have done the same thing.

- So you're saying Batyrov had a hand in Bakhrom aka's disappearance?

- You never know. But he was no longer alive when Bahrom aka disappeared. He died a year before those events.

- So he had nothing to do with Bahrom aka's disappearance, right?

- That's true. but for some reason the bitter fate of this man does not get out of my head... After Batyrov was released from prison, he sold his house in Tashkent and returned to Bekabad and lived in a rented house. One can understand why he sold his house. He could not live there where everything reminded him of his wife and children. But he could have bought a place elsewhere! Why was he forced to live in a rented house? Did he have another intention, or did he know in advance that he was going to die? What could he have spent the money from the sale of the house on? Fakhriddin Karimovich, the investigator in charge of Bakhrom aka's case, said that Batyrov had a close friend. I didn't pay attention to it then....

- Does this friend have an address? - Zamira stopped and turned to her friend.

- I need to call the investigator. We absolutely must find him.
- Can he give us any information?
- I don't know, girlfriend, I don't know. Anyway, we can get some information from him about Batyrov. Like what Batyrov spent the money from the house sale on.
- So you have a suggestion that Batyrov might have hired an assassin! - Zamira drew her logical conclusion.
- The premise is there, but could a man lying on his deathbed hire an assassin to get revenge on someone?
- Revenge is a terrible thing! A man who decides to take revenge has only one goal. And nothing can turn him from that path. Such a person is not even afraid of death....
- You're right! It is not excluded that Batyrov, anticipating his own death, hired someone for this job for a large reward....

They did not even notice how quickly they reached Zamira's house. Vazira asked her friend's permission to call Tashkent. Luckily for her, Fakhriddin Karimovich was in his office. He recognized Vazira's voice at once. They said hello. He was not surprised to hear her request. He wrote down the phone number she had called, saying he would contact her a little later. "This restless woman must have already started her search, since she's calling from Bekabad! Will she really be able to do what we couldn't do!" the investigator thought. He took out a stack of documents from the safe and began to dig through them. Finally he seemed to find the right document, put it aside, and put the rest of the papers back where they belonged. Then he called the number given by Vazira:

-Opajon, I got Dr. Zafar's address. Can you write it down?

Wazira wrote down the number and thanked the investigator.

- Wazira opa, were you able to clarify anything? As we agreed, I am always ready to help. Call me whenever you want," Fakhriddin Karimovich said at the end of the conversation.

- Thank you, Fakhriddinjon. No news yet. I'm just clarifying a few things here.

- I wish you luck. I'll be in touch.

- Thank you, you have a great day too!

Zamira glanced at the note in her friend's hand:

-Whoa, this is the street we went to! In that Almazar mahalla," she said.

- Oh, really?

- Uh, sure.

- Then let's go.

- Wazira, take your time! Let's take a break and have lunch. We'd better go later. Dr. Zafar will be back from work by then.

-I hadn't thought of that. Okay, we'll go later.

Zamira started to prepare dinner. Her friend wanted to help, but the hostess refused. "You are a guest, so feel free to relax and watch TV! I'll think of something quick," she insisted.

Though Wazira's eyes were fixed on the movie on the television, her thoughts were elsewhere: "Dr. Zafar's house is in Almazar Mahalla, is that a coincidence or a pattern? Either way, there seems to be a lot to think about here....

Who is this man, Zafar? Can I learn anything from him? What if her efforts are wasted? Is she on the right track? What is happening is like a movie!".

Zamira set the table and invited her guest to dinner. They ate together and talked about this and that. Zamira tried to keep her friend occupied with interesting stories. Although Vazira's face was smiling, her thoughts were elsewhere.....

Toward evening the friends went to the Almazar mahalla. Dr. Zafar was at home. Seeing the guests, thinking that they were clients, he invited them to his office. Zamira introduced herself and her friend. When he heard that Vazira worked for a prestigious newspaper in Tashkent, he glowed, apparently thinking that they wanted to write an article about him, and invited the women into the living room. He poured them tea that his wife had made.

-Zafar aka! I apologize for showing up unannounced," Wazira said.

- No problem. A guest is a messenger of God. No need to be embarrassed.

- I am writing an article about your friend Ahad Batyrov. You know, his hard fate will not leave any person indifferent," Vazira blushed at the lie.

- Did you know Ahad?

- I knew this man well from my college days.

- My late friend was a wonderful, sincere and kind man. He was a unique surgeon, a doctor with a light hand. I wouldn't wish his fate on an enemy.... -

Dr. Zafar took a deep breath and fell silent.

-Zafar aka, please tell me everything you know about this man. I.... I.... I don't know about this man's life in Bekabad.....

-Ahad came to our hospital on referral from the institute. He quickly gained respect in the team due to his knowledge, determination and sincerity. He was recognized as a talented surgeon. In two years he was promoted to the head of the department. Many admired him. Envious people were also not few. In recent years, there were rumors that he would become chief physician. But Ahad wasn't interested in a career. He was a born surgeon, a doctor from God.

The doctor sipped tea from the drinking bowl he held in his hand and continued:

- Ahad and I became very close friends. We were family friends. His wife Nurkhon was a beautiful, decent and sociable woman. Ahad's relationship with his wife was also admirable. Since they had no children for many years, they spoiled their children and were strict with them at the same time. Nurkhon in particular attached great importance to their upbringing.

I think people have jinxed this family. Ahad was suddenly arrested. He was suspected of the premeditated murder of a nurse named Ozoda, who worked at our hospital. During the investigation and trial, I met with Ahad several times.

He repeated every time that he had not committed this crime, that someone had slandered him, that he was not guilty of killing Ozoda at all, on the contrary, he wanted to help her, that the witnesses had been bribed. But both the investigation and the court found Ahad guilty of this heinous crime and sentenced him to a long prison term. Many people still do not believe that Ahad committed this crime. I personally wouldn't believe it either. But...what can you say...who wanted our opinion...

- Since people don't believe that Batyrov committed this crime, who do they think killed Ozoda? - Vazira asked.

- What people say! Of course, it's a sin to accuse someone without reason.... But what's the use of talking about it now? Ahad served his sentence. He passed away. He lost his wife, his children, his family, his team, everything he had. What's the point of bringing it all up now?

- Would not the soul of your friend be satisfied if we could at least justify his name posthumously? - said Zamira, who had been silent all this time.

- If he had been acquitted, if.... but... So much time has passed since then. the traces have disappeared. I'm afraid you're not up to the task ...

- Please, trust us! Just tell us everything you know. That's all we ask of you. We'll do our best. If we succeed, it will be our victory. If not, then both yours and our conscience will be clear before his memory," Vazira said so convincingly that the doctor was ashamed of his words and felt embarrassed:

- I'm sorry, sister! You're just an acquaintance, but you're so worried about him, and I'm like a close friend...

-Zafar aka, my profession is journalist. I have the right to ask questions and reveal the truth. My profession makes me behave in this way.

- You know, at that time there were rumors that the chief doctor Tashmurad Sobirov was involved in this case. But no one knows how close these words were to the truth. Apparently, he was afraid that Batyrov would take his place and organized these cases. Others said that Tashmurod dishonored Ozoda and when the girl became pregnant, he stained his hands with her blood to get rid of her. In doing so, he took advantage of Batyrov's naivety and gullibility to blame him. Thus, he killed two birds with one stone, that is, he got rid of Batyrov, who was being prepared to take his place, and of Ozoda, who was causing him problems. True, this is only a rumor. I am not able to say exactly how true it is. On the one hand, it is unfair to accuse anyone without clear evidence. On the other hand, there is a saying that there is no smoke without fire...

- And who did you hear all this from?

- I'm telling you, rumors spread among the people. What difference does it make who I heard it from?

-Zafar aka, could you tell us in detail about the fate of your friend," Wazira asked in a journalistic tone.

- The court sentenced Ahad to fourteen years in prison. I visited him in prison several times. Each time he joked: "I pay for the samosa I didn't eat[16] ".

He said that he had filed a complaint with the higher authorities and hoped that the truth would soon prevail and he would be acquitted. His depression seemed to have

---

[16] "I pay for the samsa I didn't eat" is an Uzbek folk proverb, pronounced "plachU" with an accent on the letter "u", meaning "to answer for someone else's fault".

passed. However, the unexpected second blow of fate he could not withstand and finally broke down.....

That day, his wife Nurkhon and his two sons were on their way to the prison to see Ahad. But the car they were traveling in had an accident. My friend lost his whole family in one day.....

Zafar was silent for a moment, a bitter lump seeming to lodge in his throat. Then, taking a sip of tea and calming down, he continued:

-It is said that man is more delicate than a flower and harder than a stone. And it is true. The trouble that fell on Ahad's head was a hundred times heavier than before. I thought a man could not bear such grief. Ahad endured it all, he didn't die but turned into a living corpse. That's the state of a man who has lost his last hope. I went to see him even after that. He seemed to have lost his mind. He didn't want to see or talk to anyone. I tried my best to cheer up my friend, to rekindle the spark of hope in his burnt-out heart. But I couldn't! It was useless. It was as if he didn't hear me. After that, I also had worries, and I could not visit him....

Years passed. One day he came to our house. There was no trace of the old Ahad. His hair was gray and his face was covered with wrinkles. His hands were shaking. I was happy to see my friend and invited him into the house. We talked for a long time. He said that he had no one left in Tashkent, so he decided to live in Bekabad. He lived in our house for a couple of days. Then I found him a house for rent in our mahalla. He tried to get a job. But who would hire a man who had served his time? I got him a job as a doctor on duty in the ambulance. He worked 24-hour shifts. We'd see each other from time to time. For some reason, he avoided me and other people he knew. He was rarely seen. I went to his house a couple times, but I couldn't find him. When I invited him to my place, he refused on any pretext. Although he did not complain about his health, it was obvious that he was very ill. I offered him treatment, but he wouldn't listen. He did not want to go to the hospital. One day I forcibly took him to the hospital and did a full examination. It turned out that his heart had weakened.

The only way to survive in such conditions is with medication and diet. We bought a lot of medicines. I don't think Ahad took them. His interest in life seemed to be gone...Poor, he was a victim of injustice. His heart couldn't take it. One night he fell asleep and didn't wake up in the morning. Unfortunately, his corpse lay in his rented house for a week. Neighbors informed the police when they smelled a foul odor coming from his house... As far as possible, I organized his funeral and other burial ceremonies. His personal documents and some of his belongings were given to me by the police for safekeeping....

- Can you show them to us? - said Wazira, putting her pen on the table.

- Let's go," Zafar led the guests into an inner room.

- Here are these documents," said the landlord, handing over a bundle he had taken from the top drawer of the closet. - Here are the things found in his house - two rugs, ten books, a wristwatch, a radio, a razor, two photo albums, etc.

Vazira untied the knot and looked at Batyrov's passport and diploma. A photograph appeared among the documents.

- Is that his son? - Wazira turned to Zafar.

- Yes, eldest son Zhasurbek. This photograph was among the documents in his pocket. I think the deceased friend carried it with him in prison.

Wazira turned the photo over and read the inscription on the back, "March 8, 1988."

-Zhasurbek was born on March 8?

- No, he was born on January 1, 1991," Zafar took the photograph from Wazira's hands with the words, "Well?" Looking at the inscription, he thought for a while and said: "Zhasurbek was not yet born at that time, after all! Maybe someone wrote it by mistake!", he said.

Wazira picked up a stack of books and began flipping through them. Five or six works of detective genre, ghazals by Alisher Navoi, Babur, Mashrab, Abdullah Kadiri's novel "Days Gone By"... The years of publication of the books are relatively new, so they were bought after leaving prison. Could a man deprived of his mind read such works? Why was he reading detectives? Or did he, like herself, turn to these books to carry out his plan?

Zamira pulled two photo albums out of the stack of books and began leafing through the thicker one. Vazira joined her. On the second page was a photograph of Batyrov with his wife and two young sons.

- What a happy family we had! What a pity! They were jinxed," Zamira said, unable to tear her eyes away from the picture.

- I don't even want to believe that such a family has disappeared. How beautiful they are," said Vazira, not hiding her excitement.

- And the children! They're so cute!

The women took their time and carefully looked through the photos in both albums. The pictures depicted the young years and happy moments of this family.

Vazira, looking at the photo, where only Batyrov was depicted, said:

- He looks like a kind, open, cheerful and honest man. I can't believe he's capable of crime.

- That's what I'm saying! I don't believe Ahad could have done anything evil either. But the investigation, the court... their opinions differ from ours, "the evidence, you see, was irrefutable," Zafar remembered a phrase he had heard from some investigator.

- All right, Zafar aka! With your permission, we'll go now. We've gotten a lot of information from you about Batirov. They will be useful to us in writing the article. Thank you very much again," Vazira put the album down and followed her friend, who was about to leave.

Zafar escorted the guests to the gate. Before leaving, Vazira wrote down the address of the house Batyrov had rented and the owner's place of residence just in case.

After seeing the guests off, Zafar went straight to the room where Batyrov's things were kept. He untied a bundle of documents and found a photograph of Zhasurbek inside.

Turning the back of the photo, he took another look at the inscription: "This is Ahad's handwriting. But why is the date March 8, 1988? What does this date have to do with Zhasurbek? Or did Ahad write it by mistake? Usually on the back of a photo the date when the photo was taken is indicated. I remember exactly that Zhasur was born on January 1, 1991. He is about three years old in the photo. So the photo was taken three years after his birth, around 1994. So what does this date mean? Ahad was not a man who could write anything he wanted on the back of his son's photograph.

No wonder it was written for a purpose. But what is it? He had looked at this photograph so many times, but never once had he noticed the date. If it hadn't been for this journalist, he never would have noticed. The women were attentive. But is there a secret behind this date? Or did Ahad mean something by it? March 8, 1988, International Women's Day. Stop, stop! How can you forget this date?! It's the day he and Ahad survived death! It's the date of their second birth!

Despite the fact that it was a holiday, the doctors went to work. The head doctor called him and Ahad and instructed them to visit a seriously ill man in one of the remote villages of the district. Thinking that they would be back in a couple of hours, the young men set off in a car driven by a relative of the sick man. The car traveled a long way along a mountain road. Finally, around noon, they entered the house of an old man who did not want to be treated in a hospital. After medical procedures, the old man's condition improved, and the doctors drove back in the same car. At some point the driver of the Zhiguli, driving on a narrow and bumpy road, suddenly lost control and the car fell into a ravine. Everyone lost consciousness for a while. And when they woke up, all three of them were seriously injured. Not only could they walk, but they could not even get out of the car on their own. Because the car had fallen to the bottom of the ravine, people in passing cars could not hear the voices of these poor people, who were getting weaker by the minute. It was getting dark. If it got dark, all three of them would definitely not survive...

Suddenly a cart creaked. The man driving the cart heard the man's voice coming from the bottom of the ravine and went down there. The poor man carried all three of them on his shoulders alone and took them to his home.

The man who had saved the lives of three people was in his sixties, but he looked strong and energetic for his age. Ahad considered this day his second birthday. After that, until he was imprisoned, he kept in touch with Nurali bobo. He respected this man as his father. When he went on vacation, he would take his wife and children and go to stay with him for three or four days. Nurali Bobo was childless, so he loved children very much. When his wife died, he did not know where to put himself because of loneliness. Therefore, the arrival of Ahad with his children was a real holiday for him. Despite Ahad's resistance, the old man did not hesitate to slaughter a sheep in honor of his guests and set a rich table. On a couple of occasions Zafar also took part in such a feast.

Was Ahad referring to this event?! What did he mean by it? After all, he could not have met him in the last days of his life. Maybe he had a message or a will? Perhaps he left some information about himself with Nurali's grandfather? Either way, he didn't write that date for nothing. Maybe, just maybe. Why didn't he reveal this "secret" to him? Maybe he didn't know he was going to die. He probably decided to do that just in case. Yes, Ahad was a very simple yet intelligent man.

By the way, did Nurali Bobo come to the funeral? I don't think he was there. If he had come, Zafar would certainly have remembered. Maybe he didn't hear. But if he had heard, even if late, wouldn't he have stopped by to offer his condolences? Maybe he did hear, but he didn't know where to go. Maybe Grandpa is sick and can't go out. Maybe even died a long time ago. After all, it had been years since he had seen him! Zafar had concluded that his own human qualities were diminishing with time! He could have visited the old man. Ahad would have acted differently in his place...

Thinking about it, Zafar made a promise to himself that as soon as he found time, he would visit Nurali Bobo soon. And at the same time, he would find the answer to the "riddle" his friend had left behind....

On Sunday, Zafar drove to Nurali's grandfather's village. The car traveled along the mountain roads that had once nearly killed him and entered the village around noon. He stopped the car in front of a familiar window and knocked on the door. No sound came from inside, so he opened the wooden door and shouted:

- Nurali Bobo[17] ... Nurali bobo!

- Come in, guest! - came a voice from behind.

-Hello! -I've come to visit Nurali...

-Didn't you know? Grandpa Nurali died a long time ago!

- K-o-g-d-a? - A bitter lump stuck in Zafar's throat.

- It's been about a year. You come into the house, a guest. I'm his neighbor. He was a golden man! After his wife died, the poor man was sick with grief. God gave them no children. He had no one left. I don't recognize you.

- I used to know this man. Grandpa had helped us once. I was worried that he hadn't been in town for a long time, so I decided to visit him. But as you can see, unfortunately, I didn't find him alive.

Seating his guest at an old table on the terrace, the neighbor sat down on the stairs and recited the Koran as best he could.

- Guest, you have come a long way, come to our place and have some tea," said the neighbor with the sincerity typical of the villagers. Unfortunately, Salai, the healer, had also left on business.

- Is Salai the healer a relative of Nurali's grandfather?

- No, I mean the current owner of the house. The late Nurali Bobo had no close relatives. So, uh.

- Brother, thank you very much! I'll go now," said Zafar, interrupting his companion.

- All right, all right. A cup of tea.

---

[17] Bobo the Elder

- I'm sorry, some other time," Zafar hurried to his car with his usual haughty gait.

- Have a safe journey! - said the neighbor and opened his palms for prayer.

On the way back, Zafar, on the one hand, regretted the death of his grandfather Nurali, on the other hand, was disappointed that he could not meet the so-called healer Salai. Could it have waited? Maybe Nurali's grandfather had left that "mysterious thing" at home. Perhaps grandfather had bequeathed it to the healer before his death. He didn't even ask where he'd gone! But he did say it was the "new owner of the house"! Perhaps the healer bought the house after grandpa died...

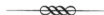

The women easily found the owner of the house that Batyrov had once rented. Uncle Sasha, an old man in his seventies, was overjoyed when he heard that the guests had come from the newspaper:

- My darlings, would you like to write an article about me?

- God willing, we will write about you too. Now we are interested in Ahad Batyrov, who rented accommodation from you. Please tell us everything you know about him," Vazira, as usual, got straight to the point.

- Oh, poor boy! He was a nice guy, paid his rent up front. I didn't notice anything bad about him while he lived, he got along well with everyone. But I could tell the poor guy was in a lot of pain!

- Did he tell you about his life, past or plans? - Zamira asked.

- He didn't talk about his life. He kept everything to himself. Several times I told him: "Why are you always so sad and resentful of life? Tell me, what's wrong with you? Maybe I can help you in some way. After all, people should support each other." To which he replied, "If I tell you about my pain, not even the stones will be able to bear the weight of my story." Don't, Father, don't ask! Don't pour salt on my wound! Yes, I remember him once saying: "I've got the only joy left in the world." The poor guy had no one. He couldn't find work for a long time. Then, with Dr. Zafar's help, he got a job. Sometime in the late summer, I think it was at night when his heart stopped. He was like that for three or four days. Although I always went to see him, this time I forgot to visit him with my worries. It was good that the neighbors, having smelled a strange odor, reported it to the police....

- Father, with whom did Ahad maintain a relationship? - Wazira turned the conversation in another direction.

- I don't know that he was close to anyone. I know he met Dr. Zafar. But I didn't hear that he had any friendships with others.... He just said hello to the neighbors, too, that's all.

- What were his relationships with women? Did he date anyone...

- What was it? He didn't care about women. I saw him only once or twice talking to Gulmirakhon, who works as a nurse in the polyclinic in our mahalla. Maybe she brought medicine....

- Can you show us Gulmirahon's house?

- Second house on the left at the end of this street. Poor thing, she's a widow with two kids. She's raising them on her own.

- Thank you very much! - Vazira went in the direction indicated by the old man. Zamira too, having said goodbye to the old man, involuntarily followed her friend.

Gulmirakhon greeted the guests coldly. When she heard that they were from the newspaper, she thought they were mistaken. Nevertheless, she invited the guests into the house. Since Vazira was in a hurry, she asked the lady of the house:

-Gulmirakhon, did you know Ahad Batyrov?

- Who's A-a-ha-ad B-a-a-a-a-y-y-ro-ov? -Gulmira stammered for some reason and was taken aback.

- Who rented an apartment from Uncle Sasha!

- Yeah, yeah, I know. I went out to give him shots a couple times at his request. The deceased was very ill. What happened?

- It's nothing. We are writing an article about this man," Vazira reassured the hostess.

- That's how!" Gulmira added, so as not to show her excitement. - I was afraid that something had happened.

-Tell me what you know about this man," Wazira pulled a pen and paper out of her bag and stared at her hostess.

- They say he was wrongfully imprisoned. His wife and two children died in a car accident while he was serving his sentence in prison. Such a nice family victimized by injustice. I cried when he told me about it. I felt sorry for the poor man...

- Has he told you about his future plans?

- What plans? He's completely lost hope in life. I don't know... In any case, he didn't tell me about it," Gulmira couldn't stand Vazira's gaze and turned away.

-Gulmirahon, remember very well, it's very important. Did he tell you anything else? - Zamira said, sensing that her hostess was worried about something.

- Didn't say anything else," Gulmira said without raising her eyes.

-All right, but if you remember anything, here's my phone number. Call me," Vazira prepared to leave, not hoping to get any more information from this woman. Gulmira reluctantly tucked the piece of paper Vazira had given her into her pocket and walked the guests to the door.

Both Vazira and Zamira were silent all the way, each thinking of her own thoughts.

- I didn't like the way that woman was acting. She's hiding something from us," Zamira said.

- Yes, she was acting strange. She flinched when she heard Batyrov's last name.

- But then when she heard that we were going to write an article about him, she calmed down a bit. Clearly, she's hiding something from us.

-What could she be hiding from us? Maybe Batyrov used her to hire people to kidnap Bahrom ak? - Zamira looked at her friend, satisfied with her conclusion. - We should compare the letter sent to your husband with Gulmira's handwriting. It's worth a try! Perhaps there will be some result.

- You're right, my friend, you're right! You are like Sherlock Holmes! - Wazira smiled approvingly.

- We can go to her work tomorrow, take her job application and compare it to that letter," Zamira was content to help her friend.

- True, but without a handwriting expert, there's no way to determine that.

- That's great. I have an acquaintance who works as an expert in the city police department. We'll ask him to help, he's a good guy, he won't refuse," Zamira winked at her friend, "trust me...

The next day, the women found the clinic where Gulmira works and managed to get her handwritten application from the human resources department.

- Look, my friend, the handwriting is identical," Zamira said, before going outside, comparing the two handwritings on two sheets of paper.

- They do look alike. But they say all women's handwriting is similar. It's impossible to come to a definite conclusion without expertise.

- It's clear without expert analysis. It's clear as daylight that both letters were written by the same person! - Zamira objected to her friend.

- Either way, we need expertise to come to an accurate conclusion.

- Let's go! Do you want forensics? There will be an examination!

When they reached the city's Department of Internal Affairs, Zamira told her friend, "You wait here, I'll be right back," put both letters in her bag and entered the building. After about half an hour, she came out satisfied:

- It's okay, man. I talked him into it. We'll have an answer tomorrow. Let's go?

- Thank you, friend. What would I do without you in a strange city?" Vazira took her friend's wrist in a friendly way.

All the way home Zamira chattered about something. Vazira, though she did not listen to her words, but either agreed or denied them, because she was busy with her own thoughts: "Did Gulmirakhon really write the letter? If tomorrow the examination confirms that it was her, what will it mean? Wouldn't it mean that Batyrov was involved in the kidnapping of my Bahrom ak, and Gulmirahon was Batyrov's accomplice? Did the mother of two children have a hand in it! Money decided everything! The need makes you do more than that, deprives a person of faith in God. It's possible that she agreed to make money in this way. But who could Batyrov have entrusted with the job? When Bakhrom aka disappeared, Batyrov was dead. Then who did he entrust with such a difficult task? Who could he have hired to commit such a heinous crime? This Gulmira knows a lot. According to Uncle Sasha, Batyrov had no other close person. People noticed his relationship with Gulmirahon, so there must be a connection. If we talk to this woman, a lot will become clear.... In any case, their efforts are not in vain...".

The next day at the appointed time they went to the police department again. Zamira, like last time, left her friend on the street and ran into the building. More than an hour passed, but the friend was not there and Vazira began to get nervous: "It seems that she didn't succeed. Or is the conclusion not ready yet? I should have slipped them some money! But Zamira said he was a good acquaintance and would not refuse her. He'll probably help her. Conducting an expert examination is not an easy thing!".

At that moment, Zamirahon came out with a satisfied smile:

- Come on, girlfriend.

- Wolf or fox?

- Wolf, wolf! Come on, let's go farther away.

Vazira silently followed her friend. Crossing to the other side of the street, Zamira took two sheets of paper out of her bag. She stopped and began to read the last paragraph of the certificate:

- The entries in both documents submitted for examination were made by the same person. What did I say! The letter was written by Gulmira...

- So she has met Bahr aka and knows where he is. We should go to her," Wazira stood up involuntarily.

- Dude, let's take it slow. Now let's think about how to proceed. If we don't act reasonably, we'll scare off the people involved. Let's go home, sit down and talk. As the saying goes, "a wedding conducted by common counsel won't upset[18] ".

- Thank you, friend. You are the wisest woman I know," Vazira praised her friend.

---

[18] a wedding held by common advice will not be upset - Uzbek folk proverb

- Oh, come on. I'm interested in this case myself. I read a lot of detective stories as a child, and I wanted to go to law school. My parents didn't agree, they said it wasn't a woman's job," Zamira said, encouraged by her friend's praise.

- Yeah, well, it's law, you're in a good profession yourself. You treat people, you get a commendation, you don't put anyone in jail. No one curses you.

- It was a youthful dream. Then my parents showed me the right path. I now love my profession and am proud of my work.

- May your hands never know pain. Ugh, ugh, so you don't get jinxed," Vazira didn't know how to express her gratitude to her friend and didn't spare her any warm words.

- Thank you, friend. May your problems be solved. May Bahrom aka return home safely.

Tears glistened in Wazira's eyes as she walked under her friend's arm....

Back home, Zamira hurriedly began to prepare the meal.

Vazira sat on the sofa and watched television, but her thoughts kept returning to Gulmira: "She was worried that day for a reason! No matter how calm she was, it was easy to see fear and panic in her eyes. How could she have written a letter to Bahrom aka? What business could an ordinary Bekabad nurse have with a man who worked in a responsible position in the Tashkent prosecutor's office. Or was this letter simply organized to distract the investigation? Then why was Gulmira trembling? Why was she so frightened? She probably knows everything! Otherwise she wouldn't be so worried. What to do now? Where to start working?".

Zamira quickly set the table. They had lunch. After the meal, Zamira made bitter green tea. Although both had the same question: "What should we do now?

- All right, girlfriend! What do we do next? We have in our hands, in the parlance of lawyers, irrefutable "evidence". What's in it for us? Will we be able to use it appropriately? - Zamira finally found the strength to speak.

- That's what I'm thinking, too. Let's analyze it from the beginning. What does the expert opinion give us? First, it confirms that it was Gulmira who wrote the letter to Bahrom aka. Secondly, it shows that Gulmira had close relations with Ahad Batyrov and helped him to realize his plan. Thirdly, it means that Gulmira also knows Bahrom aka.

- So, we need to nail Gulmira to the wall.

- She may not admit to anything right now.

- If we show her the letter and the expert report, she won't go anywhere and she'll admit everything.

- If she is really involved in Bahrom aka's disappearance, she won't confess. But if she is not involved, she may confess and tell us why she wrote the letter. Either way, we mustn't scare her off. Otherwise, she may escape.

- Where will she run away to with two children? Can she leave her home?

- Anything can happen. If she is indeed involved in this crime, it is likely that she will escape. It is possible that her partners will try to hide or destroy her. If her secret is revealed, it's understandable that her buddies won't sit idly by. That's right, Gulmira won't agree to abandon the kids and run. In that case, they have no choice but to kill the woman. It's a good thing we introduced ourselves as newspaper reporters. If Gulmira tells her accomplices that we are interested in Batyrov, they may track us down. We have to be careful.

- I didn't pay attention to that aspect of the case. After all, a prosecutor's wife thinks like a prosecutor!

- Life forces a person to think deeper, to measure seven times before cutting.

- Then what do we do?

- We should consult with Fakhriddin Karimovich. I think it would be advisable. We can't spoil what's already been done. My friend, I have to go to Tashkent. You do your work. I'll meet Fakhriddin and be back quickly," Vazira jumped up and left.

- I'll walk you to the train station," Zamira followed her friend.

- Don't tell anyone about the work we've done and the data we've gotten so far," Wazira warned her friend before getting on the bus.

- Take it easy. Have a safe trip. A big hello to the kids! - Zamira said to her friend.

After Wazira's call, Fakhriddin wondered, "What else is this restless woman up to? Did she find anything? There seemed to be an important message in her speech. Had she stumbled upon evidence? Could she have done it?! Poor thing, believing her husband is alive, even though it's been so many years since he disappeared. Perhaps that hope gives her strength. Perhaps that confidence gives her strength. Even though reputable organizations failed to handle the case, she, being a woman, did not complain about fate and rolled up her sleeves and was not afraid to go looking for him herself. It is probably the power of great love that makes a person go through fire, water and copper pipes!...".

At that moment there was a knock on the door and the secretary ushered Vazira into the office.

- Hello Fakhriddinjon, how are you, how are my sister-in-law and nephews?

- Thank you, opazhon! Thank God. How are you? How are my brothers? They're getting big, aren't they?

- It's all right, Ukajon. I wanted to consult you on some matters," said Wazira, sitting down on a chair.

- Of course. I'll be glad to help you," Fakhriddin poured her tea.

Wazira, taking her time, recounted what she had managed to accomplish in a month.

- According to Uncle Sasha, Batyrov often communicated with a nurse named Gulmira before his death.

On this basis, my friend Zamira and I went to Gulmira's house. At first sight, both my friend and I noticed that this woman was behaving strangely. We decided that she was hiding something.

Wazira pulled a stack of documents out of her bag and handed them to the investigator.

- Bravo, you're a real detective! -Fakhriddin hurriedly ran his eyes over the documents. When he had read them through to the end, he did not notice how he exclaimed:

- It's a sensation! I mean, you almost solved the crime.

- But I don't know what to do next. My head is spinning. That's why I came here to consult with you....

- It will be easier from here. Now leave it to us, you've already done your job, -Fakhriddin put the documents in a folder and stood up. - Let's go and see Tahir Gafurovich together.

- Me too? - Wazira was confused.

- Come on, don't be shy. You'll explain it to him yourself.

Wazira involuntarily followed the investigator.

Tahir Gafurovich listened to Vazira carefully. He reread the documents again and again. Then, raising his head from the papers, he said to Vazira:

- You alone managed to pull this job off! Bravo! But Vazirahon, you had no right to jeopardize your life and the lives of your children. You think the criminals don't know about your investigation? It's not a question of killing one or two people. They may have already tracked you down. Fortunately, you came to us in time.

- I was gathering information under the pretext of writing an article," Wazira began to justify herself.

- I understand, but they'll try to eliminate anyone with an interest in this case. But I can't help but recognize what you've done. Well done! You risked your life to find out so much, I can't help but admire you. Most importantly, you seem to have found the tip of the iceberg. Now leave the rest to our guys, - Tahir Gafurovich gestured at Fakhriddin. -Fakhriddinjon, although you have a lot of work to do, you will lead the group again. We will put the best investigators at your disposal. Immediately review this criminal case and prepare the text of the ruling to cancel the decision to dismiss the case and take it into your own proceedings. Today take several employees with you and go to Bekabad. First, take measures to ensure the safety of Zamirakhon and her family. At the same time, we need to work in detail with Gulmira. Naturally, she knows who Batyrov hired to commit this crime.

- Tahir aka, let me also go with them to Bekabad. Maybe I can help in some way? - said Wazira in a pleading tone.

- Good, Fakhriddin Karimovich Vazirakhon take it with you too. It might come in handy.

- Bingo.

- Only Vazirakhon promise not to do anything unauthorized again," Tahir Gafurovich said with a smile.

Wazira nodded her head in agreement.

-Vazirakhon, wait a bit in the reception room, Fakhriddin Karimovich will be right out," the deputy prosecutor stood up.

Saying goodbye, Wazira walked out of the office.

Tahir Gafurovich spoke to the Prosecutor General's office on the phone and turned to Fakhriddin:

- I'll report this to the prosecutor now. First of all, you must take measures to ensure the safety of Wazirahon and her children. Proceed with caution. Even though Batyrov is dead, his assassins could have tracked Vazira. You need to organize guards around Gulmira's house, but without her noticing. Because the criminals could either help her escape or eliminate her as an unnecessary witness. Don't forget, Gulmira is the only witness we can get to the perpetrator. We mustn't lose her. You have two hours to get organized. Then before it gets dark, go to Bekabad immediately. Oh, don't forget to conduct a second handwriting examination of Gulmira's letter as soon as possible.

- Yes," Fakhriddin hurried into his office with the chief's permission...

When Fakhriddin and several investigators arrived in Bekabad, the operatives who had left about an hour earlier had already taken Gulmira Boboeva to the building of the city prosecutor's office. The team leader occupied one of the investigators' offices and told them to bring the witness. A few minutes later, a slender, neatly dressed woman of about thirty-five, with long black braids and a pleasant face, was brought into the office.

Fakhriddin stood up and showed the woman a place where she could sit down. After examining her from head to toe, he thought: "How could such a nice woman commit a crime!" It was not hard to guess from the woman's demeanor that she was frightened. The investigator handed her a cup of tea and asked her how she was doing, asking about her work, family, parents and children. He then moved on to the target:

-Gulmirakhon, did you know Bakhrom Safarov?

- Nooooo! Who's that?

-Bahrom Safarovich previously worked in the Prosecutor's Office of Bekabad!

- No, I can't remember.

-Gulmirahon, I want to help you. Only you must tell the truth. But if you lie and try to mislead us, there's nothing I can do. You could be charged with a very serious crime. We know that you know Bakhrom Safarovitch. Please tell us the truth.

Gulmira, bowing her head, was silent for a while.

Seeing the woman hesitate, the investigator continued his attack:

- Remember, only the truth can save you. When and where did you meet him?

- No, I don't know such a person! - said Gulmira, finally raising her head.

Fakhriddin opened the criminal file on the table and slid it toward Gulmira:

- Then who wrote him that letter?

Gulmira stretched her neck to look at the paper. After reading the letter to herself, she whispered faintly: "I don't know."

- So you didn't write that letter! Did you?

- I didn't pee!

Fakhriddin pulled another paper out of another folder and tossed it in front of Gulmira:

- Here's the handwriting forensics report. It says that this handwriting belongs to you, yes, yes, to you personally! What do you say to that?!

Gulmira glanced at the paper and lowered her gaze again. After thinking for a while, she began to speak quietly:

- When I was in medical school, I met a guy who worked in Internal Affairs....

- И?

- We went out a few times. The guy assured me he was going to marry me. I naively believed him. But he turned out to be a bastard. He started avoiding me when he found out I was pregnant. Then I found out he had a girl in his village to whom he was engaged. I was desperate. After thinking about it, I decided to have an abortion. We went to the hospital. The doctors explained that it was dangerous to terminate the first pregnancy, otherwise there would be no chance to give birth later. So I agreed to keep the child, fearing that I would be deprived of the happiness of motherhood. And Bakhtiyor left me. Over time, the baby began to show signs of life in my belly. You know, giving birth without being married is worse than death. Especially in rural conditions it is a great shame for parents and relatives. I came to Bakhtiyor many times, begged him not to give up me and the child, to take me at least as a second wife. He drove me away under various pretexts. I had the only way out - to commit suicide. Once in the dormitory, as soon as the roommates went to study, I drank two packs of sleeping pills prepared in advance .... But I survived. The doctors saved my life. Then an investigator from the prosecutor's office came and began to question me about the reasons for my suicide attempt. I lied to him. I didn't tell him about my pregnancy and Bakhtiyor aka. After leaving the hospital, I was summoned to the prosecutor's office again. Then I saw Bakhtiyor aka for the first time....

Gulmira was silent for a while. Having sipped the cooled tea from the bowl, she continued:

-Bakhtiyor aka talked to me for a long time, found a way to my heart and persuaded me to tell the truth. After that Bakhtiyor aka was summoned. I was afraid that he, poor man, would be put in jail. But, no, I was wrong. Bakhtiyor aka was a good prosecutor. Considering my pregnancy, he took Bahtiyor aka's word that he would marry me and perform the wedding. With this he saved the life of me and my unborn child. I am indebted to this man for the rest of my life... At first Bakhtiyor aka and I lived well. We had a son. A year later I had another child. All difficulties and sorrows seemed to be behind us. But our joy didn't last long. Bakhtiyor aka was accused of illegal drug trafficking and was imprisoned for a long period of time. During the investigation and trial, I had to consult Bakhtiyor aka several times.

- Did you meet with Bahrom Safarovich again after that?

-Yes, when I faced difficulties in one matter or another, I went to him for help.

- When and for what purpose did you write this letter?

- When I heard that Bakhrom aka worked in the Republican Prosecutor's Office, on one of my visits to Tashkent on business, I took his reception phone number. Two or three times we talked on the phone. Three years ago, at the end of August, I had to go to Tashkent. I could not find Bakhrom aka on the phone. Then I came home and wrote him this letter.

- Were you able to meet with Bahr aka?

- No! I couldn't meet him. When I was in Tashkent, I called him several times. But each time his secretary answered that he was not at work. I did not call again, thinking that perhaps Bakhrom aka did not want to talk to me on the phone.

- Do you remember when you called him?

- It was in the fall. I don't remember exactly what day, it was so long ago....

- From where and from what phone did you call him? - The investigator continued to ask questions.

- From a pay phone booth near the Alay market.

- Who were you talking to on the phone?

- With a young man, secretary or assistant to Bahrom aka. At least that's what it seemed to me.

- Did you talk to him on the phone or meet with him?

- No, I didn't get a chance to talk or meet Bahr aka after that.

- When and from whom did you learn about Bakhrom Safarovich's disappearance?

- At that time it was talked about everywhere. Many people were surprised, as Bakhrom aka worked and lived in Bekabad. I too, when I heard about this case at work, felt very sorry for him," Gulmira sighed deeply.

- What was your relationship with Ahad Batyrov? - the investigator looked into her eyes to see the change in the woman.

Gulmira hesitated a little. She tried to avoid the investigator's glare:

- I knew a-a-a-ha-ad a-ka. I brought him medicine several times at his request. I went to give him injections when he had a runny nose. He rented accommodation from Uncle Sasha in our mahalla.

- Did he know that you were acquainted with Bakhrom Safarovich? - the investigator was cautiously approaching the target.

- No, I don't think I did.

- Answer me clearly! Did he know or not?

- Maybe I mentioned him when talking to him," Gulmira said, unable to withstand the investigator's pressure.

- What did you and Batyrov talk about?

- He was just a man of few words.

- Did he tell you he was wrongfully imprisoned?

- He spoke. He spoke bitterly about the injustice inflicted on him by the investigator, prosecutor and judges. I remember I sided with Bahrom aka then, saying that he was a good prosecutor, to which he objected: "What difference does it make whether a dog is white or black - they are all dogs anyway! They're all the same!". Then I told him about what had happened to me, particularly about the kindness of Bahrom aka. Then he said: "He may have done good for your sake, but I will never forget the suffering he caused me and my family!".

- Did he ask you for Bakhrom Safarovich's phone number or other information?

- No!

- Maybe he looked in your notebook?

- I don't know! But one day when I went to give him a shot, my notebook fell out at his house. He brought it to me the next day.

- Was Bakhrom Safarovich's phone number in this notebook?

- Yeah. I wasn't paying attention at the time.

-Gulmirakhon! You said that you went to Tashkent at the end of August to see Bakhrom Safarovich. After that you came home and sent him a letter. Is that correct?

- That's right.

- So, you sent the letter sometime in late August or early September, right?

- I wrote the letter on the day I returned from Tashkent, August 24 or 25. I remember it well because August 26 was my eldest son's birthday.

- How did you send the letter? - The investigator asked, looking at the back of the envelope.

- I think I dropped a letter in the mailbox.

- Where is it?

- We're in Bekabad.

- No, Gulmira. Think back. The letter was put in the mailbox from Tashkent. So you asked someone to put the letter in the mailbox?

- Hm-hm... Right, right," Gulmira seemed to remember the events and continued her story. - That day I went out to drop a letter in the mailbox and on the way I saw Ahad. The mailbox was quite far away. Seeing the envelope in my hand, he offered: "Give it to me. I am going to the capital today and I will put it in the mailbox there. It will reach the addressee faster that way. I agreed to give him the letter because I wanted it to reach me at least one day earlier.

-Gulmirakhon, you say you wrote the letter at the end of August. But judging by the postmark on the envelope, it was put into the mailbox on October 15 and reached its destination on October 16.

- No, no! I definitely sent the letter at the end of August. I wanted to go to Tashkent at the beginning of September. Because my son was going to go to the first grade that year. I wanted to buy him clothes and school supplies.

- But the letter reached Bahrom ka a month and a half later, in mid-October.

- Maybe Ahad forgot and threw the letter in the box late?

- No, it can't be. Because Ahad Botirov was not in this world at that time.

Gulmira thought for a moment and then agreed with the investigator's conclusions:

-Yes, that's right, three or four days after that incident I heard that he had passed away.

- After you sent the letter, did you call Bahrom Safarovich?

- Yes, I went to Tashkent again in early September. Before the trip, I called Bakhrom aka once to warn him about my arrival, but he was not at work. When I arrived in Tashkent, I called a couple of times, but no one picked up the phone.

- Did you see Ahad Batyrov after that? Did you check whether he sent the letter or not?

- No, I never saw Ahad aka after that incident. I was very sorry to hear that he had died. He was a really good man. He was a modest and harmless man.

- How do you explain the fact that you gave him the letter in August, but the envelope was dropped in the mailbox on October 15. Also, the person you asked to send the letter is deceased?

- I'm surprised, too. But Ahad was going to Tashkent that day. Maybe he forgot the letter somewhere and whoever found it threw it in the mailbox. Anyway, I don't know.

- I think you've said the right thing now. Tell us, please, why did you want to hide from us the fact that this is your letter?

Gulmira was silent, drawing an invisible pattern on the floor with the tip of her shoe. The investigator repeated his question.

- I was ashamed to admit that I had written a letter to a strange man... What would people think? After all, I don't have a husband. Moreover, when I heard that Bahrom aka had disappeared. I was scared.

- Okay, as long as you're free. We'll call you if necessary. This is my phone number, if you remember anything, call me," Fakhriddin Karimovich handed Gulmira a piece of paper.

- Thank you! If I remember anything, I'll be sure to call you. Goodbye! -Gulmira got up and went to the door.

Returning to the table, Fakhriddin thought: "I wonder what happened next. If Ahad Batyrov died at the end of August, how could the envelope given to him end up in the mailbox in October? Or did he really forget the envelope somewhere? If the envelope had been left in Bekabad, the person who found it would have sent it to the post office from here. So, the letter reached Tashkent. But it was not put in the mailbox. Later it was sent to the address by the person who found it. Who would Ahad go to? He didn't go to his uncle's house. Then who did he go to?".

At that moment there was a knock on the door and the policeman on duty ushered Gulmira in.

- Comrade Chief! May I? This woman says she remembers something...

- Yes, yes, please! You are free for now," Fakhriddin allowed the policeman to leave. Then, looking at the woman, he said:

- Well, Gulmirakhon, I'm listening to you! What do you remember?

- You know, the last time I saw Ahad aka, he didn't seem to be alone.

- Who was he with?

- Not far from the kiosk, a pretty girl was waiting for him. Although she acted as if she were alone, there was no doubt that this girl was waiting for him.

- Do you know this girl?

- No, I've never seen her before.

- Maybe she was waiting for someone else.

- No, no. That's what I thought at first, too. But I noticed that they were together. Ahad aka was walking a little ahead, and the girl was a little behind. Then they seemed to be on the same level.

- Okay, thank you and that's it! We'll check it out. If we find this girl, do you recognize her?

- Of course I do. Because there are only a few such spectacular girls in Bekabad.

- What do you think Ahad has to do with such a beautiful girl?

- That surprised me too! Because Ahadak had his own worries. He was only interested in women for business reasons, nothing more. I don't know.

- Thank you again. You've been very helpful.

- You're welcome. Goodbye," said Gulmira and walked out.

Fakhriddin began to think again: "Who was this girl? Why did the seriously ill Ahad need this beautiful girl? Or did Ahad use her for his own purposes? Usually, beautiful girls are able to pick up any man and bring him to the edge of the cliff. At the sight of beauties, any enemy will go blind, lose his mind. It's a proven method.

Could Ahad have chosen this path for revenge! It is clear that he was involved in the kidnapping of Bahrom Safarovitch. But who could he have hired to do it? Did he really involve this girl? From books he knows many stories about how one single woman by her cunning could defeat an enemy army with which a whole army could not cope. Women are usually addicted to jewelry of all kinds. And this girl, of course, needed Ahad's money. Gulmira noted that the girl was beautiful for a reason. And Ahad needed this girl's beauty. It is urgent to find this girl!".

Fakhriddin summoned several employees and told them to go to the bus station, gather information about the bus drivers running the Bekabad-Tashkent route at that time, find them and bring them to the prosecutor's office. He and Sanzharbek went to Dr. Zafar's house to examine the things left behind by Batyrov and, if necessary, to take them as material evidence.

Dr. Zafar was not at home. His wife called and summoned him. The doctor told the investigator everything he knew about Ahad. Sanzharbek recorded his words as a formality. The investigators also scrutinized Batyrov's personal belongings. It seems that they could not find anything noteworthy and put the things back. Dr. Zafar had put Zhasur's photograph separately last time. He wanted to show the photo to the investigators, but for some reason changed his mind, fearing that they would bombard him with questions: "Why did you touch his things, why did you hide his son's photo, etc.?".

- Is this all that's left of Batyrov? You didn't miss anything? - Fakhriddin turned to the owner as he left the house.

-No. -It's all— Aka, what is it? The deceased was involved in some kind of crime...

- No, no, no, no, no. It's okay. Have a good day. Goodbye!

- Goodbye.

When the investigators left, Zafar wished he had shown them the picture. He whispered: "What do they want anyway? Why are they so interested in a dead man? He had been questioned by journalists before. Or did Ahad commit a crime before he died? Or did he have evidence of another crime? No way, the poor guy walked out of prison a living corpse and died. But those organ officials are not worried for nothing. There seems to be something here."

When Fakhriddin arrived at the city prosecutor's office, several members of the group were waiting for him at the door. The witnesses brought in by the officers were mostly bus drivers who used to travel on the Tashkent-Bekabad route.

The team leader personally questioned each witness. The bus drivers were shown a photograph of Ahad Batyrov and asked if they knew the man. Two drivers said they did not know the man in the photograph and had never seen him. A mustachioed, large driver named Bazarbai, upon seeing Batyrov's photograph, recognized him immediately:

- It's the late Dr. Ahad! Of course I know him. We lived next door to him before he was locked up. He was a wonderful man! May Allah grant him paradise in heaven. Amen.

- So you were neighbors. Very well," Fakhriddin looked at Sanzharbek, who was sitting next to him.

- Well, yes, we were close neighbors. Poor guy was wrongfully imprisoned. His wife and two kids died in a traffic accident. You wouldn't wish that on anyone!

- Why do you say that the man was wrongfully imprisoned? You can't put an innocent man in jail. There is an investigation and a trial for that!

- I don't know the details. But there were rumors at the time that he was being slandered and framed. I'm just saying what I heard. But who knows?

- Okay, let's leave it at that for now. Tell me, have you seen Batyrov since prison?
- He got on my bus to Tashkent a couple of times. I told him that I would not take the fare, but he paid anyway. He seemed to be completely broken with pain and sadness. The blossoming guy was skin and bones. I felt very sorry that such a man had fallen into such a pitiful state. Later I heard that he had died.

-We'll all go there someday, Bazarbai aka," the investigator deliberately provoked his interlocutor into a discussion in order to get him talking.

-You are right, Ouka, only good deeds will be left of us in this world.

-Bazarbai aka, Ahad Batyrov told you why he is going to Tashkent?

- No way! Ahad was a man of few words. He did not talk idly. Only if you asked him about something, you could get an answer. Well, he probably didn't go to Tashkent to play. There must have been a reason! But he didn't tell me.

- Do you remember the last time he got on your bus?

-It was a long time ago. I think it was in the fall. Because I remember his buddy was wearing a black leather jacket.

- Was someone near Batyrov? -Fakhriddin jumped up from his seat.

- Yeah, I think it was the one, what was her name, the black one. Or maybe I'm wrong. Or maybe that's what I thought. Anyway, they sat next to each other and talked the whole way. Maybe they just happened to sit next to each other on the bus.

- Who was that woman? Do you know her?

- Who doesn't know her?! She's a dancer. I've seen her at a lot of weddings. What was her name, huh? Madina or Maftuna or Manzura. Anyway, her name started with an "M"!

- Would you recognize this girl if you saw her now?

- I recognize her, I recognize her. But I haven't seen this girl at any weddings lately.

-Sanzharbek, immediately contact all the artists in the city and find out the name of the dancer," Fakhriddin Karimovich turned to his assistant.

Sanzharbek hurriedly went out.

-Bazarbay aka, thank you. Wait in the corridor for a while. If the dancer is brought in, I'll need your help," the investigator stood up and left the room. - Stay here.

- All right, all right. Don't worry about me! I'll be right here. That was fast, wasn't it? I just need to take my old lady to the beshik that.[19]

- You'll make it, Father, you'll make it.

Fakhriddin Karimovich contacted Tahir Gafurovich by telephone and reported the whole situation to him. Sipping the cooled tea, he felt relieved for the first time: "This dancer must know a lot. Ahad didn't just travel with her for no reason. This is not a romantic adventure. So, Batyrov used the girl to realize his devious plans. Although this girl was not the direct perpetrator of the crime, but she had to

---

[19] beshik toh - cradle feast

be involved in any case. At least she could help Ahad find the assassin. The letter sent by Gulmira must have been left in the hands of this dancer as well. Whatever it is, it looks like we're closer to solving the mystery. The main thing is that this time we are on the right track!".

There was a knock at the door and Sanzharbek entered.

- Fahriddin aka, I spoke to several artists in the city and told them the distinctive features of the dancer. All three expressed the opinion that it was Marzia. We found her address. We have operatives on their way there now. If she's home, they'll bring her in quickly.

- Okay, so it's Marzia. The main thing is that Bazarbay's chauffeur recognizes her. It'll be easier from here.

- Our best hope is this girl. If she doesn't lead us to the perps, we're back to square one.

- No, this time it will be different. I am sure that we are going the right way," Fakhriddin Karimovich patted his pupil on the shoulder.

Even though it was already lunchtime, the investigators did not even think of going for refreshment. Time passed very slowly. That's what usually happens when you're waiting. It feels like the hands of the clock have stopped and are jumping in place. Fakhriddin seemed to have run out of patience and went out into the courtyard for a smoke. Sanzharbek involuntarily followed him. They smoked for a while under a maple tree in the courtyard of the prosecutor's office. At that moment, several operatives brought in a beautiful slender young woman.

"That's what Marziya is like! Now I can see why Bazarbai's driver's mouth drooled when he remembered her," Fakhriddin thought.

When Sanzharbek led the woman into the office, Fakhriddin, who was walking behind him, whispered in the ear of the driver, Bazarbay, who was sitting in the corridor:

- Is that her?

- Yes!" said Bazarbai, pointing to the woman who had just passed him, leaving a trail of pleasant perfume.

- You stay here. I'll call you if I need you.

The witness was taken into the office. Sanjarbek showed her a place to sit down. Fakhriddin poured tea for her:

- Please have some tea, Marziyehon.

The woman looked sharply at the investigator:

- Do I know you?

- No, but now we will correct this situation. My name is Fakhriddin Karimovich, I am the head of the investigation team, this guy is investigator Sanzharbek. Marziyakhon, we have a few questions about your service. I warn you in advance that you are required to tell only the truth. Understood?

- Yes," the woman nodded quietly. - What's this all about?

- Did you know Ahad Batyrov?

The investigator's question to the forehead seemed to take the woman by surprise. She was silent for a moment, not knowing what to say:

207

- K-k-k-k-k-k-k-k-k-k-k-k-k-k-k-k-k-k-k-k-k-k-k-k-k-k-k-k-k-k-k-k-k-k-k-k-k-k-k-k-k-ad?

-Batyrova Ahada, don't pretend! We know everything!

- I think this man is dead," Marzia's voice trembled.

- Yes, that man is dead.

- Where and when did you meet him?

Marzia thought for a moment. It was hard to tell if she was thinking about how to answer the investigator's next questions or if she was actually remembering the moment when she had first met Ahad.

The investigator repeated the question.

- It was a long time ago. I don't remember now when we met.

- At any rate, you probably remember at least a year. What was the reason you met, can you remember?

- It was the time when I graduated from high school and went to medical school," Marzia finally spoke after some silence. - Our supervisor, who had recently graduated from the institute, came to work at our school. From the first day, he let me know that he cared for me. He courted me for a long time, promised to marry me. I believed him. When we went out to pick cotton... in short, he took my virginity..... After that, he began to slowly avoid me. I demanded that he fulfill his promise and get married as soon as possible, but he lied to me, finding various excuses. Later he completely turned away from me and started to go out with another girl. I couldn't go to class out of resentment. I didn't want to live... One day, when the girls went to class, I slit my wrists to die.... But I wasn't lucky to die either. I guess it wasn't my hour of death yet. Despite the fact that I was unconscious for a long time and lost a lot of blood, thanks to the efforts of doctors, I survived. It was Ahad aka who saved me. And further he brought me back to life with his kind words and wise advice. I am eternally indebted to this man. I loved him like a brother...

-Marzia sighed deeply, wiping her tears with her handkerchief. - Then she continued in a sad tone:

- Once you ruin your reputation, it's hard to repair it. Rumors spread among people about my adventures at school. Matchmakers stopped coming to our house. My life went downhill. As a child, I dreamed of being an artist, a good dancer. Trying to compensate for failures in my personal life with achievements in art, I started going to weddings and events with singers. Soon I became famous as the most famous dancer in town. Life was getting better. Later, I heard that Ahad aka had been put in jail. I felt sorry for him. I even wanted to find him and visit him. But I couldn't. Then I heard that his wife and children had died in a car accident. I was shocked that such a wonderful family had collapsed...

- We know of the misfortune that befell Batyrov. It's the kind of thing you wouldn't wish on an enemy. Where did you first meet Ahad-Batyrov after he was released from prison? -said the investigator to distract the witness.

-We met in the street once. I didn't recognize him at all. Poor guy, he was gaunt and looked very unhappy. There was no trace of the old Dr. Ahad. He recognized me. We had lunch together. The man tearfully told me about his bitter plight, the suffering he had gone through, how he had been unjustly imprisoned, how he had lost his wife and children.

I tried to calm him down, told him that life goes on, that one should fight for life. In short, I gave him the advice he had once given me. But it seemed to me that his will was already broken and his hope for life was gone.

- Did you see him again after that? Did he ask you to help him with anything? - The investigator finally asked the question he was interested in.

- Then we went out a couple times. I wanted to help him get his life back on track. If he had asked me to marry him, I would have agreed to marry him without hesitation. But he, uh. he didn't need my help. He was a different man, emotionless and hopeless...

- Did he tell you about his plans?

- I don't think he had any plans.

- Why did you and Batyrov go to Tashkent?

- To Ta-ash-Kent?

- Yes, to the capital, Tashkent.

- No! I didn't go to Tashkent with him, -Marzia looked away from the investigator.

-Marziahon, don't try to distract us. We know a lot of things. You'll feel better if you tell us the truth.

Marziya bowed her head and remained silent. To avoid wasting time, Fakhriddin turned to Sanjarbek:

- Get Bazarbai's chauffeur," he said.

Sanzharbek came out of the office and immediately brought in a big man.

-Bazarbai aka, do you know this woman? - the investigator asked the man who came through the door.

- I don't know her name, but I know she plays. I mean, she dances.

- When and where was the last time you saw her?

-This woman I took to Tashkent on my bus together with my neighbor Ahad Batyrov.

Fakhriddin Karimovich looked questioningly at Marzia.

Marzia remained silent, eyes downcast and curling her curls on her finger.

- So, you did! For what purpose?

- I was on my way to Tashkent and met Ahad aka at the bus station. He was also on his way to the capital. On the way on the bus we talked.

- Did he say for what purpose he was going to Tashkent?

- No, I think he said he had a case. I didn't ask.

- Why did you go to the capital yourself?

- I don't remember now. Maybe I went to buy clothes for my son. It's been so long. Honestly, I don't remember.

- Do you remember the time?

- I think it was the end of August.

- Comrade Investigator, it is possible to find out," the driver Bazarbai suddenly intervened in the conversation. - . I remember then I was given a new bus "Mers", and for the first time I started driving on the route Bekabad - Tashkent. In our country, buses are issued only by order.

- Well done, Bazarbai aka, well done! I admire your cleverness," Fakhriddin Karimovich patted the driver on the shoulder. Then he turned to Sanzharbek:

- Go to the garage immediately and find that order from the ground!

211

-Fakhriddin Karimovich, what can this order give us? - Sanzharbek said hesitantly.

- To have one foot here and the other there! - said the team leader in a commanding tone instead of answering the question.

- Yes, -Sanzharbek hastily collected the papers and went out...

An hour later, Sanzharbek returned with a piece of paper in his hand:

- Here are the orders.

Fakhriddin Karimovich glanced at the order and muttered:

- So, the order came out on September 17. On September 18, the bus started to run on the Bekabad-Tashkent route.

- It was exactly September 18th. I remembered. Because September 19 was my youngest son's birthday. I brought him a bike from Tashkent," Bazarbai said.

-Bazarbai aka, Marziyakhon, you wait in the corridor, we'll continue our conversation after a while," Fakhriddin said, as if remembering something.

After the witnesses left, the team leader handed the criminal case lying on the table to Sanzharbek:

- Find information about Ahad Batyrov's death," he said.

Sanzharbek looked through the file, found document in question and handed it to the chief.

Fakhriddin ran his eyes over the paper and shrieked:

-Sanjarbek, look at this! This is where the dog was buried! What a puzzle!

- What's the matter, Fakhriddin aka, I don't understand? - said Sanzharbek perplexed.

- This certificate states that Ahad Batyrov died on August 29. And the chauffeur Bazarbai started driving to Tashkent from September 18 of the same year and took Batyrov to the capital on the same day.

- This is a misunderstanding. Maybe Bazarbai is mistaken. This can't be," said Sanzharbek, not hiding his surprise.

- Maybe, anything can be! But we'll have to check it out. You go back to the motor pool and find Bazarbay's trip sheet in the archives. Take that with you too. It might help.

After Sanjarbek left, Fakhriddin paced the room from side to side, trying to gather his thoughts: "What kind of a mystery is this? Or did Batyrov do this to create an alibi for himself? Then he is alive. Who died then, and who was buried in his place? Did he kill someone to clear himself of suspicion? Or is there some kind of misunderstanding? Where to begin the case now? What is the right way?

Should the grave be opened and the body exhumed? No, no, not yet. Digging the grave and examining the remains of the deceased is not an easy task. There is no rush! First, this situation should be well researched and clarified. Exhumation will not escape! If Batyrov is alive, he had a hand in Bakhrom Safarovitch's disappearance. And if he's alive, where could he be hiding? Then we can hope that Bakhrom aka is still alive. So much time has passed. Maybe...". At that moment there was a knock at the door, and Marzia peeped into the room:

-Can I, Comrade Investigator? Fakhriddin aka, can I go now?

- Come in, sit down, unfortunately I can't let you go yet. We need to clarify some questions, then we'll see! Marziyakhon, according to the information received from the motor depot, it turned out that the driver Bazarbai took you and Batyrov to Tashkent on September 18. However, another document says that Batyrov died in August. How can you explain this?

Marzia seemed to know about this secret and was not surprised. She silently continued to draw on the floor with the tip of her shoe.

-Marziyakhon, this is a very important fact. If you admit that you really went to Tashkent on September 18 with Batyrov in the same bus, it means that he is alive and another person died. Therefore, before you answer, think about it!

- Yes, I did go with Ahad aka to Tashkent. But now I can't remember the exact date of that trip. After all, so much time has passed since then. Maybe it was September 13 or 14.

- Maybe! But they're about to bring in a document that will clarify that one hundred percent. But I think you already know the secret! Please tell us the truth! Otherwise, you may unknowingly become involved in unpleasant events and become an accessory to a crime. But if you cooperate with us and assist in the investigation, we guarantee that you will be able to take full advantage of your rights and benefits under the law.

- I've told you everything I know. I'm not hiding anything from you.

- You knew Batyrov was alive, didn't you?

- No! -Marzia gave a brief and unconvincing answer.

- When and from whom did you learn of his death? Have you seen him since then? Or did you hear any news that he was alive?

- I heard about it like everyone else. But I don't remember who I heard it from. There were such rumors in the city at that time. I never heard from anyone that Ahad aka is alive. Everyone thought he was dead.

- Have you met him anywhere since you went with him to Tashkent in mid-September?

- No, the last time I saw him was on the bus.

- All right, why don't you wait in the hallway?

Fakhriddin sat down at the table and began flipping through the multi-volume case file lying on the table. He carefully read the testimonies of several witnesses. Then he got nervous about Sanzharbek's delay and lit a cigarette.

More than two hours later, Sanzharbek brought the man in.

-Fakhriddin aka, here are the travel logs. It took a long time to find them in the archive. Bazarbai aka really started traveling on the Bekabad-Tashkent route from September 18. This is a fact," Sanjarbek handed the documents to the head.

- Great... great... great...

- While we were looking for documents in the archive, I talked to several drivers who traveled the Tashkent-Bekabad route. Abduraim aka told me something

215

interesting," said Sanjarbek, pointing to a man about 45-50 years old standing near the door. - Abduraim aka, this man is the leader of our group - Fakhriddin Karimovich. Please repeat what you told me.

- I was driving an Ikarus at the time. It was fall. I think it was in the evening. I was coming back from Tashkent. I stopped my bus at a traffic light. A Zhiguli stopped next to me. The man sitting next to the driver looked familiar to me. I looked closely and saw an exact replica of Dr. Ahad. I was frightened. I'd been treated by him once. I remember it was a month and a half after his death. I personally attended his funeral! I wanted to roll down the window and talk to him. His eyes fell on me too. But he pretended not to know me and turned away. Then I thought how people can be similar to each other. If I had not been present at Ahad's funeral, I would have believed without a doubt that it was Dr. Ahad.

- Do you remember when this event took place?

- It was around the fall! I was driving a bus between Bekabad and Gulistan. And since the driver of the Tashkent route, Ruziboi, fell ill, my superiors temporarily put me in his place.

-Fakhriddin aka, I have brought up all the travel sheets and orders, referring to the words of Abduraim aka, -Sanjarbek took a stack of documents out of his bag and handed them to the chief. - This man really went to Tashkent on October 16-20. There is an order about it.

- That's right, that's right, I told you it was in the fall," said Abduraim, pleased that his words had been confirmed.

- Are you sure the man you saw is Dr. Ahad? - the team leader asked, approaching Abdurahim.

- Eh, if Dr. Ahad wasn't a dead man, I would have gone down and said hello to him. But I saw him at close range. That man looked just like him!

- Looks like you're right. It seems that Dr. Ahad is not dead," Fakhriddin Karimovich sat down.

- Oh, my God, really?! Then who died? After all, I attended his funeral, -Abduraim clutched his heart.

-Abduraim aka, remember well, what color was that "Zhiguli"?

- White, I'd say even milk-colored.

- You said Dr. Ahad was sitting in the front seat of the car next to the driver. Did you see the driver? Do you remember any distinguishing features? - The investigator continued to ask in detail.

- I didn't pay attention to the driver. But there seemed to be two other people in the back seat.

- You're not wrong, are you?

- I'm telling the truth.

- Can't remember at least one worthwhile detail?

- No. I didn't look at them.

- Suppose someone had a beard or a mustache.....

- No. I wasn't paying attention.

- Was there a woman in the car?

- It's hard to say. Maybe there was...

-Approximately what age were they?

- What age are you?! I only looked at Dr. Ahad in bewilderment. I didn't pay any attention to the others at all.

- In which direction the Zhiguli was traveling," the investigator continued to question.

- I met him at a traffic light when leaving Tashkent for Bekabad. He was also traveling in that direction.

- You don't remember the license plate number of the car or any distinguishing feature?

- I didn't pay attention to the license plate. But when the Zhiguli drove forward, I saw that under its rear window there was a toy dog with a moving head. When the car moved, the doggie's head also moved in time with the movement as if it were alive. You may have also noticed that many drivers place such a toy in the front or back of their car.

- What color was the "doggie"?

- I think it's gray.

- What other features of the car did you notice? For example, were there any dents or dings?

- I don't think there was anything memorable! You can't remember it all at once.

-Abduraim aka, thank you. You've been a great help. Wait outside. We may need you again.

- All right, Uka, as you say, if we must wait, we'll wait. The main thing is to make it worthwhile, - the driver Abduraim got up and went to the door.

-Fakhriddin aka, what's going on? Is Batyrov alive?! I can't believe it. Did one ordinary doctor do all this?! Did he kidnap Bakhrom aka too? -Sanzharbek hurriedly expressed his conclusions.

- Revenge is a bad thing. A man who wants revenge is like a tiger with bloodshot eyes. He's not afraid of anything.

I think Batyrov has fallen into the same state. Four years ago, we were right on Batyrov's trail. Except the fact that he's dead threw us off the trail.

- Yeah, Batyrov gave us quite a beating! How did we know he was a head taller than us! -Sanzharbek sighed heavily.

- All right, well, we're all human. But we can't let our guard down now. Batyrov is alive. That means that if we don't catch him soon, he may commit other crimes. On the other hand, Bakhrom Safarovitch could be in his hands. Usually, a vigilante is not in a hurry to destroy his enemy immediately, he wants his victim to suffer, he will try to kill her morally. From this point of view, it is possible that Bakhrom Safarovich is still alive. This requires immediate action to save him....

Fakhriddin thought for a moment, then took a paper and pen and began to write something:

-Task one is to establish that Ahad Batyrov is not dead. Quickly prepare a decision on exhumation of the body. His uncle lives in Tashkent, we need to summon him to participate in the exhumation. If the person buried in the grave is not Batyrov, we need to establish the identity of the corpse. We need to question Marzia again in detail. She seems to know a lot. We need to get her talking at all costs.

The second task is to find out Ahad Batyrov's residential address. Naturally, Batyrov is now living under someone else's name and surname. I think Batyrov must have the passport of the person who went to the grave instead of him. Establishing the identity of the dead man would make it possible to determine Batyrov's new name.

The third task is to urgently identify Batyrov's circle of contacts in cities and villages other than Tashkent and Bekabad.

Task four is to withdraw the Batyrov murder case from the court and resume work on it. The investigator who investigated the crime died, I believe, in a car accident. The details of that car crash should also be scrutinized. Batyrov may have a hand in that as well. Even the judge who tried the criminal case, if he is still alive, is in danger. It's only natural that Batyrov would get to him. God forbid, he has time to kill him. We must take measures to protect the judge! Assemble all members of the team for 9:00 p.M. We need to assign tasks. I'll brief the leadership. If necessary, we'll request additional forces from Tashkent. The main thing is not to be late. Every minute counts. Now it's time to put an end to all this.

-Fakhriddin aka, do you think Bakhrom aka is alive? Sanzharbek, writing down the orders, raised his head from the papers and stared at the chief.

- I think he's alive. Maybe Batyrov's hiding him somewhere! At least we can count on that. In the meantime, things could be different. Time will tell. Come on, don't despair just yet.

- Let him live! I feel sorry for Waziru opa. The poor woman has endured so much. She's suffered so much. But she never gave up hope for a moment! Even when everyone was sure that Bahrom aka was dead, she believed that her husband was alive. And she herself began the search. But it must be admitted that it was she who discovered the tip of the iceberg.

- You're right. This woman's courage should be an example to all of us. Okay, we'll talk about the rest later, hurry up! -Fakhriddin Karimovich stood up abruptly. - I need to question Marzia in detail. Get on with your tasks!

- Bingo!

Preparing to question Marzia, Fakhriddin wrote down some of the questions he was going to ask her and then ordered a witness to be brought in by phone.

Further questioning of Marzia did not yield the expected result. Apparently, she was tired of waiting on the street or became agitated. She answered briefly to all the questions of the investigator: "yes" or "no". She repeated that she had not been in the "Zhiguli" mentioned by Abduraim aka, that the last time she had seen Ahad was when they were traveling together to Tashkent in the same bus, and that she had not seen him again after that. The investigator's advice, explanations and warnings about the need to tell the truth and only the truth did not work.

Fakhriddin, after talking to the management, decided to let Marziya go. But she was placed under constant surveillance.

Investigators viewed her as the only witness who could lead to Batyrov.

Toward evening, Sanzharbek found out that Judge Zakir Shakirov, who had tried Ahad Batyrov's murder case, had died after a serious illness several years ago, and sent operatives to the hospital to bring the case history.

Although the cause of the judge's death was clear, for some reason Fakhriddin Karimovich thought: "Was Batyrov involved in this too? Yes, the judge was 58 years old. It is not excluded that he died because of illness. But doesn't it mean that there is some secret connection here: all three officials, who were considering the same criminal case, were in trouble? However, this Batyrov turned out to be a professional. It seems that he will stop at nothing to achieve his goal. In any case, the details of the deaths of both the investigator and the judge must be thoroughly checked...".

The next day began with the exhumation of the body. Medical workers, qualified specialists, experts who came from Tashkent, after a long examination and tests came to the final conclusion that the corpse examined did not belong to citizen Ahad Batyrov. In addition, the experts determined that the man buried in the grave was about forty years old and had died of a heart attack. Everyone was shocked.

Now there is no doubt in anyone's mind that Batyrov was responsible for Bakhrom Safarov's disappearance. For some reason, in Fakhriddin Karimovich's opinion, both the death of investigator Ikram Bozorov, who was involved in a car accident, and the death of judge Zakir Shakirov, who died of a serious illness, were the work of Ahad Batyrov. Some employees took it as a coincidence.

Experts who have studied the details of Ikram Bozorov's car crash have come to the conclusion that the cause of the accident could have been the failure of the bolts holding the front wheels of the car.

Fakhriddin Karimovich was confused: the experts noted that the car was in good technical condition. The driver also had many years of experience and did not drink alcohol. The speed of the car was also low. The car was traveling on a flat road when it went into the oncoming lane and hit a car moving in the opposite direction. According to eyewitnesses, no other vehicles were in its way. While driving, the car suddenly changed direction and crashed. The right front wheel of the car was found about a hundred meters away. The driver may have forgotten to fix them all the way when changing the tires.

Perhaps the vulcanizers were careless in securing the wheels. What if someone deliberately loosened the bolts holding the wheels in place when no one was around? Who would be primarily interested in this? Batyrov? Yeah, he'd have reason to be. But how do we prove that he was involved in this crime? He was serving a sentence at the time of the crash! Or did he hire someone? No way, who could a man in prison be socializing with? No one would believe the words of a prisoner. Perhaps Batyrov had nothing to do with the incident.

Meanwhile, experts who have scrutinized the medical history of Judge Zakir Shakirov have concluded that his body should be exhumed.

The results of the exhumation conducted the next day further puzzled the investigators. The experts concluded that there was some poisonous substance in the body of the deceased, which could have caused the slow death.

Fakhriddin Karimovich, having familiarized himself with the conclusion, asked a question to the expert sitting next to him:

-Doctor, are you saying someone poisoned Shakirov?

- No, not at all! We're merely concluding that a poisonous substance was found in the body of the deceased and that it may have caused his death. It is your job to find out how the poison got into the body!

- Can the name and chemical composition of this substance be determined?

- Possible. That would require further chemical testing. We don't know what the substance is yet.

- All right! Can you tell me how the poison got into the body of the deceased?

- This could happen in a number of ways. First of all, the poison passes through the food and medicines consumed. But other routes are also possible, such as through the air or blood.

- Can this substance be found in natural foods? Say, in mushrooms, fruits and vegetables....

-We don't know its chemical composition yet. So it's hard to say in advance. But if the poison had gotten in through natural foodstuffs, the poisoning would have happened immediately, not gradually. And the doctors would have been able to see it.

- Oh, by the way, the doctors! Why didn't they notice that the deceased was poisoned?

- The substance used in this case gradually affects the human body and incapacitates certain parts of the body, eventually leading to death. For this reason, doctors may not have noticed it. The effect of this substance on the organism can be revealed only as a result of special tests, - said the expert and stared at the investigator, "Is that enough?

- Okay, thank you. We'll talk about the rest after we get an additional expert opinion. - You can go now," Fakhriddin got up.

At that moment there was a knock at the door, and Sanzharbek entered the room with a satisfied look:

- Permission to report, Comrade Team Leader!

- Permission granted, permission granted.

- We identified the man who was buried instead of Batyrov.

- Well, well? - said Fakhriddin Karimovich, all attentive.

-Batyrov worked not only as a doctor on duty at the ambulance, but also part-time at the city morgue. I think that he got a job there on purpose in order to carry out his plan. We scrutinized all the documents from his period of employment and doubted the authenticity of the entries in one of them. When we called all the signatories to that document, they all admitted that the signatures were forgeries. It was a document on the burial of the body of citizen Askar Nurgaliyev. After that, Nurgaliyev's identity and medical history were studied.

- Who was this Nurgaliyev, did he die his death or...

Sanzharbek began to read the paper: - Askar Nurgaliyev, 50 years old, Tatar by nationality, lonely, homeless, died of a heart attack.

- These aspects correspond to the features of the corpse recovered from the grave where Batyrov was buried.

-Yes, you are! Exactly!

- I wonder how Batyrov managed to steal the corpse.

- I think it helped that he worked in an ambulance. He had an ambulance at his disposal. While on duty, he managed to steal a corpse using a forged document prepared in advance and hide it in his house. He then dressed the corpse in his own clothes and put his documents in his pocket.

And he locked the door from the inside and disappeared.

- Someone could have found the body in two or three days! Would his plans have gone awry then?

- He's a doctor! So, he understood perfectly well that in four or five days the dead man's body would change beyond recognition.

- At any rate, it looked like he had outside help. He was not able to handle that much work on his own.

- Maybe.

- So now Batyrov is walking around with Askar Nurgaliyev's passport! - said Fakhriddin Karimovich, looking at the paper that Sanzharbek put in front of him.

- Yes, he is now at large as Nurgaliyev, not Batyrov. He may even have moved to another country.

- I don't think so! He is burning with vengeance. He cannot go anywhere until he has avenged himself on those responsible for his imprisonment and the deaths of his wife and children. You'll see, the deaths of both the investigator and the judge will be Batyrov's doing.

-Fakhriddin aka, we should not forget that Batyrov was in prison at the time of the car accident.

- That's true! But Batyrov is a lot smarter than we thought. He may have orchestrated the accident remotely.

- Yes, by the way, what is known about the details of the car accident that killed his wife and two children!

- It's not like we've dealt with this issue! I have no information about it! We only heard that it happened at the time.

-Sanjarbek, this is our mistake. Now urgently prepare a request, we need to urgently withdraw the criminal case or material on the fact of the car crash! Involve one of our experienced operatives in this case. Tell him to go and investigate this matter right away.

- That's right.

- Yeah, by the way, how's the search for Batyrov going?

- At the moment, all of Batyrov's acquaintances, colleagues and relatives have been questioned.

Many people think he's dead. No one has seen or heard from him since that incident.

- The search must be resumed. Every second counts. Batyrov has already become a dangerous criminal. He will stop at nothing to achieve his goal. We must stop him. Otherwise, the consequences will be dire.

-Yes. We do everything in our hands! If there is any news, we will immediately inform you, -Sanjarbekshagom left the office....

Vazira went to the prosecutor's office every day, but was frustrated that she could not learn anything new about the progress of the investigation. Fortunately, she had a friend, Zamira. She never left her alone, cheered her up and supported her when Vazira was depressed. Although Batyrov's involvement in her misfortunes had been proven on the basis of reliable facts and gave her some hope, Vazira's anxiety increased day by day because the perpetrator had not yet been caught and nothing was still known about her husband. Every morning she went to the prosecutor's office in the hope of hearing good news, then watched the investigators until nightfall, and returned to her friend's house in the evening.

Every minute she asked the Almighty to bring her husband back to the family. It seemed to her that these days she would receive news from him. It was as if Bahrom aka would walk through the door.....

And today Vazira spent the whole day waiting. The investigators' answers to her questions were short: "we are looking", "the search is underway", "it will be found". As evening came, tired and devastated, she returned to Zamira's house. Her friend, having returned from work, was preparing dinner. When she saw Vazira, she was happy: "How are you, friend, any news?

-Batyrov can't be found!

- The main thing is that the culprit is known! Now it's not so hard to find him. You'll see, in two or three days they'll find this Batyrov. If Bakhrom aka is alive!

- So be it, friend!

-Change your clothes, Farrukh aka also called, he'll be home any minute. Dinner's ready.

When Vazira entered the inner room and began to change, her gaze fell on a photograph on the table. Taking the family photo in her hands, she scrutinized it and thought: "What a happy, friendly family. The husband and wife respect each other. The children are close by. They do not need anything. Though Farrukh is an ordinary worker, he takes care of his wife and children in such a touching way. Zamira is an angel woman and a wonderful hostess. Yes, they are simple people, but how satisfied with their lives.

At that moment Vazira envied her friend with white envy. How she would like to have her beloved by her side! Even if she was a cleaner and her husband a simple watchman, she would like to be together!

Concerned that her friend was delayed, Zamira invited her to the table again. Although Vazira had no appetite, she went into the kitchen out of politeness. They ate dinner together. Farrukh tried to cheer up the women at the table, telling funny stories. But Wazira was unable to dispel her gloomy thoughts. On the pretext of fatigue, she went to bed with the permission of the couple.

Sitting down in front of the mirror, she examined herself. When she saw two or three gray hairs on her head, she was upset: "Oh, my God! Her hair was black not so long ago! Did she turn gray in a few days? It is not without reason that suffering ages a person. She is not yet forty, and her hair is already gray!

Vazira took several photographs out of her bag and stared at them mesmerized, as if she had seen them for the first time. Looking at the photo of her husband in his prosecutor's uniform, tears came to her eyes again. She stroked her husband's face and hair with her fingers and put the photo to her eyes. Then she took the family photo in her hands, "What a wonderful time it was. I wish those days could come back. How I wish those days could come back! If only it were all just a dream! It's strange that when a man is happy, he doesn't realize his happiness. It seems to him that it will go on forever. He recognizes the value of the happy moments of life only when he encounters unhappiness."

Looking at the cheerful faces of her children, Vazira realized how much she missed them. How good it is that she has only one brother, Anvarjon, to whom she can entrust her children. Her sister-in-law is also kind and sweet, taking care of her children. They do not let them feel deprived, they look after her sons as their own children. It's a good thing she has them!

She tossed and turned all night, not knowing how to sleep. Waking up long before dawn, she somehow could not forget that photograph of Batyrov's son: "What date was written on the back of the photo? Was it the date of some holiday? Yes, yes, if I am not mistaken, there was an inscription 'March 8, 1988'." Zafar aka said: "Zhasurbek was born on January 1, 1991." Or was he mistaken? Then Dr. Zafar himself looked at this record with surprise. Perhaps later he revealed this secret. In any case, I need to meet with him again and talk about it....

Despite her friend urging Wazira to have breakfast without eating anything, she literally ran to Dr. Zafar's office. Luckily for her, the doctor was just going to work. And although the journalist's visit seemed strange to him from the very morning, he did not let it show:

- Come in, come in!

- Hello, Zafar aka. Sorry to bother you this morning.

- No, no, please come in.

Wazira sat down on a bench in the middle of the courtyard and opened her palms to pray. Dr. Zafar told his wife to prepare tea and looked at Wazira questioningly.

-Zafar aka, you must have heard, but I am the wife of that prosecutor Bakhrom Safarovich.

- Yeah, yeah, I heard that when I went to the D.A.'s office.

- I didn't lie to you last time. I really am a reporter for a newspaper. What to do, I can't just watch as a spectator and wait. In my profession, I just wanted to help the investigators as much as possible. I apologize again for bothering you so much.

- It's not a big deal. I'm sure you're on the right track and I understand your situation. I'm willing to help you as much as I can.

- Thank you, Zafar aka! If you remember that day I noticed a photograph among Batyrov's documents. Can you show it to me again?

- Of course. Last time the investigators from the prosecutor's office took away the documents and things that belonged to Batyrov, and I kept the photograph as a memento from a friend. I'll take it out now," Dr. Zafar stood up and went into the house.

Soon the doctor came out with a photograph and handed it to Wazira.

- You said the boy's name was Jasur? - Wazira asked, scrutinizing the photograph.

- Yes, Zhasurbek.

Wazira turned the photograph over and read aloud the inscription on the back of it, "March 8, 1988."

-Zafar aka, what do you think this inscription means? Is it your son's birthday?

- No, I know for sure that Zhasurbek was born on January 1, 1991. Because we used to celebrate his birthday every year on New Year's Eve.

- The same can be said about the date of this photo, because Zhasurbek himself did not exist then, right? Strange, what can this date mean? - Vazira asked, looking at the photo and the doctor.

- It surprises me, too.

- Do you think there is any event, incident or something linking Batyrov to this date, i.e. March 8, 1988?

- I don't know. Maybe...

- Dr. Zafar wanted to express his conjecture about Nurali bobo, but changed his mind, fearing it would be a waste of the poor woman's energy and time.

- Well, well, did you have something to say?

- It's hard to say. I think someone accidentally recorded it.

- Usually, on the back of the photo, the date of the photo or the birthday of the person depicted in it is written. Batyrov must have always carried the photograph with him. I don't think such a man could have written any word on a photograph that was dear to him," said Vazira, continuing to draw logical conclusions.

- I thought the same thing last time. But my hunch was not confirmed," the doctor couldn't stand it.

- So you had an assumption? - Zafar was taken aback by Wazira's questions, which sounded like an interrogation by investigators.

- It was. But my assumption turned out to be wrong.

-Zafar aka, please share your guess with me even if it is wrong!

The doctor looked at his watch and told in detail the story of the car accident that had happened to Batyrov and him on March 8, 1988, when the old man Nurali had found them and saved them from death. He also told that Batyrov kept in touch with his grandfather after that. And when he saw the inscription on the photo, he thought whether Ahad had left a letter for him and went to Nurali bobo. It turned out that long before that the old man had died. He found no one in his house. It turned out that he had traveled in vain.

- Didn't old man Nurali have anyone?

- The deceased had no next of kin. It turns out that someone lives in his house now. Unfortunately, I didn't see him either.

- This must be a distant relative of his.

- I don't know, I think he bought the house.

- Maybe if you met with the owner of the house, you'd learn something?

- I don't know. If Batyrov had left something for me with the old man, Nurali Bobo would have told me about it. After all, he wasn't a stranger to me either. I think it's just a coincidence.

- Do you think so?

- Looks like it.

- Could that date have meant something else?

- I thought about it but couldn't recall any other incident or event related to that date.

- Perhaps this date concerns only Batyrov himself," Vazira continued to question.

- I knew Batyrov and his family well. But I can't remember if there was an event in their lives related to this date. Anyway, I don't know... perhaps there are things I don't know!

- You're right. Sometimes what doesn't matter to some can be important to others. Thank you, if you remember anything, I'll be in town," Vazira thanked her host, opening her palms to pray.

- That's good. But we could still sit and talk to my wife. And I have to go to work," Dr. Zafar walked the guest to the door....

Fakhriddin Karimovich held another operational meeting with the members of the group and, analyzing the data received, was surprised that an ordinary doctor had turned into an egregious criminal. Usually such crimes are committed by morally depraved persons, prone to committing crimes, who have nothing sacred left and prefer prison to freedom. But Batyrov does not belong to this category of people. How could he turn into a dangerous recidivist in such a short period of time? The only force pushing him to such heinous crimes is revenge.

There was a knock at the door and Sanzharbek entered:

-Fahriddin aka, there are two news from Tashkent.

- One's good, one's bad?

- No, they're both good this time! Which one should I start with?

- Come on, come on, start with the best one, don't test my patience.

- Your version has been confirmed. The General Prosecutor's Office filed a control protest in the Batyrov murder case.

- That's good, but the other one?

- It turned out that Batyrov... or rather, Nurgaliyev spent the night of October 15-16 at the Rossiya Hotel in Tashkent. Marziya was also in the same hotel.

- That's it! There is no doubt now that Marzia is Batyrov's accomplice. Though she did not commit the crime herself, she obviously helped Batyrov. She will have to be arrested," said Fakhriddin with a serious look.

-With her lies, that woman has been leading us around this whole time. Let's see what she has to say now!

- Yeah, by the way, how's the stakeout going?

- Surveillance is underway. She's locked herself in her house. She hardly ever goes outside. We haven't noticed anything suspicious in her behavior.

- All right, send a task force to go get her, have them bring her in. I'll try to talk to her again. Maybe she'll admit guilt and tell me everything!

- Yes! -Sanjarbek resolutely left the office.

Fakhriddin lit a cigarette near the window. The scent of various flowers growing in the yard hit his nose. The light breeze outside soothed and tickled his tired body. He heard the joyful shouts of a group of children returning from school and involuntarily remembered his own children. It had been a week since they had arrived in Bekabad. Although he, his wife and children were used to such business trips, this time the time seemed to drag on. In this short period of time, he felt how much he missed his wife and children. The thought flashed through his mind, "Maybe I should find the time and go home?". No, it is absolutely impossible! At the moment when the situation is heated, it is impossible to leave here, not just for an hour, but even for a second. If things move forward, he will definitely go and see his family...

Fakhriddin sat down and reported to the management on the work done and asked when the protest on the fact of Batyrov's murder would be considered. He said that if Marziya admitted her guilt and refused to cooperate with the investigation, he would be forced to arrest her. Then he called his wife and asked how they were doing and how the children were. He reassured her that he had a lot of work to do, but that he would visit them as soon as possible, and told her to pay more attention to the children.

Sanzharbek's rumbling voice was heard outside. A few minutes later he ushered Marzia into the office.

When Fakhriddin Karimovich offered her a seat, he could not believe that she had changed a lot in three or four days - the girl looked gaunt and pale. What could have changed a blossoming girl in such a short period of time? Thoughts or remorse?

-Marziahon, you've been involved in a serious crime without realizing it. You may not even be guilty. I'm questioning you now as a witness. I warn you that you may be prosecuted if you give false testimony or refuse to testify. Sign here," Fakhriddin handed the paper and pen to Marziya.

Marzia signed the top of the minutes without objection.

Fakhriddin Karimovich gave his voice an official tone:

- In your preliminary testimony, you said that you met Ahad Batyrov by chance in September and saw him when you traveled together to Tashkent but never met him again. Do you have any additions?

Marzia thought for a moment, then barely audibly whispered: "No."

- Did you travel to Tashkent a month or two after that? If yes, where did you stay?

- I didn't.

- Take a good look back, October-November.

- I have no one in Tashkent, where can I stay there?

- Then please tell me how can you understand that these papers record that you spent the night at the Rossiya Hotel in Tashkent on October 15-16 of the same year? Besides, how do you explain the fact that Ahad Batyrov lived in the room next to yours on the same days?

Marzia turned pale as a sheet.

- I know that Batyrov used you for his own purposes. But if you regret what you have done and tell the truth, it will be much easier for you. Otherwise, you may become an active participant in the commission of a very serious crime.

Marziya began to cry. Sanzharbek poured water from a carafe into a glass and handed it to her. The girl drank a few sips and calmed down. Then she put the glass on the table and began to speak in a tired voice:

-Ahad aka tricked me. He once saved me from death. For this reason, I had great respect for him. So, I could not refuse his request. When he returned from prison, we met by chance on the street. We talked. He told me what he'd been through. He said that he had filed a complaint with the prosecutor's office asking for a review of his case and, God willing, he would soon be fully acquitted. We exchanged phone numbers and home addresses. Later he invited me to his house a couple of times. He gave me money and told me to use it to buy presents for my children.

During another meeting, he asked me to go to Tashkent with him. I was just about to go shopping at the Hippodrome market. So, I agreed. On the way, he told me that he could not get to the prosecutor who was studying his complaint, that the prosecutor had previously worked in Bekabad, and that he needed my help to invite him to tea and give him an opportunity to express his opinion. We traveled to Tashkent twice. When we arrived the first time in September, he said that the prosecutor had gone on a business trip, bought me and my children presents and sent me home. Then he said that if the prosecutor came back, he would call me and summon me. I went back to Bekabad. About a month had passed when Ahad aka called me and summoned me to Tashkent. We checked into the Rossiya hotel...

Marziya was silent for a moment. Seeing that she was tired, Sanzharbek poured water for her again. The girl drank and continued her story:

-The next day, Ahad aka told me to speak to Prosecutor Bahr aka on the phone on behalf of a woman named Gulmira from Bekabad. I asked why? He told me that this prosecutor had a good relationship with this woman, who had recently written a letter to him saying, "I will soon go to Tashkent and call you," and that he was waiting for a call from Gulmira. I didn't agree at first, thinking that if they knew each other, he would recognize my voice.

And he reassured me: "I'll teach you what to say. Pretty girls have similar voices, so don't be afraid." I felt sorry for him, so I reluctantly agreed. He dialed a number from a pay phone on the street. A guy answered the phone. I asked him to put me through to Bahrom aka. When Bakhrom aka picked up the phone, I changed my voice a little and told him on behalf of Gulmira that I had come by cab today with a friend from Bekabad, that I had important business with him, and asked him to go around the corner near his office for a minute. He asked me, "What's wrong with your voice?". I replied that I had a cold ....

Marzia paused and continued. The investigators were silent, holding their breath and not interrupting the woman.

- On Ahad aka's orders, I waited for the prosecutor to get out in the front seat of the cab. After a while, a young man started approaching our car. I recognized him immediately. Because Ahad aka showed me his picture. I got out of the car and met him. He was surprised and asked about Gulmira. By prior arrangement, I offered him a seat in the car, telling him that I was Gulmira's friend and that she had just gone to the store and would be here any minute. He reluctantly sat down in the back seat of the car. We got to know each other.

After that, as Ahad aka had instructed, I was to get out of the car and walk towards the store on the pretext of calling Gulmira from the store on the opposite side of the road. As agreed, I got out of the car and ran to the other side of the road. When I turned around, I saw that the car had literally sped off and driven off in an unknown direction. There was one person in the front seat next to the driver and I think there were two people in the back seat. Crossing to the other side of the road, I looked around, wondering if Prosecutor Bakhrom had gotten out of the car. But there was no one in sight. I got scared. I didn't realize what had happened and quickly went back to the hotel. Ahad aka was waiting there. After two or three hours he came back.

I jumped on him, demanding to explain why he had done it, why he had deceived me and made me an accomplice to his crimes. And he calmed me down, saying that he had demanded money for a review of his case, wanted a bribe for a just cause, so the guys would do some "educational work" with him and let him go. I asked him, "They won't kill him?". To which Ahad aka replied to me, "What good will that do me? If he dies, who will complete my work?". After that I calmed down a little. Then Ahad aka gave me a large sum of money and took me back to Bekabad in a cab. After that I did not see him...

- Who was driving the car? - Fakhriddin Karimovich stood up and approached Marziya.

- It was a man about 35-40 years old.

- Do you remember the license plate number of the
Zhiguli or any of its distinctive features?

- I didn't look at the number. It's been a long time; I
don't remember anything. Just, uh.

- Well, well?

- There was a toy puppy with a moving head on the
back window. When the car was driving, he wiggled his
head around like he was alive.

-Did Batyrov order you to get out of the car under the
pretext of calling Gulmira or did you get out yourself?

- According to Batyrov's instructions, after the
prosecutor got into the car, I was to distract him with
conversation, then get out of the car to call Gulmira, go
to the other side of the road, then return to the hotel. No
more action. I did everything he told me to do.

- Was it Batyrov who ordered to cross to the other side
of the road and look back? - Sanzharbek intervened in the
conversation.

- No, I just automatically did it.

- How many guys got in the car, do you remember any
of them?

- I think there were two of them. They were both
athletic. But I couldn't remember them.

First of all, I was already on the opposite side of the road
and far away from them. Secondly, everything happened
so fast that I didn't even have time to see them.

- When you found out that Batyrov had cheated you,
why didn't you go to the law enforcement agencies? -
Fakhriddin said, throwing a cigarette that was burning
out in his hand into the ashtray.

- Because he told me: "Nothing's gonna happen to the prosecutor. It's just that he refuses to help me, so the guys will give him a man-to-man education and let him go. I believed his words and calmed down a bit.

- When and from whom did you hear about the disappearance of Bakhrom Safarovich? - Finally, the investigator asked Marziya the question she had been waiting for.

- On New Year's Eve, rumors about it spread in Bekabad. Now I can't remember exactly from whom I heard it. But everyone was talking about it. I was scared. I began to feel guilty about these matters. I looked for Ahad aka to find out what had happened. But I couldn't find him. When I asked his acquaintances, they all said he was dead. But I knew that he was alive and not dead.....

- Knowing about the serious crime committed by Batyrov, why did you not report it to the relevant authorities? Did you know that concealing a crime is also a crime?

- Я... I'm freakin' freakin' out! Please forgive me! - said Marzia, wiping her tears with a handkerchief. The investigators "tortured" Marzia with various questions until late at night. Some questions they asked over and over again to get everything she knew out of her. By the end of the day, the experts, with her help, had drawn sketches of the driver of the car that had taken Bahrom Safarovich and his two unknown traveling companions.

Fakhriddin Karimovich, taking into account that Marziya regrets what she has done, admits her guilt, cooperates with the investigation, and has a small child to support, decided to leave her free on her own recognizance.

Marziya, who had been worried since morning that if she was arrested, what would happen to her child, who would she leave it to, was overjoyed when she heard the investigator's decision. She sincerely thanked Fakhriddin Karimovich again and again and returned home.

-Fakhriddin aka, do you think we did the right thing? What if tomorrow she runs away with the child? - Sanzharbek expressed his concern after Marziya left.

- She has a child, a house, where will she go," the team leader replied calmly. -Marzia's arrest is not a problem. We have to catch Batyrov first. What worries me more is that he is still at large. We don't know what other "surprises" he has in store for us! Every second counts! Assemble the team members for an operational meeting at 9:00 p.m. We need to discuss this. Have all members of the team come in with a detailed report on their work.

-Fakhriddin aka, may I go to Tashkent after the operative meeting?

-Sanjarbek, I realize it's been a week since we've been stuck here, forgetting our families. But that's our profession. If it's no secret, why do you need to go to Tashkent? - The head of the group gave me a meaningful look.

- My daughter's birthday. Every time her birthday comes around, I'm on a business trip. I never get to celebrate her birthday instead. And she's waiting for me and won't sleep. My head is spinning. My conscience doesn't allow me to take time off when there is such a tense situation at work.

-Sanjarbek, we can't leave our work for a single second. We will go to Tashkent and congratulate your daughter-in-law and daughter-in-law together. Call and congratulate them on my behalf," Fakhriddin Karimovich took a piece of paper and started writing something.

Sanzharbek realized that it was useless to contradict the chief and left the office. He went to the waiting room and called home. This time he apologized to his wife Maftuna, congratulated his daughter, wished her many good wishes, said that he had bought her a big doll and promised to come back in a couple of days. Then he exhaled with relief, as if a mountain had fallen from his shoulders, and plunged back into his work....

"We should visit the grandchildren. How's the daughter-in-law? Poor thing, she's been living on hope lately. She wants to do what the state authorities couldn't do. How many times I've talked to her out of it hasn't helped. She doesn't want to believe she's lost her husband forever. As long as she doesn't do anything to herself. She has to be stopped. She needs to get serious about her kids, raise them to be men worthy of their father. That's a big job. If God wills, Bahromjon will come home one day!". With these thoughts in mind, Safar aka quickly got ready, got dressed and went to Tashkent...

There were no grandchildren or daughters-in-law at home. The neighbors said they had gone to Anvarjon's house. How good it is that there are many good people in the world! A neighbor took pity on the old man, who was carrying two large bags, and gave him a lift in his car to Anvarzhon's house.

Fortunately, Anvarjon was at home. He greeted the guest warmly. Safar aka hugged his grandchildren, who joyfully flew out to meet him. He handed out the gifts he had brought from the village to them and tried to cheer them up with affectionate words.

He told his grandchildren that their father would be back soon, but in the meantime they should obey their mother and uncle. And in order to please their father when he came back, they should study hard.

When the children went to do their homework, Safar aka asked Anwar embarrassedly:

- I haven't seen your sister, she's not back from work yet?

- My sister is still in Bekabad, stopped by a couple days ago.

- Oh, my poor sister-in-law. It's hard for her. We can still bear the pain, we pray! But she can't get used to this separation, she doesn't want to be a mere observer. Maybe her heart is telling her something.

- Yeah, you don't say! If my sister hadn't sensed something wrong, she wouldn't have gone for it.

- Were you able to find out anything? Any news, Anwarjon?

Anwar told Safar aka everything he had heard from his sister on her last visit. The old man's eyes sparkled with joy.

- Oh, God! Oh, God! May our wish come true. So, if they catch this Batyrov, Bakhromjon will be found. Oh,

Lord, God Almighty, protect my son for the sake of these children! -Safar's brother had tears in his eyes.

- Safar aka, be patient, it's not much longer. God willing, everything will be fine. We all hope to hear the long-awaited news very soon. And you take care of yourselves. Have patience," Anvarjon served tea to the guest.

- Let it be so, my son. Amen," the old man opened his palms for prayer....

This time the operational meeting was longer than usual. Fakhriddin Karimovich listened attentively to the reports of the group members and gave them appropriate instructions and recommendations. At the end of the meeting Sanzharbek reported that the prosecutor's protest on the fact of Batyrov's murder had been considered by the court and satisfied, the earlier court decision was canceled, and the criminal case was again sent for investigation.

- Have you withdrawn the criminal case? - asked Sanzharbek's team leader.

- Of course! It'll be on your desk in the morning.

- Personally deal with the Batyrov murder case, merging the criminal cases into one case file. I told you about the incompleteness and shortcomings of the investigation in this case. First study the case in detail, then carefully plan and proceed with the investigation! I'll do the search for Batyrov myself.

- Yes! - Sanzharbek wrote down the chief's instructions in his notebook and stood up. - Permission to go!

- Permission granted. Have a good vacation.

-Fakhriddin Karimovich, if I'm not mistaken, the time is about 12 o'clock. Aren't you going to the hotel?

- You go ahead, I'll do some work. I've got a lot to do.

-Okay, you, leaders, work, we, ordinary people, will go to rest, - Sanzharbek tried to joke as usual.

The boss grinned and continued his work. Sanzharbek realized that this was no time for jokes and quietly walked out.

Fakhriddin learned to work at night, when no one disturbed him, and to finish the things he could not do during the day because of his interaction with many people. The same was true today. First, he leisurely went through the reports of the group members, making familiar notes in the right places. Then he gathered his thoughts and planned for tomorrow. As the first question included the task of improving the effectiveness of investigative measures to resume the search for Batyrov, wrote his name under the item "responsible for execution" and thought: "Where to start work tomorrow? Where could Batyrov be hiding? Is he hiding somewhere in the mountains or caves? Or has he dug a hole for a dwelling somewhere and dwells there? It is not excluded that he did so in order to keep Bakhrom Safarovitch captive near him. In other conditions, to keep a person so long and secretly imprisoned without anyone noticing it is a difficult thing to do, especially in urban areas. Because there are a lot of people. It's only natural that someone would notice. So, among Batyrov's acquaintances we need to identify those who live in places with such conditions. After all, a person will seek help from his acquaintances and will not go anywhere else. By the way, why did he need to keep Bakhrom aka prisoner? To see him suffer? Or is he using him for some purposes? Perhaps Bakhrom Safarovich has been killed long ago, like the others. No, no, in that case, the body would have been found long ago. If he had the intention to kill Bakhrom aka, he would have carried it out professionally like in other cases. But what good would it do him to hold him?! Yes, that's right, Batyrov is holding Bakhrom Safarovich prisoner. He must be found as soon as possible. Otherwise, if he notices we're on the trail, he may try to get rid of a living witness. We must get everyone on their feet in the morning...".

Fakhriddin came to work earlier than everyone else. Vazira was waiting for him at the door.

- Hello, Fakhriddinjon! How are you?

- Thank you, opazhon. How are my nephews? Come on in.

-Ukajon, any news?

- God willing, these days they will be. We work days and nights. You go home. Stay close to the kids. If there's any news, I'll call you first!

- The biggest suyunchi is on me! I pray to God that these days come sooner rather than later!

- Thank you! We hope so, too. Okay, oops, I'll call you later.

-Fahriddinjon... me.... me...

- Wazira opa, do you have something to say?

-Have they found Batyrov yet?

- Not yet. But don't worry, we'll catch him soon," Fakhriddin Karimovich headed for the door.

- I don't know if this is correct or not, but I have a hunch.

- Well, well, come on, I'm listening ... - the investigator turned around like he'd found gold. - Let's go into the office. You'll tell me all about it there.

Wazira followed the investigator. They entered the office. A pungent odor of tobacco hit their noses. Fakhriddin was embarrassed and opened the windows.

- Wazira opa, what did you want to say? - the investigator began to speak, not wasting time.

- When I first went to Dr. Zafar's house as a journalist, I looked through Batyrov's belongings and saw one photograph that had fallen out of Batyrov's passport.

- What was that picture? - Fakhriddin Karimovich approached Vazira.

- It's an ordinary photo of Batyrov's son. But that's not the point. On the back of the photo there was an inscription "March 8, 1988". According to Dr. Zafar, this date had nothing to do with the birthday of the child in the photo. When I found out about this, I spoke to Zafar aka and expressed to him the opinion that Batyrov might have wanted to say something by this....

-Well, well, further, - the investigator listened to the woman attentively, like a child listening to a grandmother's fairy tale.

- The doctor said that on March 8, 1988, he and Ahad Batyrov went to a remote village to visit a patient. On the way back, the car they were in had an accident on a mountain road and fell into a ravine. As they were seriously injured, they were stuck in the hole for a long time. They were not noticed by passing cars and no one heard their voices. They were unlikely to survive the cold weather as night fell. Fortunately, towards evening, an old man named Nurali passed by on a horse-drawn cart and carried the victims to the village. Thanks to this old man, both the driver and the doctors survived. For this reason, after this incident, Ahad Batyrov and old man Nurali began to maintain relations as father and son. They were family friends...

Wazira was thoughtfully silent.

- What, what happened next? - Fakhriddin Karimovich said, pouring cold tea from the kettle for his interlocutor.

- When we first saw the picture at Dr. Zafar's, the doctor was thinking about something. But he said nothing to me. After that he went to Nurali's grandfather, thinking that Batyrov had left a letter or a message through him. Unfortunately, the grandfather had died shortly before that. So Zafar returned without being able to find out anything. After that I too forgot this story. But still, I wondered whether the inscription behind the photograph was a secret. Batyrov is not a stupid man! He could not have written a meaningless date on the photo of his child, which was precious to him, and he always kept it in his pocket. Secondly, he didn't leave that photo in his pocket for nothing. He wanted someone to find it and draw some sort of conclusion. A person who doesn't know him would think the date on the photo is the child's birthday and not pay attention to it.... I could be wrong. Anything can come to mind.

-Who has this picture now?

- At Dr. Zafar's. He kept this photo as a memento from a friend.

- Thank you, Wazira opa! You don't miss details that even we investigators don't pay attention to. You should have become an investigator. No criminal will run away from you," Fakhriddin smiled, so that his interlocutor would not think that his praise was insincere.

- What should I do, ukazhon, I can't just sit idly by! - Wazira said this as if to hint to the investigator, "What should I do if you sit idly by! But in order not to offend her interlocutor she added: - I want to help you! I'm sorry we bothered you all. I wish this would all be over soon. I wish I could find Bahrom aka sooner.....

- You'll be fine, bear with me, Opazhon. I'll take the photo today. No wonder there's a mystery behind it, as you say. Thank you again for your cleverness, Opazhon!

- I'm sorry to take up your time. Well, I wish you good luck with your work. Goodbye," Vazira headed for the exit.

Fakhriddin Karimovich walked her to the gate of the prosecutor's office, then resolutely went back and ordered the secretary to gather the members of the group urgently. He sat down and waited for everyone to gather. Indeed, there seemed to be some mystery in this photograph. After all, Batyrov would not write unnecessary words on the photo of his favorite son. Secondly, it was no accident that he left the photograph in his pocket.

251

He felt that someone would see the photo and realize the cryptic inscription on it. Yes, yes, no wonder that this photo fulfills the role of a message. But to whom is the message addressed? Dr. Zafar? Or is there another person who knows about the event of March 8, 1988? Zafar must still be found! These questions can only be answered by him...

At that moment, two operatives from the group looked in and asked permission to enter. Fakhriddin Karimovich jumped up from his seat:

- Come on, let's talk on the way! - he said.

Getting into the car, the group leader told the driver: -To the infectious disease hospital!

On the way, he briefly briefed the staff on the nature of the case.

Dr. Zafar was at work. He was invited to the office of the chief physician. Fakhriddin Karimovich greeted the doctor, then inquired about the whereabouts of the photograph found in Batyrov's pocket.

- It is a memory of my friend's son. I hid it at home," the doctor replied in an embarrassed tone.

- Why do you keep the physical evidence without handing it over to the investigation? - one of the investigators intervened.

- What other proof do you have? I only have a photograph. I gave you everything else. I have nothing left of Batyrov.

- Good, good, Zafar aka, call home now, our employee will come by car and bring the picture, - Fakhriddin handed the phone to the doctor.

Dr. Zafar spoke to his wife and asked her to pass the photo through the guys who were coming up.

Soon they brought a photograph. Looking at the photograph, Fakhriddin thought: "It's a pity, such a nice boy! Then he looked at the back of the photo, where there was an inscription: "March 8, 1988".

The investigators questioned the doctor at length. They had many questions, especially about the incident of March 8, 1988. The doctor calmly told him everything he knew.

- Did you go to the village and from whom did you hear that Nurali's grandfather had died?

- From the old man next door.

- There was no one at home?

- Nurali Bobo's wife died long ago, and they had no children.

- Who got grandpa's house?

- Someone lives there. But we didn't find him at home either, they said he had gone somewhere else.

- Who is he? A relative?

- Old man Nurali had no close relatives. Someone must have bought him, but they said it was a stranger.

- Can a stranger buy a house in a mountain village? Who could it be," Fakhriddin stood up and approached the doctor. - Did you ask his age?

- No, I didn't. I was confused when I heard that Nurali's grandfather had died.

-Zafaraka, who else besides you knew about this incident? I mean, did Batyrov have a friend other than you involved in the incident?

- I don't think he had any friends closer than me. The rest of us found out later. But I remember the date because we were in that car accident together, and the incident happened on March 8.

- Good. You will show us this village," Fakhriddin Karimovich stood up.

- Will the management let me?

- We'll explain it to them!

- I'll change now," Zafar said, pointing to the doctor's white robe.

Soon the members of the investigation team, led by Dr. Zafar, drove towards the village where old man Nurali lived....

Sanzharbek took the two-volume criminal case file and studied it carefully. He reread some pages again and again. He marked the necessary places. He wrote down his comments on a separate piece of paper. Then he sat down and drew up a plan of investigation. He outlined the actions to be taken and their perpetrators.

Since the chain of events led to the Central District Hospital, he had a quick lunch and decided to work there for a couple days.

Unfortunately, a lot of time has passed since then, so most of the employees who were working at the time of those terrible events have left their jobs. New employees came in their place. Sanjarbek asked Lailo Shodieva, Ozoda's friend.

But it turned out that soon after that tragedy she quit her job, and less than a year later she fell ill with cancer and died. Sanzharbek gave the investigators the necessary instructions and, without wasting time, went to Shodieva's parents. Aunt Zhannat, seeing the bag in the hands of the investigator, thought: "Probably from the gas service or from the power grid" and hurried to tell him:

- Son, we'll get our pension in a couple of days, then we'll pay! We pay every month, even if it's late!

- Auntie, you seem to have mistaken me for someone else, I am an investigator of the prosecutor's office, - Sanjarbek took out his official ID card from his side pocket and handed it to the old woman.

- I'm here about your daughter Lilo Chodieva.

The old woman, disregarding the ID, replied:

- Well, come on in, son. - I'm sorry I thought you were someone else, I thought you were a gas man.

- It's all right! We're used to it, holajon[20]," said the investigator, deliberately adding the suffix "zhon" to annoy and get the old woman talking.

The old woman, despite Sanzharbek's refusal, led him to a cozy room inside.

- This was Lilo's room. My daughter had a short life. She didn't even have time to start a family," Aunt Jeannette wiped her tears with the tip of her handkerchief.

-Holajon, I share your pain, please accept my condolences, even if it's late. May she rest in peace!

---

[20] cholajon - auntie, auntie

Sanzharbek, in order to comfort the old woman, asked about this and that.

Realizing that he had at least somewhat achieved his goal, he moved on to the main question.

- Aunt Zhannat, did you know your daughter's friend Ozoda Kabulova well?

- She was a close friend of my late daughter. They worked together. She was sometimes at our house. She had an unfortunate fate, too. She died early, without seeing anything.

-Holajon, did Lilo tell you about how Ozoda died?

- My daughter didn't want to talk about it for some reason. But I heard from others that Ozoda was killed by a doctor who worked with her. When I asked Lilo about it, she cried immediately... Son, what happened, why are you asking me this?

- It's okay, Holajon.

We wanted to clear up some things about Ozoda's death. Is this your daughter's shelf? -Sanjarbek pointed to a table, a chair and a small bookshelf in the room.

- Yes, my poor daughter spent a lot of time here, doing her homework, reading books... - the old woman was about to cry again.

- Can I see her books? - The investigator approached the desk.

- Sure, son, don't be shy!

There were five or six fiction books and medical textbooks on the table. The bookshelf was filled with various books and textbooks in Russian and Uzbek. It was easy to guess from the dust on the table and the books that no one had looked in here for a long time. Sanjarbek took one of the books on the table.

At that moment an envelope fell out of the book. The investigator stared at it. On it there was an inscription in the "where" column - "To the Prosecutor of Bekabad city". Sanzharbek turned to the old woman:

- Auntie, did you know about this letter?

- What letter? No, I didn't know! After my daughter died, hardly anyone came here.

- This letter is addressed to the district prosecutor," the investigator showed the old woman an envelope. - May I open it?

- Of course, of course, son! You say it's in the name of the prosecutor!

Sanzharbek carefully opened the envelope. Unfolding the quadruple folded paper, he began to read the letter written in beautiful handwriting:

"Dear Prosecutor!

As I leave this world, I, Shodieva Lilo, have decided to bring you one truth. I have committed a grave crime. God punished me for my guilt – and gave me an incurable disease! As I lie on my deathbed, I hate myself. I don't understand how I could dare to do such an abomination.

I endure the pain that consumes my body day after day, but I cannot bear the torment of conscience. I feel like I'm in hell!

So I decided to put my inner feelings on paper, even if it was too late to tell the truth, to wash away the guilt before my conscience a little.

Ozoda and I were close friends. She trusted me with her secrets more than anyone else. First, our head doctor Tashmurad seduced her.

He promised to promote her to head nurse if she agreed to be intimate with him. Otherwise, he threatened to fire the poor girl and got his way. No one but me knew that they were meeting in a house in the country.

A year later, Ozoda became pregnant. Hearing this, the head doctor began to avoid her. He tried to persuade the girl to have an abortion. Ozoda stood her ground and said that she would not get rid of the child even if she died.

Tashmurad was a careerist, avaricious, cowardly and at the same time a cunning and hypocritical man. He instructed me to persuade Ozoda. In return, he promised me a bonus and gifts.

I tried to influence my friend and persuaded her to get rid of the child. But my friend was afraid that she would not be able to give birth in the future, so she did not listen to me.

The head doctor was well aware that if a child was born, his sins would be exposed, he would lose his position and be disgraced in front of the community. So, he began to look for ways to get rid of Ozoda. He needed a reliable accomplice along the way, and he chose me. Because I was the most suitable candidate for this role as Ozoda's close friend...

And Ozoda didn't even suspect that I had betrayed her, telling me all her secrets and asking for advice.

Concerned that the child in her womb was growing, she demanded that Tashmurod send matchmakers as soon as possible and arrange a wedding. She was afraid that if his father or brother found out, everything would end badly.

The cunning Tashmurad was trying to buy time by deceiving the girl, while he was plotting her destruction. When he decided to use our experienced surgeon, harmless man Ahad aka, for this purpose, I tried my best to dissuade him from this idea. But the head doctor was adamant. He wanted to kill two birds with one stone: Ozodu and Ahad Batyrov, who was gaining more and more authority in the district and in the team, and allegedly even "methought to take his place".

For this reason, Tashmurad tried to blame Batyrov for his actions. I am an unscrupulous, conniving and mean girl who naively helped him for a pittance. Before that, I spread a rumor that Ozoda and Batyrov were dating. And then I gave false testimony against Batyrov. But I didn't know Ozoda would be killed. On

Tashmurad Sobirovich's instructions, I faked my voice and called Batyrov on Ozoda's behalf and summoned him to her house. I was supposed to sneak up behind them and see them together. But that day I saw a terrible sight: Batyrov standing over Ozoda's bloody body with a knife.

I don't believe Batyrov is capable of such a thing. I'm sure Tashmurad did it. I attacked him for killing Ozoda. And he swore to me by his children that he didn't do it, said he had nothing to do with it. I told the investigators everything I saw. Unfortunately, these instructions of mine became the basis for Batyrov's accusation of murder. No one knows that he is innocent except me and Tashmurad.

I have committed a grave sin. God Himself punished me for it. I caused an innocent man to be imprisoned for a long period of time, his family ruined, his future destroyed!

I may not be able to answer before the law. Because by the time you read this letter, I'll be dead!

Forgive me for sinning! Although it's impossible. Lailo Chodieva."

Reading the letter, Sanzharbek, on the one hand, hated the girl who had abominably framed her colleagues, and on the other hand, sincerely pitied Batyrov for his bitter fate, for the humiliation he had suffered for nothing. "Poor fellow, he has indeed been unjustly accused! One single slander has brought so much misery into his life! He has lost his wife, his children, his family, his job, and everything-everything he had.And he himself has been burned in the fire of revenge and turned to ashes, his hands soiled in blood, his life turned to hell. He has no hope of life. He has managed to turn into a living corpse. It is not for nothing that people say: "Save from the scourge of fire, water and slander...".

- What does it say, son? - Aunt Jeannat said, concerned that the investigator was staring intently at the letter.

- In the letter, your daughter wrote her thoughts on her friend's death. Holajon, I'm going to have to take this letter for the case.

-Yes, son, take it if you need it.

From there, Sanzharbek called the team leader. The secretary informed him that he had gone to an infectious disease hospital and gave his phone number.

Sanzharbek dialed the number he found the chief on: -Fakhriddin Karimovich, I have two messages...

- Must one be good, the other bad?

- You guessed it. Which one should I start with?

- With a good one!

- An important piece of evidence has been found that proves Batyrov's innocence and, on the contrary, the guilt of chief doctor Tashmurad Sobirov in the death of Ozoda Kabulova ...

- Congratulations! What's the bad news?

- The person who left this evidence, i.e. the letter, the friend of Ozoda-Lailo Shodieva is not alive. We didn't catch the main witness. That's too bad.

- What are you going to do now?

-Tashmurod Sobirov, it turns out, works as head of the regional health department. To detain him...

- That's right, send the task force in quickly. We'll talk about the rest when we meet. I'm on my way to the village with the guys. There's probably no phone there. We'll be back by evening. Control everything yourself!

- Bingo!

Sanzharbek returned to the central hospital and sent two operatives after Tashmurod Sobirov. He began questioning the staff working at the time one by one. Many employees noted that they knew Batyrov as a simple, sincere person and a competent surgeon.

In contrast, Sobirov was described as an arrogant man, a womanizer, a careerist and a hypocrite. Witnesses said that at the time there were rumors among people that Batyrov had not committed the crime and that someone had deliberately framed him, but they did not know how true or false these allegations were. Some noticed that Tashmurad was at the head of the whole dirty scam, but when Batyrov was imprisoned for a long period of time, the rumors gradually dissipated.

At night, investigators returned to the prosecutor's office ...

The car drove along the bumpy mountain roads to old Nurali's village. The road became narrower and narrower. The attention of all the passengers and the driver was focused on the road. When the car reached a high part of the gorge and began to descend slowly, Dr. Zafar pointed to the abyss below:

- We had an accident in this place," he said. - Allah saved us then! We survived by a miracle.

- You're really lucky. You can't look down without fear," one of the investigators interjected.

- "There's a saying, 'Even if there's a massacre for forty days, the one who has it written in his birth will die,'" said the second investigator, looking down from the window.

Fakhriddin, sitting in the front seat, rode in silence. Though he listened to the words of his companions, his thoughts were elsewhere: "Who is the man who lives in old Nurali's house? Is it really Batyrov? No-ah, could he, having done so many deeds, live quietly in plain sight? After all, there are aksakals and district inspectors in the villages too! Wouldn't they ask him who he was, where he came from? Yes, by the way, he has false documents in his hands! Perhaps, with these documents he saves his life! If he doesn't break the order, doesn't commit a crime, who cares about him? In that case, where does he keep Bahrom aka? Or has he already gotten rid of it? What is the point of him keeping a living witness? Or does he derive some pleasure from keeping him captive? Or is it part of a revenge plan to make him suffer? He's already had his revenge on almost everyone he considered responsible for his unjust suffering. And how he had done it masterfully without anyone noticing! But why didn't he touch Tashmurad Sobirov?! It all started because of him! Or doesn't he know that he had a hand in this case? But why doesn't he know? Everyone suspected Sobirov then! Maybe he didn't have time to take revenge on him. Maybe he's looking for the right moment. There's something here we don't know. Well, let's see how this plays out.

- Stop here. We're here.

- This is the house, - said Dr. Zafar as the car pulled up to a house on the very outskirts of the village.

Fakhriddin went first to the unassuming house the doctor was pointing to. One of the officers quickly turned to the right, another went around to the left and adopted a position of observing the courtyard through the earthen wall of the house. Not knowing what to do, Zafar involuntarily followed the investigator.

The team leader poked his head through the ajar window and looked around inside. There was no one in the courtyard. He banged on the door several times with his fist. When no sound came from inside, everyone entered the courtyard. Having inspected the yard and made sure that there was no one at home, Fakhriddin-Karimovich instructed one of the operatives to invite the neighbors. He sat on a chair under an apricot tree in the middle of the yard and smoked: "Everything is open. So he is somewhere here, not far away. Yes they don't use locks and keys in village houses! Perhaps he's gone out somewhere. Word travels fast in the village. The main thing is that he doesn't run away when he finds out we're here! Well, Batyrov is a very thorough man. He's not one to give up easily. What did Dr. Zafar call him by his local name? "Salai Tabib"? Yes, yes, Salai the healer. It's better for the neighbors to introduce themselves as people who came for treatment from the district center. In any case, we mustn't scare him...".

Soon one of the operatives brought a neighbor's old man with a white beard into the yard.

Fakhriddin greeted the old man like an old acquaintance.

The elder greeted everyone by shaking hands.

- We came from the district center to see Salai Tabib. But we can't find him...

- Dr. Salai is here, he'll be late. Poor guy, wandering the mountains all day gathering herbs, doesn't know what peace is. Thanks to him, many people here have been cured. People trust him more than doctors. And... What business are you on? - said the old man, looking everyone in the face.

- We are from Bekabad... Dr. Salai... -Fakhriddin Karimovich did not finish the word.

- You are not from here," said the old man in his dialect. -Dr. Salai does not accept strangers! Oh, you shouldn't have come all this way!

- We are guests from the capital. This man is from Bekabad," Fakhriddin Karimovich was forced to tell the truth.

-Dr. Salai only treats residents of our village. Dr. Salai only treats residents of our village, and sometimes from neighboring villages. He probably won't see you.

- Let's ask him. Maybe he'll accept. We've traveled so far to hear about him.

- We came to the tabib with the hope of getting treatment, father," Dr. Zafar intervened in the dialogue.

- Well, if you came with hope, the herb will cure you, son! Until the tabib returns, come and sit with me, guests! Let's go, - the old man, jerking his body, led everyone behind him. Fakhriddin Karimovich followed him, along with Doctor Zafar. At the sign of the team leader, the operatives got into the car and drove up to the neighbor's gate and then began to observe the surroundings from there.

Frustrated that some of the guests wouldn't get out of the car, the old man approached several times to call them into the house again. He was unable to convince the guys, who sat in the car with empty and focused eyes, and went back into the house with the thought "These guys are unusual visitors".

Although Fakhriddin Karimovich chatted amicably with the old man while drinking tea, his thoughts were outside. He was worried that Dr. Salai was running late: "What if he does something else!

I don't want him to run away when he hears the strangers have arrived. Maybe we should have sent the boys to the mountains to fetch him. No, no, in the mountains, among the rocks, gorges and ravines, how could they find anyone? It's better to wait. If he is somewhere near, he will be back before dark.

The group leader was losing his patience and from time to time came out to have a word with the guys who remained in the car. He was reassured that they were keeping vigil at their "post" as they should. When the sun disappeared behind the horizon, Fakhriddin went outside for a breath of fresh air. Since the old man's yard was located a little higher up, Salaya-tabib's house was visible below. Soon it became dark. Darkness began to envelope everything around.

Suddenly, someone's silhouette appeared from the side of the mountains. The operatives tensed. A man with a bag on his shoulder took frequent steps towards the doctor's house. Fakhriddin Karimovich put his index finger to his lips and gestured to the guys sitting in the car not to make any unnecessary movements. As soon as the man entered the courtyard, the operatives ran after him.

The owner of the house, seeing the "guests" who had entered without his permission, indifferently continued his work. He took herbs out of his bag and began to sort them.

- Are you Salai-tabib? - Fakhriddin Karimovich asked, approaching the owner of the house.

- I don't receive anyone in the evening," said the master, without taking his eyes off his work.

- You'll have to take us in," Fakhriddin Karimovich introduced himself, showing a red service ID card in a thick cover from his pocket. The physician Salai stopped what he was doing, looked at the investigator with eyes widened with surprise, instantly turned pale and sat down. Then the attentive investigator realized that this man with the overgrown hair and beard and strange complexion was the very Ahad Batyrov.

- It's all over, Ahad Batyrov. You are under arrest," said Fakhriddin Karimovich seriously. - I have one question for you: where did you keep Bakhrom Safarovich for so long? Salai-tabib froze in place.

He looked at the investigator with empty eyes, as if he hadn't heard anything.

- I'm telling you, Batyrov. We know everything. Tell us the truth, it'll be easier for you! Where is Bakhrom Safarovich, where did you hide him?!

The doctor opened his mouth to say something but couldn't get it out. One of the staff quickly poured cold tea from the kettle on the bed and handed it to him. As he sipped the tea, the doctor seemed to come to his senses a little and said:

- Yes, I am that unfortunate Ahad Batyrov, who lost hope in this world and died long ago.

I don't care if you lock me up or kill me! I have no reason to live in this world. I spent most of my life in prison. The rest of my life is spent in prison, too. This house and this life is like a prison to me.....

-Batyrov! The court will decide whether to send you to prison or not. Now answer my question: where is Bakhrom Safarovich?

- What Bahrom? I don't know any Bahrom-Pahrom.

- We know everything. Don't you dare mislead us! Your accomplices have been caught. There's no point in being stubborn. If you admit your guilt and sincerely regret your actions, the court will take these circumstances into account when passing sentence.

- If you know everything, why are you asking me?

- We only ask you one thing, where you hid Bakhrom Safarovich.

- I don't know such a person!

- You stole it with your accomplices! Four years ago, Marzia called him in from the prosecutor's office. She confessed everything. You're wasting our time. Tell me, where did you hide Bakhrom Safarovich? - Fakhriddin Karimovich got angry.

- Oh, that prosecutor guy? It's true that Marzia called him in to see me. We had a man-to-man talk with this guy. I asked him why he'd wrongfully imprisoned me.

He said it wasn't his fault I was locked up. Then we parted peacefully. I never saw him again! Why? Did he disappear or something?

Fakhriddin Karimovich realized that it was not easy for him to get this man to talk, so he went on the attack from the other side:

- Then why did you kill investigator Ikrom Bozorov and judge Zakir Shokirov, who were working on your murder case? Did you talk to them in a manly way too?! - Fakhriddin Karimovich exclaimed, unable to hide his anger.

-Я? When did I kill?

- Don't you remember? 5 or 6 years ago!

- Sorry, at that time I was in prison, serving the sentence imposed by your semi-literate investigator and godless judge! So I had no opportunity to kill them! If they really left this world, I was once again convinced of the justice of Allah!

-Batyrov, stop talking nonsense! If you were in prison, then you hired a hit man for these cases! Don't try to distract us!

- Comrade Chief! I am a man who has been slandered and thrown into prison! Then I did everything to justify myself, begged, cried! But no one would listen to me. I had to pay too high a price for something I didn't do. I lost my job, my home, my children, my dreams and my hopes all at the same time. Now I have nothing to lose. I'm a dead man. When my wife and two sons died, I died with them too. All I have left is my body. I won't try to justify myself anymore. It's not me you'll have to put away, it's my body!

- All right, we'll talk about the rest there. You're coming with us," the investigator cut the conversation short, feeling that it was useless to argue with this man.

Batyrov rose slowly, took the chapan hanging on the wall in his hand, and followed the investigator to the door. Outside in the dim light he saw Dr. Zafar and stood still for a few seconds, then wanted to say something, but changed his mind and got into the car in silence.

Zafar, still not realizing what was happening, managed to say to his friend who was passing by: "Ahad, how are you, friend! Thank God you are alive!

Batyrov didn't even lift a shoulder in response.

The operatives thoroughly searched the places where Bakhrom Safarovich could have been imprisoned - a barn, a cowshed, a wood storehouse, the roof. But no traces of a man were found there....

After eight o'clock in the evening, the operatives brought in Tashmurad Sobirov, pale with fear and excitement. Sanzharbek poured him hot tea to calm him down. The investigator started the conversation from afar, asked him about his affairs, health, family, and said two or three words about the achievements of modern medicine. After a while, the anxiety on the face of the interlocutor gradually disappeared, he seemed to breathe a sigh of relief. The investigator took advantage of the moment and moved on to the target.

-Tashmurad Sobirovich, for so many years you have not been tormented by pangs of conscience?

- I don't get it! What do you mean?

- Please read this letter, maybe you will remember something! - The investigator took a piece of paper out of his desk drawer and handed it to his interlocutor.

Sobirov, worried and blushing with shame, read the letter to the end. His breath caught, he loosened his tie, unbuttoned his collar, took a handkerchief out of his pocket and wiped the sweat on his forehead. He shifted his gaze from the letter to the investigator, who looked at him questioningly and waited for him to speak. He wanted to say something but could not utter it.

The investigator was deliberately silent and paused, waiting for his interlocutor to gather his thoughts and finally admit the truth. It was not easy to refute such a terrible argument and say something in his defense. Therefore Sanzharbek did not hurry him, thinking that now this man would tell everything as it was. He poured him some hot green tea, which the secretary had just brought in, and let him breathe.

- Comrade, Prosecutor! That's right. Yes, I'm guilty. I chose the path of evil over my career. I got Ozoda pregnant. I tried hard to convince her to have an abortion. But she wouldn't agree. If the child was born, my reputation in front of my family, team and society would have been completely undermined. Ozoda also had a hard time. For a village girl, having a child out of wedlock is tantamount to death. So she demanded that I organize at least a small wedding so that she would not be disgraced in front of her parents and relatives. But I couldn't do it. In those days, such a transgression by a party man led to his expulsion from the party ranks to his dismissal from his job, and to the destruction of his future. And I did not want to lose either my job or my position. Therefore, colluding with Lailo, we spread the rumor that Ozoda was pregnant by Ahad Batyrov. Lailo was to invite Batyrov to her house on Ozoda's behalf and see them together. This was necessary for me to accuse Ozoda of having intimate relations with Batyrov and get rid of her. And so we did. But, uh, unfortunately, when Lilo went to see Ozoda that day, she saw what she saw. Yeah, it wasn't Batyrov's fault in the slightest. We sent him to Ozoda on purpose. But it cost him a lot to catch the murderer. The poor guy went to jail for a long time.

- Then why did you kill Ozoda?

- Uh, ukajon! Don't say that I didn't kill anyone. Lilo saw the crime that day. When I heard about the tragedy, I was scared. But I swear to God, I don't know who killed her!

- No one was interested in Ozoda's death but you. You see, you're the only one Lilo suspects, too. Are you trying to put the blame on someone else again? Do you even have a conscience? - the investigator's expression changed.

- Yes, I did a bad thing, I caused a man to be wrongfully imprisoned. But, uh.

- What one man! Do you know how many lives your one lie has cost?

Do you know how many families have suffered because of you? "One man" speaks!

-Ukajon, yes, it's my fault. I chickened out. I should have told you then that Batyrov was innocent. And I forced Lilo to become an accomplice to these cases. But I didn't kill Ozoda. I loved her... I was good to her! - Sobirov faked tears in his eyes.

- All right, if you plead guilty, that's good for you. Today I have to detain you as a suspect. You have three days to confess everything," the investigator stood up and approached Sobirov. - You don't know what we know about you!

- Comrade, prosecutor! I'm telling the truth. By God, I don't know who killed Ozoda!

- Leave God alone! Shameless and unbelieving people might as well not mention Allah!

- I swear on my children, I didn't kill Ozoda! If I had killed her, then Batyrov would not have left me alone!

- What? Explain what you mean!

- After Batyrov was released from prison, he came to see me. Like you, he blamed me for Ozoda's death. I told him the whole story. I swore to him for the health of my children. But he didn't believe me. I remember that's when Lilo died. There were no other witnesses. He was very angry. He could have gotten back at me. Fortunately, I was on vacation in Kyrgyzstan, or rather, I was resting in Issyk-Kul when Ozoda was killed. I showed Batyrov my airplane ticket, after which he threatened me: "I will check, but if you lied, blame yourself. After that, he never bothered me again.

- Why didn't you go to law enforcement about this?

-Batyrov threatened me: "Don't tell anyone about our meeting, think about your children." He wanted revenge...

- When and for what purpose did you travel to Issyk-Kul?

- I used to vacation there every year. I don't remember the date now. But I remember well that when I called the office on the third or fourth day of my vacation, I was informed that Ozoda had been brutally murdered. I had to go back the next day.

- Where are those plane tickets now?

- I found them at home at the time to show them to Batyrov. Must have been among my books.

-Tashmuradaka, here's the phone, call home and warn your people that our employees will come right now and take these tickets," Sanzharbek said, pointing to the phone on the table.

- Can I go get them myself?

- No, we need you here! The guys will be right over.

Sobirov talked to his wife and asked her to pass two airplane tickets lying among the books on the table through the guys.

Sanzharbek sent two operatives to Sobirov's house and continued to interrogate him himself:

- We'll check your alibi. You were close to Ozoda and should have known all her secrets. If neither Batyrov nor you were responsible for her death, then who killed her? Who would want a young girl dead?

- It surprises me, too. I knew her well. She had a good relationship with everyone. She was a kind, naive, simple-minded girl. Her only flaw was her gullibility. I never heard that she had any enemies.

- When was the last time you saw her?

- On the eve of my vacation. She asked me to send matchmakers to her house again, to organize a wedding, however small, to spare her the shame. I tried again to persuade her to have an abortion. She said emphatically that she would never do it. We had a fight. Afterward I called Lilo to me and told her that we needed to accelerate our plan regarding Batyrov. I told her that I would be away from work for three or four days and that during that time I had to prove by any means possible that Ozoda was seeing Batyrov, that is, cheating on me.

- What were you trying to accomplish with that?

- I, the fool, wanted to accuse Ozoda of cheating and send her away from me.

- When and from whom did you learn of Ozoda's death?

- I called home and worked almost every day. That day, I heard about this terrible incident after talking to my colleagues. I wanted to return home that day, but I couldn't get a plane ticket. So, the next day I flew to Tashkent.

- They say that in those days there were rumors that you were guilty of killing Ozoda. Who do you think spread those rumors?

- Many people knew that I was in a close relationship with Ozoda. In such cases, the closest people are the first to be suspected.

- Being a family man, why would you seduce an innocent girl?

- I loved Ozoda very much. I courted her for a long time. It was not easy to win her over. I gave her gifts, promised her a good career. Gradually she began to like me too. I was stupid, I didn't even think about how it would end. One day on her birthday, I gave her a gold chain. You should have seen the poor girl's joy. We drank a little wine. And two months later, we found out she was pregnant. It all started then.

Meanwhile, the operatives brought two airplane tickets. Sanzharbek examined them carefully and was sure that the person sitting in front of him was not lying. Nevertheless, he sent one of his employees to the Tashkent airport to clarify this issue. He himself interrogated Sobirov first as a witness, then as a suspect and drew up interrogation protocols. Having taken the suspect into custody, he waited for the arrival of the chief.

At night Fakhriddin Karimovich brought a heavily overgrown and strangely dressed man who looked like a dervish.

- Well, Sanjarbek, not bored?

- No-o-o-o! But..." said Sanzharbek, examining the "guest" from head to toe.

- Do you recognize this gentleman?

- I can't remember! - said the investigator with surprise. At that moment he had a thought: "Isn't this the same Batyrov?

- This man is Salai-tabib, aka Askar Nurgaliyev, aka that famous Ahad Batyrov!

- Yes? Ahadaka, how are you, are you all right? What a twist! We were looking for you at the cemetery... And you're alive! I admire you! You are a master of misleading people," said Sanjarbek, unable to hide his surprise.

Batyrov looked at Sanzharbek as if to say, "Who else is this?" but remained silent. He sat down on a chair in the corner.

- It's late today, we'll continue tomorrow. Now prepare a decision to detain the suspect," the chief said, looking at his watch.

Sanzharbek drew up documents and handed Batyrov over to IAB officers to place him in custody.

Returning to the hotel, Fakhriddin Karimovich asked his student:

- By the way, what did you do with Sobirov?

- Interrogated. He admitted that he tried to accuse Batyrov and Ozoda of intimate relations but says that he did not kill the girl. He has an alibi. At the time of the murder, he was on vacation in Issyk-Kul and presented plane tickets. However, for some reason he behaves differently. This fat man seems to be diabolically cunning. My head is spinning.

- You let him go?

- No, of course I arrested him. Anyway, he's the main cause of all the trouble. However, it seems that proving his guilt won't be easy.

- They did the right thing. It is necessary to talk to the administration of the Issyk-Kul sanatorium and check Sobirov's alibi. Who else needed Ozoda's death but him. Perhaps he went on vacation and hired a killer

- Maybe. Sobirov was more cunning than we thought. You can expect anything from him. What about Batyrov? Has he confessed to his crimes?

- As long as he pretends to be all white and fluffy. If we present him with hard evidence tomorrow, he'll be forced to take the blame.

- In both cases, we now have to rely on facts alone. They say the evidence is stubborn.

- Okay, that's enough for today. Have a good rest. We have a busy day ahead of us tomorrow," said the chief, turning towards his room. Tomorrow, call Waziru opa as well. We may need her.

- That's right. Good night!

When Fakhriddin Karimovich entered his room, the clock on his desk showed 01:30...

The investigator's morning call excited Vazira: "Is it news from Bakhrom aka! Or have they managed to catch Batyrov? Oh, God, give me strength and patience! Do not deprive me of hope! If there is justice, give me back the father of my children! My heart feels, it is ready to burst out of my chest. May it be for good."

Vazira hurriedly dressed and left. There were many people near the prosecutor's office. A neatly dressed man got out of the covered truck that had just stopped. Two policemen took him inside. Then a handcuffed man dressed in rags came out of the truck. Three policemen took him into the prosecutor's office.

"Who are they? They don't look like Batyrov, anyway. Perhaps they were brought in on another case. Whoever they are, the first man looks like a big official. Poor fellow, I wonder what he's done? The second one must be a bum," Vazira thought.

It seems that Vazira was already expected, because the policeman standing at the entrance led Vazira into Sanzharbek's office.

-Opajon, how are you? How are my brothers? You're not tired.

- Thank you, pointer. What's up? Any news?

- Yes, you are, Opazhon! We grabbed Batyrov.

-Ra-a-a-av-da-a? Is it true? And Bakhrom aka... what is he saying?" tears came to Wazira's eyes, her voice and hands trembled.

-Opajon, come on, sit here. Everything will be all right. Batyrov's been found, it'll be easier from here. But for the moment, he hasn't confessed to anything. I think we'll know soon enough. Why don't you stay here for now, we may need your help.

- Yes, of course you do. I will wait as long as you say. The main thing is that Bakhrom aka is found," said Vazira, wiping her tears with a handkerchief.

- Wazira opa, pull yourself together. Be patient, they say patience is gold.

- Okay, pointer, I'm fine. Feel free to do your job. I won't get in your way.

- This is different. I will be next to Fakhriddin Karimovich. For now, read this, - Sanjarbek threw the fresh newspapers on the table in front of the woman and left the office.

To pass the time, Wazira started leafing through newspapers. She saw a poem by poet Muhammad Yusuf[21] on one of the inside pages of the newspaper "Yzbekiston adabiyoti va sanyati".[22]

My flower, I couldn't save you,
I was a sultan who couldn't love you.
I couldn't give you my love in return for yours,
How to be, you're the good one and I'm the bad one.....
Hang me, I'd appreciate it,
Thank you for being you, thank you for being you.

"How touching! - Wazira thought. - I too have failed to keep you safe, Bahrom aka! I, too, failed to shower my love on you, failed to appreciate your care. I did not pay much attention to your poems then. Now I read them

---

[21] "Ÿzbekiston adabiyoti va sanyati" - newspaper of the Writers' Union of Uzbekistan, literally means "Literature and Art of Uzbekistan"

[22] poem by poet Muhammad Yusuf:

and my heart breaks. I even memorized the poems that you read the last time on my birthday. Every time I read them, I feel your love again, I think you are near me and stroking my hair:

You're the most beautiful woman in the world,
There are no words I can use to describe you.
You are the flower that opened in my garden of love.
You are a beautiful, lovely rose in this flower bed.

Her lips are honey, her face is ruddy, her eyebrows are bows, her eyelashes are arrows,
You're the only one with both intelligence and beauty.
Let the flowers envy you, let the sun burn with your gaze,
If you smile at the moon, I'll start to doubt you.

You are my vow, you are my throne, all my happiness is with you,
This world and this land connect us.
If everyone is looking for high love,
You are the pinnacle of love for me.

Ah, what a wonderful and carefree time it was. That day you read those ghazals in front of the guests and won applause. And how my friends envied me! If those times could come back again... If you were by my side! I would never let you be sad...".

-Opazhon, aren't you bored? -Sanzharbek entered the office, knocking quietly on the door.

- No, thank you. Reading the papers.

- Very well," the investigator took some papers from the desk drawer and went out again.

Vazira tensed, trying to hear what was going on in the next room. "Has Batyrov admitted his guilt? Or is he still leading everyone around by the nose?" she thought. - she thought. - It's clear that it was he who kidnapped my Bahrom aka! What more proof does the investigators need! On the one hand, of course, it is good that they are thoroughly investigating. In their work you can't make any mistakes at all. That's what the consequences of one mistake in the Batyrov case led to. How many people died because of it. Accusing an innocent person is probably the biggest mistake in life. My late mother-in-law had a parable that she used to tell on occasion: "A daughter from an enlightened and cultured family came as a daughter-in-law to a friendly family. The mother-in-law had a son and a daughter. She accepted her daughter-in-law as her own daughter.

One day, while the mother was preparing dinner with her daughter and daughter-in-law in the courtyard, she took off a ruby ring she had gotten from her mother and put it near the hearth. When the meal was ready, the three of them sat down to eat. When the mother remembered her ring, it was not there. First she asked her daughter, then her daughter-in-law if they had seen her ring. Both replied that they had not. The mother wondered. Who could have taken the ring if no one had entered the yard, a genie or something? The mother didn't know who to suspect and was confused. Because her daughter never touched other people's things without asking. The daughter-in-law couldn't be blamed either, because she had sworn to her family that she hadn't touched the ring. The ring was precious to the woman as it was a memory from her mother.

Despite this, she lamented not the ring, but the fact that her children had lied and behaved dishonestly and unscrupulously over a trifling thing. After this incident, relations in the family soured. A daughter-in-law is, after all, a daughter-in-law, that is, a person from the outside. Therefore, her mother-in-law suspected her more than her daughter, demanded that she admitted guilt and asked for forgiveness, even if she did not return the ring. But the daughter-in-law continued to stand her ground: "I did not see your ring and that's it!". Now the mother-in-law hated the "unscrupulous" daughter-in-law so much that she was ready to shoot her if she had a gun. She began to slander her daughter-in-law in front of her son and forced her to leave the house. The obedient son could not go against his mother and divorced his wife.

Years passed and one day the lost ring fell out of a turtledove's nest on the roof of the house. It turns out that birds are also addicted to gold. And then everyone realized that the ring had been "stolen" by a turtledove. After that, the mother was tormented by conscience all her life for the fact that she unfairly accused in the theft of a well-mannered, decent and nice daughter-in-law, thus breaking her family. Therefore, if one is not sure of someone's guilt, one should not accuse him unjustly, for this is tantamount to slander.

Thousands of reasons can give rise to any event. Some of them even exceed our imagination. It is quite possible that one small mistake will cause great trouble...".

- Wazira opa, sorry to keep you waiting. Let's move to another office. Fakhriddin Karimovich asks for you," Sanzharbek entered hurriedly.

-Ukajon, are you okay?

- He won't admit to anything. He seems to be a very stubborn man. Now you'll see for yourself," the investigator took the woman into the next room.

- Hello! Fakhriddin Karimovich, how are you?

- Come on in, come on in. How are you? - the chief stood up and greeted the guest. - Meet Ahad Batyrov.

Wazira's legs gave out with excitement. She looked at the heavily overgrown man with shaggy hair, long beard, and shabby clothes who sat at the end of the table. Batyrov looked at the woman reluctantly, then lowered his head.

-Batyrov, this woman is the wife of the very Bakhrom Safarovich whom you kidnapped," Fakhriddin Karimovich said loudly, approaching the man. - He has two small children at home. At least tell me for the sake of the children where you hid Bakhrom aka!

Batyrov was adamant. He was silent, staring blankly at one point.

Vazira stood for a while as if stumped. Then she slowly approached Batyrov and knelt before him: -Ahad aka, please find my husband! I will be your slave. I will pray for you all my life. Please find my Bahrom aka! I beg you. For the sake of my little children, please don't refuse, ...

Sanzharbek lifted a woman clinging to Batyrov's legs by her armpits.

-I know you're suffering as much as I am. But what is the fault of my children? I beg you, don't make them orphans! I know what it's like to be an orphan! Please, please find my husband! May God bless you! - Vazira was sobbing bitterly as she ran to Batyrov. She was held tightly by Sanzharbek's hands.

Batyrov raised his head and looked carefully at the woman lying at her feet, he wanted to say something but changed his mind.

Fakhriddin Karimovich watched Batyrov's emotions carefully: "Did his mother's moans touch his heart? I think he wanted to say something, but his pride or stubbornness prevented him from doing so. I think if we put a little more effort into it, he will speak. Or did this method of ours also have a negative effect on him? When Wazira said to him "What is the fault of my children?", perhaps he remembered his children and felt even more hatred for Bahromak and his family? No, no, that doesn't seem to be the case. But he did seem to soften a little. Perhaps it was Wazira's words that she knew firsthand what orphanhood was like. He had once been a kind father, a beloved husband, a good doctor who helped people out of pain! Has all the misfortunes and troubles that have fallen on his head made him completely heartless? Judging from his behavior, he knows where Bahrom aka is. But where? Couldn't stay at home because there is no way, people would notice. In the mountains or in a cave? Yes, maybe. Because he went to the mountains every day to gather herbs. No one suspected him of anything. He'd probably drop by Bahrom aka's house, drop off food. If he did not talk to him, Bakhrom aka would die of thirst and hunger! How long can a man endure without water and food? If Bahrom aka is alive, he is in danger. He could die of dehydration in as little as three or four days. Maybe we should let him go by putting a "tail" on him. But if he escapes?

If Batyrov doesn't say anything today, we must send a large group into the mountains and start searching. If we wait, we will lose time...".

Vazira, her eyes swollen with tears, continued to beg and plead with Batyrov to find her husband. She asked to spare her innocent children, not to make them suffer.

From time to time Batyrov stole silent glances at the woman. It was hard to understand what was going on in his mind. It was impossible to know whether he pitied the woman or hated her.

- Wazira opa, please stop begging him! This sub human's heart is petrified. It's useless to waste time, - Fakhriddin Karimovich stood up resolutely. - And he calls himself a doctor! Ugh at a representative of a great profession like you!

Batyrov flinched. This gesture did not go unnoticed by the investigators. Sanzharbek thought: "He is tormented by his conscience, so it is clear that he is hiding Bakhrom aka. The team leader was once again convinced that he was on the right track.

Vazira, huddled at Ahad's feet, continued to cry and beg. Sanzharbek pulled the woman's arm and tried to lift her up.

Finally, he forcibly pulled the woman away, sat her in a chair across from him, and handed her some water.

Releasing his legs from the woman's hands, Ahad tried to say something to Fakhriddin Karimovich standing in front of him, but the words stuck in his throat. He opened his mouth wide and sneezed loudly. Then he suddenly turned pale, staggered and fell face down on the floor. Sanzharbek deftly lifted him up. Fakhriddin Karimovich jumped out of the room and called the guys standing in the corridor for help. All of them lifted him up at once and ran to the car. They took the unconscious patient to the hospital. Just in case, Sanzharbek and another operative sat next to the patient.

When it was a short distance to the hospital, the sick man seemed to regain consciousness. He moved slowly and opened his eyes wide. He looked around and tried to stand up but could not. Then he looked at Sanzharbek as if he wanted to say something.

-Ahad aka, are you okay? Be patient, we'll be right back at the hospital. Everything will be fine," said the investigator, leaning toward the patient.

- Sanzhar aka, I think he wants to tell you something," said the operative riding in the front seat of the car, addressing the investigator.

-Akhadaka, do you want to say something? Speak, well, speak, -Sanzharbek raised the head of the sick man with his hand.

- He's alive! I f-go, f-go... there..." the patient fell silent. He froze with a frozen stare.

-Ahadaka! Tell me, is Bahrom aka alive? Where did you hide him?! - the investigator's repeated questions remained unanswered.

The doctors who immediately took Batyrov to the intensive care unit returned a long time later and reported that the patient had fallen into a coma due to a brain hemorrhage and it was unknown when he would regain consciousness.

Sanzharbek left the operative at the hospital and rushed to the prosecutor's office. Fakhriddin Karimovich, who was impatiently waiting for him, saw him and stood up:

-Well? Is he alive?

- Alive, but...

-What "but"? Can you talk faster?!

- He's slipped into a coma. According to doctors, it is not known when he will regain consciousness.

- Who? What a bummer! Too bad, now our job's gonna get even harder.

-Fakhriddin aka, on the way to the hospital he came to his senses, wanted to say something, but lost consciousness. He only managed to say: "He is alive".

- What, what did he say? He said, "he's alive"? Did you hear that clearly?

- Of course! I heard it with my own ears. Then I asked several times: "Where did you hide it?". But to no avail! He was in a coma. He didn't even hear my questions.

- So Bakhrom Safarovich is alive!

- I guess so, but the only person who knows where he is in a coma. I have no idea how we're going to find him.

- The important thing is that Bahrom aka is alive. We should rush to his aid. We don't know how many days Batyrov has left him food and water! If help doesn't reach him in time, he could die of dehydration and starvation. Every minute counts. I'll report to my superiors. Gather the boys immediately.

- That's right, -Sanzharbek flew out of the office.

Concerned by the events, Wazira waited impatiently:

-Sanjarbek, ukazhon, what happened? Is Batyrov alive?

- He's alive, he's alive, he's just in a coma. We'll have to wait for him to come to his senses. But on the way he said that Bahromaka is alive. Unfortunately, he didn't have time to say anything else, he fell into a coma.

- Bahrom aka... O Lord Almighty, thank you!" Wazira wiped her tears with trembling hands. She felt her whole body burning.

- Opajeon, everything's fine, why are you crying now?! You should be happy! The main thing is that what we all feared didn't happen. Now all that's left is to find my brother. Sanjarbek took Vazira under his arm and sat her on a chair in the corridor.

-Sanjarbek, if Batyrov is in a coma, will we be able to find Bahromak? - Vazira looked at the investigator with pleading eyes.

- Trust us. Batyrov is probably holding him where he lived. That's why we're sending a large search party into the mountains and the village. If necessary, we'll search every hut, every ravine, every rock. In addition to the operatives, we'll involve the villagers in the case.

Seeing the determination in the investigator's eyes and words, the woman calmed down a little, a spark of hope flared in her heart.

- Sanjarbek, can I come with you on the search?

- No, first, the village is far away, it could get messy. Secondly, the search is likely to take longer. You'd better wait here. We'll be in touch," Sanzharbek deliberately denied her, as the woman's condition could deteriorate in the mountains.

- Please, Sanjarbek, take me away, I won't interfere in any way," Vazira began to beg.

-Opajon, I'm saying this for your benefit. There aren't even sleeping facilities. And then anything can happen. Come on, you'd better wait here.

- But... well, okay, whatever you say," Vazira couldn't contradict the investigators this time.

- I'm just worried about one thing. If the search is prolonged. Bakhrom aka's life will be in danger. Ah, if only Batyrov would come to his senses sooner!

- I wish! But we can't wait for him to wake up! Please, Ukajon, start the search as soon as possible. Every minute counts. If I lose Bahrom aka when my hand is left to reach him, I will never forgive myself," Wazira said, barely holding back tears.

- God willing, everything will be fine! As long as we have such an assistant as you, we will definitely find Bakhrom aka. We will find him alive and unharmed," smiled Sanzharbek.

- Let it be so! Amen! - the woman, inspired by the investigator's kind words, opened her palms for prayer...

The "headquarters", located in Nurali's grandfather's modest hut, was full of people. Fakhriddin Karimovich, who had just returned from the mountains, was worried that the two-day search had yielded no results, and scratched the back of his head: "God, how can we go on? Are we on the wrong track again? Where did that damned man hide him? According to the villagers, he spent most of his time in the mountains. Everyone thought he was "gathering herbs". No one suspected him. No one saw him go to other villages or towns. He took clients home. He lived on the modest remuneration his patients gave him. He was not close to anyone. He didn't tell anyone about himself, about his past... But how did he manage to keep a living man prisoner in secret?! You have to feed him, feed him, keep him alive if he's not feeling well. So he must have kept his prisoner somewhere nearby. Maybe he dug a cave in the basement under his house and used a secret passage? But the guys checked every corner of the basement! There were no suspicious footprints. Where could he have hidden it? He's heard there are a lot of natural caves in the mountains. What if he found one! No, no, a natural cave could have been spotted by others. What if he dug a cave on some hill or mountainside and made the entrance unnoticeable! It's not easy to find such a place. Maybe call in the help of metal detectors or miners? In any case, they have many ways to find objects underground. We must hurry. It's been three days since we captured Batyrov. How fast time flies. We're running out of time. I just wish Batyrov would wake up, or is he already awake? The guys are on duty with him day and night. They'd let us know immediately if he regained consciousness. If Batyrov doesn't die before he regains consciousness! Then we're back to a dead end! Oh, God, when will all this end? It's been over a month since I've been home and seen the kids. But thank goodness I have a cell phone. I talk to them almost every day! I have never gone on such a long business trip before...".

- Fakhriddin Karimovich, all the groups have returned. But... they found almost nothing," Sanzharbek, greatly embarrassed, dared to distract the chief from his thoughts.

- Anybody back?

- All of them.

- You used the word "almost", does that mean there is something?

- You could say that. The fourth group came across a cave in the mountains. The guys managed to get inside for a while. But since it was late, they didn't dare to go all the way in. Perhaps there is a hole in the back of this cave that leads to the other side. The shepherds there said that they had seen the healer Salai near the cave a couple of times.

- This is valuable information! We need to go to that cave right now.

-Fahriddinaka, maybe in the morning. entering the cave in the dark....

- Tomorrow could be late. Every minute counts. Take a few of the men. We need to get funds to light the cave.

- You think Dr. Salai hid his prisoner in this cave? But they say it's too far away.

- Shepherds are sensitive people. It's not for nothing that they noticed the doctor hanging around. They didn't say that for nothing. You have half an hour. Get what you need and then we'll go.

- Yes, -Sanzharbek, realizing that the boss will not change his mind, began to perform the task ...

After a long journey in the darkness, a beautiful city came into view. There were various flowers, trees with their branches touching the ground because of the abundance of fruits, and clear water gurgling in full-flowing rivers. Eyes shone from such beauty. "What happened, have I gone to heaven, are these the gardens of paradise?" he thought. From afar, there were people walking, all dressed in white. "These must be angels."

-Ahad aka, Ahad aka, we are here! -he heard his wife Nurkhon's voice clearly from the crowd. He ran in the direction of the sound and was not mistaken. Nurkhon was leading her two sons Zhasurbek and Ulmasjon by hand through the flower garden.

- Daddy, Daddy! We missed you! Where have you been? Come quickly! - the sons shouted, interrupting each other.

- I have missed you very much, my sweet darlings. How big you are now, -Ahad ran to his children.

-Ahad aka, stop. You must still live," Nurkhon shouted in despair.

Ahad paused for a moment. Then he stepped forward again.

-Ahad aka, for the sake of our children you must live. Please come back," the woman pleaded.

- What's the point of me living without you? I want to be where you are! I would have come to you early. But I had a little business here. I had to settle accounts with someone here. I've finished my business. So now I've come back to you. Zhasurbek, my boy! Ulmasjon, my sweetie! Here I came to you, -Ahad walked resolutely towards his family.

-Ahad aka, go back. You didn't get to live in the ghost world. Your life has been a living hell. Start your life again," Nurkhon continued to plead.

- What's wrong, wife? Did you find someone else here? So, you don't want me to come?

- Are you jealous of me here, too?

- How can you leave such a beautiful woman alone?

- You're such a joker!

When the distance between them was four or five paces, someone from behind shouted: "Ahajon, stop!".

- Mom, Dad, are you here, too?

- Yes, son, we are all together. But you must go back," said his father Batyr aka.

- Dad, what are you talking about? I've been missing you and the children. I came to see you. I have no one there.

- No, son, you have to go back. You left one man at a crossroads! He needs your help.

- Mom, that man is being punished for his sin. I had nothing to do with him. I did my job.

- Don't say that, son! Yes, this man made a mistake, but he was punished for it. This is too much!

- Why would it be too much? His mistake put me in jail, I lost my wife, my kids, everything I had. Why are you taking his side, mom? -Ahad's whole body trembled.

- No, son, don't say that! Everything happens by the will of Allah. The guy's only mistake was that as a prosecutor he was inattentive to his job! But you can see that he did it with an open mind," the mother came closer to her son.

- Yes, I didn't do it on purpose. But the investigator and the judge around him knew that I was innocent! Knowing my innocence, they put me in jail!

- They received punishment for their crimes. But the man you are holding captive does not deserve such punishment. You didn't have the guts to kill him," the mother continued, seeing the change in her son's face. - He has children like yours, and a beautiful companion. At least think of them. Have pity on them, don't take sin on your soul!

- What am I gonna do, Mom? My head is spinning.

- Come back, son, come back! Another family's fate hangs in the balance. They can't do it without you. Come back, son.

The nurse who came up to get the IV saw the patient "come to life" and stared at him.

The patient looked around and asked the nurse:

- I... Where am I...?

- You're in a hospital. Calm down. You can't worry!

- What... happened to me? Where are they. my children... -Ahad raised his head, trying to stand up.

- Get down, get down! I'll call the doctor now! - The nurse took the patient by the shoulders, laid him down and hurriedly went to fetch the doctor on duty. Lying down and looking at the ceiling, Ahad realized that his memory was slowly returning. He wanted to raise his left hand to wipe the sweat from his face. But his hand did not move.

- Are you awake? Oh, thank God! -A doctor ran into the room and sat down on a chair next to the patient and started to measure his blood pressure.

- My left side doesn't work, - the patient moaned.

- It's all right. The main thing is that the danger is over. We'll treat the rest gradually. You're a doctor yourself. You're out of the coma. There could be some complications.

- How many days was I in a coma? - The patient opened his eyes wide and stared at the officer on duty.

- Two days. Luckily, you woke up quickly! You know, some people stay in comas for years.

- I need an investigator, Fakhriddin Karimovich or Sanzhar...

- They'll come. I can't let anyone in yet. You can't worry at all.

- Okay, but one man's life is in danger. Today is day four. He could die of dehydration.

- What do you mean? Who do you mean? Think of yourself! It's late tonight. We'll call them tomorrow morning. There are two policemen at the door.

- Tell them to call the investigator. I have something to tell him," Batyrov said, pleading with the doctor.

- Ahad aka, we, doctor, respect you very much. We have heard about you and admire your fortitude. Please calm down. I'll tell them. In the meantime, come to your senses.

The patient nodded his head in agreement.

The doctor on duty, the nurse and the doctors who entered the room after them examined the patient, performed some procedures and, noticing that he was calm, left one by one. Only the nurse remained in the room.

- Daughter, are there policemen at the door?

- Yeah, they're sitting outside the door.

- Daughter, get one of them, I need to tell them something.

- No, you heard, the doctors have forbidden you to socialize with others," the nurse said as she gathered her instruments.

- Daughter, honey, this is very important. It's a matter of life and death. I'll say one word to them and that's it," the sick man begged.

- Okay, I'll just give you a minute. If the doctors find out, I'm in trouble.

- All right! Hand me that paper and pen over there.

The nurse handed the patient a notebook and pen lying on the bedside table, left the room and led one of the policemen behind her.

Ahad bent a little on the bed, wrote something on a piece of paper, folded it in half and held it out to the policeman:

- Son, please give this letter to Fakhriddin Karimovich or his assistant in the prosecutor's office! They need it. We're talking about the life of a member of the prosecutor's office. And the sooner you deliver the note to them, the better. Every minute counts.

- Okay, but only in half an hour we have a shift change. I can only go to the prosecutor's office after I've been replaced," said the policeman, concerned that he was breaking the rules.

- Thank you. I'd like the note to reach them by morning.

The policeman took the note and walked out without saying a word.

Ahad thanked the nurse.

- You're welcome, Uncle. Everyone's talking about you. You happen to be a very powerful surgeon. How did you end up in this situation? - the nurse looked at the patient with a kind of pity.

- Daughter, what is there to say? It's a very long story," Ahad sighed deeply.

- All right, rest up. Get well, and then, if you want to, you can tell me all about it. Here, drink this medicine," - the nurse handed me a bowl of water.

- It's a deal, - Ahad drank the medicine and closed his eyes:

"What did I see just now? Is this a dream or ... a delusion? - Ahad tried to gather his thoughts. - I thought the nurse said I was in a coma. Did two days really go by so fast? I felt like I'd been to the netherworld. I could clearly see my children, my wife, my parents, I could talk to them. But I couldn't go near them. My mom brought me back! Eh, moms, moms, even in this situation they think of the child! Mom wanted me to live. She asked that I spare the prosecutor because he got his punishment. She told me to do it for his kids. How does she know everything? Oh, mommy, mommy!".

Ahad could not sleep; he was transported in his thoughts to the past days....

Nurkhon, still holding out hope for her husband's acquittal, wrote a complaint to higher authorities with a request to restore justice. But from everywhere she received the same answer: "Your husband's guilt is confirmed by the materials of criminal cases". She left her children with neighbors and went to visit her husband in prison.

On the one hand Ahad lamented that he had been unjustly imprisoned, but on the other hand, as if his suffering were not enough, he worried about his wife and children, whom they had begged from Allah, and the fact that he could do nothing to help them when they were in difficulty. He relentlessly appealed to the Supreme Court, the prosecutor's office and other instances, complaining about his unjust imprisonment, hoping that someone would pay attention to his complaint.

Years passed. To avoid showing the suffering that Nurkhon experienced with her children, she tried to appear confident at meetings with her husband: "Don't think about us. We are fine. Take care of yourselves. You are not guilty of anything. God willing, you'll be acquitted soon!" - she tried to encourage and reassure her husband.

Over time, it was hard to recognize Ahad as a once cheerful and successful man; he was exhausted and his complexion had changed. But during short meetings with his wife, he behaved confidently, joked and urged Nurkhon to be patient, take care of the children, sell the house and buy a smaller apartment if necessary, and spend the proceeds on the children so that they would not need anything.

He tried to convince his wife that all this hardship and suffering would soon be over.

Unfortunately, these were minor difficulties compared to the misfortune that befell the family afterward. Even the mountains might not have been able to withstand such a blow. The tears of grief that later befell this family would have melted even the rocks.....

At her husband's request, Nurkhon decided to bring her children to the next daily meeting. She hoped that seeing her children would calm her husband down a little and comfort his heart. On the other hand, she wanted to show her father and make the children happy, who were just learning to talk and were chattering away. But...

The car they were in had an accident on the road. First Nurkhon, then one by one Zhasurbek and Ulmasjon left this world forever. Although the warden had been working in this place for many years and had seen everything, in this case he did not know how to inform the prisoner Batyrov about this terrible news. For three nights he thought about it and finally decided to tell it as it was. Even a heart of steel could not withstand the grief that fell upon the head of a man unjustly condemned, who had already suffered slander when he learned of the death of his wife and children, whom he had begged from God.

The prison governor could not contain himself and cried when the prisoner, who was different from others in his behavior and who had become a very close person to him, sobbed. He brought the medical staff to their feet, instructed them to give the prisoner sedatives and perform various procedures.

This tragedy completely deprived Ahad of the will to live. Looking at one point, he lay there for a long time without leaving his cell. Fate had turned such a wonderful and talented man into an outcast. There was no one left in the prison who would not pity and sympathize with him...

When Fakhriddin Karimovich and the ten men with him approached the mountain cave, it was about twelve o'clock at night. Although it was hot below, the mountains felt cool. After a five-minute rest, they lit torches. The shepherds were the first to make their way to the cave. They were followed by the group leader. After 20-25 steps into the cave, the damp and cold air made them shiver. Thankfully, on the advice of the shepherds, everyone dressed warmly. As they went deeper into the cave, it became harder and harder to breathe. The light of the torches had also faded, making it impossible for them to move forward quickly.

Fakhriddin Karimovich stopped from time to time and looked around carefully, tapping the walls with his hands, checking for holes or cracks. And although they reached the stop, they did not notice anything suspicious. The lack of oxygen and humidity caused some of the group to turn back. Five or six operatives reached the end of the cave. The shepherds began to search carefully for the secret door. Despite his fatigue, Fakhriddin Karimovich scrutinized the rocky stones and walls of the cave, from where water was dripping. But there was no sign of any trace, secret passage or hole.

- Let's go back. I don't think anyone's set foot in this place in a long time," the chief finally allowed me to step back.

- You're right. A man who has traveled this road once is not likely to travel it next time," one of the operatives said in a trembling voice.

- There don't seem to be any holes. Better go back," said one of the shepherds, raising the torch high in his hand.

The group turned back. As they approached the exit of the cave, the fresh air outside hit them in the face, bringing with it an invigorating strength and peace. Everyone literally ran outside with their last strength. And only Fakhriddin Karimovich, raising the torch in his hand, approached the wall first from the right, then from the left and scrutinized them. Seeing him, one of the shepherds went back. They began to look for the secret passage together.

"It is quite difficult to get in and out of the cave, but perhaps Batyrov made a hole near the entrance to the cave. If you cover the entrance with stones, it's hard to find," the investigator thought. But there was no sign of a crack or hole in the surface of the stones, which were lying in disorder. They went outside, sat down on the grass and rested for a while. Some even managed to take a nap sitting on the ground. Then they set off by moonlight and reached the village at dawn.

A policeman was waiting for the investigators at the "headquarters". FakhriddinKarimovich immediately summoned him to his office.

- Hello, Comrade Chief! Permission to report! - the militiaman appealed according to the rule.

- Permission granted. What's the matter?

- The prosecutor's office sent me. Since there is no telephone service here, I came to inform you personally that Batyrov is awake.

- Really? That's good news! When did he regain consciousness?

- Last night! He asked me to give you this piece of paper," the policeman took a piece of paper out of his pocket and handed it to the investigator.

The investigator hastily unfolded the paper folded several times and glanced at the entry: "The path in the tandoor. The key is in the swallow's nest. His life is in danger, hurry!".

Having read the note, FakhriddinKarimovich turned very pale, as if he had found gold, and ran out to the porch on the left side of the yard. The others involuntarily followed him.

In a corner of the shed, covered with years of cobwebs and soot, stood a large and a small oven, and in the middle a tandoor. The group leader walked over to the tandoor, bent down and stuck his head into it.

-Sanzharbek, call one of the more nimble boys to climb into the stove and pull out the dry branches from inside! - Fakhriddin Karimovich shouted to the bewildered pupil who, like the others, could not understand what was going on.

Thinking that there must be something hidden inside the furnace, Sanzharbek brought one of the local boys standing outside without asking the chief any unnecessary questions.

- What's your name? - The chief asked the young man.
-Narzilla...
- Have you ever gone down to the tandoor?
- Yeah, but, uh.
-Narzilla Zhon, hurry, get into the oven and free him from the branches!

The young man jumped into the oven, bent down and started throwing the kindling out of it. Although the neck of the tandoor could hardly fit a man, the bottom of it was quite wide. After thoroughly cleaning its bottom, the round iron lid in its center became clearly visible.

-Narzillazhon, that's it, thank you, now come out," said Fakhriddin Karimovich, looking carefully at the bottom of the furnace. Then ordered Sanzharbek:

- We have to break the tandoor!

On Sanzharbek's order, several boys began to break the tandyr and soon demolished the old oven.

The chief quickly lifted the iron lid from the bottom of the furnace with a hoe. A well-like hole was revealed. Everyone ran up to see what was inside. And it was very dark inside. You couldn't see anything. Someone turned on a flashlight and pointed it at the bottom of the well. A wooden stepladder appeared at the bottom.

Fakhriddin Karimovich began to descend into the well by the light of the lantern. He put his foot on the stepladder and began to lower himself down. Having landed, he turned the lantern around. A long cave-like corridor, as tall as a man, appeared on the right. Sanzharbek and two other operatives also went down into the hole.

As he walked down the corridor, Fakhriddin Karimovich raised the lantern higher. At that moment, the light bulb hanging on the wall in the middle of the corridor shone.

- Yes, well, there's even current here! - said someone surprised.

- Where's the on-off switch?

- Here it is," said one of the men standing at the entrance to the well. He stepped onto a stepladder, reached up, and turned on the light. The basement filled with light, revealing a makeshift wooden cabinet in the corner.

The lower shelves were closed, the upper ones filled with various small tools. Old clothes hung on the two side walls. Various household items were scattered underfoot.

Fakhriddin Karimovich looked around and stopped his gaze on the closet. Something seemed to occur to him, and he walked over to it and opened the lower left door.

- Take these things! The secret passage should be here," he said, showing the inside of the closet to those around him. One of the employees bent down and quickly emptied the cupboard. Sanzharbek pointed a flashlight into the closet but saw nothing suspicious.

Now the chief opened the right side of the closet.

- Make room here, too!

The boys quickly removed the things that were in the closet. A thick iron door replaced the back of the closet.

- Wow! I think we've found the answer! - Sanzharbek could not hide his surprise.

Fakhriddin Karimovich bent down and pushed the iron door as hard as he could. It was locked.

-Sanjarbek, quickly upstairs, there should be a swallow's nest on the porch. The key is hidden there. Hurry up! - ordered the team leader, remembering the scraps of the text of the note.

Sanzharbek literally flew outside and saw an old swallow's nest on top of the porch.

He brought a stepladder from the courtyard, put it against the wall, and climbed up. When he reached the top, he reached down, felt the inside with his fingers, and found a thick key with jagged prongs.

Ignoring his coworkers' questions of "Is everything okay?", "Did you find anything?", "Is he alive?", "What's the matter?", he skirted into the well as quickly as he came out.

Fakhriddin Karimovich took the key from Sanzharbek, stuck his head into the closet, felt it by the light of the lantern, opened the lock and pushed the door open. The iron door opened with a heavy creak. The cave was pitch black.

The investigator pointed his flashlight inside but saw nothing but walls. So he bent down and went inside. It was a cave that could barely fit two people. So, he bent his head and walked down the corridor. Sanjarbek followed him. After walking five or six steps, they came upon a wooden door, from the crack of which a dim light could be seen. Fakhriddin Karimovich cautiously opened the door and, seeing the sight inside, froze like a stumbling block. Sanzharbek, who came up behind him, almost fainted.

The two of them rushed inside.

- There's Bakhrom Safarovich, call the guys for help! He seems to be unconscious," said the chief, pointing at the man lying at the back of the cellar. - Call the guys!

Fakhriddin Karimovich tried to approach the place where the man was lying but ran into the thick bars of the fence. He fumbled with the grating and looked for an entrance. But there was no door visible anywhere.

- Whatever happens, let him be alive! - Sanzharbek's voice trembled with excitement and, stepping back a little, he called out to the guys waiting outside who had not yet realized what was going on inside. The operatives entered the room one by one and were shocked by what they saw.

Fakhriddin Karimovich, clutching at the bars, shouted in the direction where the man lay:

-Bakhrom aka, Bakhrom aka, can you hear me? Bakhrom Safarovich, Bakhrom Safarovich!" he continued to shout.

The man lying there, hearing the human voice, seemed to move. Looking at Sanzharbek, who was standing next to him, Fakhriddin Karimovich exhaled:

- Thank God, it looks like he's alive.

- Yes, I think he moved too," Sanzharbek said, keeping his eyes on the man lying there.

-Sanjarbek, there doesn't seem to be a door here. Look, the room is surrounded on four sides by iron bars. It's a real bunker. Quickly go upstairs and find a metal cutter. Go!

- Got it," Sanzharbek bent over and stepped out.

Fakhriddin Karimovich tried several times to talk to the man lying in the corner. But the man did not make a sound. "It's been about a week since Batyrov was detained. The poor man must have weakened from dehydration and hunger. In any case, we must hurry. Every minute counts!" he thought.

The others watched the situation in the "bunker" from behind the bars. Here were almost all the conditions for living. A thick felt carpet was laid on the ground, with a few sheepskins scattered on it. At one end there was a small old TV and radio Beacon, a bed for one person and neatly folded miscellaneous clothes. In the center is a colorless dastarkhan, on it a teapot, a bowl, a plate, a cup and other utensils.

On a wooden crate in the corner were many books, newspapers and magazines. On one wall of the room was an inserted door. Many people thought that this door must lead to the toilet.

Soon Sanzharbek brought two local boys.

With a tool in their hands, they began to cut the grating where the investigator had indicated. Very quickly, a hole was formed in which a man could fit. Sanzharbek was the first to enter inside, ran up and put his hand on the man's neck:

-Fakhriddin Karimovich, thank God he is alive! - he said. Then he gently turned his head upwards. Then most of the operatives watching from behind the bars were convinced that this man was indeed Bakhrom Safarovich. At the chief's gesture, two more operatives climbed over the gap.

Passing from hand to hand, the operatives carefully carried the sick man outside. Someone dripped water into his mouth. But the patient was still unconscious and felt nothing. The ambulance crew that arrived at that moment immediately gave the patient first aid and took him to the hospital under the care of two operatives.

- Fakhriddin Karimovich, come and have something to eat. You haven't eaten anything since yesterday," said Sanzharbek, holding out to him a piece of hot tandyr flatbread brought by his neighbors.

- All right, come on. I just realized I'm hungry now," the chief took the bread in his hands and sighed with relief.

- Poor Bakhrom Safarovich, I can imagine how he suffered here! It is impossible to believe that he has lived in such conditions for so many years," said Sanzharbek, handing the tea to the chief. - The main thing is for him to recover and return to his family!

- You-you-zyz-do-rove! Batyrov supplied him with the necessary food and water from time to time. I think Bakhrom aka found himself in this position after Batyrov's capture. Seven days have done their job. The main thing is that all danger is now over.

- Yes, by the way, I didn't even have time to ask in my haste, from whom did the policeman who came this morning bring the note? Did anyone know the secret?

- Yes, I didn't tell you, Batyrov woke up and sent me a note indicating where he had hidden Bakhrom Safarovich. Here is this note," the chief took a leaf out of his pocket and handed it to Sanzharbek.

- His conscience must have kicked in! If he hadn't pointed it out himself, we'd have had trouble finding it.

- Yes, fortunately, Batyrov woke up in time. Otherwise, we wouldn't have had time to save Bakhrom Safarovich, -Fakhriddin Karimovich put the drinking bowl on top of the low earthen wall and went to the porch. He instructed Sanzharbek to inspect the scene of the event and properly formalize other procedural actions stipulated by law, then he got into the car and left for the city...

Ahad, lying on his bed and looking at the ceiling, summarized the journey he had made. He was desperate: *"Oh God, take my soul, don't torture me so much! After all, I already died the day my family died! What is the point of living!!!"*.

And he remembered everything. How difficult it had been during his first days behind bars, and how it became easier afterwards, as he began to think about a plan to escape from prison. For this, first of all, it was necessary to become a disciplined prisoner, to earn the trust of others and the prison administration. In this he could be helped by his noble profession as a doctor. With his magic fingers he treated first the prisoners, then the guards, providing them with medical care. Rumors began to spread in the prison that Batyrov was a talented doctor. His advice and the medicines he recommended helped people recover quickly. This made him famous as a skillful doctor and brought him respect among others.

Gradually, prison officials began to trust Batyrov more than the doctors in the sanitary unit when they themselves were sick and treated on his advice. His diagnosis was often correct, which increased the number of his patients.

Despite his growing reputation as an experienced doctor, Ahad was modest and unassuming, friendly, obeyed the rules of the prison without question, and tried to earn the trust of prisoners and warders alike. He behaved as if he had forgotten his past and the suffering he had endured. At night, when no one saw, he would stare at the picture of his wife and children for hours, crying silently, letting go of his pain. The situation came to the point that the prison director Salim Sattorovich trusted Ahad and asked him to help cure his daughter Zarina, who was bedridden as a child because of a car accident. Although her father had shown Zarina to various doctors over the years, their treatment was of no avail. Concerned about the fate of his only daughter, her father concluded that only Batyrov could help her.

For this reason, although it was against prison rules, he had to bring his daughter to his office a couple of times and show her to Batyrov. The actions of the imprisoned doctor began to produce positive results. But in order for the girl to fully get back on her feet, lengthy procedures were required. The father, hoping for his daughter's recovery and risking his official position, decided to smuggle Ahad out of prison from time to time and continue treatment at home. Desperate Zarina had hope for recovery and a desire to live. Seeing the change in his daughter, the father rejoiced. His actions were unlawful, and he realized that if this act was uncovered, he could not only be dismissed from his position but also prosecuted. However, he was able to convince himself that there was no other way to treat his child. At first Batyrov traveled to the house of the prison director accompanied by a member of the colony staff, but later the escort was no longer needed, as he managed to gain everyone's trust.

His serious approach to every case, his ability to keep his word, his unquestioning obedience to prison regulations, his leaving the prison at the appointed time and returning on time, and his hope to serve his sentence early, no longer bothered the warden. One spring afternoon, Ahad asked the warden:

- Salim Sattorovich, if you give me a car, I will go to the mountains to collect medicinal herbs. You can see the changes in Zarina for yourself. But for her to recover completely, in addition to the usual medicines and exercises, some herbs are also needed.

- If you write down the names of the herbs, we can bring them in," the chief objected cautiously.

- No, they are hard to distinguish by name. A person who does not know or have not seen any of these may not be up to the task. If you don't want to, you don't have to, although the treatment may take longer.

- All right, all right, tomorrow morning I'll give you my car. It's more relaxing that way. Which mountains do you want to go to?

- Towards Bekabad. I've picked herbs there before. Familiar places.

- All right, get ready for tomorrow morning. You need an assistant?

- You have a driver. What's with the extra eyes?

- You're right," the boss smiled, satisfied with his answer. - The most important thing for me is that you get my daughter back on her feet.

Early in the morning, Ahad drove to Bekabad in the prison director's official car. In the back seat of the car, Ahad sat with his eyes closed, pretending to sleep. Finally, he was overjoyed that his plans that he had made earlier had begun to gradually materialize. He mentally went over the information he had gathered in prison about the investigator Ikram Bozorov: "He quit his job because of mistakes he made. So he's at home. I know the street, the address. He has a new Zhiguli car. If he gets into a car accident, no one will suspect anything. An accident! He dies and that's it! I have to have an ironclad alibi so I can take revenge on the others. Now I'm in jail, no one can suspect me of Bozorov's car crash!

"The Zhiguli drove swiftly past, turned towards a familiar gate and stopped. A fat man of about 50-55 years old got out of the car and entered the house with a springy gait. Ahad recognized him at once. It was the same Ikram Bozorov.

Ahad got out of the car carefully so as not to wake the snoring driver, who had to wake up early this morning. There was no one in the street. Ahad waited under the cover of a tree so as not to arouse the suspicion of the cars that occasionally drove by, kicking up puffs of dust as they went by. Then, after waiting for the street to quiet down, he headed for Bozorov's car. He peered into the yard through the ajar gate. No one could be seen. A man's voice came from inside: "You're still not ready? It will be dark before we reach Tashkent! Hurry up!". Then he shouted again: "Pass me the phone, I'll warn the matchmakers that we're late." "So, he's going to Tashkent! Great! Just in time!

I have to make it before he finishes talking on the phone!", Ahad thought. He looked around. Making sure no one was around, he took a wrench out of his pocket, loosened the bolts holding the front wheels of the car slightly, and turned back in a hurry. He told the driver that he had finished his work, talked to his friend, and asked him to drive toward the mountains.

When they reached the foot of the mountain, Ahad got out of the car, went up the hill to gather herbs, and returned an hour later with a sack full of herbs. They drove back. As the car passed through Bekabad and headed for Tashkent, Ahad looked out the window with excitement

Ahad looked in the direction the driver pointed and immediately recognized the investigator's car standing on the side of the road. Although the license plate number was hard to read, Ahad had no doubt that the car belonged to Ikram Bozorov. The passenger car hit the tractor on the driver's side.

Therefore, meticulous preparations were made for the "operation". After the internal and external preparations were completed, Ahad left the prison through a secret passage at dawn on the appointed day.

In the city of Bekabad he was met by a man of Kara Namaz nicknamed "Kassob", i.e. "The Butcher". He took him to some apartment, fed him and created conditions for rest. Ahad wasted no time in injecting the poison he had brought with him into each bottle of cognac with a syringe.

The poisonous killer under the "mask" of "Samarkand" cognac was ready. All that remained was to give it to the man sentenced to death.

Ahad had practically all the information concerning the subject of the next revenge - **the** unscrupulous judge Zakir Shokirov. His address, marital status and interests were known to Ahad inside and out. The judge's habit of drinking only Samarkand cognac was considered the main factor in the development of the revenge plan. All that remained was to get him to the judge. After some thought, Ahad came to the idea that a case of cognac should be sent to Shakirov's house through the Butcher. Everything clearly worked, the poisoned cognac was delivered to the judge's wife, who was at home.

- Okay, thank you so much for everything! I'll say namaz aka you've been a great help.

-Say hi to the boss for us. He's helped me many times. God bless him! - said the Butcher, saying goodbye.

And this plan of his was also realized...

Months and years passed. Exactly six years later, Ahad served his court-ordered sentence early and was released....

Fakhriddin Karimovich, who had not slept for twenty-four hours, involuntarily closed his eyes as soon as he got into the car and dozed off. He woke up from the shaking of the car on the uneven stony road and began to mentally draw up a plan of today's work: "First of all, we must go to the prosecutor's office and report to the management that Bakhrom Safarovich had been found alive. Then I must go to the hospital and find out first about the state of health of Bakhrom Safarovitch and then of Ahad Batyrov. If the doctors allow it, I will have to interrogate them personally. Tashmurad Sobirov can also be entrusted to Sanzharbek. If we don't find Ozoda's killer, our efforts will be in vain. After all, this is where the chain of grandiose crimes began! In all his work as an investigator, he has never investigated such a complex case. It's like a movie! Batyrov is a disaster! He went to any lengths to get revenge! But he's understandable.

When Batyrov was unjustly imprisoned, an inexcusable mistake was made that led to the deaths of so many families and people! Bakhrom Safarovich, Ikram Bozorov, Zakir Shokirov made an unforgivable mistake as prosecutor, investigator and judge. And this terrible mistake cost them and their families dearly. They paid for their sin with life and blood. Could it have been avoided? Of course.

After everyone had left, Batyrov reached out, took two sheets of paper from the nightstand next to him and handed them to the investigator:

- Here, I wrote it. But I didn't have time to write it all down. After all, I'm sick. I'm scared!

- Death?

- No, I died long ago, the day my children and my wife died. All that is left of me is my body," Ahad sighed deeply.

- I'm sorry to remind you of that," the investigator was embarrassed.

- No need to apologize, you're doing your job. I'm glad you found a chance to talk to me. I was dying of boredom. They say if you share the pain that's eating you, it makes you feel a little better. You should know everything. I was afraid I'd die without telling the truth. Luckily, I woke up in time. I heard you saved Bahrom! I was glad too! I take full responsibility for my crimes. But I have no regrets. Whatever I did, I did it to avenge my family," Batyrov handed the investigator the papers he held in his hands.

After running his eyes over the paper, the investigator shook his head two or three times, as if admiring the author, and his face seemed to alternate emotions reflecting feelings of surprise, pity, and hatred.

- I have nothing but admiration for you. It is unbelievable that a simple doctor could do so much while in prison! - said Fakhriddin Karimovich.

- This was not done by a simple doctor, but by a devastated man who was a victim of injustice, who had been robbed of everything he needed for human happiness, who burned with one desire for revenge!

- Ahad aka," the investigator deliberately addressed his interlocutor with a respectful "aka" to find his way to the man's heart, "I understand everything. I sympathize with you. But our time is limited. Here you wrote everything that happened to you before you were released from prison. And beyond that.

- Yes, let us continue from here," Ahad sighed and began his story. - I came out of jail and went to my father's house in Dombrabad. But I could not live there. I could not look at my children's clothes and toys in peace. It was as if the voices of my sons were coming from every corner, and I saw the ghost of my wife. I almost lost my mind again. I had two more men to avenge. One of them was the scoundrel Tashmurad Sobirovich, who pushed me into the abyss, and the other was the prosecutor Bakhrom Safarov, who authorized my arrest. I had no right to go mad or die until I had avenged them.

When I realized that I could not stay at home for a day, I went to my uncle's house. I spent one night at his place and sold my house to one of the neighbors for half price. I got a good amount of money for the house. I needed the money to carry out my subsequent plans. I took only photo albums and documents from the house, put the money in my backpack and left for Bekabad. Since it was convenient for me to carry out my plan from there.

For a while I lived with my doctor friend Zafar. Then I rented a house, got a job at the ambulance service, working on a rotational basis - every other day. In addition, I worked part-time at the morgue. It was necessary for the realization of my plan.

At first I wanted to settle accounts with Tashmurad Sobirov, the head doctor of the hospital where I worked. But I was not sure enough about his guilt. Being a victim of injustice, I was afraid of making an unfair decision myself, of making a mistake. Of course I did not kill Ozoda, but I did not know who did. At that time, there were rumors in town that the head doctor had a hand in these cases. I thought, "If I judge only on the basis of these rumors, how will I be different from the investigator and the judge who sentenced me?" I decided to verify these rumors, but it was impossible.

I was afraid that if they noticed my interest in this case, my secret would be revealed and the plan would fail halfway through. So I had to have a man-to-man talk with Tashmurod Sobirovich. I made him swear an oath. He swore on the Koran that he really disliked me, that he wanted to blame Ozoda's pregnancy on me and thus get rid of both her and me, but that he had not killed her. I did not believe his words. Then he showed me a plane ticket and a sanatorium card confirming that he was vacationing in Issyk-Kul during the days when Ozoda was killed. After that I was forced to believe him.

- Did you see these documents with your own eyes or did you just believe what he said? - the investigator tried to clarify.

- I not only saw but also checked the authenticity of the tickets through Tashkent airport. It turned out to be true. After that, I left him alone. I did not manage to find out who killed Ozoda. But still, I did not give up my intention to find this person and avenge everything. Only that work had to be postponed. Then I decided to concentrate on Bakhrom Safarov, who held a high position in Tashkent. He was a prosecutor at that time. A lot depended on him. But he considered my case indifferently. He did not evaluate the actions of the investigator, who conducted the investigation one-sidedly, only towards the prosecution. When I was taken to him to get an authorization for arrest, I swore to him by my children that I had not killed Ozoda, begged him to restore justice. He listened to everything I said, thought for a while. I could see from his face that he was hesitating. At that moment, I had confidence in him. He was different from the representatives of this sphere. It seemed to me that he was a kind and sincere man. But he still authorized the arrest. After that, I could only hope for an investigation. I was sure that the real murderer would be caught, that my innocence would be proved...

Batyrov was silent for a while. Fakhriddin Karimovich poured him water again. Having quenched his thirst, he continued his story:

- Investigator Ikrom Bozorov was an uneducated, stupid and evil man. He didn't even want to hear me. I asked him several times for permission to talk to the prosecutor. Under various pretexts he did not allow me to meet with the prosecutor. After that, I hoped that the prosecutor would make a fair decision in confirming the indictment, remember my words and call me to him. Unfortunately, this did not happen. Bakhrom Safarov was moving to a high position at that time. He signed without reading the indictment. The investigator himself told me about it, as if mocking me. I surrendered to fate and ended up in prison. But I never doubted for a second that justice would prevail. I did not stop writing complaints to all the authorities, hoping that one day someone would hear my pain. But it all turned out to be in vain... My life was turned upside down....

Batyrov was silent, wiping away his tears with a towel. The investigator deliberately went outside and lit a cigarette to let him cry. Then he went back inside and sat down in front of Ahad, who had calmed down:

- Aren't you tired? Can we continue our conversation?

- It's okay. If you don't get tired of listening to me, I won't get tired of telling you. It'll be easier for me if I talk. Only a human being can understand human suffering!

- Then please continue.

-I knew that taking revenge on Bakhrom Safarov would not be easy. Besides, if he was killed, I would surely be the first on the list of suspects. I had no right to be behind bars again. Because I had unfinished business. I had no right to die or be imprisoned until I had avenged all my enemies. So I began to think of ways to evade suspicion. The best solution was to "die" in this endeavor, my work in the ambulance and morgue came in handy. I needed a corpse that nobody wanted. I knew that Askar Nurgaliyev, a Tatar, had no one, and that he earned his bread by begging. Even though he had suffered two heart attacks, he constantly drank alcohol. It was clear that he would not last long. I went to see him several times... After his death, I managed to get his body under the pretext of burying it. I brought the corpse home, put my papers in his pocket, and disappeared from the house. The days were hot. I understood at that time of year the corpse would become unrecognizable in four or five days. Thus, Ahad Batyrov "passed away". From now on, no one could suspect him of anything...

- Tell me, why did you leave your son's photo in your passport? What does the inscription on the back of it mean?

- Yes, in fact, I deliberately left my son's picture in my passport. That's because I couldn't say goodbye to my best friend Zafar before I left. I didn't tell him about my plans. I was afraid that if I left the letter, it would fall into the wrong hands. That's why I wrote on the back of the photo a date that only two of us could understand - March 8, 1988. On that day Zafar and I were in a car accident and survived with the help of Nurali's grandfather. In short, I hinted to Zafar that I should be found at Nurali's grandfather's house. I thought that if he understood my hint, he would find me. And if he didn't, he would keep the picture of my son as a souvenir.

- We figured as much. Anyway, it's good that you left that picture. It helped us find you. Go on.

- Thus, freed from all suspicions, I started a plan of revenge against Bakhrom Safarov. At the time, he held a responsible position in a government agency. I could not have done the job alone. I could not have summoned Bakhrom from such an authoritative organization without the help of a woman. But neither Marzia nor the others whom I engaged to do this work have the slightest guilt. I did not tell them of my purpose. I told them that my application had gotten to this prosecutor, that I couldn't get an appointment with him, that I wanted to talk to this guy in a manly way, and if he would listen, I would tell him my problems. They agreed because they respected me, because I had once cured them. You've questioned them and you know everything, so I won't dwell on the details of the events related to Marzia....

Batyrov sipped his water.

- Why did you involve Gulmira in this work? - Taking advantage of the moment, Fakhriddin Karimovich asked.

- Gulmira gave me my shots. A good woman. Once during a conversation, I found out that she knew Bakhrom Safarov and sometimes met with him. It turned out that he helped her a lot. She respected Bakhrom very much. Taking advantage of the woman's naivety, I managed to find out Bakhrom's phone number from her address book. Once, when Marziya and I were going to Tashkent, we met Gulmira on the way. She said that she had traveled to Tashkent but could not see Bakhromak, so she wrote him a letter. I suggested that she give me the letter so that I could mail it from Tashkent since I was going there. I convinced her that the letter would get there faster that way. On the way I opened the envelope and read that Gulmira would be going to Tashkent soon and would call him when she arrived. I thought of using this letter for my own purposes. In short, I saved the letter and sent it to Bakhrom's address a few days before he was kidnapped. After receiving the letter, Bahrom naturally waited for a call from Gulmira. That is why, when Marzia called Bahrom on behalf of Gulmira and invited him to a meeting, he did not hesitate to meet his old acquaintance.

Thus Marzia summoned Bahrom to the place we had specified. I and two boys of the late Kara Namaz beat him to a pulp and brought him to the house we had prepared beforehand.

We wanted to kill him and bury the body....

- Can you tell us who these guys are? - The investigator took a notebook out of his pocket and prepared to write.

- It's a secret! They did my bidding. I hired them. Don't expect me to tell you their names! - Batyrov's eyebrows furrowed and he breathed heavily.

- Okay, okay, we'll talk about this later. Go on," the investigator was forced to retreat.

- Bahrom regained consciousness when the guys tried to kill him. But I did not want to kill a man who was lying unconscious. Besides, I wanted to talk to him face to face and tell him all my resentment. I wanted to look him in the eye and show him what it was like to be punished.....

At that moment, the attending physician entered the room:

- Fakhriddin Karimovich, that's enough for today! Your time is up. Continue tomorrow. Please, let's leave the room.

The investigator looked at his watch and was forced to obey the doctor's demand. He said goodbye to Batyrov and left the room.

As he got into his car and was returning to the prosecutor's office, the driver, who was always silent, suddenly spoke:

- Fakhriddin aka, did you release Sobirov?
- Which Sobirov? - the investigator was surprised.
- I'm talking about the head doctor Tashmurad Sobirov!
- What happened to him?
- When I was in the car, he walked past me in a white coat. So, you let him go.
- What are you talking about, Sobir is in jail!
- No way, I saw him clearly. At other times I wouldn't have paid attention, but I knew he'd been arrested recently. He was brought to the prosecutor's office this morning, but I didn't hear that he had been released.
- How can he get out, he's in jail! Murtoz, are you out of your mind?! — the investigator got angry.
- I'm telling you what I've seen!
- You must be mistaken. Do you even know his face?
- He used to be our head doctor, I know, of course," the driver replied resentfully.
- I think you need to rest. You're hallucinating already.

The driver remained silent...

Sanzharbek had a headache. Who needed Ozoda's death? Tashmurad Sobirovich's alibi checked out. The airline tickets were also checked. Everything seems normal, but time is running out. If his guilt is not proven, he will have to be released. Using all his knowledge and experience, Sanzharbek once again analyzed all the assumptions. But none of them gave the expected result. The investigation seemed to have reached a dead end. He paced from side to side around the room, not knowing what to do: "We have solved so many crimes. We managed to find Bakhrom Safarovich. If we can't solve this simple crime, won't all our efforts be wasted? After all, all the trouble started with this crime. If we don't solve it, we won't achieve our goal. If we don't correct the mistake made by the late investigator and judge, we will be no different from them professionally. Yes, unlike them, we were able to prove innocence and acquit the man they wrongly put away. But it is our responsibility to find the real culprit to put an end to this case...".

At that moment the door opened and Fakhriddin Karimovich entered. He seemed to be in a good mood. At such moments he liked to joke:

- So, Sanjarbek, what's your news? Did you find Ozoda's killer? Or are you still standing there?

Sanzharbek shrugged his shoulders, saying what to do if it doesn't work.

- What are you going to do now? Today is the third day, Sobirov will have to be released," the team leader took a serious look.

- We have no other choice. There's no proof of his guilt. His alibi has been confirmed. Unless he hired someone else to kill him, he was obviously in Kyrgyzstan at the time of the crime," Sanzharbek said excitedly.

- Then we have no choice but to let him go!

- It goes like this.

- All right, prepare a ruling. We'll let him go. But if we put a tail on him, maybe he'll lead us to the perps.

- Yes," Sanzharbek sat down at his typewriter and began to write.

Fakhriddin Karimovich went to his room and smoked, opened Batyrov's letter and read it again. At that moment there was a knock at the door and Sanzharbek entered with a pile of papers in his hand:

-Fakhriddin Karimovich, here is the decision, please sign it!

Familiar with the decision, the team leader asked:

- What do we do if he escapes?

- That's also possible. What do you want me to do then?

- Come on, let's think about it! - the chief began to ponder aloud. - Batyrov did not commit a crime - that's for sure. Sobirov also drops out, since he was actually in another republic at the time. So, who killed Ozoda? Who was interested in her death? There were no signs of robbery, assault or theft. So, it's unlikely that Ozoda was the victim of another crime. Only Sobirov had a reason to kill Ozoda. We can conclude from this that Sobirov was involved in the crime, albeit indirectly! Maybe he hired someone. Or... Wait, wait, what did the driver say today?!

He said he saw Sobirov? So... he might have a brother or a little brother...

- Fakhriddin aka, kill me, but I didn't understand anything you said," Sanzharbek said, opening his mouth.

- Does Sobirov have a brother? - the chief turned to his subordinate.

- Maybe there is. But what does that have to do with the case?

- You bet I am! Find out, quickly! If we have it, we have to bring it! I'll explain the rest later. Hurry up! - Fakhriddin Karimovich's face showed signs of confidence.

Without asking any unnecessary questions, Sanzharbek silently began the task, so as not to hear a reproach in his address.

Half an hour later, Sanzharbek brought a man who at first glance looked very much like Tashmurad Sobirov:

- Meet Eshmurod Sobirov, brother of Tashmurod Sobirov, also a doctor!

Fakhriddin Karimovich invited the guest to sit down and closely examined him from head to toe: "For the first time I see such an amazing resemblance between the brothers. Just like Hasan-Husan[23]! Facial structure, height, movements are one in the same! If I had seen him on the street, I would have thought it was Tashmurad Sobirov. So, the chauffeur, seeing this man, was surprised! I shouldn't have offended him," he thought.

-Eshmuradaka, we have summoned you on the case of your brother Tashmurad Sobirov. It is known that he

---

[23] Hasan-Husan - in Uzbek families such names are given to twin sons

is suspected of the premeditated murder of a girl named Ozoda. We would like to know what you think about it," the head of the group began the conversation cautiously.

- What can I say? My brother couldn't have committed such a crime. Because he was on vacation at the time. I remember he came back a few days later. I was working at the pediatric clinic at the time. When I heard this unpleasant news, I felt sorry for the girl. But you're wrong! My brother is innocent! I think some doctor who committed the crime was jailed then," Ashmurad said calmly.

- It turned out that this doctor was not guilty. Now all the evidence leads to your brother, - Fakhriddin Karimovich deliberately lied to check his interlocutor.

- What evidence?! He was in Kyrgyzstan at the time! How can you detain an innocent man? - Eshmurad became nervous.

The team leader who was watching him thought, "Then he knows too! Even though he's trying to pretend he doesn't know, you can see in his eyes that he's lying!

- Well, our investigator will question you in detail now. Write down everything you know. **For** now, goodbye, -Fakhriddin Karimovich stood up, escorted the guest to the investigator sitting in the neighboring office and left.

Sanzharbek, who had been watching on the sidelines for a long time, stared puzzled at the chief:

- What do we do now?

- And now, comrade, investigator, quickly go to the polyclinic where Eshmurad worked and find out whether he was at work or on vacation during the days when Ozoda was killed! I think I'm beginning to understand.

-Akajon, please explain what's going on. Why do we need Ashmurad? Or do you suspect him?

- Eh, Sanjarbek, Sanjarbek! Haven't still gotten to you? Tashmurad Sobirov may have sent his brother on vacation with his passport. Look at the resemblance!

- Oh, here's the thing. That idea never occurred to me! Bravo! I can't help but admire you, teacher. I'm off," - Sanjarbek hurriedly left the office.

Fakhriddin Karimovich, not wasting time, took a pen and paper and began to make a plan for tomorrow: he wrote, drew, crossed out, smoked cigarette after cigarette, talked to Tashkent and informed the management of the information received from Batyrov.

Two hours later, Sanzharbek came in with a piece of paper in his hand:

- Fakhriddin Karimovich, as always and this time you were right! In fact, Eshmurad also went on leave at his own expense during the period we are interested in. Here is the certificate and a copy of the order.

-And now immediately contact the management of the Issyk-Kul sanatorium and ask them to fax a copy of Sobirov's signature on the documents! I know it is not easy to request information from another country. But we have no choice. Use people you know, personal connections! Ask for help from the guys at the Osh Prosecutor's Office in Kyrgyzstan. Just don't forget that today is the last day of Sobirov's detention! By any means necessary to get the fax today! If our version is confirmed, we will send one of our operatives to Issyk-Kul.

- Yes! - Sanzharbek enthusiastically began to fulfill the task, satisfied that the case he was engaged in, moved from a dead point.

Sanzharbek decided to start his work with the city telegraph. First, he talked to the management of the Issyk-Kul sanatorium and asked if there were any Uzbek law enforcement officers there. Soon it turned out that Mahmud Nosirov, an investigator from the Department of Internal Affairs of the Tashkent Region, was vacationing at the sanatorium. Sanzharbek invited him to the phone and asked him to clarify the issue. About two hours later, Mahmud Nosirov faxed copies of some documents concerning Sobirov's stay at the sanatorium.

Sanzharbek took the documents and hurried to Fakhriddin Karimovich. Upon seeing him, the group leader jumped up:

- Wolf or fox?

- Wolf, wolf! - Sanzharbek handed the chief the papers.

Fakhriddin Karimovich, apparently, had prepared himself in advance and compared the signatures in the places with a check mark "T. Sobirov" with the signature of Tashmurod Sobirov in the document received by fax, and remarked: -It doesn't look like it!

Then he compared the signature of Eshmurad Sobirov and almost shrieked with joy like a man who has found gold:

- Sanjarbek, exactly!

- So, it was not Toshmurad Sobirov who went on vacation, but Eshmurad! - rejoiced Sanzharbek.

- That's the point! To create an alibi for himself, Tashmurad sent his brother on vacation with his passport. It was their similarity to each other that helped. It was this that allowed Eshmurad to board the plane with his brother's passport and rest in a sanatorium, but it did not occur to him to put his brother's signature on the documents. He made a big mistake by putting his signature on. Now we have irrefutable proof in our hands. Now we can arrest Tashmurad Sobirov with a clear conscience. Tomorrow, we need to send one of the operatives to Issyk-Kul, let him bring the original documents! And now prepare the authorization for the arrest of Toshmurad Sobirov!

- Yes! - Sanzharbek left the office, satisfied with the work he had done.

The evidence obtained by the investigators shocked Tashmurad Sobirov, and in the end he was forced to admit his guilt:

- I didn't want to kill Ozoda. But she wouldn't agree to have an abortion. If the baby had been born, I would have been in trouble. Ozoda insisted that we should have at least a small wedding so as not to disgrace her in front of her parents. Naturally, I could not do that, because I was both a leader and a party member. I could easily have been expelled from the party and fired. My future could have been ruined. I tried to persuade Ozoda to the last minute. But she persisted.

Besides, she knew some of my secrets. She threatened to expose me if I left her. She threatened to complain to the prosecutor's office and started pressuring me. So I had to kill her. But I was afraid of the punishment. I was afraid. By blaming it on Batyrov, I got out of the situation... You know the rest.

- It is clear that you were trying to save your life by avoiding punishment. But why did you slander an innocent man, a qualified doctor? Do you know how many people have suffered because of you? - Sanzharbek got angry.

Sobirov continued to sit with his head down. It was hard to understand what was going on in his head at that moment...

By evening, Batyrov's condition had deteriorated again. The amount of sugar in his blood was increasing and decreasing. The doctors were desperately trying to save his life. Qualified doctors were summoned from Tashkent. Thanks to their efforts, his condition improved slightly by morning. Taking advantage of the moment, he asked the doctor to call the investigator, saying that he had something important to report. The doctors had to fulfill his request. This time the chief physician, taking responsibility, gave Fakhriddin Karimovich ten minutes.

When the investigator entered Batyrov's room, he realized that his condition was no better than yesterday. Still, he decided to cheer him up:

-Ahad aka, are you okay? You don't look so bad. Here, I'm here on your behalf.

- I'm not well, ukajon! It seems my days are numbered. Our conversation was interrupted yesterday. I asked the doctors to call you to talk to you. I'm sorry to bother you. You have a lot of work to do without me," Ahad grabbed the bed with one hand and turned toward where the investigator was sitting.

- Yes, by the way, I have news for you: yesterday Tashmurad Sobirov confessed to killing Ozoda! In this case, you are fully justified!

- You're not mistaken? He was on vacation in Kyrgyzstan at the time! Or did he hire an assassin?

- No, he did all the work himself. He committed the murder by sending his brother Eshmurod on vacation to Issyk-Kul with his passport. It helped that he and his brother looked a lot alike. In short, we arrested him!

-Oh, trickster! Oh, devil! Because of that rascal, I've lost everything. I'm already dying. I wish I had killed him! I made the mistake of believing his words and evidence. I wish I had taken revenge on him and now I will die with this burden on my soul," tears were in Ahad's eyes.

- He will be punished according to the law! Will you continue your story?

- Good," Batyrov wiped his face and eyes with a towel and continued his story:

- When Bahrom came to his senses, I began to choke him by the collar and demanded that he explain why he had imprisoned me unjustly. I gave him a chance to say his last word before he died. He didn't make excuses, he didn't plead, he looked straight into the face of death and boldly said: "I was then the only one who was against your imprisonment, I brought the matter up for discussion with the investigator, the regional prosecutor's office, the higher authorities, but all the instances considered that the evidence was enough to arrest you. This was in Soviet times. Nobody wanted to listen to my opinion. Yes, I was a prosecutor then. But really I was just a soldier of the Soviet government. I had to do whatever I was ordered to do. If I didn't, others would do it for me, and I would have to give up my place. I remember my conscience tormented me then. But I could not go against the "legal machine" of Soviet power. That's my fault. Now you know the whole truth. You can kill me if you want! I chose this profession. That's why I accept death too," he said. Somehow, I wanted to believe him. No matter how much I hated him, I couldn't doubt the sincerity of his words. On the other hand, if I killed him, he would die and be free of all suffering. So I decided to keep him alive, but to keep him a prisoner. I wanted my opponent to suffer as much as I did and his family to fall apart. So, I beat him again unconscious and at night, with the help of my friends, I took him to Bekabad, to the house of grandfather Nurali, whom you know. The cellar across the tandyr that you saw, I had prepared in advance with the help of two mardikor[24] s from the city. In fact, I wanted to keep Tashmurad Sobirov there for the rest of his life. But he lied to me... So the basement went to the prosecutor....

I went to the cellar every three days and provided the prisoner with the necessary food and drink. I put a television set and a radio in his cell. I brought him

---

[24] mardikor - laborers in Uzbekistan who are hired for seasonal or day work

newspapers, magazines, books. All the conditions for life I had created for him. All that was missing was freedom...

- For what purpose did you keep him? - Fakhriddin Karimovich interrupted his interlocutor.

- Purpose? There was no purpose. I could have killed him the same day. But after talking to him, I realized that he was not such a bad person, sincere, brave, from an ordinary family, achieved everything by his own efforts, and I changed my mind about killing him. Every time I went to see him, we talked for hours. In many ways, we thought alike. Had we met under different circumstances, perhaps we would have become good friends.

Unfortunately, we found ourselves on opposite sides of the barricades. I punished him for his mistake, so that from now on, whoever hears this, especially the guardians of justice, would treat their work responsibly, would not make criminals out of innocent and honest people, would not turn their lives into hell, would take pity on their children, so that those who heard this story would not be indifferent to the fate of people....

Ahad was silent for a while. At that moment the chief physician entered the room.

-Fakhriddin Karimovich, that's enough for today! The rest tomorrow. The patient needs rest! Let's go, let's go," he said in a disgruntled tone.

- One last question," said the investigator, looking apologetically at the chief physician. - Who else did you want to take revenge on?

- Finding and punishing the person who killed Ozoda was my last goal. Unfortunately, I was unable to fulfill that plan. Well, let him answer before the law now, thank you very much. It's just that if I die now, I'll be sorry I didn't get to do one more thing.

- What other case? - The investigator was surprised.

- I could not take revenge on the driver Sergei Morozov, who caused the untimely death of my wife and children. He was driving under the influence of alcohol. The court sentenced him to seven years in prison. Three years later he got out of prison and moved to Russia. I couldn't find him. I had to kill him!

- After all, he got a legitimate punishment!

- Three years in prison for the death of three people, that's a bit short, isn't it?!

- Car accidents happen because of carelessness! No driver would ever intentionally cause an accident! Fearing for Morozov's life, we checked to see if you had done any damage. Fortunately, he managed to move.

- I'd know what to do with it if it didn't move!

- Ahad aka, that's enough! We will continue our conversation later. Well, have a rest," the investigator stood up.

- Thank you, goodbye! -Ahad covered his face with his hand and squeezed his eyes hard...

Wazira had not left her husband's side for two days and was waiting impatiently for him to open his eyes, say his name and cuddle her in his arms. Safar aka and Anwar stayed close to the hospital, hoping to hear good news from inside.

Although the doctors noted that his condition was improving, Wazira still feared for her husband. All day long she prayed to God to bring him back to life. Looking at her husband's pale face, which had not seen sunlight for a long time, her heart sank as she imagined the suffering he had endured in captivity. When the nurses left and Vazira and her husband were alone in the room, she would talk to him in her mind.

In the evening, as Wazira sat looking at her husband's face, it seemed to her that the fingers of his hands moved. The woman thought it was a hallucination. After a while, the fingers started moving again. Wazira screamed with joy. Not knowing what to do, she ran to call the doctors. In no time the room was filled with doctors. One of them took Wazira out into the corridor and told her that her husband was regaining consciousness and that she should wait here and not interfere with the doctors' work.

Wazira was overjoyed that her prayers had been heard by God and that her husband was safely returning to his family.

Safar aka and Anwar came rushing in from the hospital yard, apparently, they had already been informed.

- Daughter, is he awake? - Safar aka asked, unable to contain his excitement.

- God willing, he's awake, Father, he's awake! He started moving his arms, the doctors say he's fine. Allah has heard our prayers! - Wazira hugged her father-in-law and brother, seemingly letting all the pain out of her.

- God, thank you for everything! And I was a fool to wear mourning for him early," sobbed Safar aka, wiping his tears with trembling hands.

- Sister, Safar aka, you should rejoice, not cry! The Almighty Himself has brought him back to life! -Anwar said, reassuring them.

- Eh, Anvarjon, son, these are tears of joy! These are tears of happiness! May God prolong our joy," said Safar aka with a smile.

After about an hour, the doctors' running around the room where Bahromaka was lying subsided a little. Vazira ran out to meet every person in a white coat who came out of the room and scrutinized their faces, trying to guess their mood. When she saw familiar doctors, she ran up to them and asked about her husband's condition.

Although the doctors reassured her that everything was all right, her anxiety increased over time. She whispered prayers incessantly.

At that moment a nurse came out of the room and said:

- Wazira opa, your name is called, come in here.

As Wazira followed the nurse with frequent steps, her lips whispered, "Lord, have mercy. When she entered the room, four doctors were discussing something at Bahromak's headboard.

- Please, I'll give you five minutes for the meeting. We couldn't refuse your husband's request," the tall doctor with glasses addressed Wazira. Then he commanded his colleagues:

- Everybody out!

The doctors left the room one by one. Wazira's gaze fell on her husband lying on the bed in the middle of the room, her legs shaking and her whole-body trembling.

She hesitantly approached the bed and threw herself into his arms.

- B-a-h-r-om a-ka! Bahrom akajon!

- V-a-z-i-r-a! Thank God!

-Bahrom, aka, our daddy! How we missed you! -the tears were streaming from Wazira's eyes.

- Sweetheart, my life. It's over, it's over! It's over! I'm sorry! I made you all worry! Bakhrom embraced his wife, kissed her face, eyes, stroked her hair. - How are my Jahangir, Jawahir? If you knew how much I longed for them...

- Your children are big now, you won't recognize them when you see them! They missed you too!

- How's my dad? Is he okay?

- All right. He's waiting for you outside! When he hears that you have regained consciousness, he and Anwarjon are at a loss....

- How much suffering I've caused you!

- Don't say that! We lived in hope," Vazira pulled herself free from her husband's embrace, looked into his eyes, stroked his face and hair. - You won't leave us now, will you?

- No, darling! I'll never leave you now! You're my everything!

Fifteen days later Bakhrom Safarovich was discharged from the hospital. In honor of such a celebration, Safar aka slaughtered a big ram and prepared a big pilaf in honor of his son's return. Having kept his promise, he went to the prosecutor's office to invite Fakhriddin Karimovich and

Sanzharbek to the pilaf. But they said that they had gone on a business trip to some region to investigate a murder...

Vazira could not help but be happy to see her husband and children. Happiness, comfort and warmth returned to her family. Apparently, in such cases they say that fifteen days in a month are dark and fifteen are light! Bahrom was reinstated at work. But after working for a month, he resigned of his own accord. From now on he decided to spend more time with his family, his children. Perhaps he decided that he was not fit to work in law enforcement, thinking about his unforgivable mistake, which cost many people dearly....

As they say, both happiness and unhappiness are twins. A year later, a new person appeared in their happy family. "May this little girl bring happiness to your home," Safar aka said and named his granddaughter Bakhtygul, which means "Happy"...

2011-2019.

Printed in the United States
by Baker & Taylor Publisher Services